House of Secrets

by

Kayla Danoli

Copyright

Cataloguing-in-publication data
Creator: Danoli, Kayla, author

Cataloguing-in-Publication details are available from the National Library of Australia
www.trove.nla.gov.au

ISBN: 978-0-6489423-5-1 (paperback)
ISBN: 978-0-6489423-6-8 (digital)

Cover design: T A Marshall, Mackay, Queensland, Australia

Disclaimer

This novel is a work of fiction. All characters and events are the product of the imagination of the author. While some of the characters might remind you of people you know, they are fictitious and any resemblance to anyone living or dead is purely coincidental. Although some locations also may seem real and familiar, most places referred to in this work constitute a collage of places the author has known. But they are fictitious, and any resemblance to an existing location is coincidental.

Contents

Chapter 1

"The door is locked! It's never been locked. I didn't even know it had a lock."

Flopped down on the narrow landing at the top of the stairs, I sat shaking my head in... In what? Disbelief? Confusion? All of that, and more I suspect. Never, in all the time I've spent here over all the years, have I ever known the door to be locked. Don't even remember seeing it closed.

The situation wasn't computing. My tiny mind kept telling me I was wrong. It wasn't locked – just closed. Perhaps, still being in a state of shock after what happened at the funeral home, I hadn't tried properly to open it. Yes, that must be what happened, I suggested, and bounced up off the floor.

Standing on the top step, before stepping up onto the landing again, I took a long moment to study the two doors in front of me. No, it wasn't some strange mental aberration brought on by what happened after the cremation. Nor was it just a trick of the light. Both the doors were closed. And, when I try those doors again, I have no doubt they will be locked... or so I told myself. Still, it's no good telling yourself something, if you don't confirm it. You leave yourself open to continued questions and doubts until such time as you do go back to check.

There was no surprise, no confidence-restoring click as I tried turning the knob on the first door. With my sanity shaken, but just about intact, I sidled up to the second door and tried for a confident twist of the knob. Nothing happened. "Okay, I accept it! Both doors are locked. But why...?" I asked the empty house, the universe, and anyone else who might happen to be listening. "Any and all explanations are most welcome," I added as encouragement, but still received no enlightenment in return.

After trudging downstairs again, I plonked down into one of the overstuffed ancient lounge chairs. Maybe tomorrow will be different. Should I go home and sleep on it? Maybe then I'll be more intelligent and better able to apply logical thought to the situation. "That would be the best approach," I announced as I scrambled out of the chair. "Tomorrow… I'll sort it out tomorrow."

As I locked the front door behind me and made my way to my car, I realised if I felt even remotely so confident about tomorrow, I might enjoy a better night's sleep. All the way home, today's events and incidents ran through my mind on an endless loop. By the time I was in my own kitchen, still no clarification or inspiration had arrived. I poured two fingers of single malt scotch, dropped in a couple of ice cubes, and took it through to my lounge room.

"Just the one…," I reminded myself as I settled into my favourite chair. "A clear head is required tomorrow." *Tomorrow*… What is likely to have changed by then? The short and honest answer was 'nothing'. And I knew it. Nevertheless, I would be at Lillian's house again in the morning and, by whatever means, I would discover the reason for the locked doors.

But, in spite of my best efforts, today's incidents would not leave me alone. Memory of the cremation service and what happened afterwards didn't require too much effort to recall. My mind rolled over the entire event, and continued on to my arrival at the house. The images were vivid. There I was unlocking the door and then racing across the ugly front room carpet and up the stairs … And up to those two doors. There my mind bogged, stuck in a groove, and refusing to move forward. Try as I might, the image of those two doors would not go away.

Sometime later, my brain was weary and my eyes grew heavy. I felt myself swimming through a thick void towards sleep. Spending the night in your favourite chair, while easy to do, is never recommended. Not if you don't want to end up stiff and almost crippled next morning. Images of Aunt Lillian flitted through my mind as I took myself to bed and invited sleep to come.

As Morpheus finally accepted the invitation, one last thought about Aunt Lillian anchored itself front and centre in my mind. Why was she *Aunt* Lillian? Whose aunt? On occasions throughout my adult life, I wondered about it, but never to an extent sufficient enough to cause me to find out.

Chapter 2

This morning I was up later than usual, famished, and feeling decidedly below par. Yesterday, thanks to the funeral, lunch didn't happen. And, the smear of vegemite on a slice of overdone toast for dinner last night, while enough at the time, now had me wanting more than cereal for breakfast. Poached eggs on toast seemed easiest, fastest, and involved the least faffing about.

Although the two eggs atop their golden slices of toast were dispatched about half an hour ago, I remained parked at the breakfast bar sipping my morning's second mug of coffee. What is this dread preventing from me getting on with my day? The morning is disappearing at a rapid rate and I have done nothing and been nowhere. "Shake yourself. Get up and do something." I delivered the command in a voice loud enough to cause my neighbours a moment of concern. As my sluggish body began to obey, my final thought before falling asleep last night again pressed its case for attention.

Who was Aunt Lillian? Or, more precisely, whose aunt was Lillian? She was a big part of my life since my earliest memories, and I suspect even from before then. My mother always called her Aunt Lillian. I suppose, as I grew up, I followed suit, trusting in my childhood assumption she was my mother's aunt. The adult version of me had a problem with the concept. Although never into the family history thing, I remained unaware of any family connection between my mother and Lillian Cavendish. Never having known my grandparents only served to further complicate the matter. Only Lillian's and my mother's birth dates placed them in the right timeframe to allow for an aunt/ niece relationship to be a possibility.

With both my mother and now Lillian deceased, there was no one to ask about it. At least, no one I knew of anyway. Lillian never married – or so I believed – thereby negating any chance of gleaning family history information from her offspring. Perhaps some dark story underlies Lillian's life.

Maybe a proverbial 'skeleton in a cupboard' has remained hidden for decades. Well, now she is gone, uncovering the truth is unlikely to cause anyone with a close connection any significant degree of discomfort. Is it likely her will might shed some light on the situation? Of course, there is always the chance the document could further compound the question. Now I think on it, I can't help wondering whether some dark secret also lies lurking in my mother's background.

It's time I made a move. My mind is taking me into dangerous territory.

Today was not going well so far, and my arrival at Lillian's house did nothing to change my assessment of it. The front door was unlocked and stood a little ajar. I froze on the spot, while my hand clasping my key continued to reach for the door. No damage was evident. Whoever was here must have a key. But, *nobody should be here. Nobody should have entered this house after I left yesterday.*

As I eased the door open wide enough to enter, I breathed a sigh of relief when it didn't squeak or make any other sound to announce my arrival. My rubber-soled shoes and the carpet combined to silence my footsteps as I crept towards the centre of the front room. There, I faltered, unable to continue further for a moment or two. What to do? Where to go?

In front of me, the sight of the staircase snaking up to the upper floor held me transfixed. I let my eyes run up those stairs until they reached the landing above. Then, they could go no further. Confronted by the two closed doors, my eyes continued to stare at them. I was unable to drag them away from those doors, until a sound from the kitchen startled me.

"Oh, my goodness, Miss Sinclair, you did give me quite a turn. I didn't hear anyone come in, so finding you here in the front room, almost frightened the daylights out of me."

"I think both of us are dealing with the same reaction, Rita. I hadn't expected anyone else to be here, and when I found the front door open… Well, it did have me on edge for a bit. As I don't suppose you've come in today out of habit, why are you here?"

"Yesterday morning, I remembered I hadn't cleared out Miss Lillian's fridge. There were a few leftovers I wanted to put in the rubbish before tomorrow morning's collection. I had thought to come here after the funeral to deal with the fridge. Then, after it was over, I just didn't feel up to it."

"You shouldn't have put yourself out. I would have done it. But I am pleased you are here. There are a few things I would like to ask you about, if you have the time."

"I do have an appointment this morning, but I have a few minutes. I was going to put this rubbish out, and then write you a note. Now you're here, you've saved me having to do it. Anyway, it might be easier to tell you, rather than to write it."

My stomach tightened. Nothing was great about today so far. Why should whatever Rita wants to tell me be any different? I gestured to Lillian's ancient lounge chairs and suggested we sit before beginning our discussions.

"Well, I might be telling you stuff you already know but, with your being away all last week before Lillian passed, I thought I should mention a few things – just in case. Lillian left you a note. I was going to put it on the kitchen table before I left so you wouldn't miss seeing it. It might cover everything I was going to mention anyway."

"I'll read the note later. In the meantime, please go ahead with the matters you wanted to discuss."

"Okay… well, the first thing you should do is to contact your aunt's solicitor, Mr Breen, at Whitby and Breen."

"No. It would be Mr Whitby I need to contact. Mr Whitby was Aunt Lillian's solicitor."

"True, old Mr Whitby was Miss Lillian's solicitor … until he retired a few months ago. When he retired, all his clients were transferred to the young Mr Whitby. Miss Lillian wasn't impressed by the young man, and didn't think he had enough experience for her liking. She probably caused a bit of a kerfuffle when she insisted her files be transferred to Mr Breen instead."

"Oh, I see. Right, I will make an appointment to see Mr Breen, but is there anything specific I need to discuss with him?"

"I really couldn't say, Miss Sinclair. I wasn't privy to Miss Lillian's personal affairs, but I think it might be about her estate. You know, whatever is in her will and such matters."

"After being away for the week, when I called in on my way home on the day before she died, you said she was sleeping. I didn't go in to see her because I knew I would see her the next day. Then, next morning, she was gone by the time I arrived. I'm still trying to cope with the way it panned out. Tell me about what happened during those days I missed in the lead up to her death."

"She had everything organised you know. Everything about her funeral was arranged with the undertakers, and they were paid in advance. Mr Breen had an appointment with her on the Monday afternoon after you left. It seems she had arranged his visit beforehand too. I kept out of the way while he was here, so I don't know what went on, but he didn't stay long."

"Did she appear worried about anything, or did anything unusual happen while I was away?"

"Miss Lillian came downstairs. I didn't think it was possible for her even to get out of bed. Although, she did seem much better – stronger somehow – just before you went away for the week, but I still didn't think she could get out of bed on her own. After making sure the monitor was turned on and working properly each night, I slept in my own room on Friday, Saturday and Sunday nights. The monitor was silent all night but, when I went to her bedroom on Monday morning, the door was locked. I tried the door to the office, but it was locked too. Those doors were never closed before, let alone locked."

"What did you do? Finding the doors locked must have sent you into a panic."

"I didn't know what to think. 'Panic' doesn't describe it. At first, I thought she had locked herself in there and maybe done herself some harm. Although she never said as much, there were a couple of times over the last weeks when I thought she was depressed; sick of the way she was. So, maybe you can imagine what my thoughts were when I found the doors locked."

"It would have been enough to send me into a major panic. How did you work out she was downstairs?"

"It took me a while. I banged on the door and called out, and generally carried on for a bit before I thought to go back to my room and check the monitor. I discovered it had been turned off. Well… then I didn't know what to make of it. If something had happened to her during the night, the monitor would have woken me. It didn't because it was turned off. So, then I thought she might have turned it off so it wouldn't wake me and I wouldn't be aware of whatever she was going to do. I couldn't bring myself to think about what might have happened – about what she might have done. I started searching the house."

"When you found her, where was she?"

"She was asleep down here in the back room."

"How did she manage to get out of bed without your help?"

"That's just it, Miss. Not only did she get out of bed by herself, but she came *downstairs*. After I convinced myself there was a chance she might not be in her room, I searched everywhere upstairs. When I couldn't find her anywhere up there, I came and looked for her down here. You might remember she always had what she called her 'daybed' in the back room. She hadn't come downstairs for months, so it hadn't been used for some time. But, when I found her, there she was... fast asleep in the back room."

"Goodness, it's a wonder she didn't have a fall as she came down those stairs on her own. I wonder whatever possessed her to want to be down here."

"I don't know, Miss, but she was quite determined to stay downstairs. There was a trundle under the daybed. So, to be near her at night, I've been sleeping on the trundle. She had arranged for Mr Breen to come to see her on Monday. I thought his scheduled visit might have prompted her to move down here. She would have thought it most improper to meet with him in her bedroom. After he left, I wanted to call the ambulance to help take her back upstairs. She refused, and insisted on staying in the back room."

"Maybe she thought it would make things easier for everybody if she were on the ground floor rather than upstairs. Nevertheless, I find her actions strange. I'm sorry I made the decision not to see her when I arrived back the night before she died."

"It never occurred to me to mention it to you at the time. As you say, I don't know what her reason was for coming downstairs. All I know is, the effort involved took a lot out of her. Throughout the week you were away, she slept a lot. When she was awake, she gave me plenty of instructions regarding what I needed to do if anything should happen. Most of those instructions related to you, Miss."

"Rita, I know it's a bit late in the game, but do you think you might bring yourself to call me Sophie, rather than calling me Miss Sinclair all the time?" She looked a bit surprised but nodded, and I continued with the questions. "What were the instructions you were to pass on to me?"

"Well, Miss… Sorry … Sophie, there's not much to tell. Like I said, I was going to write you a note, but all I had to tell you was to talk to Mr Breen, and to make sure you read the note Miss Lillian left you. I'm sorry, but I can't tell you more."

"No, of course not. Lillian was a private person, and wasn't in the habit of sharing her personal information with others. My problem is, I'm still trying to get my head around everything that happened after I left for my week away, and I'm still trying to come to terms with my guilt at not being here at the end. I do have one question though. Your room is at the far end of the landing upstairs. How did you manage after Lillian decided to move herself down here?"

"The trundle under Miss Lillian's daybed isn't the most comfortable thing I've ever slept on, but it was obvious she wasn't doing so well. I assumed the monitor remained locked in her bedroom. Although, because of her condition, even if she hadn't moved down here, I would have slept in her bedroom with her to be close-by should anything happen."

In spite of her attempt to avoid being obvious, I saw Rita steal a glance at her watch. I remembered she had an appointment. "Rita, thank you for coming today. I know you have an appointment, so I don't want to delay you. When I talk to Mr Breen, I will remind him about your pay."

"Don't go worrying yourself about me. As I said before, Miss Lillian had everything planned and arranged. She made sure my pay – holiday pay and everything included – was paid into my bank before she passed. It was as if she knew exactly when it was going to happen. So uncanny the way she arranged everything beforehand. If there is nothing else for now, I really must be off. You and Mr Breen know where to reach me if you need to talk to me."

After she made a quick phone call, I watched her rush down the path and out onto the footpath. As she closed the gate, a taxi pulled in alongside the kerb. Rita gave me a quick wave through the window as the cab sped off again.

Then I was alone. The house felt… felt what? Oppressive? Eerie? For a few moments, I was apprehensive. It was as though I was trespassing. "Stop it. There are no ghosts here," I chastised myself aloud. "Whatever this nonsense is, don't continue with it. Stop it and get on with what you need to do."

It was all well and good telling me to get on with it, but to get on with what? I felt there were things I needed to do. Important things I must do. Right then, I would have given anything for a note listing what those things were. Everything had happened without me, without my involvement in any way. As a result, I was like a ship adrift without a sail or a rudder. I didn't know what needed to be done – or what had been dealt with already.

Aunt Lillian's note…! Of course, if she arranged everything else, she was bound to have organised me as well. It probably will tell me everything I need to do and by when. I rushed back to the kitchen and opened the cupboard where Rita had indicated I'd find the note. A plain white envelope was propped up against Lillian's favourite two Royal Albert tea cups. Its only adornment was my name scrawled across the front in black ink in Aunt Lillian's familiar hand.

After ripping open the envelope and extracting its contents – a single white unlined sheet torn from a small pad – I remained anchored in front of the cupboard. Slowly, I unfolded the page and prepared to read the last words Aunt Lillian had for me.

I don't know what I expected, but I know it wasn't the words Lillian left me... brief, to the point and unemotional. No fond farewell. No explanations or encouragement. Just a few sentences and a brief list followed by her signature. The disappointment I felt on first glance at the note turned to something else as I read:

…Everything is arranged in the hope of avoiding stress or concern for anyone as a result of my passing. Nevertheless, to avoid the occurrence of even the remotest chance of a cock-up as is so often consistent with human nature, there are a few things you must attend to immediately after I shuffle off. The list is as follows….

'Cock-up'….! Where did that come from? I never heard her use such language. Was this some new found freedom resulting from the sure knowledge of her impending demise? Lillian's note had so rattled me, I couldn't continue reading it to the end. As a result, for a few moments longer, I remained ignorant of the things I was supposed to do. Albeit, at this late stage of proceedings, there can be no doubt, whatever they were, they would now be done a bit later than she intended they should be.

Flopped down on a chair I dragged out from the kitchen table, I read the note again; through to the end this time. With more than a touch of trepidation, I returned to the list of things I was supposed to do. I shouldn't have worried, and just stuck with being disappointed. Although wordy, there were only two instructions: contact Harrisons, the undertakers, to arrange to collect her body, and talk with Tom Breen at Whitby Legal Services.

Her instruction to contact Harrisons included the assurance *everything has been arranged with them and they will know what to do.* Reassuring, but cold comfort somehow, given the present circumstances. Regardless of Harrisons' being aware of what was required of them subsequent to Lillian's death, with her funeral now consigned to history, I would talk to them today. They might know how and when everything was arranged, but I didn't. Although Harrisons' part in the story was over and done with, I still needed to know how it came about.

My call to Whitby and Breen Legal Services proved in keeping with the rest of the day so far. Mr Breen was in court and was not expected in the office at all today. Tomorrow was looking no better for an appointment. He was fully booked, and the court case he was involved with could drag on for another day or so. I settled for leaving a message to the effect I needed to speak with him as soon as possible. While I felt more than a twinge of urgency about it, I managed to avoid suggesting the matter was urgent in case it made him put off seeing me until he had a large slab of time available to deal with whatever I wanted to discuss. In reality, I would be happy even with just a few minutes squeezed in somewhere in his busy schedule.

Harrisons broke my run of 'outs' for the day. Frank Harrison was only too happy to meet with me and suggested a twelve o'clock meeting. I imagined he was squeezing me between his busy morning's work schedule and his lunch break. As I didn't think our discussions would take long, I didn't feel too guilty about taking up a few minutes of his lunchtime. In the end, traffic was lighter than I expected and I arrived at the funeral home about fifteen minutes early. Not exactly a great place to wander around in to fill in time until my appointment, I was pleasantly relieved when he invited me into his office almost the minute he saw me set foot in the place.

His first comments were clear indication he was concerned I had come to complain about some aspect of Aunt Lillian's funeral.

"Quite the contrary, Mr Harrison, I've come with questions, not complaints. I understand Lillian Cavendish made all the arrangements for her cremation some time in advance of her death. I was away for the week immediately prior to her passing, and knew nothing about any of her arrangements beforehand. Is it possible to share some of those details with me?"

"Of course; I wasn't aware you had been out of town, and I admit to being a bit surprised when I didn't hear from you until after we had collected the body. What would you like to know?"

"If I'm honest, I still haven't come to terms with how pre-emptive she was; how organised. It was impossible for her to know the exact date she would pass away, so how far in advance had she made the arrangements for her cremation?"

"O-oh, her first contact must have been about four months beforehand. At the time, it was just a general enquiry about what was available, indicative costs, etc. The sort of enquiry people with a close family member in palliative care make as their loved one's end draws near. Then, we didn't hear from her again for about three months. Our next discussions were by phone. She outlined what she wanted and how things should proceed, and asked for an itemised account to be mailed to her.

While it was a little unusual perhaps, it didn't create any problems. We mailed her the information she required. About a week later, we received her reply authorising us to act in accordance with our quote. She included a cheque for the amount quoted … and a little extra to cover any unforeseen incidental costs. It was received about a week before her death. You are familiar with what happened next."

"Yes … at least I suppose I am. When I went to the house to see her on the Monday morning after I arrived home on Sunday night, her nurse already had called you and you had removed the body. I contacted you later in the day to confirm the arrangements Lillian had put in place."

"Correct. We told you the cremation was scheduled for ten o'clock on Wednesday morning, and you expressed your surprise we could have everything in place so soon. But, for us, there was no surprise involved. She had requested her cremation take place no later than two days after her passing."

"Right, but it must have been difficult for you to drop everything in order to accommodate her request. It's not as though you are sitting around with loads of spare time just waiting for people to die." Frank Harrison studied his hands clasped on his desk for a few moments. When he looked up at me, he seemed uncomfortable, troubled even.

"It wasn't a problem. You see, she told me she would pass away sometime this week. And she did, in the early hours of Monday morning."

I found myself shaking my head in disbelief as I struggled with her accuracy of her foretelling her own death. Whether it was because I had run out of questions or because I was too stunned to think of anything else to ask, all I had left to do was to thank Frank for his time. As I gathered up my bag and stood to leave, his question stopped me in my tracks.

"If you don't mind my asking, Miss Sinclair, was there a problem after the service? While I don't want to pry, did something unpleasant happen as everyone was leaving?"

"Thank you for your concern but, no, there was nothing unpleasant. Unexpected – curious even – but not unpleasant... At least, I don't think so. But, no, it had nothing to do with the service, and was nothing for you to be concerned about." As I made my way out to my car, I hoped I was right.

How could she predict with such accuracy when she was going to die? Do people get some premonition – some sign –the end is approaching? After leaving the funeral home, I sat in my car for a while, too stunned to do anything else. My questions found no answers, but a nagging thought continued to lurk. I refused it an opportunity to develop, but who could I talk to? Maybe I should go back to Rita for a more in-depth conversation about Aunt Lillian's last days.

With no better ideas of what to do, I went home. I couldn't face the thought of going back to Lillian's house today. A few minutes of sitting in my lounge room with my mind in neutral forced me to my feet and had me gravitating towards my mother's old photo album on the bottom shelf of my bookcase. In a state of nostalgic melancholy, as I turned each page with care, I read the captions under the photos.

They were all there: all the photos of my childhood taken at various places, at various times, and with a limited number of other people. Aunt Lillian seemed almost a fixture in my early years. There were a few photos in which she didn't appear and, for some of those, I suspect she was the photographer. I knew this was not in my best interest, but something made me want to wallow in it for longer than I should.

Not much before five o'clock, a phone call saved me from myself. It was Miss Dodson, Tom Breen's clerk. A window in Mr Breen's busy schedule had opened up at four o'clock tomorrow afternoon. Would I be available to meet with Mr Breen then? Of course I would be available. I just wasn't sure how I was going to hold my curiosity and impatience at bay for so long. But, with twenty-four hours to wait before I could find out any more from Lillian's solicitor, I had to find something to do to keep unpleasant thoughts in check.

There were things I wanted to talk to Rita about. Perhaps I could call her to see if she might be free for a chat. Her daughter answered and told me Rita had gone to check on a potential new position. She didn't know when her mother would return. Rather than have Rita call me back, I told her daughter I would try her again, maybe some time tomorrow. With no better ideas about how to fill in time for the rest of the evening, producing something for dinner was my only option, followed by surfing TV channels for something to occupy my mind.

Chapter 3

After another late start to the day, and as if on automatic pilot, I made my way to Lillian's house. Again, there was a feeling of trepidation as I unlocked the front door. What is this all about? Why do I feel this way? I decided it might be something subconscious telling me I was intruding. After I was living in my own place, I would never go into Lillian's house if she were not at home, unless she asked me to check on something while she was away. The explanation I came up with helped eased my tension a little.

Everything was just as it had been yesterday. The only difference being Rita wasn't there. I knew it was pointless, but I couldn't help myself. As I climbed the stairs to the upper floor, I felt my tension levels rising again. By the time I stepped up onto the landing, my stomach was a roiling mass. No surprises awaited me. The doors were still locked. I walked to the end of the landing and stood outside the door of the third bedroom. This had been the live-in carer's room. Again, I had an overwhelming feeling I was about to intrude. I tried ignoring it.

The door was closed, but not locked. I pushed it open and hesitated for a moment before crossing the threshold. No sign of Rita's presence remained. Her personal effects were gone. The bed had been stripped and remade ready for its next occupant. There was nothing more to do or see on the upper floor, so I traipsed down the stairs again and continued through to the back room where Aunt Lillian had set-up her daybed. Rita's handiwork was evident there too. No longer was there anything personal about the room. Now it was just a room in-waiting for someone to make use of it.

While my tour of the house probably was useful in some way, it wasn't helping answer any of my questions, especially the main one: where would Lillian leave the keys for those two rooms upstairs? Instinct told me there had to be something important stashed away in those rooms. Why else would Lillian lock them? Did Lillian lock them? It wasn't Rita. So, who else might have locked them? I told myself I would do better to start looking for the keys.

Lunchtime had come and gone by the time I admitted defeat. After searching every possible nook and cranny in the house, I still had no keys. I thought it might be worth calling Rita again to arrange a meeting. When no one answered, I gave up, locked the door behind me and went home. There remained only a couple of hours to fill in before my meeting with Lillian's solicitor.

Due in no small part to my inability to settle to do anything worthwhile today, I arrived at Whitby & Breen's rooms about fifteen minutes early for my meeting with Tom Breen. Nevertheless, I barely had claimed a chair in the reception area when Miss Dodson appeared and showed me to his office. As I followed her, I thought I glimpsed a familiar shape disappearing into another office further along the corridor. While I was intrigued by what I thought I saw, what came next was nothing short of amazing.

Once the initial pleasantries were over, Tom Breen moved straight onto the business in-hand. "I assume you have come to discuss the late Miss Lillian Cavendish's last will and testament?"

"Well, I suppose it is why I am here. All I know is Lillian left me instructions to contact her solicitor in the event of her death. I understand you are now her solicitor."

"Yes, you are correct as far as it goes. But I have asked her previous solicitor, Mr Whitby senior, to join us. From his long association with Miss Cavendish, he is better informed about her intentions. Do you have a problem with Mr Whitby's presence at this meeting?"

"No, not if you think it beneficial."

It was just as well I didn't object for, as soon as I finished speaking, James Whitby entered the room. I wasn't losing the plot. It was James Whitby I had glimpsed in the corridor earlier. Then, Tom Breen took charge of the meeting by opening the discussion of Lillian's will.

"Are you aware of Lillian's intentions regarding her estate?" I shook my head. "I see. I assumed she would have discussed the matter with you." Tom Breen's face registered genuine surprise. I heard a soft chuckle from James Whitby.

"I apologise for having to plead ignorance, Mr Breen, but Lillian did not discuss either her intentions or her will with me. Should I read something into her actions? You see, I'm not surprised she didn't discuss anything with me. Perhaps, if you knew Aunt Lillian better, you would be aware she was an extremely private person, with a strong aversion to any display of emotion." By the time I finished saying my piece, James Whitby was laughing out loud.

"Too right, she was. She was all of what you described and more, and came across as something of a formidable figure – until you came to know her well. Apart from anything else, she was an exceptional accountant."

"I see… Well, we'll move on to the contents of Lillian's will shall we?" An exasperated Tom Breen looked over at me before giving James Whitby a curt nod, which I think might have served as a reprimand.

It's as well I arrived early. We seemed to be going nowhere so far. I settled for a smile and a nod in response to Tom's question.

"Right then; starting from the top, Lillian appointed you, Sophie Sinclair, and James Whitby, as joint executors of her estate."

My appointment came as a surprise. There was nothing surprising about Whitby's appointment. I expected he would be the executor. Tom Breen's voice cut through my surprise.

"Shall I continue? …Unless you have questions about anything so far?"

James Whitby's chuckle was almost inaudible when Tom asked his question. I shot Whitby a questioning look, but asked Breen to continue.

"Miss Cavendish's will is straightforward and does not present as an onerous task for the executors. There are only four minor bequests, each of five thousand dollars: One to each of two organisations whose work Lillian had supported for decades, and one to each of the two carers who looked after her during the last years of her life. Everything else – the house, cash, personal effects, and investment portfolio – goes to you, Miss Sinclair."

"Isn't anyone else mentioned? Members of her extended family…?"

"You would be aware Lillian never married," James Whitby said, "so there are no immediate family; no offspring."

"Yes, I knew she never married, but I thought there would be members of her extended family out there somewhere. I admit I never met any of them, or even heard Lillian mention family connections. Nevertheless, I thought there would be relatives she might mention in her will."

"As I said, Miss Sinclair, no one else is mentioned, and no other bequests have been included. Now, we have prepared the papers for probate and the hearing is booked for early next week. It is unlikely there will be any problems with the granting of probate, so everything should be finalised by close of business on Wednesday next. Letters to go to each of the beneficiaries have been prepared and, unless you wish otherwise, they can go out in today's mail."

"Unless Mr Whitby has other ideas, please send the letters out today."

When James indicated he had no objections, Tom reached for his phone and instructed Miss Dodson to add the letters to the day's mail. The advice to beneficiaries taken care of, he returned to the contents of the will.

"There is only one other clause of any consequence, and it gives instructions to her executors. It related to her desire to be cremated, and provides instructions on what to do with the ashes subsequent to her cremation. Miss Sinclair, you will be able to study all of this in detail later. Here is a copy of Lillian's will for your records. Mr Whitby already has a copy."

"Thank you, I will read it later." I looked at the document Tom placed on the desk in front of me. It was obvious Tom Breen was anxious to be done with the reading of Lillian's will. He had barely slapped the copy down on the desk before continuing.

"Only a couple of other matters are left to deal with: transfer of ownership of the house, and transfer of the various contents of the investment portfolio into your name. In the latter case, transfer of the investment portfolio, this is best left until after probate is granted and a copy of the death certificate has been obtained – all of which should be in place by the end of next week at the latest.

In the matter of the house, transfer of the property title to you also will be delayed until the grant of probate documentation is to hand. As I said, any delay is unlikely to extend beyond next week but, to expedite the transfer of title, we have prepared the requisite paperwork for signature. If you sign these documents now, as soon as the probate is through, they can go to the Titles Office."

He pushed a folder across the desk towards me. As I reached for it, James Whitby cleared his throat.

"Ahem... If I might make a suggestion, perhaps Miss Sinclair needs time to consider the future of the house before signing the paperwork. If she should decide to sell the property in the near future, the house could remain in the estate until it is sold and ownership could then be transferred to the new owner. With such an approach, only one transfer is required, instead of two in fairly quick succession."

"As I didn't know about the bequest, I haven't thought about it. But, I am confident I won't be selling the property in the immediate future."

Tom Breen reached across and snatched back the folder containing the documents. He did not look at all pleased with the way things were progressing. Good old James Whitby stepped in to rescue the situation.

"As one of the executors, and a solicitor, I suggest Miss Sinclair and I take some time, to discuss between ourselves, the contents of Lillian's will before we progress further. Tom, I am aware you need to rush away in the next few minutes. If Miss Sinclair has no objections, perhaps you might take your leave now, while I finish up here this afternoon. I could bring you up to speed in the morning on any decision or conclusion we reach."

No further persuasion required. Tom didn't breathe an audible sigh of relief, but his demeanour suggested there was one. As soon as James finished speaking, Tom was on his feet and bidding us goodbye. While Tom clattered down the back steps on his way to his car, James settled into Tom's recently vacated chair. His face told me he was enjoying every moment of what just happened. I was dying to ask what it was all about, but thought better of it.

"My apologies for Tom, he's a bit tense today. He had to rush off because it's his Rotary Club's handover dinner tonight. He is being installed as president of the club for the next twelve months. It's a big night in the Breen household I gather, particularly for Mrs Breen. Now, returning to the matter at hand, is there anything about Lillian's will you wish to discuss? You indicated you weren't interested in selling the house at the present time. If you are sure you want to keep it – even if you hold on to it for only six months – I would recommend you sign the documentation for the transfer of title to you."

"Thank you. At this stage, I have no ideas about what to do with the house. Somewhere down the line, if I do decide to sell, then I'll contact Mr Breen – or yourself."

"I think you've made a wise choice. It is a valuable property, and its value will only escalate over time. There is one thing I wanted to ask you about. On a couple of occasions during our meeting, you raised the issue of Lillian's having existing family members. Was there a reason? Is there something you know about which has the potential to cause us problems?"

"Not as far as I know, except… Well, I don't know if this is even worth mentioning." He assured me, if it was a concern to me, I should run it by him. So I did. "There was an incident – I suppose it's the best way to describe it – after Lillian's cremation service. When the service began, apart from Frank Harrison and his assistant, there were five of us seated in the chapel. The whole service only lasted about twenty minutes before we were making our way out of the place. I was last to leave and, as I approached the door, three men came towards me and blocked my way."

"Did you know those men?"

"No, never seen them before. They must have come in late and sat in the back row. I didn't hear them come in, but the piped music was a tad loud."

"What happened? Did they threaten you in any way?"

"They invited me to join them at the pub further along the street for 'a bit of a wake' as they put it. I wasn't feeling particularly sociable after the service, and I didn't much like the look of them. I politely refused their invitation and went to continue on my way out of the chapel. They bunched up in front of me to prevent my leaving. Not being in the mood for it, I demanded to know what their game was. Their reply told me in not these exact words: I should be more polite. I would be seeing a lot more of them in the future. They had come to claim their rightful inheritance as relatives of the deceased."

"Who were those men? Did they give you their names?" I shook my head and he rushed on with his next question. "What happened after they 'enlightened' you as to why they were there?"

"Alarmed by the way the situation was developing, I was desperate to leave the chapel and escape. I don't know whether it was good luck or by design but, just then, Frank Harrison's assistant came striding down to where we stood.

As he approached he called out: *Ah, Miss Sinclair, I'm glad I caught you before you left. I forgot to ask you about the flowers, and only remembered on my way down to lock up when I saw you were still here. Is everything okay, or do we have a problem?* I was never so pleased to hear or see anyone. You might know Frank's assistant. He's a big lump of a bloke who looks as though he works out regularly."

"Yes, I have seen him around. I take it his arrival was well-timed?"

"Well, it was amazing how quickly the three men disappeared out the door. It only took my rescuer moments to ask me what I wanted to do with the flowers purchased to decorate the chapel for the service. I didn't want to take them home, so I suggested they go to the local aged care facility to help brighten the residents' lives. In the time it took to exchange those few words, and for me to walk outside, the men had disappeared. I assumed they went to the pub as intended. I wasted no time scrambling into my car and driving away."

"What can you tell me about the men – apart from the fact they were rude and offensive?"

"Nothing much other than they were scruffy looking. They looked as though they were from the rougher end of town, if such a description means anything to you. I couldn't help but think how disgusted Lillian would be if these were family connections."

"You haven't heard from, or seen those men since?"

"There's been little enough time. The service was on Wednesday and today is Friday."

"True, but, if you should encounter them again, don't hesitate to call the police … and me."

Having signed the title transfer documents, I was about to leave when another question occurred to me. "Mr Whitby, does the surname 'Millard' ring any bells for you – perhaps associated in some way with Aunt Lillian?"

"I can't say it does. Why do you ask?"

"Yesterday, I went to Harrison's and collected the condolences book they had open at the service for attendees to sign. The three men were accommodating enough to sign the book. Millard was the surname they used."

On my way to the door, another question niggling me since I spoke with Rita yesterday, flashed to the forefront of my thoughts. "Do you know if Lillian changed her will or made a new one recently? I believe Mr Breen visited her early last week, and I wondered if it was for something along those lines."

"No, it wasn't anything so significant. She wanted to make sure, as it stood, her will was still okay and nothing needed to be changed or fixed in any way. Tom was able to assure her it was fine and there was no need for concern. Their meeting only lasted about ten minutes. Oh, you have just reminded me... There was something for you. Hang on a moment while I fetch it."

I didn't know how to respond to the item he placed in my hand. A range of emotions tried to fit the occasion, but confusion was the one to succeed. I settled for a brief 'thank you' and left.

Although my intention was to go home, as I drove away from Whitby & Breen's rooms, I changed course. I had things to do … at Lillian's house.

As I unlocked the front door, my left hand clutched the small parcel James Whitby handed me as I left their office. My gut instinct insisted the right place to open the parcel was at Lillian's house. But now, here in her kitchen, I hesitated. "Open the bloody thing. It's unlikely to be Pandora's Box," I snarled aloud.

Why would something so small and insignificant-looking create so much uncertainty? About the size of a cigarette packet, the parcel was wrapped in brown paper. Whatever it held was lightweight. In fact, it felt light enough to suggest it was empty but, when I shook it, it was obvious it contained something. Apart from my name scrawled across the front of it in Lillian's familiar hand, there were no other clues on the wrapping.

I slit and peeled back the brown paper to expose a small cardboard box. A couple more swipes with the sharp paring knife severed the adhesive tape holding the lid in place. My hesitancy continued but, after a couple of deep breaths, I forced myself to lift the lid… and then gasped.

"You crafty old woman…!"

Taped to the bottom of the box were two keys. I didn't need to think about it. Of course they would be for the two locked doors upstairs. But, why all the faffing about? Couldn't she have left the securely wrapped parcel somewhere in the house? Was she concerned Rita might open it? I rejected the suggestion. She had never found fault with Rita, and never questioned her honesty. No, there had to be something more to this story. Something to delay my unlocking those doors until after I met with her solicitor.

After spending the last two days desperate to gain entry to the two locked rooms, why was I still standing here in the kitchen staring at the keys in the box? I ripped the keys free of the tape holding them in place and looked at them lying in the palm of my hand. For the first time since opening the box, a doubt crept in from somewhere. Were they the keys to the upstairs rooms? Did they look like door keys? What else could they be? I headed to the stairs.

My stomach tightened with every step I climbed. An all-pervading sense of dread filled me. Then I was standing outside the locked door of Aunt Lillian's bedroom. To go blundering into her bedroom seemed disrespectful. I would feel I was trespassing. Wracked with such rubbish thoughts, I took a few sideways steps to stand in front of the second locked door.

In accordance with 'Murphy's Law', the first key I tried wasn't the right one. The second key slid into place easily, but the lock was stiff. For a moment I feared the key might break before the lock released. Then, with a resounding click, so deafening in the silent house, the door was unlocked. Filled with trepidation, I eased open the door and hesitated before entering.

Chapter 4

Once a bedroom, for the last decade or more, it had served as Lillian's office. This was her study, her escape from the real world where she could lose herself in her books and memorabilia – or deal with the more mundane business of everyday life such as replying to mail and paying accounts. I had spent little time in there and only on rare occasions. I had no reason to come into this room, and always felt it was her private space.

Still feeling a little uncomfortable being there, I stood beside the big old wooden desk and slowly scanned the room. Where a bedroom might have built-in cupboards, one wall of this room was lined with bookshelves. Bookshelves crammed to capacity with books of all shapes, sizes and coloured covers. Lillian remained an avid reader right up until the last couple of months of her life. This room reflected her love of the written word. But her study was a mix of both old and new. While some of the books, and the prints on the walls, appeared to have been acquired decades ago, the latest technology also was there.

As my eyes fell on the twenty-seven inch screen standing on the corner of her desk, I remembered her buying a new computer and the monitor less than twelve months ago. Around the same time, she also bought a large colour laser multifunction device, after having moaned for some time about being restricted to monochrome printing and copying. The big beast of a machine had required the purchase of another small cupboard for it to sit on.

A jumble of two drawer filing cabinets and small cupboards ran along the wall under the windows, and additional bookshelves and filing cabinets adorned the wall behind her desk. Rather than holding prized printed volumes, these bookshelves held current files, work in progress, and other more personal folders and items.

See, no ghosts in here; nothing scary, the little voice in my head began chanting as soon as I stepped into Lillian's office, and it kept delivering its message as I scanned the space. Nevertheless, I still felt uncomfortable being there. Since I stepped into the room, a thought had been developing. As it grew, it worked on elbowing all other thinking and emotions out of its way until it occupied 'centre stage'.

Why had Lillian locked this room? Yes, it was her private office. But, what was so sensitive in here, she needed to lock people out? Questions come easily; answers not so readily. I knew, over the next few days, I would spend time searching this room for those answers. Before then, there was the other locked room to investigate, Lillian's bedroom. I could think of no reason Lillian wanted people kept out of her bedroom.

Back on the landing, I inserted the second key in the lock on the bedroom door. It released easily with an almost inaudible sound. Still, I hesitated before going inside. Behind this door was Lillian's private space. A place she had not left for a couple of months – until less than two weeks ago when she decided to take herself downstairs. After a couple of deep breaths to steady my nervous apprehension, I pushed open the door and strode in.

Confronted by the rumpled, unmade bed, my newly found resolve faltered. Of course the bed would be unmade, I told myself. By locking the door when she relocated to the back room downstairs, Lillian prevented Rita stripping and remaking the bed. Nevertheless, the sight of it made me a bit weak-kneed. I collapsed onto the bedside chair. A chair I had occupied for so many hours over the last couple of years as I kept Lillian company and we held long conversations.

Apart from the bed, nothing else about the room caught my attention … Or so I thought, until I noticed one of the built-in cupboard's doors was slightly ajar. Lillian must've been in a hurry when she vacated this room. It's the only reason she would leave a cupboard door ajar. Feeling compelled to remedy the situation, I gave the door a shove.

Nothing happened. Something prevented the door from closing. A second, harder shove produced exactly the same result. Again, this was out of keeping with Lillian. She was tidy and fussy about such things, almost to the point of obsession. I needed to put it right for her, to close the door properly.

It was then, Lillian delivered her next surprise. Or, should I say 'shock'? Shelving, from top to bottom, occupied this part of the cupboard. The uppermost shelves held neatly folded underwear. But, the lower shelves caught my attention. I had found the reason the door wouldn't close properly.

I remembered the bottom couple of shelves had been empty. Now, a number of large photo albums filled the second bottom shelf. The uppermost album didn't quite fit and protruded slightly beyond the edge of the shelf. The temptation was too great.

After removing the album, I had to check out its contents. While I don't know what I expected, I know it wasn't what I discovered. The first large black page of the album held about a dozen small photographs, each one fixed in place by four white photo corners. Yellowed with age, all the photos were of people, either in groups or as individuals. Captions handwritten in white ink under some of those of individuals provided no more than a first name.

A photo of a cute little girl with pigtails and gaps in her smile was labelled 'Esme'. Another, of possibly a young teenager, was captioned 'Isabelle'. As I read the names under a few of the other photos, I realised they contained only images of girls of various ages, and there were none of adults or males. Also missing were images of Lillian. Were these photos of friends or family? Because of the various ages represented, I was inclined to think they might be family.

What about the group photos? None of those were labelled. Why? Were the identities of the people involved not known, or was it because Lillian didn't need to write their names for posterity? Sitting on the floor in front of the cupboard with the album open in my lap, I took a closer look at each of those photos. Time slipped away unnoticed. My stomach grumbled, alerting me to the fact it hadn't been fed since breakfast, and it was now dark outside. Only one resulted conclusion from my exhaustive scrutiny of those twelve photographs: they were taken over a period of time. Judging by the clothes and hairdos involved, they were captured over a span of several years.

It was enough to make me stop and take stock of the situation. I tried weighing up what information might be gained from the time required to examine each of the photo albums. If the captions were no more informative than the ones I'd seen so far, it would be a pointless exercise. As I didn't know anything about Lillian's background, or her family, none of the names I came across was likely to mean anything to me. I slapped the album closed and placed it on the empty shelf above the one containing the other albums.

As I scrambled to my feet, a distant thought tried making its presence felt, but remained lurking in in the background of my mind. It accompanied me home, and it wasn't until after dinner it chose to reveal itself.

Its origin stemmed from my weighing up whether to continue examining the albums, and then realising, without prior knowledge of Lillian's family history, the albums were likely to be a waste of time. The keywords in my thinking were 'family history', and it put me behind the eight ball before I even started. Never having been involved in the family history thing – never even having felt inclined to research my own family history – I had no idea where to begin or how to go about tracing Lillian's background.

"Lou...!" Of course, why had it taken me so long to think of her? ... Louella Radford, genealogist extraordinaire, and long-time friend of my mother. Mum and Lou were friends almost since the day they started school together. Their friendship faltered a little during the years of Lou's disastrous marriage, but returned as strong as ever after her husband died. Her husband, much older than Lou and a brute of a man in many ways, died after only seven or eight years of marriage, leaving Lou well off and with investments guaranteeing an ongoing substantial income. Instead of returning to her career as a medical researcher, she turned her hobby into a new career and became a professional genealogist.

Too late to call Lou tonight, I would try to talk to her first thing tomorrow morning. Thoughts of Lou lifted my spirits no end, and special memories of times spent with her accompanied me to bed. As I was about to enter university at the tender age of just seventeen, my mother died after a short but aggressive illness. Both Lillian and Lou were there for me then, and had stayed with me ever since. Now, only Louella remains. As I drifted off to sleep, I made a mental note to start spending more time with Lou … before she too was gone from my life.

*****

Remembering Lou always was an early riser, I didn't feel the need to wait until a civilised hour rolled around to call her this morning. At only a couple of minutes past seven o'clock, she answered on almost the first ring. After the usual pleasantries and apologies for having neglected each other for too long, I moved straight on to the reason for my call.

"You might not be aware, Lou, but Aunt Lillian passed away earlier this week. I'm hoping you might have some spare time to help me with something."

"I returned from England yesterday, and only heard about Lillian last night while dining with a friend when I went to collect my dog she looked after while I was away. I was devastated to learn about Lillian and not be here for you when it happened. How are you holding up? And, as for having spare time, you know I'm retired and have all the time in the world to do as I please. What do you need my help with?"

"Family history…"

"Eh? Like your mother before you, you never showed any interest in researching your family. Has something I should know about happened?"

"No… and it's not my family history I'm interested in. It's Lillian's background. Come to think of it, you've probably already researched her."

"Oh, I see. Lillian… no, I've never looked into her tree. What did you want to know?"

There was no mistaking her disappointment it wasn't my family I was interested in. Ignoring her reaction, I gave Lou an abridged version of my encounter with the three Millard men after Lillian's cremation. In spite of James Whitby's advice not to worry about them, should they turn up again, I felt it would be better to know about them.

"Goodness, Sophie, of course we must find out all we can about those blokes. I don't remember Lillian's mentioning the Millard surname. Nevertheless, they might be hiding somewhere in her tree. Best we get stuck into learning everything about Lillian Cavendish. What are you doing for the rest of today?"

Moments later the call ended. Throwing me into a spin for a few minutes. We agreed to meet at Lillian's house at ten o'clock. What did I need to do beforehand? Was there something I should prepare or take with me? It was too early in the day for such decisions, so I arrived at Lillian's equipped only with a laptop, notebook and pen. Lou just about needed a trailer to transport all the stuff she brought. After several trips up and down the stairs carrying stuff from Lou's car to Lillian's office, I left Lou up there setting up while I made coffee.

From my earliest memories of Lou she had worn caftans and jangling jewellery. It was somehow reassuring to find age had not robbed her of her style. Today she arrived wearing a calf-length floaty creation in swirls of bright colours, and with what must be the best part of a kilogram of costume jewellery occupying her neck and wrists. Over the years, her hair had been every imaginable colour, and never the same colour on two consecutive visits. Today it was tightly permed in a semi-Afro style, and was the fire-engine red colour currently favoured by many teenagers. Also retained was her other signature feature: her love of dramatic and excessive eye makeup, including extra-long false eyelashes. And, as had always been the case, it didn't matter what she wore, it always looked 'right' on Lou.

As I entered the office, Lou cleared a space on the desk for our coffees and the plate of out-of-date dry biscuits I found in a cupboard. The biscuits weren't too bad – if you dunked them. Lou, in full-blown genealogy mode, made sure we didn't dally too long over coffee and stale biscuits. She was determined I should share her enthusiasm. But, as I soon discovered, my role was no more than to bring and fetch in response to Lou's demands. As lunchtime approached, I realised there was nothing to eat in the house. I escaped to the nearby shopping centre in search of food.

On returning from my 'hunter-gatherer' expedition, I found Lillian's office much transformed. Her computer had been replaced by Lou's laptop and, when I entered, one of the printers was spewing forth reams of paper. Lillian's once tidy workspace and clutter-free desk now were something else. Despite Lou's resistance, I insisted she take a break, and lunch was to be eaten in the kitchen, and not in the paper strewn office.

I won the skirmish, but not the battle. My hoped for hour-long lunchbreak lasted about half an hour. As soon as we were in the office again, the questioning began: who were Lillian's parents? When was she born... or how old was she when she died? How could I not know the answers to those questions? Then the big one: who provided the information for her death certificate? It was just another one I couldn't answer. Did I have a copy of the death certificate? My negative response didn't win me any Brownie points either. By the end of the five-minute inquisition, I felt mildly irritated and grossly inadequate. But, I was grateful for the subsequent few moments of heavy silence. They allowed me time to think about the information Lou wanted.

Somebody provided the information to complete the form to register Lillian's death. Since it wasn't me, who was responsible? Who else knew such details? While, sometime prior to her death, Lillian arranged with Frank Harrison everything to do with her cremation, I doubted she shared such personal information with him. The only other person she might be comfortable sharing it with was James Whitby. I wished I knew more about the legal requirements associated with someone's death.

My approach to life had long been: when you want to know something, ask somebody who probably knows about it. So, I did. "Lou, in the case of a normal family death, how would information for the death certificate be collected?"

"In most situations, the then head of the family would provide it. It might be a surviving spouse, or one of the deceased's children. In the latter case, it might be necessary for them to consult with uncles or aunts to ensure complete and accurate information. If the deceased was a young person, a parent would provide the details."

"Is there some delay between when a death is registered and when the death certificate becomes available?"

"It's usually a few days, and could be as long as a couple of weeks or so. Is there a problem with her death certificate?"

"No, I am not aware of any. Lillian died last Monday morning, and today is Saturday. Would a death certificate be available before sometime next week?"

"Okay, I see your point. We still don't know who provided the information for the certificate. Have you any ideas about who it might have been?"

"Nah, not really; the best suggestion I can come up with is her solicitor – her former solicitor – James Whitby. He might have been in possession of the requisite information. Perhaps, in much the same way as she arranged her funeral prior to her death, she also might have pre-arranged for this part of the process as well."

"Good thinking… She had a lot of time for James, and might have trusted his integrity enough to allow him to hold such personal information. Let's give him a call."

"Lou, it is Saturday afternoon. We are not going to call James Whitby today, no matter how important any of this stuff is. It will have to wait until next week. If there is nothing else we can do in the meantime, let's call it a day and go home. Do you agree?" She required some persuading.

As I waved her off home, I wondered whether today achieved anything. "Ah well," I told the empty house as I gathered up my things to leave, "at least today has us set-up and ready for Monday's onslaught on Lillian's family history."

*****

My visit to Lillian's house on Sunday was more out of habit than for any real purpose. After sorting and tidying all the paper Lou had strewn about the office, I spent about an hour studying the photographs in the same album as I looked at earlier. Although no better informed by it, I had developed a suspicion some of the girls making frequent appearances in the photos were important to Lillian. Perhaps they were important enough to be close family members. I knew jumping to such conclusions at this early stage of our research was pointless, but the suspicion persisted.

Reluctant to dig through Lillian's personal papers without Lou there to supervise, I didn't stay long, and spent the rest of Sunday cranky about having to wait for the business world to re-open on Monday before any further research into Lillian's background was possible.

So, Monday morning found me out of bed early and marking time at Lillian's house until Lou arrived.

When ten o'clock slipped by with still no sign of Lou, I was about to write-off the day and go home. "Just in case…," I told the kitchen as I decided to delay my departure until after I had a coffee. "She probably will turn up any minute now," I confided to the kettle as I waited for it to boil. And, I was right. Lou arrived just as I sat down with my coffee.

"Yes please, I would like one of those too," she said by way of a greeting as she waved a satchel at my coffee. "Everything seemed to take longer than usual today, and I was beginning to think I wouldn't be here before lunch. Never mind, I'm here now. So, what have you done since I left on Saturday?" As my short answer was 'nothing', it barely allowed her to pause for breath before she continued. "I've been to all sorts of places this morning; almost waited on their doorsteps for them to open. … Hasn't done me much good though. We need to obtain her basic information before we can do much more."

"I thought we agreed on Saturday, there was nothing more to be done until today."

"True… and now here it is, Monday. Who do you think provided the details for Lillian's death certificate, the undertaker or the solicitor?"

"While I know she made all her funeral arrangements in advance with Frank Harrison, I'm more inclined to think it was her solicitor. Oh, and I don't mean Tom Breen. Theirs was a recent association. If she entrusted such personal information to anyone, I think it would have been James Whitby."

"Right, so where do we get hold of this James Whitby bloke. Do you know him personally, or are we going to have difficulties getting him to hand over the information we need?"

"Apart from the fact I have known him for years, he and I are joint executors of Lillian's estate. As we spoke only last Thursday, I don't foresee any problems approaching him for the information."

My comment was enough for Lou to start organising me. I was to call James to ascertain if he had the information we required. If he did, I was to arrange to see him straight away. If he couldn't provide the details, I was to ask him to suggest someone who might be able to help. Although James is retired now, on occasions he does spend time at the office. But, he also spends a lot of time playing golf and volunteering for a couple of community organisations. I didn't bother alerting Lou to the fact I didn't have a hot line to the retired solicitor, or to the possibility I might not be able to contact him at all today.

My call was put through to Miss Dodson. I still haven't worked out whether she is a secretary or an articled clerk. Regardless of her position, she always gives me the impression she is not particularly fond of me. Today was no different.

"The senior Mr Whitby is not expected in the office today. If you could outline the nature of the business you wished to discuss with him, perhaps I could help you with it."

No-o, I had no intention of giving her any clues whatsoever … if for no other reason than her attitude brought out my dark side. "As you might or might not know, James Whitby and I are co-executors of an estate. I have an urgent matter in relation to the estate to discuss with him. Is there somewhere I might contact him?"

"We do not give out such information. If Mr Whitby should call, I will advise him you wish to speak with him."

There was a loud 'clack' in my ear as she ended the call. So, what now…? I could either go to Lou and admit defeat, or come up with an alternative. The only alternative to come to mind was to call Frank Harrison. While there was no harm in doing so, the little voice in my head kept telling me it would be a waste of time. Lou interrupted my procrastination.

"Are you making a coffee down there? I could use another one – and something to go with it if there's anything in the cupboards. My extra-early breakfast this morning was hours ago."

Chapter 5

Our coffees and a plate of dry, not too fresh biscuits accompanied me up to the office. My work yesterday tidying and organising the office had been destroyed, and chaos ruled once more. While Lou occupied the only chair in the room, I perched on a small cupboard near the window. Our coffee break wasn't nearly as long as I would have liked, but Lou made it clear it was time to get back to work. I trudged down the stairs to return the tray to the kitchen. My phone rang as I rinsed our mugs. James Whitby.

"James… Thank you for calling, and my apologies for interrupting your plans for the day. Miss Dodson gave me the impression I was unlikely to hear from you today."

"Ah, yes, Miss Dodson… very efficient, but she can be something of a tyrant. I'm sure she thinks Tom Breen and I are her personal property. More importantly, as a result of this call, you will now have my number. Call me any time you have something you need to discuss with me. Now, what is the urgent matter you wanted to talk to me about?"

"When we last spoke, I asked you about a family named Millard. Not knowing whether or not those three blokes at her funeral were relatives of Lillian's gnawed at me until I felt compelled to try to find out. I supposed it is a bit like being forearmed in case their threats do come to anything. Anyway, I asked an old family friend, Louella Radford, who is a professional genealogist, to help trace Lillian's family tree. The truth is, we don't know enough about her origins even to make a start on it. We wondered who provided the information for her death certificate and I thought it might have been you."

"Are there no records at the house you could use?"

"No, and no certificates or anything similar; nothing."

"So typical of Lillian; she always was so guarded about her private life. When I was about to retire and her affairs were being handed over to Tom Breen, she gave me an envelope to hold on to. I offered to pass it to Tom, but she insisted I keep it, and it was to be opened only on her death. While it was intriguing, I also found it a bit concerning – from a legal point of view. Nevertheless, I did as she asked and only opened the envelope after Frank Harrison called to advise she had passed away. The short note inside contained the relevant details required to complete the death certificate. I registered the death and advised Frank Harrison accordingly."

"I knew you might be the only person she would entrust with the information. As her death certificate might not be available for a few days yet, might I have a copy of what she left you?"

"Of course, I could drop you a copy now. Where are you, at your place or Lillian's?"

As he was about to go to golf, he said he would drop off a copy of her note on his way past. About ten minutes later, he rang the doorbell. He didn't stay. On the doorstep, he simply handed me the copy of Lillian's note, told me the original had to remain a part of her legal documents, and left. I wanted to read it alone, and took it through to the kitchen.

Oh yes, this is what Lou needs to start unravelling the mysteries of Lillian's background. Her parents' names, where she was born, her date of birth… the latter detail made me catch my breath. Not long before my mother passed away, Lou and I engaged in a fierce debate about when Lillian was born. Although we knew her birthday was in February, none of us knew how old she was. Mum said she had no idea of Lillian's age, and refused to enter our debate. It didn't deter us, and Lou and I continued our guessing game. As revealed by Lillian's note, both of our guesses were a long way shy of the mark. Lillian Cavendish was born in February 1922!

You didn't need to be a genius at maths to work out the grand old lady's age when she died. A wave of emotion engulfed me as I remembered Lillian the way she was the last time I saw her alive – and told her I would be back to annoy her before she even had time to miss me. I had estimated she was in her early nineties. In reality, if she had lingered on for a few more months, she would have been in line for a letter from the Queen. My few moments of maudlin reflection came to an end when Lou called my name.

"Sophie, where are you and what are you doing down there?"

In response, I wandered out into the front room to find Lou standing at the top of the stairs.

"Ah, good, there you are. What do you plan on doing for lunch today? I've done as much as I can do for the moment. So, I thought if you were planning to go somewhere for a bite to eat, we might go now. It's a bit early, but not too early for lunch. What do you think?"

"Well, I was thinking along the lines of a sandwich. I stocked up on some groceries over the weekend so we wouldn't have to interrupt what we were doing here."

"It would be handy – if we were actually doing something. But, as it's not the case, do you still want to make sandwiches?"

Our conversation happened as Lou was coming down the stairs. When part way down, she looked towards the front door. "By the way, who was it rang the doorbell earlier?"

"Come out to the kitchen. I have something for you to read while I make our lunches." I turned on my heel and headed for the kitchen. After a slight hesitation, Lou followed me. I pulled out a chair and indicated for her to sit. "It was James Whitby who rang the bell. He came by to deliver a copy of a note Lillian left with him sometime prior to her death. As soon as we finish lunch, you should be able to make some progress on tracing her family history."

Silence reigned for the few minutes it took me to make the sandwiches. When I brought them to the table, Lou was staring off into the distance. "Are you all right?" I asked quietly. "Is something wrong?"

"Eh…? No, nothing is wrong. Do you realise how old Lillian was?" I nodded. "Damn! If she had lasted just a few more months, she would have appeared in the births index. I would have found her and been able to forge ahead, instead having to waste all this time."

Unsure how to react to Lou's outburst, I decided no response might be the best option… at least for the few moments until I weakened. "Yeah, but she didn't. So, how does the information on her note help with your research?"

Somehow, I avoided voicing my irritation at Lou's comment and the thought it gave rise to: Lillian hadn't chosen to die at the age of ninety-nine out of sheer bloody-mindedness, or just so she could make some inquisitive family historian's life all the more difficult. Although, if I were honest with myself, I would admit she was determined to ensure her life remained a 'closed book' right to the end.

"Yep, what we need to get started is right there in her note. The traditional way of doing family history research is to start from the known and work backwards through the previous generations. If we followed such an approach, the 'known' would have been about Lillian – and it's exactly what we didn't know. Her note gives us the missing information. So, now we can go back to her parents and, in this case, work forward through to Lillian and her wider family. Her note gave us not only the place and date of her birth, but also her parents' names: Frederick Cavendish and Annie Grace Morgan."

"Okay, but where will you start? What will you look for first?"

"Well, First, I'll look for Fred and Annie's marriage, and then I will search for children of their marriage to see where Lillian fitted in the family's structure, and who her siblings were, if there were any."

"Why do we need to know about her siblings? How are they important to finding out about Lillian?"

"We know Lillian never married and never had any children. Well, maybe my statement needs qualifying. It's what we *believe* to be the case, and our research is likely to confirm it to be true. But, if we want to know about any connection she had with the Millard name, we will have to look at other members of her family and what they might have been up to along the way."

"Is it going to be difficult? So far, all we know are the names of her parents. Do we have enough to get started?"

"More than enough…"

"Right, well, come on eat your lunch, so we can go back upstairs to do some work."

While Lou worked her laptop interrogating various online sites, I was at a loose end. Just sitting watching someone else work soon loses its appeal. I went nextdoor to Lillian's bedroom and those photo albums in the cupboard. It occurred to me I had only looked at the first two pages of the only album I had opened. Should I look at one of the other albums, or stick with the one I started on, and go through to the end of it before starting another? After a moment or two of hesitation, I decided to continue with the one I looked at yesterday.

More photos of young women filled the next few pages. Captions were few and far between, and none of them indicated when or where the photo was taken. "This is boring and getting me nowhere," I grumbled to the empty room. I slammed the album closed and reached for a different one. No, I told myself, the decision was to look right through this one before moving on to the other albums. With a deep sigh, I opened the album again and flicked through to the last page I had looked at.

Nothing changed as I worked through the album until, towards the last few pages of it, when something about one of the photos caught my eye. Its caption said 'Esme'. Wasn't it a name I'd seen earlier? I turned back to the first page. There was the photo of the cute little girl with pigtails and missing front teeth – and with the name Esme below it.

After flicking backwards and forwards a few times between the two photos with the same captions, I was convinced they were the same person. In the first photo I estimated Esme to be aged about six or seven, while in the later one, she might have been at the start of her teenage years. Her appearance had changed quite a bit, but I managed to convince myself both photos were of the same person. With the album tucked under my arm, I scrambled to my feet and hurried back to the office.

"Lou… Lou, I know you're busy, but can you spare me a moment to look at something please?" She didn't look too happy about the interruption, but gestured for me to bring the album to the desk so she could see it. I did the flipping backwards and forwards between the two photos performance for her a few times, until she grabbed my hand to make me stop.

"Stop flapping things about, and let me look at those photos properly." After a few moments, she nodded. "Yeah, I'd say they are the same person, but with several years between when the two were taken."

"I don't know if you've found anything yet, but I'm wondering whether this Esme person might be someone close to Lillian. Close enough to be a sister maybe?"

"If you can be patient for just a few minutes longer, I might be able to tell you. I'm waiting for an electronic copy of a certificate, which might provide us with a few answers to questions like such as those." It was a long forty minutes before a loud ping announced the arrival of something in Lou's inbox.

"Ah, maybe it has arrived," she said as she worked the mouse overtime. "Okay, now let's see what we have here. Yes, it's a certificate I asked for. Hang on a moment while I print it out." The big printer sprung to life and spat out two sheets of paper. I grabbed them, slapped one on the desk in front of Lou and held onto the other one.

Not being familiar with death certificates, it took me a moment to work out what it told me. Then I started going through it aloud, in the hope Lou would correct me if I misunderstood anything. "Right, this appears to be the death certificate for Annie Grace Cavendish, whose maiden name was Morgan. Okay, it's a good start. It confirms the name Lillian gave us for her mother. And, it says this woman was married to Frederick Cavendish for what looks like quite a while before she died. So, it would appear we are talking about Lillian's correct parentage." Lou's only response was to nod and keep reading her copy.

After working my way down the certificate to the last item, I paused for a moment. "Here where it says 'issue', I assume the word means 'children'?" It was a moment or two after I'd asked the question before Lou answered.

"Yes, they are Annie's children. It appears she had four daughters, but only two of them were alive at the time of her death. It only takes a moment or two of simple maths to work out, from the date Annie was married and the ages of the children, the deceased daughters were her youngest."

"But, it doesn't tell us the names of those girls. What were their names and when did they die? And, I suppose the other question I should be asking is whether it is important to us or not."

"Well, I could be wrong, but I suspect one of the deceased daughters might be the Esme we've been looking at."

"Can it be Esme? If it is Esme, she couldn't have been very old when she died. Judging by the ages of the other daughters, maybe Esme was still a teenager when she died."

"It's quite possible she did die young and, if it is Esme, she would have been only about nineteen at the most when she died."

"How do we prove whether it is Esme or not we're talking about here?"

"If you go and find something else to do for a few minutes, I will try to confirm whether it is or not. Now, stop talking to me and let me get on with what I'm trying to do."

I didn't have anything else I wanted to do, or needed to do. But, I was almost bursting to know whether the deceased daughter was the girl without front teeth in the early photo of Esme.

While Lou beavered away at whatever family history research requires, I wandered back to Lillian's bedroom and opened her wardrobe. "God, what am I going to do with all this stuff?" I murmured as I ran my hand over the various garments occupying just about the whole hanging space in the cupboard. Further investigation revealed drawers were crammed full, the bedside cabinets were just as well stocked with all manner of bits and pieces, and her dressing table was a veritable wonderland of cosmetics and jewellery.

Up until then, I hadn't given any thought to what I needed to do if the house was about to become mine. It felt a little disrespectful to be thinking about clearing out and getting rid of good stuff, when Lillian was only so recently departed. Nevertheless, it would have to be done – even if the house should end up not being mine. What was an appropriate period of time to wait before doing anything about her personal possessions? I suspected the longer I waited, the harder it might become to do what needed to be done.

Finding the prospect of the task ahead too overwhelming to deal with at the moment, I took myself back to the office. Lou remained much as she was when I left: hunched over her laptop and furiously scribbling in a notebook. I risked interrupting the process. After all, I wouldn't want her to think I wasn't interested in what she was doing.

"How is it going? Has the little bit of information we have been useful?" My audacity earned me a brief glare from the researcher. In my opinion, it was uncalled for. I felt my enquiries reasonable and justified, so I persisted. "Are there any other revelations you care to share with me?"

"If you shut up long enough for me to finish what I'm trying to do, I might well have some interesting information for you. In the meantime, try being patient – and quiet – until I'm finished."

Feeling suitably chastised and put in my place, I stomped across to my now familiar perch atop the small cupboard near the window to sit and sulk for however long it might take. It felt as though she was deliberately stretching out the time it took to do whatever it was just to annoy me. In reality, I probably indulged in my sulk no more than a couple of minutes before Lou threw down her pen and sat back in her chair.

"Well, well, well… Such goings on… Who would have thought it?" Her comments made more to herself than to me.

"I, for one, wouldn't have thought it… mainly because I don't know what 'goings-on' you are talking about. Perhaps, if you shared some of the details with me, I might be able to give you an opinion."

"Eh? Sophie, what are you saying? You are not making much sense, and you're sounding a bit put-out about something. What is wrong with you?"

"You appear to have found something interesting, shocking even. Would you like to share it with me? Come on, Lou. I can see you have disappeared into your own world, but do you think you might like to let me in too? I am supposed to be a part of this exercise, and I was the one who asked you to become involved."

"Of course I'll tell you what I found. I was trying to get it all square in my mind before I tried explaining it to you. Do you think it might be time for coffee? If you go downstairs and make us a coffee, I'll join you in the kitchen in a few moments. We can talk about what I've found while we drink our coffee."

A few minutes later, we were seated at the kitchen table with our coffees and a plate of dry biscuits between us. To avoid any further delay in finding out what Lou discovered, I initiated the discussion I wanted to have. "Okay, Lou, you have the floor. Tell me what your research has uncovered so far this afternoon."

"Well, I haven't focused on any one particular aspect of Lillian's life. Instead, I've tried piecing together the family from when her parents married. I've established Lillian was their first born, arriving about fifteen months after her parents' marriage. She was the oldest of four children, all girls. After Lillian, there was Isabelle, Gladys and Esme."

"So, as I suspected, in the album I was looking at, the photos labelled 'Esme' were of someone close to Lillian– her youngest sister. Some of those other photos also might be of Lillian's sisters. I wonder why she didn't label all of them. I'm sorry, I seem to have interrupted you. Is there any more to tell, or am I going to have to wait for the next instalment?"

"No, there is more. Frederick Cavendish, Lillian's father, died in 1940. At the time of his death, one daughter already had predeceased him. As his certificate shows Lillian, Isabelle and Esme as his surviving children, we can assume it was Gladys who had died."

"She must have been quite young. Although we don't know when she was born – unless you have discovered her birth and not told me about it – isn't it likely she was only a few years old when she died?"

"It seems a sound assumption. The daughters' births were too recent to appear in the index. But, Frederick's death certificate gives the ages of the surviving children at the time of his death. Simple maths gives us approximate birth dates, but accuracy is a problem with given dates. Someone might be listed as nine years old, when they were about a month short of their tenth birthday. While it's accurate at the time, it is not much help in determining in which year they were born. Likewise, a child's age might be given as 'ten', when they were only a couple of months past their ninth birthday. They might have been in their 'tenth year', but not yet ten."

"Okay, I can see the problem associated with the process, but how does it help us with the Cavendish children?"

"Didn't I say? Right, maybe I didn't. Well, judging by the ages on the death certificate, a Cavendish child was born every two years. Given Lillian was born in 1922, Isabelle arrived around 1924, and Gladys' birth likely occurred in 1926… or there about."

"Does it then follow we can assume Esme was born in about 1928?"

"Yes, I think it safe to assume she was born then."

"Right, if we accept your rationale – and your maths –Gladys wouldn't have married. By your calculations, she was about fourteen years old when she died." Lou nodded her agreement. "Good, but we are still left with two daughters who might have married and produced offspring at some point: Isabelle and Esme."

"I have discovered a little more. At the time of the death of Lillian's mother, Annie Cavendish, there were only two surviving children, Lillian and Isabelle. Therefore, Esme, as well and Gladys, predeceased her. We might be tempted to assume Esme died young and might never have married. But, as every piece of information in family history must be confirmed by evidence, I will search for a marriage when I get a spare moment."

"It doesn't sound like she was married, but I suppose it is worth checking before we accept it as fact. How old would she have been when her mother died?"

"Again, it is as speculative as every other date we have but, when Annie Cavendish died in 1953, Esme would have been about twenty-five at the most … if her assumed birth date of 1928 were correct. The problem with our calculation is, we don't really know how long before Annie's death Esme died."

"Then, if she was twenty-five, she was old enough to have married and had a child – if she married young. If we accept our assumptions are correct, it only leaves the life of the other sister, Isabelle, to investigate to discover whether or not she married and produced children."

"Ye-es, so it would appear."

"You don't sound too sure. I feel there is about to be a 'BUT' involved in all this. Am I right – or, is there something you are being cagey about?"

"For a genealogist, there is far too much speculation involved to feel comfortable accepting what we've discussed as being true, or even close to accurate. Much more research is required before I start feeling confident about any of what we have come up with so far."

"So, what are you going to look at next? And, is there anything I can help you with? Bear in mind, I don't know much about how any of this stuff works."

"I am going to have to go soon. I have a meeting to attend this evening. So, we'll have to wait until tomorrow to learn more about the Cavendish family. There is something you could do in the meantime if you feel inclined."

"Of course, what can I do?"

"Perhaps you might buy some decent biscuits for our morning and afternoon teas. I'm a bit over those dry biscuits you've been churning out so far."

"Well, you are in luck. The biscuits we've just had were the last of Lillian's supply. I planned to visit the supermarket on my way home this afternoon. If there is anything else you want added to the larder, you should tell me about it before you leave."

Having confirmed there was nothing else she wanted added to my shopping list, Lou left about twenty minutes later. After washing and drying our lunch and afternoon tea things, it was still early. I didn't feel like leaving Lillian's place yet, and I was suffering an acute awareness of not having contributed anything to our efforts to discover any connection between those three Millard family members and Lillian. Out of force of habit rather than for any particular reason, I headed back upstairs.

Chapter 6

At the top of the stairs, I hesitated. Where to go, the bedroom or the office? Still feeling a bit uncomfortable about going through Lillian's personal belongings, I settled for the office. "And, now I'm here, what am I going to do?" I asked the empty room as I lowered myself onto the chair so recently vacated by Lou. With no suggestions forthcoming, for a few moments, I just sat there letting my eyes roam at will around the room. Having visually explored all in front of me, I swung the chair around to face the bookshelf and cupboards behind the desk.

Still nothing worthy of a poke-around suggested itself to me. Perhaps I should have gone home instead of coming back up here. I suppose the time will come when I do have to explore what lurks in all the cupboards and filing cabinets, but nothing indicated it should happen today. As I was about to vacate my seat and go nextdoor to the bedroom, my eyes wandered to the line of drawers on the right hand side of the desk. "…Might as well check out the drawers while I'm sitting here," I told myself aloud.

The desk looked old, and its manufacture supported its vintage. Made from all good, honest timber, with not a piece of cheap ply or manufactured alternative to timber used anywhere in its construction. Four drawers ran down each side, and a long shallow drawer ran the full width of the desk's well. All drawers were fitted with attractive brass plates and handles. Yes, the drawers were worth a look, I told myself as I fingered the handle on the top right hand drawer.

Opening it did not rival entering Aladdin's cave or finding the pot of gold at the end of the rainbow. Its contents were of the mundane office variety: notebooks, small calculator, plastic tray with partitions containing pens, erasers and paper clips, a pair of scissors, and a medium sized stapler and packet of staples. I felt a slight wave of disappointment wash over me. I don't know what I expected to find, but part of me must have been hoping for something more exotic. After closing the drawer and telling myself to get on with it, I opened the one below it.

"Now, this is more like it. There has to be something more interesting amongst this lot." There were a few files in manila folders, and underneath them were two hard-covered journals. At first glance, the files didn't appear particularly interesting. Not interesting enough to warrant spending time reading them right now anyway. I stacked them on top of the desk and removed the first of the books.

It appears Aunt Lillian had expensive tastes. The black *faux* leather-covered expensive brand of hard-covered book looked intriguing. As I ran my fingers over its tactile surface, a thought flashed in from left field. There were no diaries. It caused me to delay opening the book while I thought about the apparent lack of diaries. After reminding myself this was only the second drawer I'd opened. Common sense suggested diaries were probably in one of the other drawers.

I flicked open the book in front of me to its first page. *January 2020* written in jumbo-sized copperplate occupied the centre of the page. Turning the page answered a few questions. It appears Lillian shunned traditional diaries in favour of keeping a journal. A journal eliminated blank pages for days when there was nothing of note to record, and allowed as much, or as little, to be written whenever its owner saw fit.

I flicked to the last entry. It was written on a Tuesday about three months ago. The date tied in with my memory of when Lillian was experiencing difficulty getting out of bed and became bedridden soon after. It wasn't a long entry, and was written in a hand more shaky than in the early pages. Ignoring my almost overwhelming discomfort, I forced myself to read her last entry.

'Heartrending' is the most apt word I can think of to describe it. It recorded Lillian's frustration and disgust at her diminishing ability in almost every aspect of her life. She acknowledged her future was short, and her life was drawing to its close. Instead of any hint of sadness or disappointment about her looming demise, she wished it a speedy arrival, and for her life soon to be over.

She wished for nothing more than to end her dependence on others, and to cease being a burden to those who had taken on caring for her. There was a brief comment about endeavouring to put in place everything necessary to deal with her demise when it came, and how she hoped she would not overlook some critical aspect of those preparations.

At last the floodgates opened, and those tears I'd held back over the last week now welled up and rolled down my cheeks. Since my mother's death, Lillian and Lou had been my support network. But, it was Lillian who became the surrogate mother to this seventeen year old university undergraduate. She picked up the reins the moment my mother died and remained a steadfast part of my life until last Monday. And now, my rock was gone. Along with the tears and the feeling of grief, I felt cast adrift on the ocean of life.

"Pull yourself together! This is nonsense. Get up and do something useful. Sitting here blubbering doesn't make anything right – or better." I slammed the journal closed and sprang up out of the chair. Telling myself to do something useful was all very well, but what constitutes 'something useful' in the here and now? Nevertheless, I felt compelled to exit the office but, once out on the landing, something seemed to draw me into Lillian's bedroom.

For a brief moment, I wondered whether this might be an 'out of the frying pan into the fire' type situation. I didn't have to belong to Mensa to realise spending time in her bedroom could only result in my becoming even more maudlin. Regardless, here I was in the bedroom. Now I'm here, what am I going to do? I suppose I could look at some of those other photo albums but, if the lack of captions continues, it will be a pointless exercise. In spite of acknowledging the fact, almost as if pulled by some strange magnet, I was drawn once again to the built-in wardrobe.

With all the lower doors standing wide open, I stood back to study the contents for a moment. Apart from the photo albums, everything was as you might expect to find in a woman's wardrobe. Granted, quite a few of the garments were more modern and fashionable than might be associated with someone of Lillian's advanced years. I don't think Lillian had ever seen herself as old, or considered herself to be as ancient as she was. Why should she? She didn't look so old, and her brain had never withered as the years rolled by. Her mind was as sharp as ever, right up until the end.

The top sections of the cupboard I could just about reach, but it would be much easier if I stood on a chair to open them. I dragged over the chair from beside the bed and climbed up on it. It allowed me to open the upper cupboard doors with ease. I would need to move the chair along to open the other two doors, but opening those might be something for another day. The contents of the two sections I opened were not what I expected, and now held my full attention.

Recycled shoe boxes and copy paper boxes, all stacked neatly, filled one section. The second section appeared to be a jumble of books and folders. Why would she keep this stuff in her bedroom when her office next door appears to have more than ample storage capacity? Did she consider this stuff more personal – more private and confidential – than material kept in the office?

There was only one way to find out: going through it all, piece by piece. And, there was nothing more I wanted to do. But the afternoon was fast drawing to a close. If I didn't visit the supermarket soon, I would need to be there early tomorrow morning to accommodate Lou's request for something better than dry biscuits. Without closing the two upper cupboard doors, I dragged the chair back to beside the bed.

I closed the bedroom door behind me, but the little voice in my head told me closing the door was not good enough. It reminded me Lillian had sought to keep private the things in her room, and now I had left them exposed for anyone who ventured in there to see. I galloped down the stairs and out to the kitchen cupboard where I had stashed the small cardboard box containing the two keys for the upstairs rooms. Moments later, the bedroom door was locked, the key was back in its cardboard box, and I was locking the front door behind me on my way out to the car.

*****

A phone call just as I was about to leave for Lillian's place this morning left me wondering about the rest of my day. Lou wouldn't be joining me today as a job, which could stretch on into tomorrow, had come up. I gave the bags of groceries waiting to be loaded into my car a rueful look. My rushed provisioning run just before closing time yesterday now could have been done at my leisure this morning. After hesitating for only a moment, I loaded them into my car. Lou's absence today was no reason for me not to do anything.

My motivation might have been due in part to a flashback to the treasure trove of material I discovered in the top section of Lillian's wardrobe. I wouldn't know if it were important until I went through it. Confident it would occupy me today and maybe tomorrow, I set off with a brighter feeling about the day.

With the groceries stashed, I raced up and unlocked the bedroom door. Moments later, standing on the chair, I was hauling material out of the cupboard. Being a one-man operation, the process necessitated climbing on and off the chair many times before all of the material was stacked on the floor. The original plan was to take it all through to the office. In the end, I took only whatever I was about to work on into the office. This meant sitting on the floor amidst the rescued material to sort it out.

About half an hour later, quite a bit of it was sorted into discrete piles according to its content. There were several journals from many years prior to the one I looked at yesterday.

Correspondence folders required restraint until everything else was sorted into relevant piles. The sorting done – and before I succumbed to the lure of those folders – a coffee might be a good idea. Once I started studying the material in detail, I knew I would not take a break.

Soon, my coffee waited on the big wooden desk while I fetched something to work on. My original thinking was to begin with one of the folders. By the time I went to collect one, my interest had shifted to one of the recycled copy paper boxes. It wasn't as heavy as I expected, but did seem to hold quite a bit of material. I plonked it down in the middle of the desk and gently eased off the lid. My strangled yelp echoed loudly through the silent house.

Where on earth did all this stuff come from? …And, why did Lillian have it? Although I hadn't done more than remove the lid, already I could see a pair of baby's bootees, a rattle, and something I thought might be a teething ring. These obvious baby's items lay on top of neatly folded baby's clothes. Judging by the prevalence of the colour pink, they were meant for a little girl. As far as we knew, Lillian never married and never had a child. Why would she store a box of baby's things… and from whose baby?

Without removing anything from the box, careful but perfunctory inspection of the clothes produced no clues as to whose they were. Stunned, I sat back and tried to work out what to do next. Should I check the other boxes to see if they too contained baby's things? Or, would my time be better spent trying to find out about the baby to whom all this stuff belonged at some time in the past? With no clear course of action in mind, I returned to the other material on the bedroom floor.

It would be time well-spent if I just lifted the lids on the other boxes to gauge what they contained. In one of the other boxes, amongst unrelated material, I found a child's tiny pair of shoes. Although not an expert on such matters, I allowed myself to imagine they might have been a child's first pair. Apart from those, a look in each of the boxes without disturbing anything produced nothing more relating to children.

It was obvious, if I wanted to know more about whose baby, I had to search for documentary information. The question was where to find it? Would there be something recorded in the journals? Perhaps, but how long ago, and was the relevant journal amongst the pile on the floor in front of me? Somewhere amongst Lillian's papers, maybe there were letters or certificates which would explain everything. All such thinking did was reiterate what was becoming a standard question: where to look, and for what?

My attention turned to the stacks of thick folders. There were eight of them and all filled to bursting point. Again, I assured myself having a quick flick through each of the folders wouldn't be a waste of time. It should give me some idea about the contents of each one. I grabbed the top folder off the stack closest to me. With the clip holding everything so tightly in place, flicking through the contents was no easy task.

What I envisaged as a quick and straightforward process proved to be time-consuming and an exercise in frustration. Nevertheless, by the time I stopped for a late lunch, I had a reasonable understanding of what each of the folders contained. Although why Lillian went to the trouble of filing some of the material in such a way remained a mystery. One folder contained what looked like of outgoing correspondence. I hoped a closer inspection might produce chains of correspondence which would provide insight into the issues being discussed.

The contents of another folder made me catch my breath. I had to explore it in detail before anything else. As I carried it to the office, my stomach tightened and an uneasy feeling began developing. No point in rushing into bad news, I told myself as I placed the folded on the desk. Perhaps a quick sandwich before tackling what lies ahead might make sense … and provide an opportunity to stall a bit longer.

In spite of my best delaying tactics, it was time to face the contents of that folder. With my resolve somewhat weak and tenuous, I trudged upstairs and flopped down at the desk. As I dragged the folder over to me, doubts flood in. Maybe I should leave well enough alone ... Maybe Lillian had her reasons for keeping her life so private ... Maybe I had no right to pry. There might be something to the old adage about letting sleeping dogs lie. "Open the folder," I snarled.

Without reading the top document, I turned to the second document in a plastic pocket. The item it contained caught my eye earlier when I flicked through the folder. This was the cause of my trepidation and the lead ball in the pit of my stomach. I took a deep breath and began reading. Expecting to discover Lillian had a child at some point in her life, I had to read the birth certificate twice from start to finish before I began to understand. This was not a birth certificate for a child of Lillian's. It was for a daughter born to Esme Harding (nee Cavendish) and her husband, Bert Harding.

So, do the children's things belong to Lillian's child, or her sister Esme's daughter? On face value, it was strange for Lillian to keep a box of her niece's baby clothes. On the other hand, she might hold on to a box of her own child's things. Well, whoever the owner of those clothes was, they might be the start of a family lineage which connects to the Millard name – and the blokes who accosted me at the funeral home.

Born in 1946, Ruby was Esme's daughter, and Lillian's niece. Since Ruby's birth, sufficient time had elapsed for at least a couple more generations of the line to occur. Would children of the most recent generation of Esme's line be considered close enough relations to have valid claim on Lillian's estate? As I sat staring at the birth certificate, I found myself wishing Lou was here to help make sense of it. A thought tried to elbow its way through to the front of my thinking. Although I continued staring at the birth certificate to help it, the thought remained bogged in a dark corner.

After chiding myself for having stalled my investigation so early in the folder, I reminded myself there were more documents to examine. Perhaps, as I worked my way through the folder, the story would unfold and all would become clear. With some semblance of resolve, I flipped over to the next document: another certificate in a plastic protective pocket.

"What the…?" My exclamation was so loud, it startled me … and probably brought the neighbours running to their windows.

In the pocket in front of me was a death certificate … Esme Harding's death certificate. But, this was far from being an ordinary looking document. Just about all of its margins were filled with handwritten notes. Before tackling the tiny writing, I concentrated on the details in the body of the certificate.

"Now, let's find out what happened here. Can that be right…?" Stunned by what I read, I flipped back to the previous certificate for Esme's daughter, Ruby, for a quick check before returning to the death certificate. There was no error in my maths. Esme died about two weeks after her daughter's birth. The certificate listed a couple of unhelpful causes of death, which I think simply meant it was due to complications associated with the birth.

The thought struggling for attention almost came through to the front. It urged me to take another look at the date. And, yes, I knew there was something significant about it. But what…? While it was tragic she died so soon after her baby was born, the little voice in my head was suggesting there was something else I should be aware of. I reached for the notebook in which I was recording facts as we uncovered them. As I entered the date of Esme's death, my eyes slid up to entries I'd made while Lou was here.

"She was still a child herself!" I was stunned when the realisation dawned on me. Esme was born in 1928, and here she was dead a little before her eighteenth birthday in 1946. Even I can work out she became pregnant not too many weeks after her seventeenth birthday. "What else does this certificate tell me?" I asked the empty room before turning to the handwritten notations.

It confirmed everything I knew so far about Esme: her husband was Bert Harding, and she was survived by one daughter, Ruby, aged two weeks. Well, there were no surprises so far. Now for the marginal notes… where to start?

Having decided to start at the lower left-hand corner and proceed clockwise around the margins. The writing appeared a little clearer now it was removed from the plastic pocket, but it still resembled small ants crawling around it. A quick forage in the desk's drawers produced a magnifying glass. I took a deep breath and began reading.

A few minutes later, I slumped back in my chair, too stunned to fully comprehend everything I had read. Sitting there – probably with my mouth hanging open – I allowed the details to bounce around in my mind for a while, until they finally settled into one cohesive story. I scribbled my interpretation of it in my notebook:

Esme was not married to Bert Harding as she claimed. Bert Harding was a married enlisted man with a family, who claimed no knowledge of Esme or her child. As a result of investigations carried out after the mother's death, Esme Cavendish's child, born two weeks before her mother's death, was determined to be illegitimate, and the records were to be amended to reflect the true situation surrounding the birth.

I re-read my note. Although a potted version of all the formal jargon written on the certificate, my note covered all the salient points. Nevertheless, it remained difficult to comprehend all the implications arising from the certificate. While it was a tragic end for young Esme, what about her baby? What happened to Ruby after her mother's death? Did she survive? If she did, what became of her?

With no more to be extracted from the death certificate, and no real answers gleaned from it, continuing through the folder was the logical next move. I flicked over to the next item: another certificate in a plastic pocket. This one caused no real surprises. It appeared to be an amended birth certificate issued for the illegitimate baby, Ruby Cavendish. My intention to continue with the folder diminished as another idea gained credence. I closed the folder and headed back to Lillian's bedroom – and the stack of journals on the floor.

The one covering the time period I was interested in took some finding as not all of the journals had their relevant date range listed on their cover. There was a chance I would be wasting my time scanning the journal entries, but I figured the death of her youngest sister would rate at least a mention in Lillian's journal of the day. My search located more than 'a mention'. A whole family saga unfolded over several pages. But, to find the beginning of the story, I had to flip back through the pages to almost the start of the journal.

Chapter 7

Although not yet seventeen, the young Esme defied her parents and moved to the city to commence nursing training. Lillian's record of the event and the upheaval it caused in the family, suggested, apart from Esme's age, the parents did not consider nursing an appropriate occupation for their daughter. It appears, as soon as Esme left for the city, her parents considered asking the police to bring her back. After all, their daughter was a long way from attaining her majority and legally being able to make her own decision regarding her life.

While Lillian and Isabelle appeared to share their parents' views on the matter of Esme's becoming a nurse, the two daughters counselled against involving the police. They argued it would cause the family embarrassment, and could impact on their father's position as a local councillor. Better to maintain an unsullied image in the town, than to give the locals something to gossip about.

Okay, the family's feeling about the young Esme leaving home to begin nursing are quite clear. It's probably fair to assume things were a bit strained between the parents and their youngest daughter, and I imagine they worsened when Esme became pregnant. I skimmed pages in the journal looking for the next mention of Esme, to gain a possible insight into how the family reacted to the news of the pregnancy. After having worked through a lot of pages without finding Esme's name mentioned anywhere, I paused to think about the Cavendish family's situation.

A stray thought had me open the folder at Ruby's birth certificate. Aha, so that's how it played out. At first, I thought the parents would insist Esme came home to be looked after … and possibly have any 'necessary arrangements' made. It wasn't the case. Esme didn't give birth in her home town, or anywhere close by. In fact, the birth certificate shows Ruby was born close to where she had been nursing. Perhaps it speaks volumes about the family's reaction to the news. I returned to skimming pages in the journal.

At last, Esme's name appeared again. Some simple maths suggested she was then about seven months pregnant. The note Lillian recorded in her journal suggested her feelings towards Esme had softened somewhat. When she contacted Esme, she learned her baby sister was no longer working. Unable to hide her condition any longer, she went to the matron to resign, and was told they were about to sack her anyway *as they were not blind to her unacceptable condition.*

There followed some process of re-establishing the sisters' relationship. Lillian discovered Esme was staying in a church-run hostel while awaiting the birth of her child. No further mention of Esme appeared until shortly before the baby's birth. Lillian's next journal entry suggests she was struggling to cope with Esme's impending event. The following few brief entries over the subsequent period of time indicate Lillian's increasing concern for her sister.

The next journal entry relating to Esme was a long and touching record of Lillian's emotional turmoil as Esme's due date approached. It was obvious the family had cut Esme from their life when she left to go nursing, and they continued to shun her from then on. While Lillian appears to have tried to mediate the situation towards the end, she records her efforts were rebuffed by the family. She was left with having to decide whether to turn her back on Esme and stand with the family, or to defy them and make some overture to her sister.

It appears the latter option won out. A week before the baby was born, Lillian took holidays from the accounting firm where she worked and travelled into the city. There appears to have been some communication between the sisters before Lillian went to visit Esme at the hostel. In her journal, Lillian later recorded how shocked she was by Esme's drawn and haggard appearance. After their first tentative meeting, Lillian returned to the hostel the following day and was shocked when the woman running the place told her Esme was no longer there.

Complications arose and, although about two weeks early, Esme went into labour and was admitted to hospital. Armed with the name and address of the hospital, Lillian went to find her sister – and drew a blank. The hospital had never heard of any Esme Cavendish. After a few tense and sometimes heated minutes, Lillian established a young woman by the name of Esme Harding had been admitted the previous night. When Lillian asked to at least see the woman to ascertain whether it was her sister or not, her request was refused. The woman in question had been in labour for several hours and doctors feared, if she did not give birth soon, they would have to intervene.

Rather than leave, Lillian opted to remain at the hospital to await further news. A couple of hours later, she was told Esme had given birth to a healthy but small baby girl. It was late afternoon when Lillian was finally allowed to see her sister. She later recorded how, from the moment she saw her, it was evident how long and difficult Esme's labour had been. With Esme so exhausted and weak, Lillian kept her visit brief. There was no mention of Esme's registering under the Harding surname until Lillian's visit the following day.

Esme, reluctant at first to discuss the matter, succumbed to Lillian's continued questioning, but not to the extent Lillian wanted. When pressed about how strange it was for her 'husband' to be invisible at such an important time – and why Esme had been staying in a hostel instead of at home with him – Esme explained he was enlisted and still overseas. Lillian's entry in her journal following her visit indicates she was not quite satisfied by Esme's explanation. The next entry shows she pursued the matter again on her next visit to Esme.

While it appears not all the details were forthcoming, Esme admitted she and Bert Harding were not married. She claimed he was sent overseas just as they were about to seek her parents' permission to marry. Lillian recorded her belief permission would be withheld. The family had disowned Esme, and Lillian felt sure they would not be inclined to grant her any favours. Almost as a postscript to the entry, Lillian added Esme's final comments on the matter: *If the hostel knew she was unmarried, the baby would be taken from her soon after birth and put up for adoption.*

Those few journal entries left me unsettled, and saddened by people's unkindness to others. I needed to take a break … I needed a coffee … And I needed time to come to terms with everything gleaned from Lillian's journal. Maybe the best thing to do was to call it a day; go home and let everything I learned today distil overnight.

*****

After I left Lillian's house yesterday, one thought troubled me. It persisted and managed to keep sleep at bay for some time.

I remained unaware whether Lou would be joining me at Lillian's today. Perhaps I should call her to suggest she not bother to come today. What even vaguely acceptable sounding reason could I give? Anyway, the curiosity such a call might generate would make her all the more determined to turn up. It wasn't about not appreciating Lou's efforts, or needing her expertise. It was about all I learned yesterday making me feel this was something private between me and Aunt Lillian. Lou's presence would seem an intrusion.

Questions swirling through my head fought for attention all the way to Lillian's house. Did Lillian have a child at some time, or was it only Esme who gave birth to a daughter? What happened to baby Ruby after Esme died. Was Bert Harding Ruby's father, although he and Esme were not married? Was baby Ruby given to Bert Harding to bring up when he returned from active service? So many questions, but the big one: where to start my research today?

As I approached the house, instead of pulling in onto the driveway, I eased in against the kerb out front. Half expecting Lou to be waiting on the front doorstep, it came as a pleasant surprise when there was no sign of her. For a few moments, I studied the house. Almost a copy of so many to be found in the area, there was nothing remarkable about it.

It was an ordinary, unadorned, two storied square box, the colour of butter, with its only enhancement a few bits of russet-toned trim. Set in the middle of a mid-sized block of land, it had a minuscule front garden and a larger pocket handkerchief-sized backyard. All of it sat tucked tidily in place behind a white picket fence fitted with a double gate for vehicle access and a single gate for foot traffic. The smaller gate was surmounted by a plain, no-nonsense arbour which, for many years, was enhanced by a climbing rose until the rose bush was deemed to be too much trouble and was removed some years ago. After months of neglect, the once lush lavender-filled garden bed along the inside of the front fence now looked forlorn and had more gaps than plants. Window boxes on the ground floor front windows once were resplendent with red geraniums, but they too were long gone.

My mind wandered around to the rear of the house and its tiny backyard. Carers, Mavis and Rita, always drove their cars along the back lane and in through the double gate in the back fence to park in the back yard. Due to the narrowness of the lane, entry to and exit from the yard could be a difficult manoeuvre requiring much 'backing and filling'. For years, until Lillian gave up driving, I parked there too. As Lillian was getting on a bit and traffic was increasing, she decided it was cheaper to use public transport – mainly taxis – rather than pay skyrocketing car registration and insurance costs. She always parked on the driveway in front of the house but, once she sold her car, I commandeered her favoured parking spot.

"Enough procrastination," I announced with a sigh, before easing out from the kerb and turning onto the driveway. Making a coffee to take upstairs with me provided opportunity to fritter away a few more minutes, and gave me time to work out what to tackle first today. As I stood over the kettle waiting for it to boil, someone calling my name startled me.

"Sophie. Sophie, sorry I'm late. Where are you?"

"I'm in the kitchen, Lou. Would you like a coffee to help start your day?"

"Oh, yes please. It seemed the more I hurried, the later I became this morning and, of course, then I got stuck in traffic. After the hectic day I had yesterday, a nice quiet day of research is what I need today – along with coffee and a nice biscuit to get it started."

Upstairs, Lou commandeered the only chair in the office. For a brief moment, I contemplated adopting my usual perch atop one of the small cupboards before a better idea occurred to me. I marched into Lillian's bedroom, picked up the visitor's chair from beside the bed, and carried it back to the office. My former perch, the top of the small cupboard, provided a nice side table.

"Right, so where shall we start today?" Lou demanded. "Have you had any bright ideas in my absence?"

"Ye-es… and no, I dug up a few interesting snippets yesterday, but I'm not sure how to progress further with some of it. Here are the notes I scribbled out as I found pieces of information. You might like to read them while you have your coffee. Then, we'll talk about what we going to do next." I was determined not to be put off by Lou's sceptical look.

So, while she drank her coffee and came up to speed with what I discovered, I grabbed the journal I worked on yesterday and retreated to my chair and its makeshift table. The little voice in my head was reminding me not to let her see I didn't know what I was doing. With a false show of confidence, I flicked through the journal to where I left off yesterday, and began working forward as I searched for the next mention of either Esme or Ruby.

Eureka… there it was. A quick scan of the next long entry in the journal suggested it might answer at least some of my questions, but I noted it contained no reference to Bert Harding. Aha, maybe it's something Lou could work on. With her expertise in finding out all there is to know about people, maybe she will be able to fill in the blanks about Mr Harding. I risked interrupting her reading of my notes to suggest it to her.

"Hmm… As I imagine it's all comparatively recent stuff, it will be a bit more difficult. Nevertheless, I'm sure I will be to dig up something about the fellow. As soon as I finish my coffee and set up my laptop, I'll get started on tracking him down."

With the matter of Bert Harding seemingly under control, I returned to the long entry in Lillian's journal. The first thing I discovered was it was more than just one entry. It was a series of entries over a period of time running together to paint a picture of a situation lasting almost three weeks. After her birth, Ruby appears to have been a bit 'fragile' (as Lillian described it). But, after a couple of days, Ruby began putting on weight and behaving as any normal baby would.

By the time a mother and her baby normally would leave hospital and begin establishing their routines and lives together, some concerns had arisen regarding Esme's condition. Lillian didn't specify the nature of those 'concerns', but the increasing length of time Lillian spent by Esme's bedside each day suggested they were serious. Then, it was all over. The young mother had lost her struggle to survive.

Lillian's words left me in no doubt her youngest sister's death hit her hard. A flood of sadness tinged with guilt swept over me as I read Lillian's personal account of her remorse and anguish at the loss of her sister. Although of no consequence to Lillian now, my intrusion into such private commentary caused me extreme discomfort. The tears welled up, stinging my eyes. I struggled to hold them back. The last thing I needed was Lou cross-examining me about them.

After regaining some measure of composure, I pushed on with the next journal entry. While not lengthy, it was no less poignant than the previous one, and covered arrangements Lillian put in place for her sister's funeral. Esme would not be going 'home' to be buried. In spite of Lillian's efforts to unite the family in providing a peaceful end for Esme, it was not to be. Isabelle sided with her mother in rejecting any suggestion the Cavendish family had a daughter named Esme. How could they do that? Even after her death, they continued to disown her.

The next journal entry indicates the family's foolish pride achieved nothing but to strengthen Lillian's resolve … and consolidate the wedge between her and the rest of her family. I thought for a moment about how a family – how a parent – could be so cold-hearted and react in such a way to one of their own. It was a waste of time. There was no way I would ever understand it.

While waiting for the funeral to occur, Lillian continued visiting baby Ruby in hospital. She persuaded the nursery staff to allow her to hold her niece, and to help bath and feed her, insisting the baby should not miss out on knowing the love and care other infants receive from their mothers at this early stage of life. The only day Lillian didn't visit Ruby was the day of the funeral because … as she noted …she was concerned Ruby would sense how distraught Lillian was, and it would upset the child.

God, I'm going to have to walk away from this journal for a while; find something else to do. It is so depressing. If the journal continues in this vein, I am going to need a box of tissues – and probably a stiff drink too. "I'm going to fetch some water before we both die of thirst. I'll be back soon. When I return, if you can tear yourself away for a few moments, perhaps you could tell me what you have discovered so far," I said as I left the office.

Lou grunted by way of acknowledgement, and I bolted down the stairs. I loaded a jug of water and a couple of glasses onto a tray ready to take upstairs. But, I wasn't ready to go back up yet. I needed more time to settle a bit before returning to the journal. My watch told me it was almost lunchtime; just what I needed.

"It's almost lunchtime, Lou," I called up to her. "How about I make it while I'm down here and we take a break now?"

"Okay, I'll be right down."

Not too artistically slapping slices of cold meat and salad on a plate doesn't take long. Lou joined me in the kitchen just as lunch was ready. I was impressed by my self-restraint as I allowed her to clear most of her plate before I asked for a report on her morning's efforts.

"Make us another coffee first, and then I tell you while we drink it."

The suggestion worked for me, so I made the coffees and we took them through to the relative comfort of Lillian's ancient lounge chairs. "Right, you have the floor and I'm all ears. What have your labours uncovered this morning?"

"Well, I'm not sure whether it's positive progress or not. As you suggested, I focused on tracking down Bert Harding. I now believe I'm safe in saying Harding was not the father of Esme's daughter, Ruby. While maths might not be my strong point, I didn't need a calculator to work out he couldn't be the father. Esme was right when she said he was enlisted and overseas. Thanks to his service records in the archives, it's obvious he just wasn't around at the right time."

"So, is it likely she was involved with Bert Harding and somebody else at the same time, and was confused about who was responsible?"

"No. No, I think it unlikely she was involved with Bert Harding at all. It took me a while to get to the bottom of an event in Harding's life. It wasn't until I read his statement to the court, the details of a particular period became clear. The incident in question began about six months before when I think Esme became pregnant. During a two-day furlough before being shipped overseas, Harding gave his wife a 'going away present' to nurture and care for over the ensuing nine months."

"He was married? And his wife was pregnant? What was Esme thinking, getting involved with someone like him?"

"Now don't go jumping the gun, wait until you've heard the whole story before forming conclusions. After nine months overseas, Harding and his mates were brought back to Sydney, where they spent a weekend in barracks before moving on. It seems anyone with family in the Sydney area was given a twenty four-hour furlough to catch up with their family.

For the last couple of months of her pregnancy, Harding's wife – and their two young children – moved back in with her family to await the birth. As soon as Harding was released on furlough, he went to his in-laws' home to see his wife … only to be told she had gone into labour and had been admitted to hospital."

"The story is becoming more sordid by the moment. Don't tell me his wife was admitted to same hospital as where Esme was nursing."

"I'm afraid it is exactly what I'm going to tell you. Anyway, getting back to my story… Harding went to the hospital to await the birth. He wanted his wife to know, although it was by pure good luck, he was there with her. In those days, husbands weren't allowed anywhere near the delivery room, but he stopped a young trainee nurse and asked her to deliver a message to his wife. It seems she did so and then, during the subsequent hours he spent waiting to see his child and its mother, the same young trainee nurse took pity on him and kept him plied with cups of tea, and the odd dry biscuit when she could find one."

"Are you suggesting the young nurse was Esme? I'm sorry, but such a situation between Esme and her lover at such a time is beyond my comprehension. Nevertheless, if there is any more to this story, you had better tell me about it."

"You are still jumping to conclusions, and I think you missed the main point of this story. It doesn't matter. I'll do a recap at the end of it. When he finally left the hospital, Harding went back to his in-laws' house to share the good news, and telephoned his brother to tell him as well. His brother suggested they should have a drink to celebrate the occasion. Harding's wife's two brothers agreed. The four men made a big night of it and were quite drunk by the time they were chucked out of the pub at closing time.

Harding slept late the next day and surfaced feeling pretty seedy. He hung around at his in-laws' house – to use his words – *until he got himself together* before going back to the hospital to see his wife and son one last time before he shipped out again.

The visit didn't end so well for him. Things were okay while he was with his wife but, when a nurse brought his son in for him to hold for a few minutes, she smelled the booze on him. Believing it was inappropriate for someone in Harding's state to be handling a child, she reported his condition to the matron, who promptly had him thrown off the premises."

"As you say, it didn't end well for him. I can't say I feel any sympathy for him, but I do feel for his wife in all of this. So, what happened after his undignified exit? You said something about him telling the story in court."

"Well, having been chucked out of the hospital, he collected his gear and headed back to barracks. The problem was, he was supposed to be back at barracks by noon. It was 12.45pm when he signed in at the gate. He was charged for his late return. The following day, Harding and the rest of his platoon were sent up north somewhere, and he was away from home for at least another six months. At his appearance in court during the week after they left Sydney, he was shown some leniency due to the compassionate circumstances involved. He was sentenced to three weeks confined to barracks."

"Okay, if it's the end of the story, how does it prove he couldn't be Ruby's father?"

"Oh, for goodness sake, pay attention and I'll spell it out for you. The only connection he had in any way with Esme was if she was the young trainee nurse who paid him a bit of attention during the birth of his son. Harding was shipped overseas at least six months before Esme became pregnant, and didn't return to Sydney for nine months. At the time his son was being born, Esme was already about three months pregnant.

Whether you like it or not, Bert Harding just wasn't around at the right time to have been responsible. My guess is as follows: Esme had an affair with some unknown bloke. It seems likely she was the nurse who took care of Harding while he waited for his son to be born. To avoid having Ruby registered as illegitimate and taken from her for adoption as soon as she was born, Esme looked around for a fictitious father ... And remembered Bert Harding who she probably considered was a nice bloke."

"Ye-es, but then, who was the father? How does any of what you have found help us find a connection to the Millard surname? After all, that is the purpose of this whole exercise."

"We probably will never know who the father was. What we achieved today was to eliminate Bert Harding from the equation. I'm not saying it's the end of the story, or the hunt for information. All I'm saying is, Esme's history has come to an end. Now we need to move onto the next generation, to Ruby. If you think about it, there could be a couple of generations added to Esme's line since her death. The connection you're looking for might have happened during any one of those generations. So, instead of haranguing the narrator because you don't like the story, accept it, and push on with the research."

Chapter 8

Lou stood up, indicating our session was over. Feeling more than a little stupid and totally embarrassed, I mumbled my apologies for my behaviour.

As Lou walked over to the stairs, she checked her watch. I copied her and was surprised at how much time had elapsed since we'd eaten.

"Sophie, I think I might go back upstairs to pack up and go home. Tomorrow we'll start trying to find out what happened to Ruby."

"Look, I hope you're not rushing off because of the way I've behaved. I am sorry for the way I carried on. It was uncalled for, and I suppose it was an indication of how frustrated I am with trying to find out whether those Millard blokes do have any claim on Lillian's estate."

"God no, I'm not so thin-skinned as not to be able to handle my findings being questioned. It happens all the time. The only reason I'm going to leave early is to avoid the afternoon traffic. I'll be back here tomorrow, but I might be late again, say, sometime between ten and eleven, if it's okay with you?"

"Yeah, it's fine with me. Before you go, I'd like your opinion on something." Lou indicated for me to ahead and ask. "Regardless of what ends up happening with this house, is it likely to cause problems if I start throwing out some stuff?"

"As executor of Lillian's estate, I believe you have the right, but it might depend to some extent on what you were thinking of getting rid of."

"Rubbish collection is tomorrow and there is almost nothing in the bin here. I thought I might make a start on cleaning out her wardrobe. Oh, only anything not good enough to go to the local Op Shop. Underclothes, and scuffed and well-worn shoes, might be a safe place to start. There's plenty of room in the bin for a few big bags of rubbish this week."

"It sounds like an ideal opportunity to make a start on what is likely to develop into a major task before all her personal stuff is dealt with."

While Lou was busy upstairs packing up to go home, I spent the time cleaning up after our lunch. About fifteen minutes later, I waved her off. Then, it was time to make a start on clearing out Lillian's wardrobe. Armed with several large plastic bin liner bags, I headed upstairs to Lillian's bedroom.

Emptying all the underwear and other bits and pieces of clothing from the storage baskets and shelves in the wardrobe took less time than I imagined – and filled two bags. Then it was time to look at the shoes. Sitting cross-legged on the floor in front of the shoe rack at the bottom of the cupboard, I shovelled pairs of shoes into another bag. When I finished with the obvious 'beyond saving' ones, only two pairs remained. While both pairs were still in good condition, they had seen some wear. After considering them for a few moments, I decided they too could go in the bag.

With the three full bags of rubbish tied off and parked near the bedroom door, I then realised I now had to move them downstairs, and out into the bin. It sounded a straightforward operation, until I felt the weight of the bags. Lugging those bags, one by one, down the stairs was an exercise fraught with danger. It could result in a tumble – and a tragic outcome.

To remind myself just how treacherous it might be, I went out onto the landing and surveyed the stairs. No, I was not going to attempt carrying the bags down the stairs. Then, for no particular reason, I looked over the railing directly across from the bedroom's doorway. Beneath me was an unoccupied ugly expanse of carpeted floor.

"It might … just work. And, if the bags do any damage, the carpet is crying out to be replaced anyway." I told the empty house as I turned on my heel and returned to the bedroom. "Exactly how heavy is one of these bags?"

There was no denying it, the one I tried lifting was heavy, but I could struggle it up to a height of about a metre off the floor. "That's high enough," I tried reassuring myself before plonking it back on the floor. "Let's give it a go."

After dragging it over to the railing, with a lot of struggling, sweating and swearing, I managed to work the bag up and perch it on top of the railing. A quick peek over the side to reassure myself nothing untoward would happen, before I gave the bag an almighty push to launch it off the railing. A moment later, I heard it land with a satisfying soft thud on the floor below. Another quick look over the railing to check for damage revealed no cause for concern.

With the trial 'drop' considered a success, the remaining two bags received the same treatment. With the last one (the bag of shoes) launched, I ventured downstairs for a closer look at the results of my initiative. To my relief, none of the bags had split or disgorged its contents in any way. "Right… now what?" I asked the universe. The prospect of lugging each of the bags out to the bin did not appeal. More creative thinking required.

If the bags can't go to the bin easily, why doesn't the bin come to the bags? Bringing the bin in to where the bags lay piled up on the floor in the front room seemed a logical solution. For a brief moment, I considered the possible impact of such a move on the ancient carpet. I already had decided, the first thing whoever ended up with the house would do is get rid of the carpet. So, running a wheelie bin over it was unlikely to cause anyone too much indigestion.

As I dragged the bin into position to load it, I realised a good deal more grunting and sweating would be required to lift each of the bags up and into the bin. Creativity came to the rescue again – and helped save my back from further stress. By putting the bin on its side on the carpet, with a bit of pushing and shoving, it was possible to 'shovel' in the bags with comparative ease. The stressing and straining came when it was time to upright the bin again. It wasn't easy but, after only a few moments, it was once more on its wheels. I felt a certain degree of satisfaction at the sight of the full bin in position ready for emptying in the morning.

Not only satisfying, the episode of filling the bin with unwanted material also helped my mind settle again after struggling with this morning's findings. Should I go home now, or should I go back upstairs to read more of Lillian's journal before I call it a day? It was a no-contest. It was still far too early to slope off home. And, with Lou gone for the day, I had the luxury of sitting at the desk to work in comfort. I ran up the stairs.

Settled at the desk with the journal open at the last entry I had read, and confident the saga of Esme's illegitimate child would continue in the next entry, I turned the page. I was right, and then braced myself for disappointment. The next couple of notes were so brief, I doubted they would be much use in discovering what happened after Esme's funeral. My focus now was on Ruby, and the question of what happened to her after her mother's death.

For a little while after discovering Esme's death, I had hoped there might be some sort of miracle. Bert Harding would come forward to identify himself as the father, and take baby Ruby home for him and his wife to raise along with their other children. Now, with Lou's research having erased Bert Harding from the picture, the original question remained: what happened to Ruby? When no father came forward to claim her, was she adopted out anyway, in spite of Esme's ploy to avoid it?

Those next entries recorded nothing more than a continuation of Lillian's daily visits to the hospital to spend time with the baby, and to talk to various staff. Were Lillian's discussions with staff about arranging for Ruby to be offered up for adoption? Her next journal entry went some way to answering my question. She wrote:

Discussions with senior hospital staff are going nowhere. They continually say what I am suggesting is unacceptable and perhaps not allowed, but cannot explain why this is so, or even if it might be the case. Exasperated by the lack of progress, my frustration boiled over today, and I told them I would be seeking legal advice on the matter. I told them, if the matter were not resolved forthwith – or I received a further negative response from them – I would be seeing them in court. Time is rushing by and I must return to work within the next few days, and Ruby will be going with me!

Good God, Lillian wanted to take the baby. Did she want to adopt the child, or just bring it home to become part of the Cavendish family? Would she bring Ruby up by herself, or did she have some other arrangement in mind? Did she think the family's attitude would soften once she brought the baby home, and they would welcome it into the fold to be brought up by Lillian's mother? All I know of Annie Cavendish is what Lillian has recorded about her in this journal, but it is enough for me to guess she was more likely to reject the baby, than welcome it with open arms. I couldn't help but wonder, if Frederick were still alive, what would be his reaction to his first grandchild.

Again, the following entry was brief. True to her word, Lillian consulted a local solicitor on the matter of Ruby's future. I imagined her triumphant air as she wrote the final sentence to the entry: *He assures me there is no obstacle to my legally adopting Ruby, although he did acknowledge some might question my suitability due to my unmarried status.*

At last, things are becoming clearer. Lillian didn't want just to take Ruby home, she wanted to adopt her. Now I think on it, such an approach is totally in keeping with the Lillian I knew. She would want everything signed, sealed, and nailed down properly, to eliminate any possible challenges or problems in the future. She was like that. She took no chances, cut no corners; always wanted everything accurate and precise.

My mind went into hyperdrive and paused my reading. In 1946, how would an unmarried woman cope with bringing up a child alone? What challenges would a single, professional woman face in terms of her career, her family, and the community in general? Regardless of how I looked at it, it would be a near-impossibility for Lillian to maintain her career at the same time as raising a child.

In spite of how bleak my mind painted the picture, I knew Lillian continued with her career well into her seventies before retiring. Perhaps, once a child went to school, it would be possible to fit work in around her school hours but, for those first few years of Ruby's life, it would be impossible to care for the child and work at the same time. Still, I was yet to discover how the various negotiations about Ruby's future panned out. So, I continued with the journal entries.

The next few entries told me nothing more than negotiations were continuing, and the tone of the entries left no doubt about Lillian's increasing frustration and anger. Then, the next lengthy journal entry told a different story. From the tone of it, I could almost picture Lillian's elation as she wrote the words. The key passage of the entry said it all: *at last, there is success, but only after my solicitor threatened to take the hospital to court for unlawful rejection of my application to adopt the baby in order to profiteer from possible other more lucrative adoption arrangements.*

I felt tears sting my eyes. She had done it! It appeared Lillian had won the battle to adopt Ruby. "Pull yourself together," I snarled. "It happened decades ago. Don't go getting all soppy about it now. Read the journal." After sniffling a few times and wiping my eyes on my sleeves, I turned the page to the next entry. The next page comprised of what were no more than a series of short statements of fact:

Signed the documents today; everything is now legal.

Told I can take her home tomorrow. So much to organise. Back to work next week.

Called Lorna Green about a possible live-in position. She seemed interested.

Not much idea what's needed, but so much to buy just to get us home okay.

Need to think about a nursery. Which room?

What have I done? I don't know about babies. How am I going to manage?

Collected Ruby today. Somehow boarded the train and arrived home okay.

Reality was about to hit Lillian, and she recorded the beginning of her steep learning curve in her next few entries. While it was a monumental day for Lillian, it appears it was an unsettling occasion for Ruby. Boarding the train accompanied by a baby, a pram, and more luggage than when she arrived in the city, proved more than Lillian could manage single-handed. She was forced to seek the assistance of a porter, who then arranged with the conductor to help her off with everything at the end of the trip.

The whole exercise was so distressing for Ruby, she bawled as loud as her little lungs would allow from the moment Lillian took her from the hospital. And, the situation didn't improve after they arrived at Lillian's house. On their arrival home, the first problem to deal with was the complete lack of 'baby equipment'.

There was no cot or bassinette, no appropriate baby's bath, or soap, or shampoo, or even a soft baby's brush. And, then there was the matter of feeding her. Yes, Lillian had bought all the necessary equipment, including a container of formula powder but, somehow, it all seemed so much easier and straightforward when she helped the nurses at the hospital. Now, it just felt scary. On top of everything else, it had been a big day and Lillian was tired. Her excitement meant she hadn't slept well last night, and today's events left her exhausted. And, still Ruby had not stopped crying. Her entry in her journal said more than the words she wrote:

Tomorrow promises to be another big day when I go shopping for a long list of everything I need to care for this baby. What do I do with Ruby while I go shopping? I doubt I'll manage anything if I have to take her with me, but what alternative is there?

For want of a better option, Ruby slept in her pram on her first night at Lillian's place. Having screamed and cried ever since leaving the hospital, Ruby eventually tired herself out and fell asleep at about nine o'clock. After refusing to take more than a little of her bottle during the day, she didn't sleep long before hunger woke her and the squalling began again. At least, then being hungry, Ruby was happy to take her bottle.

With her hunger sated and contented for the time being, Ruby slept for a few hours. Lillian's journal entry about their first night at home, suggested she regretted her decision to adopt the baby: *If I had not been so foolishly confident, and had only fostered the child, I could give her back when I realised I could not manage. Still, what's done is done and there is no point in rueing the decision.*

An early phone call next morning must have lifted Lillian's spirits no end. According to the journal, Lorna Green called to say she had considered Lillian's offer of the position as live-in nanny to Ruby, and would accept it. They arranged for Lorna to come around straight away to help ensure Lillian's shopping list included everything necessary for the baby, and to stay with Ruby while Lillian went shopping. Once Lillian returned from her shopping expedition, Lorna would return home to collect her belongings in readiness to move in with Lillian. Lorna's sister, who was living with her at the time, would continue to live in Lorna's house and look after it.

Who was Lorna Green? I had never heard her name mentioned by either Lillian or my mother. In the hope I might learn something of the woman, I skimmed the next few journal entries for Lorna Green's name. After checking the whole of the next page without success, I gave up. Would Lou know who Lorna was? After giving the question some thought, I decided it was probable Lou wouldn't be able to shed any light on Lorna.

Lou appeared not to know about Ruby, or her adoption by Lillian, so it was unlikely she knew about Lorna. Who else was there who might know? Although no one came to mind at the time, later in the evening, James Whitby's name flashed in from nowhere. He had known Lillian for decades, but did their acquaintance date back far enough to take in the Lorna Green era? Come to think of it, James hadn't mentioned anything about Ruby when we talked about Lillian's background. I might still ask him about Lorna, although I think it a waste of time.

Time had slipped away unnoticed while I sat pondering Lorna Green. It was late. I was hungry and it was time to go home. I closed the journal and, as an afterthought, removed it from the desk and stashed it in the small cupboard I had been using as a table. The journal was mine to study, and I did not want Lou getting her hands on it. Like as not, she would take it home and I would never see it again. Although Lou has been a part of my whole life in one way or another, and I like her a lot, she does have some not exactly endearing characteristics.

A few minutes later, I was ready to leave. Tidying the kitchen and making sure everything was secure for the night was done on auto-pilot. My mind was a swirling mass of thoughts and ideas about Lorna Green and Ruby's transfer from the ordered world of the hospital's nursery to Lillian's unprepared home. It wasn't this house, but the previous one she owned. Locking the front door behind me also was an automatic act requiring no conscious thought. The real world around me didn't elbow its way into my conscious thought until I was walking to my car.

I glanced over at the rubbish bin waiting on the footpath; just a last minute check. No problems; all was as it should be there. Then, my eyes slid past the bin standing proudly out front and continued across the road to a car parked there against the kerb. While not new, there was nothing special about the vehicle. I guessed it to be about five years old. The vehicle itself was the problem. The same vehicle had been parked there earlier this afternoon when I put the rubbish bin out.

The street is wide with a nature strip running down the centre. I couldn't remember seeing the car parked in this street on any previous occasion. Shrubbery on the nature strip made it difficult – almost impossible – to have a clear view of the driver. Still, I felt reasonably confident the driver was a man, and I was almost sure there was more than one person in the vehicle. I thought a second person occupied the front passenger's seat. As I could make out only the vague shape of the second person, there was no way of knowing its gender.

Alarm bells were ringing in my mind. Was I sure it was the same car I saw earlier? Even if it were the same car, what of it? The people might be waiting for the occupants of the house behind where the car is parked to come home. It wasn't working. The more I tried convincing myself there was no cause for alarm, the more concerned I became. My discomfort level, rising by the second, won the battle over my common sense. After rummaging in my bag as if checking for something, and then giving myself a head-slap for forgetting whatever it was, I returned to the front door, unlocked it and went inside.

"Okay, now I'm back inside, what am I going to do?" I whispered to the silent house. It didn't reply, and its silence made my thumping heart seem almost deafening. With only one light switched on in the front room, I tiptoed up the stairs. The small high bathroom window had no curtain and overlooked the street. I opened the bathroom door just wide enough to slide through sideways, and closed it again as soon as I was in the bathroom. For several seconds, I stood glued to a spot just inside the door as I allowed my eyes to adjust to the blackness surrounding me. Even after my eyes adjusted, I made my way to the window by braille, rather than by sight.

Several decades ago, when this area was no more than a few squiggles on a drawing board, forward-thinking planners opted for subdued street lighting in their new development to avoid the harsh glare of the more traditional lighting found in heavier trafficked areas. Nevertheless, the soft orange lighting was more than enough to be able to see the same car still parked in the same spot across the road. I knew the occupants of the house it was parked in front of were away on holidays, so it was unlikely anyone would come out to question their continued presence.

After employing the 'cautious door' routine again, I was standing on the landing outside the bathroom. I dragged out my phone and keyed James Whitby's number. It dialled for what seemed a long time before going to message bank. After leaving a brief garbled apology for calling the wrong number, I ended the call. Common sense had gone off duty for the night, and I was heading for full panic mode. Desperate times call for desperate actions. I dialled '000' and asked for the police.

I imagined the officer who took the call rolling his eyes at having to deal with yet another suburban 'Nervous Nellie'. But instead, he was patient, and I somehow managed to convey the nature of my concerns with sufficient clarity for him to respond. With nothing more constructive for me to do, I slipped back into the bathroom to keep an eye on those keeping an eye on me. About ten minutes after my call, a patrol car entered the street and cruised towards this end of it – and the parked car.

Although no siren was employed, the red and blue flashing lights were enough to alert those in the car to the possibility they had outstayed their welcome. The patrol car cruised along at a slow pace as if it was there for nothing more than a routine patrol of the street. I saw the parked car shudder as its engine came to life. By then, the police vehicle was close. Too close for the car to gun the motor and roar away from the kerb. Such an action would amount to an admission of up-to-no-good, and was bound to get it followed and pulled over.

When the patrol car was about ten metres from the other vehicle, the driver of the parked car signalled his intention to pull out. Without any change of speed, the police cruised past the parked car and continued to the end of the street where it made a U-turn around the end of the nature strip and started along my side of the street. The parked car, now no longer stationary, trailed the patrol vehicle to the T-junction at the end of the street, before turning left and disappearing from view.

As soon as the other car was out of sight, the police pulled into the kerb, and sat there idling for a short time before resuming their slow travel along the street. Once they became mobile again, it was a short trip of only about fifty metres before they pulled in alongside the kerb in front of Lillian's house. I raced down the stairs and was waiting in the front room when they rang the bell.

Chapter 9

"I hope my call wasn't a waste of your time, Officers. When the car was parked there for so long with nobody getting in or out of it, I became concerned. They appeared to be watching this house and it started alarm bells ringing for me."

"You did the right thing calling it in. A vehicle parked for no good reason for an extended period in a quiet suburban street such as this is worth having us take a look. To give us an idea of how long it was parked there, can you tell us when you first noticed it?"

"Well, I don't know when it arrived, but it was there when I put the bin out at around 3.30pm. I was going to go home soon after, but decided to stay and do a bit more first. My 'bit more' took about four hours."

"Was it always parked where it was when we saw it, or did it move around a bit in the street?"

"No, where it was parked tonight was where it had been the whole time."

"We have asked for a check on the plates, but we haven't heard back yet. Have you any idea why someone might be so interested in this house, or who might have been in the car?"

"Oh, I would only be guessing…"

The senior officer suggested even guesses might be handy, and encouraged me to share my thinking with them.

"As I said, I don't *know* who they were, but a couple of things happened recently which influence my thoughts on the subject. The elderly owner of this house passed away a week or so ago. I and a local solicitor are joint executors of the deceased's estate. In her will, the house was left to me. Three men – strangers – turned up at her cremation service. They ambushed me as I was leaving the chapel. While their comments to me did not include a direct threat as such, they were aggressive. There was an implied threat in the message they gave me. In effect, they believed they were relatives of the deceased woman and, as such, were entitled to her estate (with particular reference to the house) and they would be coming to take what was theirs."

"Is the estate subject to some dispute at the moment?" I shook my head. "Are there any grounds for their claim to the estate?"

"Therein lies the problem. Apart from the fact they are not mentioned in the will, none of us who knew the deceased ever heard her mention them. The deceased woman never married and, as far as we know, had no offspring. We are in the process of trying to discover whether there might be some link through one of her sisters. Our research has been happening over the last couple of days, and hasn't progressed far yet."

"Did the three men in question give you their names?"

"By process of elimination, I worked out, from the condolences register at the chapel, their surname was 'Millard'. They only gave initials of their first names."

There wasn't much else I could tell them, and they had even less to share with me. When they asked what my plans were for the rest of the night, I told them I was going home as soon as they were finished with me, and I wouldn't be back here until tomorrow morning. "Those three blokes don't know who I am or where I live – as far as I know. Now they have gone, I feel it's safe to go home without worrying about whether I'll be followed or not. But, I know I will keep an eye out for their car, or any other car paying me too much attention."

As I finished speaking, the senior officer's phone buzzed, and he moved away to take the call. It wasn't a long call, but it did appear to be intense. The moment the call ended, the senior officer came back to talk to me. His jaw seemed set a bit tighter than it was before the call.

"Now, before we were interrupted, you said you were going home, but were a bit nervous about the possibility of being followed. How would you feel about one of our unmarked cars following you home … just in case? Although we don't believe there is much likelihood you would be followed, one of our cars keeping an eye on things might make us all breathe easier."

"If it doesn't pull your officers off something more serious than my situation, I would feel safer."

"Okay. An unmarked will be here in a few minutes. You should be in your car and ready to drive out of here the moment it cruises past. It won't stop here so, when I give you the word, just leave in your normal fashion. Don't speed or do anything silly on the way home."

While it did seem they were going to a lot of trouble on my behalf, I wasn't going to knock it back. I thanked them and, as I picked up my bag ready to leave, the senior officer had more to say.

"Hmm… there is one other thing. It's obvious you must have a key to this place." I nodded and he continued. Would you consider allowing a couple of our officers to stay in the house tonight? We don't expect any trouble, but you never can tell, and it's better to be prepared should it happen."

"No, I don't have a problem… But there is nothing much to eat in the place … And I'm not sure the sleeping arrangements will suit your people."

"Don't worry about food. The officers will bring whatever they need to survive. As for sleeping arrangements, they will be on duty all night, so there won't be any sleeping."

"So, how are you going to put this arrangement in place?"

"Once the two officers in the unmarked see you safely home, they will come back here. We will wait here until they arrive, and then will leave them to it for the night. By doing things this way, they won't need a key to get in. Then, in the morning, they will stay on here until you arrive. So, again, there is no need for any officers to have a key. What time do you think you might return tomorrow morning?"

"I'm usually here before nine o'clock, but I could be here earlier. I know you said you didn't expect any problems tonight, but will the officers who stay in the house be in any real danger? Although, I suppose anyone planning on breaking into the house would change their mind when they realised somebody was here."

They told me not to worry about the house or the officers who would be spending the night there. And, nobody would know the place was inhabited overnight. It would remain in darkness the whole time. As an added precaution – or deterrent perhaps – a police car would patrol the street every hour for the rest of the night. After only a couple more minutes, the senior officer received another phone call. When it ended, he announced it was time to be in position, and gave me a few last-minute instructions on what I had to do, and how it would all happen. Then, I climbed into my car in readiness for the next dramatic phase of the evening.

Although I knew the car following me was keeping an eye out for anything suspicious, I was on high alert the whole way home. If anything untoward did happen during the trip home, I was unaware of it. Nevertheless, I was still a ball of nervous tension as I unlocked my front door and went inside. The unmarked vehicle following me home didn't stop. Without any change in speed, it drove past and disappeared around the corner at the end of my street. A few minutes later, I saw it cruise past again – and I felt myself relax a little.

Earlier this evening, I was feeling famished but, now I was home, I seemed to have lost my appetite sometime during the ensuring period. After a long hot shower, I settled for toast and a mug of soup. It was still early, but all I wanted to do was to go to bed. That much I was sure about, but whether I would sleep or not was another matter.

By the time I did go to bed, I had just about worn a track to the front windows from constantly checking for strange cars parked in the street. Although no cars were spotted, I spent a restless night with little sleep involved.

*****

I just knew this was not going to be one of my better days. After crawling out of bed late and dawdling over breakfast, I didn't seem to be able to find the next gear. Any forward momentum seemed to be at a snail's pace. As a result, I left for Lillian's place later than usual. After battling morning peak hour traffic all the way, I arrived at Lillian's a bit short on good humour, and almost right on the dot of nine o'clock. The only good thing so far this morning was discovering Lou hadn't arrived before me. An early arrival by Lou would have made life interesting for a moment or two. I hadn't mentioned to the police she might be first to arrive, because it didn't occur to me at the time.

After thanking the two officers who spent the night there, and apologising for any inconvenience it might have caused, I saw them off from Lillian's front doorstep. Still sluggish and more inclined to procrastinate than get on with anything, I made another coffee and drank it in the kitchen before hauling myself up the stairs to Lillian's office.

For some unknown reason, I was having trouble getting started on the journal again. As another fine piece of time-wasting, I wandered into Lillian's bedroom and opened her wardrobe. What more can I throw out without fearing repercussions? All the hanging garments caught my attention. My intention was to sort them into two groups: those to go to the op shop, and those to be thrown out.

As the hanging space was packed tight with all manner of outer clothing, trying to sort them out while they were hanging in there was impossible. A few at a time, I hauled them out and placed them in four piles on the bed. Only those garments to go to the op shop would go back into the cupboard for the time being. All the others would go into garbage bags ready for the bin. Garbage bags… I hadn't brought any upstairs with me and I only had one left from those I brought up yesterday.

Going downstairs for more garbage bags was a further opportunity for procrastination – and I didn't hurry about it. As a means of expediting the task, those garments not going back into the cupboard were dumped in another discrete pile to be bagged up later. At the end of sorting through the first pile, it was obvious far more was being thrown out than was going back into the cupboard. If it was any indication of how the rest of the piles would be divided, I hadn't brought up nearly enough garbage bags, and the amount I wanted to throw out would exceed the bin's capacity.

The pile of 'throw-outs' became so large it spread out over too much of the bed. There was a danger of material from it becoming mixed in with garments in other, as yet unsorted piles. The simple solution would have been to start bagging to prevent the pile of throw-outs from taking over the bed, but some subconscious 'thing' seemed to prevent it happening. Instead, my inspired workaround-solution was to drag all of the throw-out pile off the bed and onto the floor. I addressed the untidy mess on the floor, "There, how's that? Now see how much of the house you can take over by the time I'm finished."

While I kept sorting through the garments, the little voice in my head kept telling me I should be working on the journal while it was peaceful before Lou arrived. Of course, it made sense but, try as I might, I seemed unable to face the book again this morning. "What is wrong with me?" I snarled. I did want to know what happened next. I did want to know who Lorna Green was. So, why wasn't I in the office devouring more of what the journal had to tell me? What was I afraid of? I knew I had an almost tangible dread of what I might discover next.

At some point during my 'beating myself up exercise', I realised quite a bit of the morning had slipped by since I arrived at the house. My watch told me it was long gone ten o'clock. And, there was still no Lou this morning. Within the blink of an eye, my mind conjured up the worst possible scenario: perhaps she had been involved in an accident on her way here, or worse still, perhaps she wasn't coming at all today because something serious had happened during the night.

Such thoughts were doing me no good at all, so I took myself downstairs for another coffee. As I dawdled over the coffee and a couple of chocolate biscuits, my mind roamed free until it decided to focus on the incidents of last evening. Nothing had happened, and perhaps I had been jumping at shadows when I became agitated about the car parked across the street. If I think about it, why would anyone want to break into this place anyway? I am unaware of any hidden treasures here worth the effort to steal them. I seemed intent on being my own worst enemy today. It would be nice to have the occasional happy thought. Maybe I should have pulled the bed clothes up over my head and stayed in bed.

Lou's call saved me from myself and my depressing outlook on life. "I am sure you are aware I haven't arrived today. And, it now looks as though I won't be coming at all, and maybe not tomorrow either. Visitors I was expecting next week changed their plans and arrived last night. As soon as they leave, I'll be back to work on Lillian's story. Is there anything pressing you need me for?"

"Yeah, although I've been busy, I had noticed you weren't here. I was worried you might have had an accident on your way over, so I'm pleased you called. No, I don't have anything I need you to do. Oh… There was something I was going to ask you: do you know of Lorna Green at all? Have you heard Lillian mention her?"

"…Never heard of the woman, from Lillian or anyone else, until you just mentioned her. Should I know her? Sorry, I've got to go. If she is important, maybe we could look into Lorna Green the next time I'm there."

How glib it rolled off my tongue! I assured Lou it wasn't anything urgent or important. Lorna Green was just a name I came across somewhere and wondered about the connection, nothing more. Lou's not knowing Lorna was as I figured, but I thought it worthwhile checking all possibilities, no matter how unlikely. Having drawn a blank with Lou, where to next? There was still James Whitby to try. After checking it was a civilised hour to be calling the solicitor, I keyed his number.

"James… Sophie Sinclair… Are you free to talk for a couple of minutes?"

"Sophie, this is as good a time as any. What can I do for you? Do we have a problem with Lillian's estate, or those three ruffians perhaps?"

"No, it's nothing of the kind. In the course of my research into Lillian's family history, I came across the name Lorna Green, and wondered if you knew anything of the woman or her connection to Lillian."

"Lorna Green, eh? Well now, maybe it does ring a bell. I have a vague recollection of the name from somewhere in the distant past. Can you give me a moment please?"

The clack of a keyboard being given a solid workout was all I heard for the next few moments. Then the keyboard fell silent. I assumed, having found what he was looking for, James was reading through some document to refresh his memory regarding the woman. When he came back on the line, he seemed hesitant.

"Uhmm… Lorna Green… How did you… Do you think she might be important in establishing whether those three blokes have a sound claim against Lillian's estate?"

I heard the little voice in my head chanting a warning: Be prepared, a fob-off approaching. No matter how hard I tried to ignore it, I couldn't. I already had come to the same conclusion without any prompting from 'the voice'. It took a few heartbeats to work out how to handle the impending situation.

"James, I understand the need for client confidentiality and how it governs a solicitor's life. I'm not asking you to breach such confidentiality. All I want to know is whether she might be significant in establishing any connection between Lillian and those three blokes, regardless of how tenuous any such connection might be."

"Yes, of course… I wasn't trying to be difficult. Where are you at the moment, Sophie?" I told him I was at Lillian's house and would be there all day. "Good… Look, there are a couple of things I need to do first but, if you will still be there in about an hour's time, I could drop by to talk to you. Would it be okay if I came then? Oh, are you there on your own, or is Louella Radford with you today?"

"As I said, James, I will be here for the rest of the day. So, please drop by whenever it suits you. I am here on my own. Louella is dealing with something else today."

If I thought my conversation with James would put my curiosity about Lorna Green to bed, it did nothing of the kind. Now, I was even more curious about her. And, why does James Whitby feel the need to come here to discuss her face-to-face with me? I knew I had a long hour's wait ahead of me, and I also knew I would be incapable of concentrating on anything else until James arrived. Nevertheless, I somehow managed to force myself to go back upstairs and continue sorting through the garments I'd removed from the wardrobe.

True to his word, James arrived just a little more than an hour after our call. The cake box he carried in with him had me on high alert. If he felt the need to bring a cake, I was not going to be told anything I wanted to hear. The cake, coupled with his apparent uneasy demeanour, nudged my dark side to life. My tongue had honed itself almost razor-sharp by the time we were in the kitchen.

"I suppose, if we're going to cut whatever's in the box you brought, you would like a coffee to go with it? You could have delivered whatever the bad news is over the phone, and saved yourself the expense of the cake and a trip to this house."

"Sophie, just make the coffee, and then we will talk. By the way, the only person I've heard mention 'bad news' is you. Whether what I have to tell you is bad news or not is up to you to decide after we've talked. All I will say until I'm sitting here with coffee and cake in front of me is to assure you I didn't come here to stonewall you."

After a feeble attempt at an apology, and feeling I'd made a right goose of myself, I sat down opposite him at the kitchen table. If I'm honest, I suppose I expected him to start telling me whatever he came to say as soon as I sat down. I'm sure the delay I had to endure, while he ate a little of his slice of cake and washed it down with a few sips of coffee, was my punishment for my earlier outburst. Once the old rogue had decided I had suffered long enough, cordial relations were re-established.

"While what I can share with you does come close to breaching client confidentiality, I am comfortable with what I am about to do. What I did not feel comfortable about was talking about it over the phone. Now, Lorna Green… I must admit I had to go through her file to familiarise myself with the story from way back then. What I think it's safe to say at the outset is Mrs Green does not figure directly in Lillian's family tree. There was an association, but Lorna was not part of the family."

"Okay… Are you telling me I shouldn't bother trying to find out any more about Lorna Green; I shouldn't bother digging any further into the woman's life?"

"No, it's not what I was suggesting. Many years ago, long before Lillian established her own practice, she was also heavily involved with a community-based group with a particular focus on improving the lives of women from lower socio-economic backgrounds. My late wife also was involved with the group, and she and Lillian were friends. Out of the blue one day, Lillian called me and asked for an urgent appointment. I agreed to see her after hours, after everyone else had left the office. She arrived with another badly beaten woman in tow. The woman was Lorna Green."

"Why did she bring Lorna to you? Why not go to the police?"

"You need to understand the world was a different place back then. A beaten wife was of no consequence in the overall scale of things in the area where she lived. Lorna's husband was a brute of a man, who put her in hospital on several occasions, and Lillian was determined to help her put an end to it. She sought to achieve it by some legal means, rather than going to the police. I won't go into details. Suffice to say, we were successful in securing an intervention preventing him from ever harming her again.

It was only about a year or so later, when her husband, in another of his drunken rages about something or other, battered their son, who still lived with him, to death. The husband was jailed for life. He liked to throw his weight around in prison, and his often uncontrollable rages had him offside with both his fellow prisoners and the authorities. One day, about twelve months after he was sentenced, he met with a fatal 'accident' in the showers."

James's phone interrupted his story. After signalling I was going upstairs, I gave him privacy to deal with his phone call. While I still didn't know the whole story, all he had told me so far kept my mind occupied while I wandered around aimlessly upstairs. When he called to me from the front room to let me know his call was finished, I was more than ready for the next instalment of the Lorna Green story.

Chapter 10

James waited in the front room for me to race down the stairs, and then gestured towards Lillian's ancient lounge chairs. "Unless you were planning on indulging in more cake and coffee, perhaps we could make ourselves comfortable out here."

"Right, when you are comfortable, James, please may I hear the next episode of the Lorna Green story. The fact Lillian felt compelled to do something to protect Lorna all those years ago doesn't surprise me. Lillian often came across as brusque but, underneath the tough façade she developed for herself, she was a softie with a heart of gold. Quite early in my life, I saw through her outer shell."

"Well, with Lorna's husband and son dead, she was alone in the world. But, she did quite well out of her husband in the end. He hadn't made a will before he died. So, having died intestate, his estate could have gone to the Crown. Again, Lillian came to me. This time it was to help Lorna mount a court case to secure her deceased husband's estate. At the outset, none of us realised the extent of his estate."

"So, Lorna did all right out of his death. It's good to know she was compensated – albeit belatedly – for what she suffered at his hands."

"It wasn't all smooth sailing. All was going well until an illegitimate daughter came forward to claim her share. In the end, Lorna got the house, car, and other possessions, but the cash component of the estate was divided equally between Lorna and the girl."

"God, it's a cruel world we live in. While I suppose I understand the illegitimate daughter had a right to claim, I find it difficult to feel any sympathy for her over the loss of her father. I don't suppose anyone challenged the legitimacy of her claim?"

"Not at the time, and the estate was divided up accordingly. Lorna ended up with the material possessions – house, car, furniture – but, once the cash was divided, neither of the women received much. For the girl, whatever she gained from the exercise was a windfall. In Lorna's case, the money wasn't enough to live on for very long. Lillian brought her back to me again. I organised for the money she received to be invested. It didn't earn her a fortune, but the little it paid every year didn't impact on the pension we managed to arrange for her. Lillian insisted, now Lorna held possessions in her own name, she should make a will – to prevent everything ending up with the illegitimate daughter if anything happened to Lorna. You see, Lillian never was convinced the girl was Lorna's husband's child."

"I can understand why neither Lillian nor Lorna would have thought too kindly of the girl, but it seems she had a legal right to lodge a claim as she did – unless there is more to the story. Was anything else going on in the background?"

"A while later, another case I was involved with brought something to light to cast some doubts in my mind about the girl and her mother. It must have been about two years after the estate was settled, when I was given some information in the course of interviewing another client who was facing a whole string of charges. He happened to mention the girl's mother's name. It seems the man, my then client was alleged to have killed, was one of the mother's regular 'clients'. It appears the mother was into supplementing her pension with a fairly lucrative sideline."

"Oh, this is starting to intrigue me. Don't stop there. I'm sure you looked into the mother's sideline a little further. What did you discover?"

"I did confirm Lorna's husband had been a client of the mother, but not one of her more regular visitors. On face value, it was plausible the girl could have been Mr Green's daughter.

But, when I thought about it, it was just as possible the girl was by one of the mother's other clients. When I started digging into the story, the first thing I discovered was the mother's death a couple of months beforehand. Anyway, to cut a long story short, there was no way the girl could prove she was the illegitimate daughter of Lorna's husband. My research stirred up something of a hornets' nest, and eventually led to another of the mother's clients coming forward to claim paternity.

It seems he had been a favourite and moved in to live with the woman, and lived off the earnings of her flourishing enterprise for some period of time. He kept an eye on the customers and made sure they didn't get out of line. He was on a cushy number until the woman became pregnant and reached the stage where she couldn't 'work' for several months. It appears there was consensus the child was his. But, now the mother wasn't bringing in the cash, the arrangement had lost its appeal. He moved on in search of a different living arrangement more suited to the lifestyle he required."

"Was there anything you could do about it? So long after the estate had been settled, and in spite of the new evidence regarding the girl's paternity, it seems unlikely there would be much you could do to reverse the court's earlier decisions."

"It seems the man in question did not get on with the daughter at all and, being possessed of something of a vindictive streak, he was happy to provide dates, times and places, to support his claim he was the girl's father. The court bought his story. It was helpful the girl admitted she and her mother had hatched the scheme to improve their financial situation after the mother saw Mr Green's death notice in the paper and recognised him as one of her former clients.

The earlier decision was quashed, and an order was issued for the money the girl had received from the estate to be recovered and paid to Lorna. Of course, by then, there wasn't more than a few pounds left for the court to reclaim. So, Lorna didn't reap too much benefit from it. But, although the girl didn't result from it, Lorna then had her husband's infidelity confirmed beyond doubt."

"Okay. So far, this story seems to give Lorna a losing hand all the way along. I understand Lillian's ongoing support of the woman, but I am curious about why she called Lorna Green at the time of the adoption of baby Ruby. Are you aware of the circumstances surrounding Lillian's phone call?"

"Once the adoption was finalised, Lillian came to see me. She wanted to put in place something to give Lorna Green custody of Ruby if anything happened to Lillian before the child reached her majority. I drew up two documents, one of which simply stated what should happen in the case of such an eventuality. The other document was Lillian's new will which, along with everything else, provided for the same outcome to occur. Obviously, sometime later, her first will was superseded by the one currently before the probate court."

"Why would Lillian want Ruby to go to Lorna Green? I'm sorry, but I don't understand."

"And I'm sorry I don't seem to have made myself clear. Lillian hired Lorna Green as a live-in nanny for Ruby. In return for free board and lodgings, Lorna looked after the baby and did a bit of light housework while continuing to collect her widow's pension. She lived with Lillian for quite a few years."

"So, Lorna had no familial connection with Ruby, and was outside of Lillian's family tree?" James nodded his confirmation. "In which case, there is no possible Millard connection to Lillian via Lorna Green. I'm sorry, James. It seems I've been chasing a false lead, and I've managed to waste a good deal of your day as a result of it. Thanks for sharing those details with me, and thanks for your patience. I'll try not to bother you again, but I will keep you informed if anything emerges from my research."

Oh yes, super sleuth, Sophie Sinclair, is an expert at 'wild goose chases', I chided myself as I climbed the stairs after I'd waved James Whitby on his way. Best I stick to the more tangible stuff in future – like sorting out garments and other personal belongings. At least it's a task I am equipped to make decisions about.

I returned to sorting the clothes in the bedroom, but my heart wasn't in it and I only stuck at it for a few minutes. The problem was, my curiosity was fully charged again, and it kept tugging my mind in the direction of Lillian's journal. "Why not…?" I asked aloud. With Lou otherwise engaged today, I had the desk to myself again – and it was so much more comfortable to work on the desk than my little makeshift table.

The next few pages of Lillian's journal made for fairly mundane reading, with the exception of the occasional mention of Ruby's weight gain, or how she seemed to be settling in. It took me a while to realise the time elapsed between journal entries was increasing with each page. And, it came as a shock when I worked out the next entry I looked at was written some six months after the previous one. Had life become less noteworthy, or was it a case of Lillian's now being too busy with the baby to have time to record anything but the more critical or exciting events?

With growing monotony, I turned page after page of well-spaced entries about nothing of import. Then, I almost missed it. Entries were becoming more frequent. I sensed a period of high activity starting to develop, and checked back a couple of pages to see if I had missed something on my way through. No, I hadn't, but comments about frequent shopping expeditions and the *exorbitant prices of everything these days,* were out of keeping with the contents and tone of previous entries.

All became clear about a page further on. While the entry wasn't long, it spoke volumes: *Today is Ruby's first day of school ... not sure who of the three of us was most nervous, but we all shed a tear or two anyway. Don't know why I felt this way, but I'll mark it as another of life's experiences.*

So, Ruby had reached school age, and mention of 'the three of us' suggests Lorna Green remained a part of the household. The entry caused me to stop and dwell on what Lillian's life must have been like then. The emotions expressed about Ruby's first day at school suggested Lillian had developed a strong – almost maternal – bond with the child. Somehow, the notion of Ruby's adoption proving such a rewarding experience for both the women gave me a warm, fuzzy feeling.

The next several entries related to how Ruby settled in and was progressing at school. As the end of first term approached, Lillian arranged a meeting with Ruby's teacher to check on Ruby's progress and behaviour. Judging by the glowing report on the meeting as recorded by Lillian, it went well. Ruby was proving to be a budding genius. But, I had reached the final page of the journal.

Should I fetch the next one to continue reading about Ruby's progress, or should I find something else to do for the remainder of the day. When in doubt, have another coffee. So, after heaving myself out of the chair, I wandered down to the kitchen. My mind was so occupied with conjuring up images of life in Lillian's home at the time, I knew I wasn't going to achieve much more today.

At about 3.30pm, I opted for an early finish. The decision drove me to the bathroom window to scan the street out front. There was no sign of the car from last night, or any other suspicious vehicle lurking in the street. As I tidied the kitchen in readiness to leave for the day, the sound of the front door bell turned my stomach into a squirming mass. It also seemed to affect my legs. They didn't seem able to move, and I remained frozen to a spot on the kitchen floor near the sink.

Who knows I'm here? "Stupid question," I murmured to the kitchen, "anyone who isn't blind could see my car parked on the driveway." For a brief moment I hesitated. I reminded myself I had checked the street and there were no suspicious cars out there when I looked. It could be anyone ringing the doorbell; not necessarily the blokes from last night. Although I tried hard, the little voice in my head kept asking: so who else might it be?

Standing here in the kitchen wondering about it wasn't going to provide any answers. Answer the door, I told myself, but be careful. "Who…" As I walked to the front door, I started to ask who was there. I didn't get more than one word out before the doorbell rang again cutting me off. By then I was at the door anyway, so I opened it a fraction… and gasped.

"Has something happened? Why are you here?"

"It's okay, Miss Sinclair. Nothing has happened to concern you at this stage, but we would like to ask you a few questions if you don't mind."

The two police officers who spent last night here in the house stood on the doorstep. I ushered them in and offered them coffee, which they accepted. Instead of sitting in the lounge to talk as was my original intention, the officers followed me into the kitchen and made themselves comfortable at the kitchen table while I fussed with the coffee. As they didn't display any inclination to move, we remained seated at the table. The suspense, not to mention my curiosity and foreboding, reached a critical level. Overlooking polite etiquette, as soon as the three of us were seated, I encouraged them to get on with whatever had brought them to the house again so soon.

"We wondered whether you noticed any strange cars about the place today – either parked or just cruising the area. Or, perhaps anyone at all – on foot, on a bike, or whatever – who seemed interested in this house?"

"No, I hadn't noticed anything or anyone at all. But, it is fair to say, I haven't checked the street regularly. Now you're asking, I have to admit I can't say I've even heard a vehicle on this street since I arrived and you left this morning. Why are you asking? Is the reason for your visit something I should be aware of, or perhaps, concerned about?"

"Not really… No, we just wanted to follow up to make sure nothing else had happened."

While it sounded plausible, I wasn't buying any of it. Everyone knows the police are under-resourced these days. I didn't doubt for a moment there were other serious matters these two officers should be dealing with, instead of paying what amounted to a follow-up courtesy call to me. As I am not fond of surprises, especially the unpleasant variety, I was determined to extract the whole story about their visit.

"At the risk of appearing rude and ungrateful, all I have heard from you so far is rubbish. You would not come all this way just to ask me those questions. So, it's time for you to stop playing games, and to tell me exactly why you are here? And, while I think of it, did you discover whose car it was parked across the street from here last night? …. Aah, yes, of course … maybe you do know who owns the vehicle, and it's why you are here."

"Well, yes, we have identified the owner. Look, the last thing we want to do is alarm you, or give you any cause for concern. It's why we were being… It's why we were just checking there had been no further incident we should be aware of."

"I'll consider whether to believe you or not after you tell me who owns the car."

"As it is not normal policy to divulge such information, I'll need a little more information before I can make a decision. To start with, explain your relationship with the Millard brothers? How much have you had to do with them, and how well do you know them?"

Once again, I reiterated the story of my encounter with the three men, who I assumed to be the Millard brothers, after Lillian's cremation service. "It was the first and only time I met them. They didn't introduce themselves but, from the condolences register, I concluded their surname was Millard. I haven't seen them since – unless they were the people in the vehicle parked across the street last night."

"So, what is their relationship to… er, what's her name... Oh yeah, Cavendish … what's their relationship to Lillian Cavendish?"

"None, as far as I know. After their comments at the funeral home, I thought it a matter of some urgency to establish if there was any relationship. As the executor of Lillian's will, I needed to know whether those three blokes did exist somewhere in her extended family tree, in case they made a claim on her estate. For the last few days, it's what I have been attempting to do.

And, I notice you still haven't told me who owns the car. Nevertheless, your questions regarding the Millards suggest there is a connection. Perhaps, it is now your turn to provide some direct answers."

"Ye-es, while it goes against our normal procedure, in this case, maybe you do need to know. The car which caused concern last night is owned by the oldest of the Millard brothers. Their names are not unknown to the police. Oh, there's nothing major, just petty stuff: breaking and entering, shoplifting, robbery with menace, and causing a disturbance. All three have been charged with the latter offence after brawling in pubs and other public places. Although there was nothing major in the past, a current case under investigation has their names all over it."

"What sort of 'major' are we talking about in relation to the case under investigation?"

"A local businessman remains in a critical condition in hospital as a result of being seriously assaulted by two men when an extortion attempt failed. We still need a little more to have sufficient evidence to charge the Millards, but I'm told an arrest is likely within the next couple of days."

"I see … and thank you. If I was uneasy about being here alone today before you arrived, I think I've now changed to being terrified. Do you have any advice? What should I do to avoid ending up like the chap in hospital?"

"At this point in time, we have no clues as to their intentions regarding this place – or you. It might be their intention to do nothing more than to break in and rob the place or, if they gain entry, they might claim squatters' rights. A more worrying scenario is if they intend applying strongarm tactics to persuade you to look favourably on their claim to the estate. As none of them seems to have indulged in any form of employment for some time, it is likely they are looking for a means of continuing their lives of leisure ... and this house alone would go a long way towards achieving it for them."

"Ri-ight, so what am I supposed to do? I am not the only one I need to think about. A long-time friend, a professional genealogist, is helping me look into Lillian's family history. Although she is not here today, she has been coming here to undertake the necessary research. Yesterday she left early, but she might not always do so. If something untoward is to happen, she also might be in danger."

"There are a number of measures we would like to put in place, if you agree. First, we would like to install two officers here again tonight. Patrols of the street will continue, but on a more random arrangement than our previous hourly schedule. While, we realise having an officer here during the day might get under your feet a bit, we would recommend one officer be here during the day. How do you feel about such measures? Do you have any objections, or suggestions?"

"No, I don't think so. The only thought I have is about me when I'm not here. If they choose to follow me when I leave here, am I likely to be attacked at home?"

"It is a possibility – and it is not one we had overlooked. How do you feel about moving in here, at least for a few days until we see how things eventuate?"

"It would feel a bit weird I should think. Having someone here during the day would not be a problem and, maybe, having the other officers here at night might make it a bit easier to cope with sleeping here. Uhmm… yeah, I think I could do it. When is all this likely to be put in place?"

"Today … as of now … If it suits you, we could bring in the daytime officer now, and the night shift could take over this evening. The only thing I would suggest is for you to go home to collect a few things to see you through the few days you might be staying here. Do you feel safe enough to go and fetch some things?"

I hadn't felt anything but safe until he asked the question. Still, it made sense to fetch some things, if I was going to be staying here for a few days. As I picked up my bag and was about to head out to my car, the senior officer stopped me as his offsider came back inside. I hadn't seen her go out but, when she came back in, she was still holding her phone in her hand.

"The day shift officer will be here within the next half hour," she announced.

"Good. Miss Sinclair, if you wouldn't mind waiting until the other officer arrives, we will accompany you to your house while you do what you have to do, and then we will follow you back here. It's possible such precautions aren't necessary, but it's best not to take any chances."

If I didn't have any concerns before, my stomach was letting me know it wasn't too fond of the way things were developing. Telling myself there was nothing for me to worry about was a waste of time. Not for one second did I believe it was true.

About twenty minutes later, a female officer arrived, and we all gravitated to the kitchen. The senior officer suggested we might all have another coffee while everyone became acquainted. Gail Olsen, the day shift officer, was about my age and looked about twice as fit as I am. Well-tanned, and her ready smile made her dark eyes twinkle. I couldn't see how having her around all day might be any problem. Besides, if she had nothing much to do, to avoid boredom, she might keep Lou and me supplied with coffee while we worked.

As soon as the coffee and introductions were done, I gave Gail a quick tour of the place before I headed home – with the other two officers close behind. Having devoted some thought to what I might need over the next few days, it didn't take long to gather those things, load them into the car, and be on my way back to Lillian's house. When I pulled onto Lillian's driveway again, the two officers in the unmarked vehicle continued along the street, and had disappeared from sight by the time I reached the front door.

Gail met me at the door and helped carry my few belongings inside. The thought of sleeping in Lillian's house still felt a little weird, and the prospect of sleeping in what had been the carer's bedroom was unsettling. Nevertheless, everything was now in place. This would be my home for the next few days. I idly wondered exactly how long a 'few days' might be … and how long it would take me to adjust to having people around me 24/7.

While much of the day had slipped away, at last tranquillity had returned to Lillian's house. With nothing better to do after I announced I was going upstairs to the office to continue my research, Gail opted to watch TV for a while. When I came downstairs later, she had given up on surfing the channels in vain for something decent to watch, and was reading a book. Probably to break the boredom, or out of politeness rather than genuine interest, she asked what I had been researching.

It was yet another opportunity to tell the story of my encounter with the Millard brothers, and to explain my search to find any Millard family connection to Lillian. Perhaps I had misjudged her earlier. As our conversation progressed, not only did she appear interested, but she demonstrated a better understanding of how to undertake family history research than I possessed. My reassessment of the officer led me to think Gail might prove handy to have about the place over the coming days.

Chapter 11

Last night was my first attempt at sleeping in Lillian's house since her death. I don't think a lot of sleep happened, and the way I feel this morning tends to confirm it. The two officers on duty in the house all night were not responsible in any way for the lack of sleep. How they filled in their night after I went upstairs is a mystery. I stayed up until nearly midnight in the hope it would help ensure a good night's sleep; it didn't work.

After chatting and surfing TV channels until after eleven o'clock, the officers excused themselves as they had work to do. While the female officer did an inspection tour of the inside of the house, her male partner prowled around outside checking for any unwelcome visitors or anything else out of place. I was in bed by the time they settled down with a pack of cards in the kitchen.

The changeover of 'guards' occurred at seven o'clock this morning, when Gail arrived to relieve them and spend the day with me.

"Will your friend be joining us today?" she asked as I made myself toast and coffee for breakfast.

"Her name is Louella Radford. I don't know whether she is coming or not. I haven't heard from her since yesterday morning, when she suggested she might not be able to come again today. She had unexpected visitors arrive."

"What will you do if she doesn't come?"

"I suppose I'll spend the day in the office trying to dig up more information on Lillian Cavendish's background. How much I will achieve is debatable, as I don't have a clue where to look for information. So far, my contribution has been to read through Lillian's journals for clues to help Lou target specific records."

"Would you object to my helping with the research? I wouldn't get in the way, and won't intrude if you think it's too personal for me to know. Of course, if your friend, Lou, comes today, I'll stay down here and leave the pair of you to get on with your research upstairs."

It was almost nine o'clock when Lou phoned to confirm she wouldn't be coming today, and the situation it might continue on into tomorrow as well. As soon as Lou's call ended, I apprised Gail of the situation, and suggested we make fresh coffees to take upstairs with us before starting work for the day.

Once we were settled in Lillian's office, Gail wanted a precis of where we were at with our research into Lillian's family history. I explained how Lillian, the oldest of four daughters, never married, but stepped in to adopt her youngest sister, Esme's illegitimate daughter, Ruby, after Esme died. We speculated on how the story might have unfolded in the future, and Lorna Green's part in it. Then the hard questions came.

"How far have you gone with Ruby? I mean have you reached the stage where she might have been old enough to marry or maybe have a child of her own?"

"No, I've only reached the stage where Ruby has started school. I assume the story continues in the following journal when I locate it, but it looks like being a long haul, and many journals further on, before I reach the stage where Ruby might be producing offspring."

"What about Lillian's other sisters, did they marry and have families?"

"Isabelle was the only other Cavendish daughter to survive to adulthood. I hadn't thought about her, but I suppose she would have married and had children. Although I hadn't considered it before, any of her grandchildren would have a distant – and, in this case, tenuous – connection to Lillian via Isabelle."

"Well, while you pore over the journals, I could spend some time looking for a possible marriage for Isabelle."

"It might prove difficult. I don't have any dates or names to help you and, as I understand how this stuff works, any marriage of Isabelle's is likely to be too recent to be in the marriage index."

"Yes, but it might have rated a mention in a local paper. Give me anything you know about when and where she was born and her parents' names. I might draw a blank, but it is worth a try."

I gave Gail all the information and estimations I had about Isabelle. Although it didn't amount to much, she scribbled everything on a page of her notebook. As she booted-up Lillian's computer, I went to search in Lillian's bedroom for the next journal. Of course it was too much to hope they would be stacked in order, and each one would have its date range written on its cover. My hunt for the correct book provided an opportunity to correct the situation. As I checked each one, any missing their date range were dealt with. By the time I was finished, all of them were stacked in correct chronological order. Then, armed with the one I came to find, I returned to my makeshift desk in the office.

Gail looked over at me as I pulled my chair up to the cupboard I was using as a table. "Aw no, that won't do. There has to be something better around here somewhere. Have you noticed any little tables anywhere in this place?"

As I shook my head and started to say no, a recollection flashed to mind. "I'm not sure, but there could be one in the carer's room. I'll check."

"Hang on, I'll come with you. If there is something suitable, we'll carry it back here."

The piece of furniture I had in mind, resided under a tailored floral cover, and was against the wall in a corner of what had been the carer's room for the last few years. Its unveiling revealed a small, dark timber rectangular table with an almost full-length drawer running across the front of it. While it wasn't the most stunning piece of furniture I had ever seen, I could see nothing about it to warrant its being hidden under a cover. Gail and I marched it along the landing and installed it in the office. Within minutes, as I began my trawl through the next journal, I experienced the bliss of working at it.

Entries in this book were not added on any regular basis, and seemed to occur only when something of significant note happened. I smiled at one entry considered sufficiently noteworthy to deserve recording: the loss of Ruby's first baby tooth and the tooth fairy's subsequent visit. The random timing of entries meant this journal covered a much longer timespan than might be expected. Most of its contents focused on milestones and incidents associated with Ruby's school days … none of which were helpful to my quest to discover any Millard connection.

In the interests of thorough research, I skimmed every entry until I finished the book as the day was drawing to an end. A check on the time told me Gail's shift should end soon and the 'night crew' would replace her. I glanced in her direction. She was intent on something on the computer screen and, at the same time, furiously scribbling notes on a pad next to her keyboard. Reluctant, to interrupt her, I eased my chair away from my desk, and almost tiptoed to the bedroom to retrieve the next journal from the stack.

When I returned to the office, Gail was slumped back in her chair reading the notes she made. I felt it was too late in the day to start reading another journal, so I flopped down on my chair and asked Gail for a report on her day's research.

"I found a write-up in the paper about Isabelle's marriage to Lloyd Stubbs in early-1954. She was getting on a bit by the time she married. Early in my research, I suspected she lived at home and cared for her parents before the wedding. Then, after my initial reading, I assumed Isabelle and her husband continued to live with the parents in the family home after they were married. But, with a bit more digging, I discovered I didn't have the whole story.

It seems Frederick Cavendish, Isabelle's father, died in 1940. I'm not aware of anything significant about his death, but it left Isabelle's mother, Annie Cavendish, still living in the house with Isabelle. A funeral notice for Annie Cavendish (nee Morgan) gave her date of death as 29 December 1953."

"…And Isabelle was married early in 1954?"

"Yep, the end of March 1954."

"My mind interprets the scenario as Isabelle having put off her marriage until after her mother died. Was it by choice or obligation, I wonder, or was her mother invalided in some way and required care? Maybe it had something to do with the will of one of the parents. Perhaps there was a clause which stipulated the family home was to pass to Isabelle after the deaths of both parents – but only if she continued to care for them until such time as they were both deceased. Maybe there was something else in one of their wills which forbade Isabelle from marrying until after both parents were dead."

"It certainly sounds like something along those lines was involved. Both of the parents' wills should be available. We could request copies, instead of sitting here speculating about what might have been in them."

"It makes sense. What do we have to do, and how long would we have to wait for the copies?"

"Do you have a credit card?"

"Doesn't everybody these days?"

"Okay, I'll order them on line and you can pay for them with your credit card. It's still early enough for them not to have closed for the day yet. If we are lucky, the copies of the wills might be in your inbox sometime tomorrow."

To a sceptic from way back, it all sounded too simple to me, but I told Gail to go ahead and order them anyway. I paid for them and gave my email as the delivery address. In doing so, I hoped I would be pleasantly surprised when I checked my emails tomorrow morning. Then, there was no time for Gail to do anything else. The night crew had arrived and it was time for her to leave.

"If those wills arrive, don't you dare open them before I'm here in the morning," she called over her shoulder on her way out to her car.

After a few words to the new officers, I left them to do their checks and settle in while I went back upstairs to tidy the office.

Of course, I didn't just tidy up. I returned to plodding through the journal I started earlier today. While it was interesting to follow glimpses into life in this house over an extended period of time, I encountered nothing which required notetaking. Simply put, it was interesting but not useful. Having skimmed the last page, I closed the book and checked the time. It was just gone six o'clock. Sounds of the TV evening news drifting up from downstairs confirmed the time.

On my way to the kitchen, the only thing on my mind was what to have for dinner. I had raided my fridge for food to bring with me when I went to collect my belongings for my 'few days' at Lillian's house, but nothing I brought with me suggested an exciting meal for three people. In fact, for obvious reasons, my food came in one-person-sized lots of everything ... and would require some creative thinking to turn any of it into a reasonable meal for three.

As I stood inspecting the contents of the fridge and waiting for inspiration to strike, Jodie, one of tonight's officers, came into the kitchen.

"I hope you don't mind our rearranging the contents of your fridge a bit so we could fit our food in too. Will it be all right for us to reheat our meals here in the kitchen later?"

With any luck, my sigh of relief went unnoticed as I surveyed the extra containers stacked on one shelf. "Feel free to make yourself at home. Anything you can find to do to relieve the boredom on your long shift is fine by me."

"Thanks. By the way, do you play chess?"

"Not really. I've tried, but lose concentration after the first couple of moves."

"We also brought Scrabble. We could give the game a workout after dinner if you are interested."

"Sounds great; I'm still not comfortable about sleeping here, so anything to help keep me up late might result in a better night's sleep."

Later, with the kitchen redolent of reheated curry meals, my taste buds let me know my uninspired omelette left a lot to be desired. Nevertheless, I told myself it was food, and it would prevent hunger adding to things likely to keep me awake tonight. Once dinner was over, we cleared the kitchen table and sat down to the promised game of Scrabble. As someone who earns their living through wordsmithing, I congratulated myself on perhaps having something of an unfair advantage.

It didn't take long for my pride to suffer a nosedive. Those two officers were good – bloody good – and, by the end of our first game, proved themselves superior to me. I did recover some pride in subsequent games, and have to admit to having enjoyed several hours at the kitchen table with them. It was well after eleven o'clock when our last game ended. The officers had to do their routine periodic patrols of the place, and I needed a shower and sleep. Not too much later, I was in bed and telling myself to relax and let sleep come. In hindsight, I think it arrived within minutes.

After what seemed like only a few minutes later, shouting woke me. As I clawed my way out of my deep sleep, I was unsure whether there had been shouting, or if something from my nightmare woke me. With every muscle tensed ready to spring, I lay rigid in bed as I waited for my eyes and ears to adjust. The house seemed ablaze with lights. I'm sure there were not so many lights turned on when I went to bed. Almost convinced it was real shouting and a dream didn't wake me, I strained my ears for any suspicious sounds.

The thud of footsteps running, followed by more shouting, had me out of bed in a flash. I struggled into my robe as I raced along the landing and down the stairs. Just about every light in the house was switched on.

"What's going on? What's happening?" I demanded while descending the stairs.

No one answered. Another burst of shouting emanating from somewhere outside, told me I was alone in the house … and my 'night crew' were busy dealing with something happening out there. When realisation finally sunk in, I froze where I stood in the front room.

Should I go back upstairs and lock myself in my room? … But, my room – the carer's room – didn't have a lock. Only the office and Lillian's bedroom were lockable. Where did I put the keys after I unlocked them? With the two officers outside somewhere, should I stay down here to defend the place if someone should try to enter? And, just how might I do that – me in my dressing gown and with not a potential weapon in sight?

How long I stood there dithering is a mystery, but it probably amounted to no more than seconds, before I was jarred back to reality. While the wail of sirens approaching at speed unglued my feet, my indecision remained. Should I go back upstairs, or stay down here? More sounds adversely impacted my struggling decision-making process. Car doors slammed. More shouting. This time several people seemed involved. Flashing lights lit up the street and another siren announced the impending arrival of still more police. The pounding of many boots around the house and out on the footpath created the illusion I was at the centre of a marathon.

A stream of bad language, accompanied by grunts and thumps, floated in on the night air. More shouting and slamming of car doors mingled with another torrent of offensive language. Two-way radios squawked and phones rang, and the shouting became reduced to the odd command above the murmuring of many voices. A vehicle was started and, after idling for a minute or so, drove off. A few moments later, a second car came to life and followed the first one out of the neighbourhood.

Heavy silence descended to cloak the house. Then, feeling relatively safe, I ventured over to peer out of the front door. The street was empty and the front yard devoid of people. With my stomach still a tight nervous ball, I tiptoed out onto the doorstep. After a quick scan of the scene in front of me, I was about to step out into the yard.

"Where the hell do you think you're going? Go back inside and stay there."

Shocked and terrified, I scuttled back inside before I had time to register who owned the voice barking at me. After a moment, I realised it belonged to Ryan, the male member of my current 'night crew'. While I understood the need for safety, I felt entitled to know what had happened and, more importantly, what the situation was now. If I couldn't go outside, did it mean the danger – whatever it was –remained? Had my life been in danger, and was it still the case? Common sense made me do as I was told. I stayed inside, but hovered just inside the front door.

Time crawled past. The ten minutes before my night crew officers came inside felt more like half an hour. "Well…?" I demanded as Ryan led his offsider into the front room.

"Well, what…?" He looked genuinely perplexed by my question and exchanged a questioning look with his fellow officer.

Was he being cute, or was his reaction real? I was too tense to work it out, and opted for a more direct approach to find out.

"You know damned well what I was asking. What was all tonight's action about, who was involved, and what is the current situation? Do you need further clarification? Oh, and I suppose there is one other big question: am I safe now?"

Jodie stepped in to save the situation. "Of course you need to know what happened. Perhaps we might do a debrief over a coffee, what do you think?"

Did I need a coffee at this hour of the morning? Probably not. But, if it meant finding out what went on tonight, I would make us coffee. Manners dictated I should ask if they would like something to go with it.

"A piece of toast of some sort would go down well," Ryan suggested.

When the two pieces of fruit loaf I flung into the toaster popped up, I slapped butter on them and took them to the table. Then, with sustenance supplied all round, my patience was at an end.

"Right, now which one of you is going to lead off?" I watched two pairs of eyebrows rise and then exchanged questioning glances. "That's enough. At this hour of the morning, I am not in the mood for this crap. What … happened … here … tonight?"

Neither officer would meet my eyes. Then, Jodie looked up, took a deep breath and went to speak. Ryan cut her off before she could utter a word.

"Discussing it with you would be contrary to standard procedure. As the senior officer here, I have to ensure everything is done by the book."

"To hell with 'standard procedure'. Either I am briefed on this evening's activities now, or I am having a conversation with whoever is the commanding officer on duty at your station tonight. Which is it to be?" I felt my jaw tighten as I glared at Ryan. He glared back and, for a moment, I thought I might have to action my bluff. The little voice in my head suggested, give it one last try. "Well, which is it?" I demanded and thumped the table for emphasis.

Again, Jodie stepped in to save the situation. She gave Ryan a hard look and growled, "Neither of us is the senior officer. The last time I looked, we were of equal rank." Ryan squirmed on his chair. Jodie threw him a warning look before turning to me.

"Of course you want to know what all the fuss was about tonight. I know I would want to if I was in your position. But, Ryan is correct. In some situations such as this, the resident already is so upset by events, it is deemed best not to divulge too much information to avoid upsetting them further."

"I am not some dotty old lady who can't handle the information. I have a right to know. I want to know. And, one way or another, I will know the details of what happened here, and to what extent I was in danger. Is there anything about what I've said you don't understand?"

Jodie shook her head and looked uncomfortable. "No, I understand. Before I start, I have to say we don't know whether you were in danger or not. We believed there could have been a break-and-enter on the house. If anyone did gain entry and encountered you here, you could have been in danger."

"Then, why am I staying here? Wouldn't I be safer in my own home?"

"We can't be sure such a move would be better. Whether the Millard brothers might break into the house, or if they might intend harming you – or worse – in a bid to secure their claim to Lillian Cavendish's estate, is unclear. We don't have the resources to provide 24/7 protection of this house and your place as well. By having you stay here, we can concentrate our resources only on this place."

"Okay, I see your point, but what was the intention of tonight's event? …And, were the Millards involved."

"Well, while we can't be sure about their plan at this stage, entering this house was a definite part of it. Nothing more is clear. Maybe we will know more after they are interviewed. Of the three people involved, only one was a Millard, the youngest brother. The other two with him are repeat offenders from way back for break and entering, shoplifting, robbery, and assault."

"Am I misreading the situation, or do the police have a particular interest in the Millard brothers?"

"Over the last twelve months, one or all of them are suspected of having been involved in a number of crimes. While we know the Millards were involved, there has never been enough evidence to charge them. So, yes, if an opportunity presents to nab at least one of them, we will grab it. Tonight, our surveillance of this house paid off with one of the brothers now in custody."

"They didn't actually enter the house. So, what charges can you bring against them? I admit to being surprised they tried anything when there were lights on in the house."

"There were no lights on. After you went to bed, we turned off all the lights and sat in darkness in here when we weren't patrolling both inside and outside. The other thing we did after you went to bed was to strap on our cameras. When we heard a strange noise outside, Ryan snuck out to investigate, and managed to capture footage of young Millard trying to gemmy the backdoor, while his mates looked on. Ryan and I were connected the whole time. So, when he whispered details to me of what was happening, I called it in, and then went out to help with the take-down.”

“Reinforcements seemed to arrive quite soon after all the fuss started.”

“A patrol car was in the next street. They were redirected to here, while a van was dispatched from the station to help out. In the end, there were six officers here.”

“So, if they were watching the house, they would know I was here. In spite of it, they still attempted to break-in once the place was in darkness. They must have known they would have to deal with me.”

It was Ryan’s time to stop sulking and join the conversation. “Even if they hadn’t been watching the place, the moment they arrived they would see your car in the driveway and know you were inside. As Jodie said, while we don’t know their original intent, your presence here wasn’t going to deter them … and it probably is best not to think about what might have happened to you.”

There was little comfort in any of their information. In spite of their insistence, I refused to go back to bed. I remained too on edge to sleep, and besides, the sun was beginning to come up. It was five o’clock, and not much before the usual time I am up every morning. Forget sleep. It was almost time to think about breakfast.

Chapter 12

News travels fast it seems. Gail, my daytime officer, joined me in the kitchen after seeing off my 'night crew' officers.

"I hear tell you had a bit of excitement here last night. How are you holding-up? Are you okay?"

"Just about… I'd feel a lot more relaxed if I knew what those three blokes intended last night. Whether it was to rob the place, to wreck the house, or if I was to be the recipient of some 'special treatment' … or, maybe their plan was for a combination of all three."

"I haven't heard how the interviews are going, but I suspect it will be a long, slow process. Those three guys are old-hands at being questioned. But, one of them is a weaker link. I suspect he will come in for some extra 'special' attention. Sorry, but there isn't anything else I can tell you about last night. Now, what about today, do you feel up to continuing with our research?"

"Yes, it's what I planned to do today. I haven't heard anything definite from Lou Radford, so I don't know whether she will be joining us or not. Anyway, we can carry on from where we left off yesterday, and worry about what to do after she arrives."

A few minutes later, we carried our coffees up to the office. I went to fetch the next journal in the series while I waited for my computer to boot up. As I sat back at my desk again, Gail reminded me to check my emails in case the copies of the wills had arrived.

"O-oh, yes. They are here." Copies of Frederick's and Annie Cavendish's wills were in my inbox. After I hooked up Lillian's printer, it was soon spewing out volumes of pages. "Which one should I start with, and what am I looking for?"

"Let's take one each. As you go through it, make notes of anything pertinent – particularly anything about any bequests and any conditions attaching to them."

After sorting and stapling the pages, I handed Gail the top copy. When I sat down, I realised I had left myself Annie's will to work through. It had fewer pages than Frederick's. I skimmed most of the first page which was taken up with the usual jargon at the beginning of such a document. Then, it was on to the bit about who got what. So many words…! It was as if Annie had aspirations of becoming a novelist. Several paragraphs rambled on about Isabelle and how she had remained in the family home and cared for her parents *all the while with one eye on what she might acquire at the end of it all.*

"What a harsh, ungrateful comment to make." I read those paragraphs again and, to my dismay, found Annie insinuated much the same thing a couple of times, before stating outright her opinion of Isabelle.

"Have you found something interesting? What comment are you on about?" As Gail asked her questions, she never lifted her eyes from the copy of Frederick's will she was reading.

"Sorry, I shouldn't have interrupted your reading. Let's wait until we both finish going through the wills before discussing what we found."

Once Gail agreed to my suggested approach, I ploughed on through the rest of Annie's will, while maintaining my extreme dislike for the woman. By the time I reached the end of the document, my dislike had turned to disgust. While I didn't know the circumstances surrounding the family's living arrangements, I still felt Annie's comments about, and her criticism of Isabelle, were unjust. I slammed the document closed and sat back to ponder Isabelle's situation following her mother's death.

Isabelle was left very little by her mother. While Annie made quite substantial bequests to a couple of charities, she left only a small amount of cash to her daughter. She even went so far as to bequeath what appeared to be a significant family heirloom piece of silverware to one of Annie's long-time friends. And, as others of her friends had, over the years, commented on other pieces of silver in the house, Isabelle was instructed to allow them to choose whatever they especially fancied from the collection. While I found all of it disgusting, when I came to Annie's comments relating to Lillian, my disgust turn to anger.

It seems Lillian's move to reconnect with her youngest sister, Esme, just before Esme passed away offended the family who, months before, had disowned Esme. The final blow, as far as the rest of the family were concerned, was struck when Lillian adopted Esme's illegitimate child, Ruby. As a consequence of Lillian's behaviour, she too was disowned by the family. Annie's will spared no vitriol in outlining how disappointing and insulting Lillian's actions were for her family. The final consequence of all this was for Lillian to be cut out of the will, with the added instruction to the executors for Lillian not to benefit by any means from Annie's estate.

My faith in human nature was restored to some extent a bit later. Amongst the probate paperwork were documents relating to a challenge to Annie's estate. A claim against the estate was lodged on behalf of Annie's only grandchild, Ruby. No simple matter for the executors to deal with, the claim ended up in court. It appears the court did not take long to rule in Ruby's favour. A small amount of cash was placed in trust for the child until she obtained her majority.

"Good for you Lillian," I chirped.

Startled by my outburst, Gail almost sprang up off her chair. "What…? Did something happen?"

A few moments later, after I outlined what I discovered, Gail echoed my response. "Good on Lillian. It does my heart good to see such family bitterness defeated – and in such a good way. Lillian didn't seek anything for herself, although she probably was entitled to do so. But, she made sure the next generation, Ruby, didn't suffer the same elimination from the family as her mother and aunt encountered."

"I think you would have to go a long way to find a more bitter and twisted woman than Annie Cavendish. It's not surprising Lillian never mentioned her family. While they might have disowned her, it's not surprising she did not want to be associated in any way with them. I suppose there is no accounting for the way families behave or how they treat their own, but this will leaves a particularly bitter taste for me. How are you going with Frederick's will? Are there any 'gems' in that one?"

"Not really. Although it's a major document to read, it is fairly straightforward. Most of his estate was left to his wife, Annie. There are a couple of interesting bits. But, in reading his will, you need to remember he died a long time before Annie … and before any of the nonsense relating to Esme and Lillian occurred. All of which seems to be all of Annie's doing."

"Tell me about those interesting bits. I could do with something uplifting after Annie's will."

"He didn't leave the house to his wife. Annie was to be allowed to live there for the rest of her life, or until she remarried. The house was to go to Isabelle, but only if she complied with certain conditions. She had to continue to live there and care for her mother until her mother's death. In order to discharge her duties faithfully, she must not seek employment outside the home, or undertake any other employment which might interfere with her role of carer and housekeeper. She must not marry, nor carry on a relationship with any man, until after her mother's death. If Isabelle contravened any of those conditions, she must leave the house immediately and with only her personal possessions. In the event of such a contravention of the conditions, ownership of the house would pass to Annie."

"Slave labour…! I must have led a sheltered life, but I wouldn't have thought it possible for a middle-class Australian family. The parents effectively robbed Isabelle of the right to a life of her own, and blackmailed her into compliance with the promise of the family home at the end of it all. Instead of dying when she did, Annie might have survived for another decade or more. Isabelle would have been well into middle-age by then, with the opportunity for marriage and family having passed her by."

"Oh, he did allow Isabelle some compensation in return. He set up an allowance – an annuity I suppose – to be paid to her until such time as Annie died and Isabelle was no longer tied to caring for her. Of course, the financial support also disappeared if Isabelle did not comply with the terms of Frederick's will. Following her mother's death, any monies remaining in the trust fund were to go to Isabelle."

"As no one knew how long Annie might live, it would be difficult to estimate how much money was required to set up the trust fund. It then raises the question of how much, if any, was left in the fund at the time of Annie's death."

"At this stage, we don't have anything to tell us about Isabelle's financial situation when she finally was free to live a normal life, and to marry. We discovered she married in the year after her mother's death, but we don't know if there were any children from the marriage. Unless, like Lillian, she lived to a grand old age, Isabelle is likely to have died some time ago."

This was not going as I hoped. While the rest of the stuff we learned today was interesting, it didn't help my quest to establish whether there was a family connection with the Millards. "I know we don't have any information about Isabelle's or Lloyd Stubbs' deaths to help us narrow down the search parameters, but is there any way we might be able to search for their deaths?"

"Hmm… maybe… I'll have a think about it. In the meantime, I should carry out a patrol of the premises."

"While you're about it, I'll make coffee. Don't waste too much time thinking about how else we might search for information. It's something Lou can do the next time she shows up."

"Are you worried about her?"

"No-o, not really. It's just out of keeping not to have heard from her, but she does have a busy life, and a business to keep her occupied. Any time she spends with me on this research is as a favour. I did offer to pay her usual rates, but she refused."

"Give her a call to see what her situation is and when she might be here again."

"God, no, I couldn't. It would seem like I was hounding her for not turning up. She will let me know in her own good time what's happening. I suppose it's safe to say Lou has always been something of a free spirit. Reliability was never one of her strong points."

As I put our coffees on the kitchen table, my phone played its tune. "Speak of the devil…" I said as Gail dragged out a chair, "It's Lou." I took my phone out to the front room.

"Is everything okay?" Gail asked as I returned to the kitchen again.

"Since yesterday, Lou has been researching on the other side of the country for a big client of hers. She doesn't mention details of course, but I think it might be a bit like my research except, in this case, it has something to do with a disputed significant estate. It could be another couple of days before she can head back east again. So, I suppose this is my big chance to see what I can achieve without her."

"What we can achieve. It seems I'm going to be here every day for a while yet, so we'll just keep going with whatever we can until she comes back."

I took advantage of the call to ask Lou for guidance on finding the deaths of Isabelle and Lloyd Stubbs. Over coffee, I passed on Lou's suggestions to Gail.

"I had intended trying something similar when we went back to the office, so it's reassuring to have her confirm my approach. I'm sure Lou pointed out whether we find anything or not will depend on how long ago they died. If their deaths were too recent – in comparative terms – they won't appear in the deaths index yet."

Buoyed up by the thought further progress might be a possibility today, I didn't want to waste time hanging around in the kitchen. As soon as I finished my coffee, I scraped back my chair and stood ready to head back upstairs. Gail got the message, downed the last of her coffee, and was only a couple of steps behind me as I headed for the stairs.

"Right, I'm going to see what I can dig up out of the deaths index. Sophie, have you got something to be going on with in the meantime?"

"Yep, I'm not stuck for something to do. There's a whole pile of journals waiting for me in the other room. This seems like a good time to get started on the next one."

Disappointment greeted me again as I made a start on the next journal. As I skimmed page after page, all I saw were entries noting Ruby's various achievements. It appears the girl was bright and doing quite well academically, but there were vague references to what I interpreted as Ruby's having transgressed in some way at school. There were a couple of changes of schools along the way, all of which involved first class, expensive, private schools. Although the reasons were not given, Lillian seemed to visit Ruby's school on numerous occasions. More often than what I considered might constitute normal parent/teacher review meetings.

On one such school visit, Lillian recorded a police officer also attended. Frustratingly, she omitted any details of the reason for the visit to the school or why the officer was there. Nevertheless, as I continued skimming the pages, I was forming a definite picture of a problem child. What had Lillian taken on when she adopted her niece? Was the misbehaviour simply a case of Ruby's reacting to her past circumstances, or was it as a result of something genetic in her make up? I couldn't help but wonder if knowing something of Ruby's father might help us understand what was going on. Gail's yelp halted any further pondering about Ruby's behaviour.

"Here he is. I've found Lloyd Stubbs' death entry in the index. He and Isabelle weren't married for too long before he died. Do you want to order a copy of his death certificate?"

What a silly question. Of course, I wanted a copy of the death certificate. Again, Gail took charge of ordering a copy online, and I simply filled in the credit card information.

"The information the certificate provides might be enough to answer some of our questions, but I keep looking to see if there is an entry for Isabelle's death. If we are lucky, Lloyd Stubbs' death certificate might come through sometime this afternoon. If not, it should be here in the morning. Still, it would be good also to be able to obtain Isabelle's certificate. It would tell us if anything happened after Lloyd died."

I left Gail to continue attacking her keyboard while I returned to Lillian's journal. A monotonous picture was emerging of a young girl with serious problems … or perhaps one of a spoiled brat. Again, there were inferences rather than direct comment, but I didn't have to be too bright to work out Ruby was causing Lillian more problems than she was worth. And, as I progressed through the book, those problems seem to be escalating in frequency and severity. Lillian didn't deserve any of it. She must've been almost at her wits end as she tried to deal with Ruby's behaviour.

One interesting fact I did discover related to when Lillian bought this house. Although I can't be sure, it seems as though Ruby's behaviour had reached the point where Lillian felt compelled to move, not only to a new address, but to new employment as well. For a few moments, I sat and thought about how the scrapes Ruby was getting herself into might have impacted on Lillian's career as a chartered accountant. No matter how understanding or forgiving the firm's client base might be, Ruby's antics would not have reflected well on Lillian. Perhaps it's why she felt she had no option but to move and try to make a fresh start in a new position in a new location.

Lunchtime had rolled around unnoticed, and it was almost one o'clock when I realised how late it was. "I'm going downstairs to make lunch, Gail. You should stop too, and take a break before we eat."

As we were finishing lunch, Gail received a phone call and wandered outside to take it. I remained parked at the table. Instead of clearing away the lunch things and stacking them in the dishwasher, I sat there staring off into space. Why is it, every time we stop work for more than five minutes, I have trouble getting started again? Maybe it's the prospect of trudging through another of Lillian's journals documenting almost every conceivable step in Ruby's life. Was this how all parents were about their offspring: so proud of, and wrapped up in, a child's life? Was everything they did so worthy of recording?

Now, there's an interesting concept to contemplate. Did Ruby fulfil some maternal need in Lillian, to the extent Lillian became as besotted with the child as a natural mother might? I was still pondering the question when Gail returned from taking her phone call.

"Are you okay, Sophie? I expected to find you back upstairs and hard at it again by now. Instead, it looks as though you haven't moved since I left. Shall I stack these dishes in the dishwasher for you?"

"No, I'll do it. Nothing is wrong. I was just kicking around a couple of thoughts – questions really."

"Did you come up with any answers?"

"Not yet… but, perhaps, you might have some thoughts on the matter." I outlined my questions about why Lillian was so fixated on every little thing Ruby did. "Do you think it might be nothing more than some maternal instinct thing in play here, or was there something else driving her to record almost every little detail of Ruby's life?"

"Interesting… I hadn't thought about it but, now you ask, it is interesting. Before I joined the police, I was at university. I was going to be a psychologist. By the time I completed my basic degree, I knew it wasn't what I wanted to do. If you don't mind, I'll have a look through a couple of those journals to see the sorts of things Lillian recorded."

Of course I didn't mind. If Gail was busy with the journals, it meant I wasn't … and I welcomed the excuse to take a break from them for a while. As soon as we were upstairs, Gail grabbed the last journal I'd looked at and took it to her desk. I took another of the journals I had finished with and placed it on her desk, so she had plenty to provide her with a more complete view of the situation. The little voice in my head told me I could fetch and go through another journal from the bedroom while I waited for Gail to finish with the two she had. In spite of its strenuous efforts, it couldn't convince me I needed to go through another one just yet.

In need of something else worthwhile to do, I decided to check my emails. My work as a freelance journo had been banished to oblivion for the last few days. I hadn't even checked my emails since we received the copies of the Cavendish wills. My inbox confirmed my lack of attention. It sported a long list of unread emails. One caught my attention. Suddenly, I was perched on the edge of my chair waiting for the attachment to open. It would be a shame to interrupt Gail, I told myself, and took great care not to alert her to anything exciting happening on my side of the office.

There it was: Lloyd Stubbs' death certificate. Best not print it just yet, I told myself. The printer would be a dead giveaway about having found something interesting. So, I enlarged the scanned copy of the certificate on the screen and set about acquainting myself with how to interpret the information it provided.

Ah yes, this was the 'right' Lloyd Stubbs. It gave his wife's name as Isabelle Cavendish, and the correct date of their marriage. His address told me they were living in the Cavendish family home. And, why not, I thought. After all, once her mother died, it was Isabelle's house. It appears Lloyd died of a heart attack. I skimmed over the information about his burial, to reach the last block of information on the certificate.

It provided information about Lloyd's children. "Well, well, well…" I murmured. "How about that!"

"How about what," Gail demanded.

"Oh, sorry, I didn't mean to interrupt you." Gail gave me a 'gimme' gesture I couldn't ignore. "It appears Lloyd Stubbs died without any surviving issue. There was one child who predeceased his father and died as an infant. I assume it means Isabelle's line ends with her."

"Possibly… It depends on what happened after her husband died and how old Isabelle was at the time."

"Let's see… Lloyd died in 1970. Isabelle would have been about forty-six when he died. I suppose it's still young enough for her to remarry – and maybe even to produce a child."

"Yeah, at her age, she might have remarried. But, having a child… I suppose it could have been possible, but it might have been pushing the boundaries a bit. And, after losing one child as an infant, she might not feel inclined to go there again."

"Hell! Look at this."

"I would – if you printed me a copy to look at." I set it to print. "While I'm waiting, what is it I should look at?"

"Lloyd Stubbs' age at death… I didn't notice it before, but he was sixty-seven years old."

"It looks like Isabelle swapped looking after one geriatric for another. I should get back to searching for Isabelle's death. I doubt there were any children but, in the interests of being thorough, we should see if she remarried. If she did, it would be too recent to appear in the index and, without knowing her new married name, I wouldn't be able to find her death."

"Well, let's hope she had enough of looking after other people and decided to remain a widow. If she was anything like Lillian, you might have a long search ahead of you, even if she did remain 'Stubbs'."

"I'll start checking for Stubbs' deaths from the end of the 1991 deaths, which are the end of the indexed period, and move back through the years from there."

With nothing else I felt inclined to do, I decided to make us a coffee and bring it up to the office. I pushed my chair back and stood up – but it is far as I went.

"Ye-e-s!" Gail yelped. "I've found her. She never remarried, and died in 1989. Do you want the certificate?"

"Might be a good idea to have a copy on file, just to prove we looked into every possibility."

A few minutes later, I had used my credit card to order her death certificate, and we were sitting in the kitchen with fresh coffees and feeling chuffed with our progress today. About half an hour later, tonight's 'night crew' arrived. It was Ryan and Jodie again.

Chapter 13

With the night crew busy settling in and undertaking their routine initial patrols, I disappeared upstairs to the office again. Gail might be gone for the day, but there was nothing stopping me continuing our research.

A half-formed question had fought to assert itself since we ordered Isabelle's death certificate. Back in the solitude of the office, the silence worked its magic. The niggling question finally managed to dominate my thinking. Who ended up with the family home? While I knew it wasn't of any consequence to the research I was supposed to be doing, rampant curiosity insisted I should find out. I wished I'd paid more attention, or been more involved, when Gail looked for wills. But, how difficult can it be?

Abandoning my own computer, I went and sat at Lillian's. Okay… So, now I'm here, what do I do next? When all else fails, and you don't have any other ideas, have a look at Google's search history. It only took a small dose of logic to work out where to go to find something to do with wills. So, I double-clicked on the appropriate entry on the list of sites visited – and held my breath.

"Yep, this looks promising," I told the empty office … And then spent a couple of minutes working out how to navigate my way around the site. "Not nearly as difficult as I expected," I announced with a hint of triumph after a further few minutes of fumbling around.

I found an entry in the index for Isabelle's will. Now, how the hell do I order a copy? A little more exploration of the site took me to the right place to 'click to order' a copy. After entering all the information required, I once again employed my credit card and, moments later, I had completed an order for a copy of

Isabelle's will. Basking in the sense of achievement, I sat back to contemplate why I thought it was important to obtain a copy in the first place.

The only remaining family members had been Isabelle, Lillian, and young Ruby. Then, on Isabelle's death, only Lillian and Ruby remained. Regardless of whatever she felt about Ruby, would Isabelle leave any part of her estate to Lillian? After Lillian's having been shunned by the family for so many years, it was difficult to form an opinion on whether Isabelle would maintain the same stance to the bitter end, or if her impending demise might encourage a softening of the relationship? "Well, with any luck, I'll find out tomorrow," I told the universe. Bearing in mind, Lillian never mentioned her sister, Isabelle, or having inherited the family home, it seemed unlikely anything changed.

Rather than waste time sitting around doing nothing – and I didn't feel inclined to go downstairs and be sociable – I made a start on the next journal of Lillian's life. I had only glanced at the first couple of pages when Jodie tapped lightly on the door.

"It's gone six o'clock. I wondered if you were interested in dinner sometime soon. Ryan and I will probably take our meal break shortly, but we can wait a bit long if you'd like to join us."

"How did it get to be so late? I'll come down now. My intention was to do a stirfry for dinner. I don't know what your plans are, but I could make it big enough for the three of us."

Jodie assured me a stirfry had infinitely more appeal than a tuna sandwich and a cup of soup, and she proved a dab hand with a knife as she helped chop vegetables. Another game of Scrabble was suggested for after dinner. I begged off, citing having looked at enough words for one day.

Over dinner, I took the opportunity to ask about the outcome of last night's activities. I don't know whether they didn't have any information, or simply were playing by the rules, but they claimed not to know what happened to those taken into custody. It wasn't worth pressing them about it. My relationship with Gail is on a much better footing than with these two officers. If

Gail hears anything, I'm reasonably confident she will pass it on to me.

As soon as dinner was over and the cleaning up done, the two officers commandeered the kitchen table for a game of chess. I beat a hasty retreat to the office. Although I didn't feel up to wading through Lillian's journal, I did not want to be downstairs and faced with the prospect of being roped into another game of Scrabble or some other time-wasting pursuit. So, having installed myself in the office, there was nothing for it other than to plough through another journal.

My mind glassed over about five minutes after I started skimming the pages. All I registered about it was it appeared to be more of the same about life with Ruby. After about twenty minutes – and quite a lot of pages – something was trying to grab my attention. "What...?" I demanded aloud. "Nothing jumped out at me." The universe didn't provide an answer, but I knew better than to ignore the little voice in my head telling me I had missed something important. I grabbed a number of the pages already skimmed and flipped them back. This time I would make myself read every word.

Try as I might to find something significant, there was nothing, no incident or event of any importance. I inserted a bookmark and closed the journal. It was time to reflect, not time for more reading. It only required a couple of minutes before a thought started to develop. All was no longer sweetness and light on the home front. To see the full picture of the situation, I had to read between the lines; not just the words on the page. Things seemed to have become a bit tense in Lillian's household. But, it was only to be expected.

Ruby was by then a teenager and was testing her boundaries. Even today, parents tell of struggling to cope with their children's teenage years. Perhaps it was more difficult for Lillian without any natural maternal attachment to Ruby to help her through the rough times. Although the entries in the journal were brief and a bit cryptic, there was no mistaking the stress Ruby's behaviour generated for Lillian and Lorna Green. Nevertheless, my gut instinct was telling me whatever was going on at the time was about more than just a rebellious teenager.

Maybe I should not try reading any more tonight. It would have been so easy for me to skim over all this without picking up on the real story of how things were for Lillian at the time. It might be better to come at it again when I'm fresh tomorrow. But, one question continued to nag me: was any of this important … *really* important in the overall scale of things? The question stayed with me long after I went to bed. Another one soon joined it: What happened to Ruby?

In all the time I knew Lillian, I don't recall ever hearing mention of Ruby. Had the difficulties of her teenage years escalated to the point where Lillian and Ruby parted company? Legally, until she turned twenty-one, Ruby couldn't leave home to start her own life elsewhere. Regardless of how rugged life became during those years, I can't imagine Lillian being driven to the point where she would kick Ruby out. It wasn't in the nature of the woman I knew as Lillian Cavendish.

I did eventually fall asleep. But, it was for a few hours of troubled sleep which found no answers to the questions gnawing at me.

*****

While it wasn't a restful night, it wasn't disturbed again by any form of unlawful activity. I hadn't long come down for breakfast when Gail arrived and the night shift left.

"You look dreadful," Gail announced. "Did something happen again last night?"

"No. I just didn't sleep well; probably a legacy from the previous night. But, I am itching to be back upstairs this morning. In fact, I think I'll take my coffee up there with me now. Don't feel you have to rush up too. Do whatever you need to do down here, and join me when you are ready."

I drummed my fingers on the desk as I waited for my computer to boot up, and then for my emails to load. Yes! There it was, the copy of Isabelle's will. The printer seemed to be spitting out pages for quite a while before it fell silent again. Some of the pages had curled and managed to get themselves out of order. Sorting them into the correct order and stapling them seemed to take forever but, at last, I was ready to put my feet up and sip my coffee as I read Isabelle Stubbs' Last Will and Testament.

Just to frustrate me I'm sure, the first page contained nothing but legal gobbledegook. The real substance of the document didn't begin until the second page. Having learned my lesson last night, I forced myself to read every word and not skim over any bit of it. This part of the document started with what amounted to an inventory of the various members of Isabelle's extended family, both living and deceased.

Although I knew some of the details already, I stuck to my rule of reading every word. At the end of the section, I knew as much about Isabelle's surviving family as I did at the outset. I knew only Lillian and Ruby remained. And, Ruby might as well not have existed, because she did not rate even one mention in the will. It appears Isabelle's husband, Lloyd Stubbs, was an only child. With Lloyd and his parents having predeceased her, all who were left were the two members of Isabelle's family. Apart from charitable institutions, Isabelle wasn't left with too many options for what to do with her estate.

Forcing myself to consider Isabelle's situation for a moment before carrying on to the next section, I felt a hint of excitement starting to build. Would she do the 'right' thing, or would she remain bitter and twisted to the end? "Only one way to find out," I murmured to the empty room.

The next couple of pages, while jammed full of legal-ese, told an amazing story. Isabelle had come to the end of her life as a well-heeled widow. More to the point, as the inventory of her estate attested, she had been a very wealthy woman. The estate comprised two parcels of real estate, one of which was the family home. Then followed an almost endless list of jewellery, silverware, furniture, vehicles, books, and collectables. There was a string of investments, shares, and bank accounts, the latter all healthy indeed.

Apart from a bequest of five thousand pounds to a women's benevolent group I'd never heard of, everything else went to Lillian. I continued through to the end of the document to see if anything or anyone had intervened in the probate process, thereby altering the final outcome of Isabelle's estate. No, there it was, confirmed in the Grant of Probate just as Isabelle had intended.

"Bloody Hell … what happened to all the stuff?"

"What happened to what stuff?" Gail asked as she strode into the office. What have you found? You sounded shocked."

"Yeah, not a bad description, but 'dumbfounded' would do just as well."

I handed Gail the copy of Isabelle's will to read while I sat in silence and contemplated all I gleaned from the document. The question of what happened to everything from Isabelle's estate after probate was granted continued to dog my thinking. I don't remember seeing mention of anything resembling the material from Isabelle's bequest contained in Lillian's will. Did Lillian dispose of everything; turn it into cash perhaps? Was some of it part of the cash I inherited? Argh, it was no good sitting here tying myself in knots about it. Sorting it out was beyond my capabilities. The only person who might help make sense of it all was James Whitby. As soon this morning reaches a civilised hour, I'll try giving James a call.

Further thought on the matter was interrupted by a long low whistle from Gail. She looked up at me with eyes the size of saucers. "Wow, the old girl wasn't short of a crust was she? And it all went to your Lillian. If you don't mind my asking, does it mean you inherited the residue of Isabelle's estate when Lillian died? I mean, was some of what you inherited from Lillian, some of the material listed here in Isabelle's will?"

"I don't mind your asking, but I don't have an answer for you. I'm not aware of any of it being a part of my inheritance, and I certainly would have noticed the old family home if it were listed."

"So, what are your thoughts now? As I'm sure you want to know, how do you propose to find out?"

"The only thing I can think to do is to talk to the solicitor, James Whitby. Although, if he knew about this situation, I feel sure he would have mentioned it. Regardless of what's happened, or who knows what, such a sizeable estate can't just disappear into thin air. There have to be records of somewhere showing what happened to it all after Lillian inherited it. I plan to ring James this morning to set up an appointment with him."

"Hmm, it's probably the best thing you can do. What are you working on now?"

"What else but Lillian's journals? I've still a long way to go, and a whole truckload of questions needing answers. My hope is, as I slog through those books, I'll have a better idea of how things played out in Lillian's life, and maybe they will shed some light on what happened after Isabelle's death. Do you have something to keep you occupied?"

"I have a couple of ideas I might follow up, but I'm sure I won't get stuck for something to keep me busy."

We worked in absolute silence until Gail suggested she would make coffee, and asked if I wanted mine brought upstairs, or would I take a break and have it downstairs. A check on the time told me the morning had disappeared in a flash. It was almost ten o'clock. My intention had been to call James Whitby around nine o'clock before he went to golf, or became involved in whatever else he had planned for the day. I placed the call as I followed Gail down to the kitchen.

James took a while to answer but, just as I was thinking I'd missed my opportunity, he picked up. He sounded out of breath and I was concerned about what I might have interrupted. "No. No, you didn't interrupt anything important. I was pruning my roses when I heard my phone ringing. By the time I shed my gloves and wellies, and rushed in to pick it up, I fully expected it to have dialled out."

"Then I must apologise to your roses for interrupting their spruce-up, but I was hoping you might have some time soon for an appointment with me."

"Don't worry about the roses. I welcome anything more important to do than dealing with those prickly monsters. What's your timing like today? Would twelve o'clock be okay for an appointment? We could combine it with lunch at the little bistro just along the street from my office."

Of course it suited me, and I informed Gail about the appointment when I joined her in the kitchen for coffee. "Okay, if we leave here at 11:45, we should be at the bistro in time for your twelve o'clock appointment."

"Oh, I hadn't intended dragging you along as well. I imagine it would be a very boring session for you, and I'm not sure James would want to discuss legal matters in front of you."

"Unfortunately, you don't have a choice. If you are going somewhere, I have to be with you. No, there's no need for such a look. I won't be sitting with you. I'll be parked at a nearby table from which I can keep an eye on everything happening around you. I'm sorry, but it's how it has to be. Anyway, I'm quite looking forward to having a bistro lunch on my expense account. Thank you for inviting me."

"Well, I don't remember inviting you, but you're welcome. As soon as I finish my coffee, I'll gather up the bits of paper I need to take to my meeting with James. I wish I knew how he is likely to react to all this; to my opening another can of worms for him to sort out."

There wasn't much time to waste thinking about it. By the time we'd rinsed our coffee mugs and I'd gathered up the documents I wanted to take with me, it was time to go, and we were on our way out to my car. As we headed along the street, my mind was filling with questions, and not all of them questions James could answer. I couldn't help wondering how Lillian reacted to finding herself the last of the family left standing – apart from Ruby – and then discovering Isabelle's bequest. These questions might never have answers ... *unless*

Lillian was generous enough to document her feelings in her journals. I felt a sudden renewed enthusiasm for examining those journals.

In the meantime, there were more important matters to deal with, like how Gail envisaged my meeting with James should play out. Only one way to find out, I asked her. "Gail, are there any rules, protocols, or whatever, I should be aware of as far as this meeting is concerned? Is there anything you want me to do, or not do, while we are at the bistro? You'll have to tell me how you want to play it."

"If I'm honest, I would have preferred the meeting was in Mr Whitby's office. It's a more enclosed space and easier to police. If it were, I would have been sitting outside his office keeping an eye on anyone who came near his door. Since it's not at his office, but in the bistro, we will just have to adjust to the setting. The only thing I would suggest you keep in mind is not to keep looking in my direction. It would be a dead giveaway to anyone who was scoping the place."

To my surprise – and delight if I'm honest after Gail's comments – the bistro was almost empty. A small hole-in-the-wall type place, it had Italianate aspirations. From its dark stained timber furniture and red and white checked tablecloths, to the Chianti bottle candle holders, and the prints on the walls, it was determined to be Italian. A quick glance at the menu displayed on the board outside was the only slight departure from the theme. While not unexpected, Mediterranean cuisine predominated, but diners were offered a good range of other dishes to choose from as well.

James was already there and had selected a table in the back corner. While it was one of the least popular spots diners would choose, it suited our purposes to perfection. Another vacant table a couple of metres away served Gail's purpose as well. As our tables were adjacent to the back wall of the bistro, it meant any interference would come from in front of us, making Gail's surveillance an easier task.

Our meeting lasted less than two hours, not bad considering

it included having lunch as well. James insisted we order before knuckling down to business. And then, while we waited for lunch to arrive, he requested only an overview of what I wanted to discuss, rather than diving into the real business of the day. I have to admit to being guilty of bolting my food down in a bid to move things along to the discussion I wanted to have. With our meals finally dispatched, I fished the copy of Isabelle's will out of my satchel.

"James, in the interests of not wasting too much of your time, perhaps you could glance through this while you're sipping your coffee." His eyebrows crawled up his forehead before settling down again and drawing together across the bridge of his nose. It was obvious I'd taken him by surprise and it was not what he expected the meeting to be about.

It was a struggle not to fidget with impatience as he painstakingly worked his way through the copy of the will. I wanted to shout, 'just go to the estate inventory page, or the grant of probate document attached at the back', but I bit my tongue and held my silence until he was finished.

"This is amazing. I don't know what else to say, except to admit I know nothing of any of this. While I can imagine you have a whole host of questions to ask me, maybe it would be helpful at this juncture if you told me what prompted you to make this appointment. Tell me what you want to know."

"What happened to it, to all the stuff Lillian inherited? Please don't think I'm questioning why none of it came to me. I'm just curious to know what she did with it. Maybe knowing would help me understand the woman she was and what was going on in her life back then. And, if the Millard name crops up in your investigation, it will confirm whether those three blokes are related to Lillian, or simply unconnected opportunist who read the funeral notices in the papers."

"Your questions don't come as a surprise. I want to know what happened to all Isabelle's stuff as well. And, as you say, it might uncover any Millard connection. May I keep this copy of Isabelle's will?"

"Yes, take it with you. I can print another copy when I'm back at the house… which reminds me. We should be getting back. I don't think Gail was too happy about us being out and about. Her brief seems to be to keep an eye on me, but also to keep an eye out for any sign of a break-and-enter. She can't do both while we are sitting in this bistro."

"No, of course you must go. I will look into this." James waved Isabelle's will at me and frowned. "I'll follow everything through to develop a timeline. And, I'll go back through the history of Lillian's will. I know the one submitted for probate was not the first will she made. There might be some answers to be found in searching various files. I'll give you a call when I know more."

Gail made no secret of her relief to be heading back to the house. As soon as we arrived, she carried out one of her patrols of the place, checking every window and door and prowling around the yard. Having found nothing to cause her concern, she joined me in the office, and stirred Lillian's computer to life again.

While she waited for a site to load, she asked, "Was your meeting successful? Did you gain any answers?"

"All I can say at the moment is, I think my meeting with James was worthwhile. It didn't gain me any answers but, in time, it might. It seems he is as much in the dark as I am, and knew nothing of Lillian's inheritance from Isabelle. I've no idea how long it will take him to find any information, but there's not much I can do except wait."

"Is there nothing you can do here while you're waiting?"

"I didn't mean to create the impression there wasn't anything I could be going on with. I still have a stack of journals to go through, and today's development has me hoping Lillian's journal entries might provide some indication of what happened. So, for me, it's back to wading through the journals. What about you? Is there anything you've thought of which you'd like to follow up, or are you going to have to sit around and be bored for the rest of the day?"

"Bored…? Never; I do have something in mind to look up. It might prove a waste of time, but I think it's worth a look. I'll try not to disturb your reading."

True to her word, Gail spent the remainder of her shift interrogating various websites. With no interruptions, I managed to finish another journal. It told me discord between Lillian and Ruby – and Lorna Green to some extent – was escalating. A sense of foreboding filled me as I went to fetch the next journal in the series. While it was too late to start reading it now, it would give me a valid excuse to avoid another game of Scrabble after dinner.

Chapter 14

Changeover of the police crews was as swift and efficient as usual. As I walked Gail to the door, she leaned in close and murmured, "Don't you go finding anything too exciting before I come back tomorrow." I gave her a mock questioning look. "You've picked up the scent and now you're experiencing the thrill of the chase. I know you will spend hours in the office tonight, chasing down every possible clue you come across."

"I will go and hide in the office to avoid Scrabble, but I don't know how much work I will do."

After spending a few minutes with the night shift officers, I retreated upstairs until it was time for dinner. Although the only logical thing for me to work on was another journal, the extent and details of the estate Lillian inherited from Isabelle kept interfering with my concentration on the words in front of me. It was hopeless to continue with the journal, so I put it aside and let my thinking go wherever it chose regarding Lillian's inheritance.

The only member of her close or extended family still around at the time was Ruby. In spite of the previous successful challenge to Annie's estate, I always doubted there was any way Isabelle would break with the family stance and leave anything to Ruby, her illegitimate niece. And, Isabelle's will confirmed she didn't. So, if she intended keeping the estate within the family who would inherit it was a no-brainer. But, although Isabelle left everything to Lillian, would Lillian consider using it to benefit Ruby in some way? Such a move would be in keeping with what I knew of Lillian. Would the fact the relationship between Lillian and Ruby was becoming strained make Lillian reluctant to do something for Ruby with at least part of the inheritance?

Such thinking seemed to want to persist. I knew it was a waste of time to try reading the journal. I put my feet up, lounged back in the chair, and stared off into the distance to let my mind roam wherever it wanted. If Lillian had made such a move, there would have to be documentation of some sort. The cash and the family home were the two stand-out items. Lillian might have set up some form of trust account for Ruby using the cash from Isabelle's bequest.

It was a considerable amount of cash, and would have stood Ruby in good stead for her adult life. Perhaps it could have been set up as an annuity which came into effect when Ruby turned twenty-one. But, such an arrangement required trustees to oversee the money and its allocation. There would be records and other documentation surrounding the establishment of the arrangement and its subsequent management. Who would hold such documents? A solicitor seemed the most likely candidate, but who and where? Maybe it's something else James Whitby needs to look into.

Then, there is the family home to consider. By the time Isabelle died in 1989, Lillian was well-established here in this house and had her own accounting practice in town. I don't remember her ever not living in this house, and I don't recall any mention of her having gone back to live in the family home at any time. Did she sign the house over to Ruby at some point? Perhaps when she turned twenty-one? There would certainly be a record of any such transaction. The changeover would appear on the title deed. In fact, a copy of the title deed might prove useful, as it would record changes in ownership over the decades since the house was built. Could I obtain a copy of the title deed? I suspect not. So, perhaps it's something else James Whitby might have to do.

What about all the silverware, furniture, and other collectables? What happened to all those items? I can't say I've ever seen silverware of any note in this place. As a professional running her own business, Lillian might not have been too wrapped in the prospect of spending hours polishing the family silver. Good quality silverware probably would fetch a reasonable price if sold through the right channels. I could imagine Lillian finding such an approach appealing. Again, the proceeds from the sale of silverware, and anything else for from Isabelle's estate, might have been used to set up something for Ruby's future.

About then, the little voice in my head reminded me it was all very well sitting here speculating on what *might* have happened, but it wasn't getting us any further with establishing what *did* happen. There was nothing for it but for me to have another conversation with James Whitby, unless he should find the answers lurking in the stuff he already was looking into. It which case, it might be best to wait. The word I dread – patience – seems to apply in this case, and has no way around it for the moment.

"Right then, it's back to reading the journal," I reminded myself aloud, as I swung my feet down and reached for the current journal. I hadn't progressed past the first three pages when Jodie came up to ask if I was joining them for dinner this evening. Dinner…! God, I hadn't given it a thought and had nothing planned. When I admitted my shortcomings, Jodie laughed.

"On our way home this morning, we talked about how you've been feeding us while we've been here, and how it's not the way it's supposed to work. We decided tonight was going to be our treat. It took us a little while to work out how we might go about it. We hoped you wouldn't mind settling for a roast dinner with all the trimmings. It should be delivered in the next few minutes."

The very thought of a roast dinner just about had me salivating and, when the doorbell rang about two minutes later, I almost swooned with anticipation. The aroma was divine, and the food lived up to it in every way. Afterwards, we all complained about having stuffed ourselves a little beyond the comfortable limit. I felt as though I should run up and down the stairs a few times to help work it off before it had a chance to settle around my waist and hips. The predictable game of Scrabble was suggested as something suitably light after such a big meal. I don't think they were surprised when I again turned down the offer.

Back in the office, I avoided becoming too comfortable at the desk while I tried reading Lillian's journal. After my big heavy meal, there was a real chance I'd fall asleep if I was too comfortable. Nevertheless, dinner somehow had renewed my interest in Lillian's entries. I told myself, reading those books wasn't a race from start to finish in the shortest time. It was more like a literary stroll which provided time to observe and assess what lay between the lines, as well as taking in the actual words.

It seems life hadn't become any easier. As the weeks and months dragged on, Lillian's entries became less frequent and shorter. No words were wasted on describing relationships in the household, but it wasn't difficult to work out Ruby's attitude had worsened and Lillian was struggling to cope. At one stage, Lillian found it necessary to order Lorna Green to take a few days off. To go home and try to relax for a bit, and to consider whether she wanted to return at all. So, it appeared it wasn't just Lillian's life being made a misery, but poor Lorna Green was suffering as well.

Then, the bombshell dropped. Breaking point had been reached …But whose breaking point: Lillian's or Ruby's? Just one succinct entry spoke volumes about how things were in this house at the time: *Ruby ran away sometime during last night.*

Poor Lillian! I wished she had recorded more information on what led up to Ruby's night-time flit. Was there a monumental row during the evening? Or, was it just a case of an ideal opportunity occurred for her to make a clean getaway, and she took it? I added the event to a timeline I was creating of the family's significant events. The timeline made depressing reading. There was nothing I would call a happy event recorded anywhere along it. Because of the circumstances surrounding it, even Ruby's birth, which should have been a happy event, had unhappy repercussions for several family members.

Spurred on by the entry for the first interesting event I'd come across in a while, I rushed on to see if more details were provided and what happened in the aftermath of Ruby's disappearance. It occurred in 1961. Some simple maths told me she was only fifteen when she left. A day later, the next entry recorded the girl as 'still missing'. The following day, Lillian recorded having reported Ruby's disappearance to the police. As Ruby was under age, and Lillian was legally responsible for her, Lillian felt she had no other option but to report the girl's disappearance.

Reporting it to the police seems to have been not a simple – or pleasant – procedure. Lillian's entry after the event suggests she found the ordeal embarrassing and confronting, and she left the police station feeling they believed her responsible for the girl's absconding from home. The entry gave me pause for thought. Although Lillian's entry didn't go into great detail, it said sufficient for me to realise how upsetting she found the experience. Up until then, my thinking had been coloured by my knowledge of my association with Lillian over so many years. I couldn't help but see Ruby as an ungrateful little wretch.

The new line of thinking trying to assert itself imagined a different situation. What if life had been so horrible – so oppressive – it compelled Ruby to face a life on the streets rather than endure it any longer? Was Lillian's approach to raising a child so strict and authoritarian it became unbearable for the young girl? Granted, Ruby was in a rebellious teenage period of her life. Perhaps it contributed to her act of defiance. Lillian never appeared headstrong or dogmatic about anything, but she was one of the most self-assured people I've known. Still, as a middle-aged spinster accountant running her own business, Lillian would be unfamiliar with raising a teenage girl. If Ruby proved to be a headstrong, rebellious teenager, it might have contributed in equal part to the major upheaval in the household.

Scant entries were added to the journal over the next few months. To this outsider-looking-in, it appeared as though nothing of any consequence occurred over the next year. Lorna

Green continued to be a part of the household but, after Ruby's disappearance, she ceased to live-in. Instead, she then came in daily for a few hours to act as housekeeper for Lillian.

No further mention of Ruby was frustrating. I considered abandoning the journal in favour of an early night. Just one more page, I told myself, and then I'm off to bed.

The one last page I'd promised myself did not result in an early night. The police had located Ruby. Rather than raise the neighbourhood's eyebrows by having a police vehicle disgorge Ruby at Lillian's front door, the police arranged a taxi to take Ruby home … with a plain clothed police officer accompanying her in the cab to ensure she did go home. Lillian's record of the event told me Ruby arrived home about mid-morning to find only Lorna Green there. Lillian rushed home after a call from Lorna.

A flood of short entries followed Ruby's arrival. In reality, they covered only the day of the arrival and the next day. None of them said anything of any consequence. Then, the following day, the next major event occurred. It appears Lorna moved back to live-in so someone was there to keep an eye on Ruby during the day, as the matter of Ruby's return to school remained unresolved.

Over the previous twelve months, when she was only working a few hours every morning, the now elderly Lorna developed the habit of taking an afternoon nap. The first couple of days after Ruby was home, when Lorna went for a nap, Ruby retired to her room and amused herself in some way. On the third day, Lorna and Lillian were confident the same situation would apply. Ruby had other ideas.

As soon as Lorna retired to her room after lunch, Ruby slipped away. Lorna was unaware it had happened. The door to Ruby's room remained closed when Lorna emerged from her nap. She heard Ruby's small radio playing music as she walked past. Busy with finishing off some ironing and preparing dinner, Lorna never gave Ruby a thought, and Ruby's absence downstairs wasn't noticed until Lillian returned home from work.

Lillian, fearing the girl might be ill – or sulking about something – rushed to knock on Ruby's door. After a couple of attempts at knocking received no response, Lillian opened the door. The radio was still playing, but there was no sign of Ruby. And, no sign she had been in there at all during the afternoon. Although fearing a repeat of Ruby's previous escapade, Lillian decided to give the girl until after dinner to reappear.

They still didn't know where Ruby had been or what she had done during her almost year-long absence. But, the girl had returned looking as though she had been living rough, and was so thin as to cause concern. It seems Lillian discussed the matter in some depth with Lorna:

Lorna said I was right to wait until dinner time. She was sure Ruby would be back in time to eat dinner, and commented on her observation Ruby hadn't stopped eating since she arrived home.

I told her Ruby needed all the food we could get into her to put some meat back on her bones. Come to think of it, I should have my doctor give her a check-up. Who knows where she has been, or what she might have picked up over the last twelve months?

Lorna agreed it would be a good thing, but wasn't sure I could convince Ruby it should happen. If Ruby was difficult before she disappeared, she is a determined young miss now and is not likely to be persuaded to do anything which has little appeal to her.

It seems their gamble paid off. According to Lillian's next entry, they always sat down to dinner at seven o'clock:

At a few minutes before seven, Ruby marched through the front door with a skinny young man in tow and announced 'this is Ken'. She hoped we didn't mind, but she had invited him to dinner with us. She said they would like to have a chat with me after dinner. Then, Ruby announced she and Ken should wash up for dinner, and took Ken to show him the bathroom.

Lillian's whole record of the event was a long and detailed narrative. It made for riveting reading. So much so, I had the page half turned before I'd read the last sentence. The thought of Lillian and Lorna's reaction to the situation had me stifling a fit of the giggles. If, as Lillian recorded the event, it was how it played out, top marks to Ruby for a clever strategy – and guts to deliver it. I was relieved to find the next page continued Lillian's narrative.

Yes! It was how I pictured it. Lillian recorded both she and Lorna were left standing with their mouths hanging open in astonishment as Ruby escorted Ken upstairs to the bathroom. Although I knew it probably wasn't, I hoped Lillian's record of the conversations was as near to verbatim as possible, and not just her interpretation of what was said. The narrative continued and I eagerly devoured it:

"What's this all about then?" Lorna demanded as the two youngsters clomped up the stairs.

I wished I knew. Some advanced warning would have been wonderful. Still, whatever it's all about, I suspect I'm not going to be happy about it. No doubt, whatever it is, will require a heap more 'kid glove treatment' on my part. I can't help but wonder if the day will ever come when we will be able to stop tiptoeing around her. When we can stop living with the fear she might abscond again. It still feels as though the least thing could set her off again.

Lorna was left to clean up after dinner, while the other three moved to the sitting room. Lillian observed Ruby appeared awkward and unsure of herself. Their 'chat' seemed to have trouble getting started. In a bid to help initiate the conversation, Lillian asked Ruby if she was okay with Ken sitting in on their chat, or did she want to discuss something more personal, just with Lillian. It appears Lillian recorded her chat with Ruby verbatim, possibly in case it might need to be recounted later in some legal arena:

No, I want Ken here too. He needs to be here. I ... I mean WE... have something to tell you ... to ask you. Ken and I want to get married.

Married! Ruby, you are fifteen; far too young to be married. You should be thinking about going back to school to finish your education, not about getting married. What's this nonsense all about? Has something happened to bring about such a request?

We wouldn't be here if I wasn't underage and didn't need your permission to go ahead with it.

This is ridiculous, Ruby. What about Ken? Ken, how old are you? Do you need your parents' permission as well? Are they likely to sign the papers you need to get married? I don't think the pair of you have thought this through. Where would you live? Ken, do you have a job? How are you going to pay for everything you need just to live, never mind the extra expense of caring for a baby if one should come along? Perhaps, if you could explain to me why you want to marry, maybe I would understand what this is about.

I'm pregnant… and we want to keep our baby and bring it up as normal parents do. We don't want the child taken from us and placed in an orphanage and being adopted out by someone else… by strangers.

Pregnant! Good God, can this get any worse? Ruby, I need time to think about this. Time to take on board everything you've told me. But, there is one thing I can tell you right now: I will not be giving you permission to marry. If for no other reason, I owe it to your mother to do all I can to prevent you making a total mess of your life.

You mean, like my mother did?

What happened to your mother was tragic. When I learned of her situation, I went to her with the intention of bringing her and her child back to live with me. Fate proved it wasn't to be. And, yes, had circumstances been different, you might have been placed in an orphanage, with hope of adoption sometime in the future.

Well, isn't it what happened? Wasn't I supposed to go to an orphanage after my mother died, and wasn't I adopted anyway?

In spite of Lillian's refusal to sign the permission forms, it seems she did score a couple of small victories. She persuaded

Ruby to stay at the house, although she would not allow Ken to stay there as well. And, she managed to drag Ruby along to Lillian's GP for a check-up. According to her journal entry, the GP was not impressed with Ruby's condition and expressed concern for the welfare of the baby.

After what appeared to have been a week of constant rows and tantrums, Lillian relented. She agreed to sign the required permission documents to allow Ruby and Ken to marry, but only on the proviso Ruby continued living with Lillian until she was married. Afterwards, and subject to their having found suitable accommodation, the couple could start their married life together in their new place. If no suitable accommodation had been obtained, Lillian would allow the young couple to continue living under her roof until other suitable arrangements were in place.

While Ruby was unhappy about the requirements, she agreed on the basis she saw it as the only way permission would be forthcoming. But, the other condition Lillian wanted to impose, Ruby would not agree to. Lillian wanted her to wait until after the baby was born – maybe a month or two afterwards – before the marriage took place. Ruby was unrelenting in her insistence the baby should be allowed to legally have its father's name and, therefore, the wedding should take place as soon as possible, and before the birth.

With each party having made their position on the matter clear, Lillian's entry recorded her belief the wisest thing for her to do was to sign the permission to marry document and have the wedding go ahead. Her utmost concern appeared to be for the unborn child. As she recorded, against her better judgement, she realised her continued refusal to sign the papers could result in Ruby's absconding again. Her entry records her struggle with nightmares of Ruby giving birth alone at night in a squat, or out on the street in some shop doorway.

As I read those series of journal entries, the lump in my throat developed to the point where I felt tears start to well up. Torn between doing what was best of each and all of those involved must have been a distraction for Lillian. I couldn't help but think back to when she made the decision to adopt Ruby, her baby sister's illegitimate child. She could not have envisaged the level of grief and anguish the child's teenage years would bring.

So, in what she must have hoped would result in at least an uneasy peace between them, Lillian signed the required paperwork. Later, she recorded spending a long, sleepless night questioning her decision. Still, it was done, and now she had a quiet Registry Office wedding to arrange – or so she recorded in her journal.

A gentle tap on the office door interrupted my reading. Jodie eased the door open a fraction and stuck her head in. "We were doing our routine patrol of the yard and house, and I noticed the light was still on up here. It's midnight. I wondered if everything was all right, or if you forgot to turn the light off when you went to bed. Is everything okay?"

"Midnight…! Thank you, Jodie. Everything is fine. I just lost track of the time, but I will call it a night now you have alerted me to how late it is."

I didn't think I would be able to sleep, dying to know as I was about what happened next in the Ruby's wedding saga. But, I was wrong. Sleep was swift in its arrival – and so were the dreams which accompanied it… not disturbing enough to wake me up, but sufficiently so to make for a restless night's sleep.

Chapter 15

After so few hours of restless sleep, I surprised myself by being wide awake at five o'clock this morning. Disinclined to make pleasant conversation with the two officers downstairs, I elected to wait until Gail came on duty before going down for breakfast. So, once I was dressed, I snuck along the landing to the office, closing the door behind me before turning on the light.

The dilemma was what to do for the next couple of hours until Gail came on duty. I knew it was a while since I checked my emails, and I also knew there was a reason, at least in part, for not having done so. By now, my editor would be edgy about the non-arrival of the article I was supposed to submit a week ago. I did advise him a family bereavement would delay things for a day or two, but many more days than promised now had elapsed. All the interviews and research were done. All I had to do was write the article, but there just didn't seem to have been time to do it.

Today… I told myself. I will write the article today and send it off. Who was I kidding? Not me! I had too many questions in need of answers to spend time writing an article. A series of pings as emails flooded into my inbox refocused my attention for the next little while.

My eyes went straight to an email from Lou Radford. Geez, I'd forgotten all about Lou. How long had she been away? If I'm honest, I can't say I've missed her. Gail stepped straight into Lou's research role, and has proved much easier to work with. While I've known Lou for most of my life, and she is good at what she does, she can be a bit abrasive at times; a bit dictatorial. I hesitated for a moment before opening her email, and my dread didn't lessen any when I saw the length of her message.

For Lou to spend so much time composing the message, I felt sure it would tell me something I didn't want to know. Read it and get it over and done with, I told myself as I moved the cursor to the start of her message and began reading:

Apologies for my prolonged absence. I expected my client's work would entail spending only two or three days in Western Australia, but it did take a little longer. As I was about to wrap up everything and head home, a fortuitous call from a cruise line company delivered an offer I couldn't refuse. As part of the entertainment offered to passengers on some of their cruises, they include a family history course and workshop. For a number of years, they have used the same well-known genealogist to run those courses. He became seriously ill a few days before his next cruise departed, and they asked me to step into the breach at short notice. The cruise has finished, but it will be another few days before I am home. I'll call you as soon as I'm back and have sorted myself out again.

So, it wasn't such bad news after all… I would be able to carry on working with Gail for at least the next few days. It's best I keep Lou unaware of my research during her absence. There is no point upsetting Lou by telling her how well I've managed without her. The way things are going, the questions are going to keep cropping up long after the police decide I no longer need a protection detail looking after me. It brought something else to the front and centre of my thoughts: to remember to ask Gail if she had any idea how much longer the police might have officers stationed here.

Voices floated up from down below. Gail had arrived and the other two officers were about to depart. I heard farewells exchanged and the front door slammed. Time to go down for breakfast. As I headed for the stairs, I heard water running in the kitchen. Gail would be filling the kettle – and I was more than ready for coffee.

"Good morning. I had a sneaking suspicion you were already up and about before I arrived," was Gail's greeting as I walked into the kitchen.

"Yeah, thought I should spend a few minutes catching up on *real* work. My editor hasn't sent me any nasty emails yet, so I can probably ignore my bread-and-butter job for another day or so. There is something I need to ask you about. I'm not sure you will know the answer, but I was wondering how much longer a police presence is likely to be maintained here."

"Yep, a good question – but, as you suggested, one I can't answer. I had dinner last night with someone who works a lot closer to the top brass than I do. I asked them much the same question. I didn't get a definite answer, but there is some suggestion protection might be maintained only for another couple of days, and is certain to be removed by the end of the week. There, now you know as much as I do."

I couldn't help feeling the timing was right on the money. If Lou was back in town sometime during the next few days then, by the start of next week, it was likely she would expect to return to the research we were doing here … unless another client pops up in the meantime. The thought spurred me on. For some reason I couldn't quite identify, I had a compelling urge to have my research a considerable way further advanced by the time Lou reappeared. Today's unexpected extension of time was a bonus. So, sometime today, a call to James Whitby might be in order.

Although I knew he would have called me if he uncovered anything important about the outcome of Lillian's bequest from Isabelle's estate, I felt a call might hurry things along. Even if he were still digging into it, anything he had found so far might be useful. The prospect of having nothing more positive to do, other than to continue reading Lillian's journals, was frustrating. It could take pages before I arrived at entries relating to Ruby's wedding. But, I had learned my lesson well. I knew better than to skim the entries in a bid to speed up the process. That's the way critical nuances are missed.

We hadn't been upstairs long when Fate intervened to brighten my day. As Gail and I were settling down to work, the phone call shattered the silence of the office. It was from

James Whitby. He suggested coming to the house to discuss his findings with me, but I could tell the offer was nothing more than a polite gesture.

"James, might it be easier if I came into your office and we went over everything there? At the very least, it would save you having to bundle everything up to bring it here, and would avoid the possibility of one vital piece of paper being overlooked."

He sounded relieved when he accepted my suggestion. Then, as I bundled up the various notes from my research since I last spoke with him, I told Gail of James' call. "We'll meet at his office in about an hour's time. I'll take my notes about anything our research has turned up in case it proves relevant to anything James has found. I'm sorry but, if you are going to come with me, maybe you should bring something to read. You might be in for another long, boring wait outside his closed door."

It was pointless trying to do any further research before we had to leave for the meeting. With my excitement level so high, I wouldn't be able to concentrate on anything I tried to read. We settled for another coffee, accompanied by a whole lot of speculation about what James might have discovered. I checked the time so often, I'm sure I almost wore the hands off my watch. Time seemed to be running slow today. Gail drove us to the meeting in the police vehicle. I couldn't sit still.

"For goodness sake, Sophie, stop fidgeting. It won't get us there any sooner. Seriously, anyone would think you were sitting on an ants' nest."

We were shown into James' office as soon as we arrived. A few moments later, niceties exchanged and Gail having determined we were safe in his office, she was occupying a chair across the hall from James' door. Once the door closed behind her, James chuckled. "How are you coping with having a constant watchdog? And, how much longer is the situation likely to continue?

"I like Gail and she is good to have around. She has been helping me with my research, and seems to know more about how to do it than I will ever know. The scuttlebutt she has picked up suggests the police protection detail will be gone by the end of the week at the latest. My other bit of news is Lou Radford is likely to be back next week."

He cocked an eyebrow at me as simply replied, "I see." I gained the distinct impression he wasn't looking forward to dealing with Lou any more than I was. "Well, let's not leave Gail sitting out there any longer than necessary. Let me acquaint you with what I have discovered so far." As I pulled my chair up to his desk, he opened a substantial file.

"After studying the copy Isabelle Stubbs' will, the easiest place to start my research was with the old family home. The title deed in itself tells an interesting story. Lillian's great-grandfather built the house… Uhmm... I can't remember the date, but I'll look it up for you after I tell you the story of the house. Anyway, great-grandfather died relatively young, as was the tendency in those days. The surprising thing about his death was, although his wife and son were still alive and living in the house, he left the house and much of his estate to his youngest child, his daughter Elizabeth."

"So, he bypassed his son and heir, and left it to a younger daughter…? It must have raised a few eyebrows – and made life interesting in the family home. Sorry, I shouldn't interrupt. I suspect the rest of the story is just as intriguing, so please do go on."

"Yes, I don't imagine life was a lot of laughs once the house belonged to Elizabeth. Nevertheless, she retained ownership even after she married, and on her death, the house and the then entire estate went to her only son, who became Lillian's grandfather. Subsequent progression followed the more traditional route with the property coming down through the male line. When the grandfather died, the house passed to his son, Lillian's father, Frederick Cavendish. Things became a little more complicated in the next generation.

Frederick didn't have any sons, only four daughters. For some reason, he chose not to leave the house to his wife, Lillian's mother, Annie Grace Cavendish. It left him only his daughters to consider. Although he had two surviving daughters, whom to pass the house onto presented no problem to Frederick. In his eyes, there remained only the one daughter worthy of consideration, Isabelle. Lillian, having started on her career path by then, wouldn't give up her career to comply with all the conditions he wished to put in place. So, he probably didn't suffer a moment's hesitation in bequeathing everything to Isabelle."

The next part of the story I already knew, so I saved him the trouble of repeating it. "There were provisos attached to the bequest. Isabelle's mother was to be allowed to live in the house until she died, and Isabelle was to care for her full-time for however long until her mother's death. To compensate Isabelle, he set up a small annuity for her. After the mother died, Isabelle was finally free to marry. But then, after only a few years, her husband also died. When Isabelle died leaving no surviving offspring, her only remaining family consisted of her sister, Lillian, and her illegitimate niece, Esme's daughter, Ruby... And, Ruby, as the stain on the family's name, was never going to be considered."

"I think you've about summed it up. Left with few options, Isabelle left most of the estate, including the house, to her sole surviving sister, Lillian."

"Now we've established so much of the story, the big question arising is: what happened to everything after Lillian inherited it?"

"Ah, well now, we only have the title deed to refer to, and it insists ownership of the property still remains with Lillian Cavendish."

"But, if Lillian still owned the house when she died... And I inherited all of Lillian's estate... Does it mean...?"

"Does it mean you own the Cavendish family home? Yes... Or you will, when the transfer of title to you occurs."

"Isabelle has been dead since 1989. What's happened to the house since then? It will have become almost a wreck if it's been unoccupied for so long. More importantly, what's the situation with the house now? Have the rates and insurance been paid?"

"I had one of our investigators check into the current situation with the house. It seems it's been a rental property since soon after Isabelle's death. There were a number of tenants along the way, but the current tenant has leased the property for some years now. It is what you might call a quasi-religious group. Their initial intention in leasing the property was to set up a home of some sort for homeless and unwanted children. It's likely their intent appealed to Lillian's maternal instincts.

For the first few years, everything was okay but, in more recent times, their focus changed from fostering and adopting out those children. They now are more of a religious cult using the house as their headquarters. According to the agency managing the property, at the current time, they are considerably behind with the rent. The bailiffs are likely to descend on the property early next week to seize goods and property in a bid to recover the outstanding rental monies."

"To me, it sounds as though taking over ownership of the property now means I will also be taking over a whole truckload of other problems. Do you have any advice or suggestions on how to proceed?"

"It might not be as bad as it sounds. The group's current lease expires in about two weeks. They were advised some time ago the lease would not be renewed. Then, due to the debt collection agency having no success in recovering the outstanding rental money, they were given a week to vacate the premises. When they refused to do so, a court order was obtained and, hence, the bailiffs will visit next week. By the time the lease expiry date rolls around, they should be well gone from the premises. Then we will move to transfer ownership of the property to you."

"Okay, I understand you're telling me to be patient and to allow the various processes in place to simplify the situation. It won't be too difficult for me to do. The other thing about Isabelle's will intriguing me is the amount of the family's furniture and silverware she inherited and then bequeathed to

Lillian. What happened to all the other stuff? There are a couple of bits of furniture in Lillian's house which could be of the right vintage, but I've never seen any silverware. I suppose she might have sold off stuff to avoid having to work out what to do with it. Oh, and there was a second property. What happened to it?"

"You might be forgiven for thinking she sold the contents of the house, but our investigations tend to suggest otherwise. Within the last week, I put in motion the necessary paperwork to transfer to you access to another property – not the second one mention in Isabelle's will. In this case, it's a lock-up in one of those 'Fort Knox' type storage places. Apart from the usual facilities, this storage place also has individual storage buildings – a bit like small sheds. Those with a volume of material to store, and deep pockets to go with it, can purchase outright one of those buildings. Lillian owns such a facility at the storage place in question. While I don't know what she kept in it, I'd be willing to bet it was some of the stuff she inherited from Isabelle."

"Crikey, where does all this end – and what am I going to do with it all if it's what's stored there?"

His advice was not to worry about any of it for another week or two, until various processes already in place were complete. I was happy to go along with his suggestion. But, his revelations didn't end there. He also advised they had yet finished investigating the second property mentioned in Isabelle's will, and then returned to discussing other aspects of my inheritance.

"There is one other aspect of Lillian's will we decided to look into."

"Don't tell me… It was all a hoax and I didn't inherit any of it?"

"Not so, I'm afraid. Everything about the inheritance stands. We were interested in any earlier wills Lillian might have made. As you are aware, the will we have been discussing – her last and current will – was made by Lillian about twelve years ago. She was not one of our clients prior to when she made the will, and I wondered whether any previous wills might've been made with her former solicitor. If there were, it doesn't change anything now. My interest was purely out of curiosity. What I discovered does give rise to some interesting thoughts."

My pulse had become rapid and my breathing shallow. "I hope you're not going to keep me in suspense for more than a couple of heartbeats. If you do, I'm likely to expire from a lack of oxygen before you get round to explaining it to me."

"It would never do to have you expire in my office. Lillian did make an earlier will in which she was going to leave everything in trust to her niece, Ruby, or, in the event of Ruby's predeceasing her, everything was to be held in trust for any natural offspring of Ruby. So, had Lillian not made a new will more recently, her estate would have gone to Ruby's children. Again, because of what prompted our investigation in the first place, and out of rampant curiosity, over the next week or so, I intend to investigate what children Ruby may have had."

"Well, I might be able to help you a bit with your research. Ruby was pregnant at age sixteen and wanted to marry. At first, Lillian was against the move but relented and all the paperwork was in place for the marriage to go ahead. It would have taken place soon after Ruby turned sixteen, and the baby was due a month or so later. So, there's a fair chance there was at least one child. Whether it survived to adulthood is another matter."

"What else can you tell me about Ruby's life afterwards, and what was the name of the man she married?"

"Now, there's something I can't help you with. My research hasn't progressed past the point where the necessary paperwork was in place to allow the marriage to occur. Give me another couple of days and I might be better informed. As for the name of her intended husband, all I can tell is his name was Ken."

"Okay, it looks as though, between the pair of us, over the next few days, we might be able to dig up a bit more on Ruby's life after marriage. There is one other thing I need to tell you about. While my investigator was out and about looking into the

Cavendish family home and anything else relevant to Isabelle's estate, he did come across something interesting."

"Why do I have the feeling 'interesting' is another way of saying 'more problems'?"

"Perhaps, but I don't think so. He looked into the storage facility Lillian owned – as much as he could anyway. Confidentiality rules stymied him from gaining too much information, but he did manage to wheedle one piece of information out of the bloke in charge of the place. It seems Lillian bought her lock-up about thirty years ago. In the fifteen years he has owned the business, he doesn't recall Lillian or anyone else visiting the facility."

"Thirty years ago would tie in nicely with Isabelle's death and when Lillian inherited Isabelle's estate. Perhaps we should take a look in her lock-up. What do you think?"

"I agree, but… there needs to be a bit more paperwork in place to prove you are now the rightful owner before we will be allowed access. Although I was flying blind to some extent, I started the process to acquire the requisite piece of paper a couple of days ago. With any luck, everything will be in place within the week."

"You said you were 'flying blind'. Are you suggesting there could be some complication with the required paperwork?"

"No. What I was alluding to was without having completed my research into Ruby's life, it meant I wasn't in any position to answer all the possible questions if any arguments arose. Nevertheless, it doesn't affect transfer of ownership of the storage facility. We now know the lock-up was purchased by Lillian and it now forms part of her estate. The shed is not something she might have inherited from Isabelle. I'll give you a call, hopefully in a day or so, when everything is in place for us to go and talk to the owner of the storage facility about providing us with a key to Lillian's lock-up."

"He might not hold a key to it. After all, it has been a while since anyone's opened it, and the business changed hands during those years."

"And, to avoid further delays, we will take a sturdy pair of bolt cutters with us when we go to visit him."

Since there wasn't much more to be said, and I was struggling to absorb all I already had been told, my meeting with James Whitby came to an abrupt end. As he held his office door open for me, James reiterated he expected to call me again in a couple of days.

Gail was sitting with an ancient magazine and an almost empty coffee mug when I emerged from James' office. Her relief was evident on her face when I asked if she were ready to leave.

Although little conversation occurred during the drive back to Lillian's house, the questions came thick and fast once we were seated at the kitchen table with our lunchtime sandwiches and coffee.

Chapter 16

Eager to return to Lillian's journal after my meeting with James, I was reluctant to waste time over lunch. I was pleased when Gail received a call which cut short her questioning about my discussions with James. She wandered outside to talk to the caller. I threw everything into the dishwasher and bolted upstairs to the office. So engrossed in Lillian's journal, I didn't notice how much time elapsed before Gail came up to join me. Her face was pensive when she marched in and plonked down behind Lillian's huge desk.

She cleared her throat to catch my attention. "Ahem, my call was from my senior officer. You have me for the last time tomorrow. Tonight will be the last time there will be a night shift deployed here."

"So, the police have decided it's safe for me to be alone now and there is no likelihood of the Millard brothers coming to bother me? What's happened to change the situation?" I had mixed feelings about the police protection coming to an end. The night shift crew had been a pain, although I couldn't say why I thought so. On the other hand, Gail was good company and had helped with my research.

"The Millards will not be coming to annoy you any time soon. As we speak, all three of them are behind bars awaiting their court appearances. It seems the third brother had proved elusive for a while, but they located him a couple of days ago and took him into custody last night. There is a string of warrants out for their arrests, both across this state and interstate. Word is, all three of them will be spending quite some time behind bars in the future. So, with them out of circulation, you won't need protection."

"Yes, I suppose it is good news – but there is a downside to it. After tomorrow, you won't be here helping me with my research. Perhaps I should get as much work as I can out of you while you are still here."

"Right, so what do you want me to start on?"

Hers was a good question, but not one to which I had a ready answer. I stepped my thought processes up a notch in a bid to think of something for Gail to do. Nothing came to mind. So, instead of giving her a task, I reverted to running through a list of all we'd achieved so far in the hope some further line of research might occur to at least one of us. Of course, I could give her one of Lillian's journals to read, but somehow it would feel like breaching confidence. They were personal records of her life, and I didn't feel inclined to hand them over to someone else to read. In the end, I admitted defeat.

"If I'm honest, I don't know what else we could or should be looking for. My mission at the moment is to find out about Ruby's wedding and the birth of her child, presumably soon after they were married. I don't even know Ken's surname, so it won't make research any easier."

"Okay, you go on with reading your journal while I look through our notes to see if any possible research jumps out at me."

Gail had barely opened my information folder when her phone chirped again. "Oh, I seem popular today. I have to take this." She was already out the door by the time she finished speaking. Now I could get on with reading the journal, instead of having to think about something for Gail to do.

Although I read every word, and without rushing, I covered the next couple of pages of the journal in a short time – and had reached the next bombshell. While everything was in place and ready for Ruby's marriage to go ahead, things didn't go to plan. The morning after Lillian signed the last of the paperwork for the marriage, Ruby didn't come down for breakfast. By lunchtime, Lillian began to suspect Ruby hadn't just slipped out to tell Ken the good news. When Ruby still hadn't returned by the evening,

Lillian accepted she had staged a repeat performance of her previous disappearing act.

The next couple of one-line entries told me Ruby hadn't returned after being missing for a couple of days. Lillian must have been half out of her mind with trying to decide whether to go through the rigmarole of reporting Ruby's disappearance to the police, or if she should just accept the situation and focus on cancelling the wedding arrangements. In the end, it appears she decided on the latter course of action.

After the entry in which she recorded the last of the wedding arrangements were cancelled, the next entry in her journal was five weeks later. By then, it was close to Ruby's baby's due date, and the entry gave me a sense of Lillian's concern about the impending birth. Several months elapsed before Lillian again recorded anything in her journal.

I read on through the journal, searching for any mention of Ruby or her baby. There was none. Whatever was happening at the time, I think it's safe to assume Lillian heard nothing more of Ruby or the baby for a long time after Ruby disappeared. I couldn't help but wonder if she ever heard from Ruby again.

No doubt, if there had been contact of any sort, Lillian would have recorded it in her journal of the day. Perhaps, as I continue reading through those journals, I might find out more about Ruby, but something told me she and her child were a lost cause. When Gail returned from her phone call, she found me staring into space as I pondered what became of Ruby and her child.

"What's happened? Did something happen while I was away? Sophie, talk to me," Gail demanded.

"Nothing happened. I was just thinking about the next episode in Lillian's life, and how she didn't deserve the worry and strife it brought with it. It angers me to see someone who acted solely out of kindness and compassion be treated with so little respect and consideration."

Of course my comments ignited Gail's interest, and another lengthy question-and-answer type discussion followed. Part way through it, we went downstairs for another coffee. After examining what we knew from every possible angle and having indulged in fanciful speculation, the only thing left to do was to carry on with our research. As we rinsed our coffee mugs, Gail suggested, "Two questions are gnawing at me: did Ruby get married, and did the baby survive. If you carry on with the journals, I'll see if I can round up any clues which might help answer those questions."

My temptation was to tell her it would be a waste of time as both those events were likely to be too recent to appear in any of the records we could access. But, as I didn't have any other suggestions as to what she might do to fill in her time, I wished her luck and told her to go ahead. It came as no surprise she had found nothing by the time the night shift normally came to relieve her. The next time I checked the time, I realised she had stayed later than she should, and I took her to task for it.

"It's okay. I don't have any plans for this evening. You're probably aware, when I leave this afternoon, it will be the last of the police presence at this house. There will be no night shift taking over this evening. I really wanted to find out what happened to Ruby and her baby, but it is time I left. So, it looks like I'm never going to know. Here's my card. If you do find out what happened, and you have a bit of spare time, please think about letting me know."

Somehow it felt like saying goodbye to an old friend as I watched her climb into the police vehicle and reverse down the driveway. Then, with a wave to me, she was off along the street and gone from my life. I felt bereft as I wandered back inside, and was at a loss as to what to do next. After wandering aimlessly around downstairs for a few moments, I decided the most practical thing to do was to check the fridge for what I might use to produce an evening meal.

Over reheated leftovers, I ignored the bigger picture and focused on my immediate future. I figured there were at least a couple of days more before Lou Radford might return. How could I fill in my time productively? Then the big question hit me: what does my future look like now? ...Or, more precisely, where is my future now? Do I go back to living in my own home, or do I move in here properly and continue to live in this house? It was all too difficult to contemplate over nothing more than reheated leftovers. When in doubt, take the easy way out – do nothing. So, in line with such thinking, I would be spending tonight at Lillian's place. Tomorrow might be soon enough to work out what happens next.

Although I didn't have to escape from the night shift crew tonight, it made sense to stick with what had become an established routine. I went back upstairs to read more of Lillian's journal. By about ten o'clock, my eyes were heavy. I had about three pages of the book left to finish. Although its entries covered a lengthy timespan, I had not picked up any subtle nuances or learned anything of any consequence. I pushed through to the end of the book, slammed it closed and fell into bed.

While I knew the Millard brothers were behind bars and I was safe, my nightmares had missed the relevant news flash. In their ignorance, they continued to visit me all night and woke me several times.

*****

After not such a great night's sleep, I was in danger of falling headlong into Lillian's journal if I tried to read today. It seemed prudent to find something else to do, but something unlikely to waste a day of valuable research time. Breakfast lasted longer than usual as I pondered the situation. By the time I went upstairs to begin work, I had decided on a course of action to keep me busy for at least part of the morning.

Perhaps I was taking the long way around in my search for a Millard connection to Lillian Cavendish. Might it shorten the process if I started from the Millard end and worked backwards towards the Cavendish family connection – if there was one? Having convinced myself it was worth a try, I then had to work out how to go about it. All I knew about the Millard family so far was there were three sons. Who were their parents? If

I could establish their parentage, it might take me back to the right era to find a Cavendish connection.

With nothing more to go on than a guesstimate of the brothers' ages, I didn't like my chance of discovering anything useful. It all was likely to be too recent to find anything in the indexes of births or marriages. The old adage of 'nothing ventured, nothing gained' came to mind and spurred me to make a start.

Trying to guess the ages of the Millard brothers occupied my mind for longer than it should have, but achieved nothing. I slumped back in my chair in frustration. Then my eyes slid towards the card Gail left on the desk yesterday. Do I dare to call her? So much for saying she was gone from my life! With no way of knowing what she might be doing, a call might catch her at the most inconvenient moment. Nevertheless, as if controlled by some external force, I reached for my phone and keyed in her number.

After apologising profusely for the call and promising not to make a habit of it, I asked if I had called at a bad time.

"No, I was sitting at my desk catching up on paperwork. What can I help you with?"

"My plan was to see if I could find out anything about the Millard family, but I fell at the first hurdle. I tried working out the ages of the three brothers to give me an approximate starting point for my research, but it was hopeless. So, I wondered if you had any information or any ideas about their ages."

"Hang on a moment while I look up something."

She came back to me after only a second or two, and I learned my guesses were a long way off the mark. The only good look at the men I has was after Lillian's cremation. I'll put my confusion down to my emotional state at the time. My memory pegged the men as quite young, possibly in their thirties. Gail's information, probably from some official police file, had them a lot older. After my brief call ended, I did a spot of quick maths to realign my thinking.

Based of Gail's information, I estimated the eldest Millard son's age to be in his early fifties. If I worked on the assumption their family followed what was the case with many families, subsequent children would have arrived at roughly two-yearly intervals. If this applied to the Millard family, it would place the other two brothers in the latter half of their forties. Amazed, I sat back to consider my brilliant piece of deduction… and ended up with a new question begging for an answer: so what? How did it help me work out what to do next? It didn't, and I was reduced to taking desperate measures.

Would I find the Millard surname in any of the indexes for the 1970s? Following through on my idea kept me busy until mid-morning, by which time I was desperate for a caffeine top-up. I reviewed my morning's work over coffee. While I had found a few entries for the Millard name, there was nothing to indicate a connection to any of the people I was researching. Then, my deductive powers, revived by caffeine, led me to think about newspaper archives. I had no clue what I might find, but I could think of no other option worth trying.

After eventually navigating my way to the National Library's online newspaper archives, I typed in the Millard surname and held my breath. Expecting no hits, I was surprised when my search produced a few. So, where to start? Without given names to help identify the most likely hits to explore, I chose to look first at one from 1973. It opened up as a section of a page from a newspaper. I eventually found where the name was highlighted in a small area of the fuzzy reproduction.

It proved to be a death notice for a Rose Millard. I didn't know anything about any Rose Millard and was sure the death notice would be of no interest. As I was about to 'swipe left' after giving it no more than a cursory glance, the little voice in my head told me to do it properly. It made me pause and read the notice. "Can this be right?" I asked the empty office. "Is it possible I've struck gold on my first attempt?"

While I had nothing definite to suggest she was one of 'my' Millards, everything about her seemed to fit with the little I knew about the Millard family. Her details seemed about right. She was only thirty when she died, and was survived by her husband, Keith Millard, and three young sons. The names of the three sons would have been useful, but the 1973 death notice wasn't about to be so helpful. Nevertheless, I felt reasonably confident I had found the brothers' parents: Keith and Rose Millard.

Determined to exercise my recently gained family history research skills, I convinced myself Rose Millard might have left a will and it would be worth my while to spend a few minutes checking the index. My next challenge was remembering how to find the online index to wills. The old saying, *if at first you don't succeed...*, applied in this case until my perseverance paid off. I found two entries for the Millard name.

Without any real thought, and in the belief neither of them would prove useful, I clicked on one and waited for the relevant entry to open. I knew it was too good to be true. My run of luck seemed to have run out. The entry I selected related to a will from the early 1900s. I had one other entry to try. Almost sure it would prove irrelevant as well, I had the mouse at the ready to click out of the index as soon as the entry opened.

I gasped. The entry related to the will of one Keith Raymond Millard, and was for probate granted in 1987. My breathing was shallow and fast as I tried to find where I could order a copy of the will. After bringing my credit card into the action once more, there was nothing for me to do but wait for a copy to arrive. Then, it was time to sit back and assess what I had gained from my last couple of hours' work.

As it was almost lunchtime, I decided to review my progress over a sandwich in the kitchen. While munching on lunch, I scanned my notes spread out on the table in front of me. What little I'd learned about the Millard family so far didn't indicate any connection to the Cavendish mob. For the brothers to think they had some claim on Lillian's estate, there had to be a link. Without some connection to the Cavendish family, their claim would be nothing more than an extortion attempt. As loath as I was to do so, the latter possibility was gaining credibility in my mind.

In spite of everything, I felt a touch of sympathy for the Millard brothers. When their mother died in 1973, they would have been young children. If my new estimation of their ages was close to the mark, the youngest brother would have been no more than a toddler when his mother died. Then, only about fourteen years later, they lost their father as well. Although I don't know what other family they had around them at the time, life would not have been easy for the three boys.

Back in the office after lunch, my mind still dwelt on the death of Keith Raymond Millard and the probable impact it had on his sons. With no ideas on where else to look for anything on the Millard family, and with my computer still logged into the State Archives' site, I decided to check for any other mention of the Millard surname. It was unlikely to produce anything useful, but it would fill in time and make me feel as though I was doing something worthwhile.

It would be handy, and would avoid a mega-dose of frustration, if I knew how to navigate around the State Archives' site to find what I was looking for. After some time wandering around hopelessly lost on the site, and due to more by good luck than any intelligence on my part, I found a further mention of Millard. It was in relation to a coroner's inquest into the death of Keith Raymond Millard.

After a quick look at what appeared to be a mountain of documents presented at the inquest, I finally decided the report of the coroner's findings might provide me with sufficient information to satisfy my curiosity. Again, more action for my credit card – and then the wait for the information began. Was there something else I could do, somewhere else I could go for information? As a rank amateur at this family history research lark I had hit the proverbial brick wall. Maybe it was as well Lou Radford might reappear soon. I hoped my patience would hold out until then.

Although it was only mid-afternoon, I found myself stumped for inspiration about what else to do – other than go back to reading Lillian's journals. While they were great and a good source of information, it was like taking the long way around to find out what you wanted to know. But, when no other option is available, reading a journal takes on renewed appeal. After a quick stroll to the bedroom next door, I was back at Lillian's big desk with the next journal from the stack open in front of me.

My mind wasn't focused on the job – and my heart wasn't in it either. After slogging through about four pages of nothing more interesting than Lillian's attendance at a performance by the Australian Ballet and coffee with an author after the launch of the author's new book, I lost interest. It seemed as though even Lillian had lost interest. Entries were sporadic and brief. I stopped reading after an entry about Lillian's employment of a new junior for her accounting practice. The girl happened to be a former school friend of Ruby's. It was time to do something else.

One of the things I needed to do was make a decision about where I would live in future, in my house or Lillian's. Regardless of where it was going to be, I needed to visit the supermarket. While shopping for food is not my favourite pastime, it did take up the remainder of the afternoon. Then, in acknowledgement of my reclaimed freedom to be out and about alone, I walked the few blocks to the local park and strolled around until dusk made its presence felt.

Chilled to the bone but invigorated by my time in the fresh air, I looked forward to a dinner of one of the nice steaks bought earlier this afternoon.

Chapter 17

After dinner, and about twenty minutes spent surfing TV channels without finding anything interesting, I hauled myself out of the lounge chair and resigned myself to reading more of Lillian's journal. If nothing else, it would help put me to sleep. Armed with a mug of hot chocolate to keep me company and sustain me through the ordeal, I settled down behind Lillian's desk with the journal I abandoned earlier.

The next couple of pages continued in much the same vein as the previous ones. Just as I was about to give up on the book, the next entry caught my eye. To refresh my memory, I flicked back a couple of pages to the entry about employing the new junior, Jacqui, who had been a school friend of Ruby's. Returning to the next mention of Jacqui, I devoured the brief but intriguing entry.

On one day each week, Lillian kept her office open for a couple of hours after other businesses closed for the day. This allowed clients, who couldn't come during the day, to meet with their accountant. On those days, to deal with the late appointments, one of the office girls came in late in the morning and stayed on until the last client left in the evening. In the second week of her employment, Jacqui was scheduled on the 'late shift'.

Jacqui started packing up to leave as Lillian showed the last client out. On her way back to her office, Lillian scuttled Jacqui's plans for a quick getaway. She asked, if Jacqui had nothing urgent to do after leaving work, could she spare Lillian a few minutes before she left. But, if Jacqui needed to get away, it could wait until another time. As well as recording her request of the new junior, Lillian's entry noted a look of apprehension crossed Jacqui's face in response to the request.

Lillian's chat with Jacqui was about one thing and one thing only: Ruby. She asked if Jacqui had kept in touch with Ruby, and probably was excited by Jacqui's answer of 'on and off since school'. But, any excitement Lillian felt was short lived. Jacqui admitted she had seen Ruby a few times after she absconded when she was fifteen, but only a couple of times after Ruby discovered she was pregnant. At the time, as far as Jacqui knew, Ruby was living rough either in squats or on the street.

Then, when the pregnancy occurred, Jacqui said Ruby seemed to take a hard look at her life. She talked of going back to Lillian, of marrying Ken, and of making something of a life for her baby. It seems Lillian had more questions than Jacqui had answers. She wanted to know about the baby, and about Ruby and Ken's marriage. Jacqui admitted the last time she spoke to Ruby was after the baby was born.

Ruby did not have the baby with her when Jacqui encountered her in a shopping arcade in the centre of town. Lillian recorded Jacqui's discomfort when asked whether the baby was a boy, and recorded Jacqui's response verbatim:

I don't know. Ruby didn't have the baby with her when I ran into her. She said the baby was about three months old by then, and she had left it with a friend to look after while she went shopping. She didn't refer to the baby by name, or say anything else to indicate whether it was a boy or a girl.

A more positive answer came in response to Lillian's question about Ruby's marriage. As far as Jacqui knew, there was no marriage… not to Ken anyway. During their last meeting, Ruby told Jacqui she hadn't seen Ken in about six months and she didn't know where he was. But, one of their friends had told her Ken had 'gone up north, possibly to the Northern Territory' for some work he picked up.

Nothing more about Ruby, the baby or Ken, appeared in the next couple of pages of the journal. I couldn't believe Lillian would do nothing more after all Jacqui told her. While I wasn't sure about what she could do, knowing Lillian as I did, I knew she would not simply accept the news and move on. It spurred me on to keep reading, as I felt I soon would come to an entry confirming Lillian's attempts to locate Ruby.

I was wrong. Maybe I misjudged Lillian. Perhaps she decided enough was enough of Ruby and all the consternation she had caused over the years. She decided to wipe her hands of the girl. The trouble was, I only half believed it. As a result, I kept reading – and hoping. About a dozen pages further on, I found my eyes no longer would focus properly. I knew it was late but I didn't know how late. I took my watch off when I had a shower after my walk in the park. Then I discovered the office clock had stopped at five o'clock either this afternoon or this morning.

It was time for bed, but my mind continued to work at breakneck speed. I closed the journal, put my feet up and tried to relax in the hope slowing down and relaxing would allow me to feel sleepy. It didn't. Now I had stopped reading, the questions were coming thick and fast. Perhaps this was how Lillian's life was as she tried coping with not knowing what was going on in Ruby's life.

What had happened between Ruby and Ken to prevent their marrying as planned? Where did Ruby have the baby and what was it? How and where was Ruby living? How was she supporting herself and her child? Had life with Lillian been so bad, no matter what Ruby's life had become, she preferred it to returning to live with Lillian?

Damn… too many questions with no answers – and they were starting to do my head in. Sitting thinking wasn't relaxing me at all. If anything, I was becoming more revved up by the minute. Maybe a nightcap would help, I told myself, and headed for the stairs. With no idea what form my nightcap might take, I found myself peering in a kitchen cupboard. No-o... coffee would only help keep me awake... and I couldn't handle another mug of hot chocolate. One of those about every six months was as much as I could manage.

As an unexpected, but welcome surprise, at the back, and out of place amongst the other occupants of the larder, I found an unopened bottle of scotch. "This will do nicely," I told the universe, "and it's high time someone opened and sampled it." After a tentative initial sip, I deemed it worthy of further assessment … and poured about two fingers' worth into a tumbler. As I drew in its bouquet and taste of peat, its warmth flowed through me. I do remember draining the tumbler, but nothing afterwards until just after five o'clock next morning. Lillian's ancient lounge chairs aren't comfortable to begin with, and are almost crippling if you should fall asleep in one.

*****

While my outlook on life remained as gloomy and confused as ever, in addition, I would now spend all day dealing with a stiff neck and shoulders. Coffee and a couple of poached eggs on toast didn't do much to restore my equilibrium. So, in desperation, I took myself off for a lukewarm shower, and finished with a stinging cold rinse off. It wasn't great, but it did clear some of the cobwebs and allowed me to feel half human again.

What else would I do next except drag myself along to the office to confront those journals again? In a weak attempt at procrastination, I told myself I should check my emails before doing anything else. All of a sudden, the day seemed much brighter. There in my inbox was the copy of Keith Raymond Millard's will I ordered yesterday. Expecting to print the usual three or four pages, I checked the printer's paper tray. There weren't too many sheets in it, but I estimated there was heaps more than enough.

I set the file to print while I busied myself with installing a new battery in the office clock. At about the same time as I finished with the battery, the printer stopped and beeped several times. "What the…?" I yelped as I read the error message on the screen: "No Paper! What do you mean by 'no paper'? There was plenty," I told it – before I noticed the piled-up tangled mass of paper in the output tray. "Jesus, how many pages did I ask it to print?"

A quick check on the file it was printing told me there were still a number of pages to go. After removing those already printed, and feeding the machine again, I set it to finish the task. The Archives had sent me a massive file. I was now curious to discover how a will could involve so much paper. The larger documents ordered previously consisted of no more than three or four pages. Come to think of it, this file had cost considerably more than any I'd ordered before.

When the printer finally finished and I sorted all the pages into their correct order, I found I had not only a copy of Keith Millard's will, but also the probate file ... and a copy of Keith Raymond Millard's death certificate. The latter being a real bonus, I pushed the rest of the printout aside while I studied the certificate. "I think I did hit pay dirt with this one." I shared my excitement with the universe. "I'm sure this is the father of those three brothers."

"Okay, so what does it tell me," I murmured as I dragged my notebook over closer in readiness to record pertinent details. The first thing I noted was Keith Millard was still a young man when he died just before Christmas of 1986in a work-related accident on a construction site. "What about his sons, what happened to them?" I asked the certificate. Some quick maths told me they were still young lads when their father died. After having lost their mother a decade or so earlier, and then their father, who did they have left?

The section of the certificate dealing with 'spouses' caught my attention. Yep, there was his marriage to Rose, with the added comment *deceased.* But, the next piece of information took my breath away. I read the entry twice. And, then read it again – just to be sure I hadn't imagined it. A second marriage took place in 1975. The bride was none other than one Ruby Cavendish, who was a spinster at the time of the marriage.

So Ruby did eventually marry and, if the information on the certificate was accurate, the Millard wedding was her first marriage. Were there children from the marriage? As Ruby was only about twenty-nine at the time, it's quite possible the marriage produced offspring. The implications of my deliberations hit me: if Ruby and Keith were the parents of a Millard offspring, their child could have legal claim to Lillian's estate. A call to James Whitby seemed in order to acquaint him with the outcome of my research.

If there is a claim on the estate, my dilemma about where to live in the future might disappear. Apart from a considerable amount of cash, the other significant item in Lillian's estate was her house. While they might not be interested in living in the house, if they ended up with it, it would fetch a premium price on today's Real Estate market. Yes, I could see why the Millards would be keen to confirm their family connection to the Cavendish family. The thing I don't understand was the recent events.

Why would they try to break into the place, when all they had to do was establish the family connection? Why threaten and try to intimidate me, when it simply was a matter to be thrashed out by solicitors and the court perhaps? Is there something about the Millards' potential claim to the estate, something with the potential to negate it from the outset? Oh God, I'm going down the track again where my brain becomes so overloaded with questions, it ceases to function at all. Yep, definitely a call to James Whitby required... but, perhaps I should wait until a more civilised hour.

Feeling more than a little despondent, I slumped down in my chair to ponder what the future might bring. Whatever happened, I had no doubt it would be complicated and throw my life into turmoil for some period of time. Maybe I should give up on researching and concentrate on producing the article my editor is going to be demanding any day soon. Who was I kidding? With so much more begging to be discovered about Ruby, the Millards, and everything else to do with Lillian's family and estate, how could I concentrate for long enough to write even the first paragraph of an article?

About then I realised I hadn't completed reading Keith Millard's death certificate, let alone looked at his will. Well, if

I'm going to talk to James Whitby later, I should at least know as many of the facts as possible. I hauled myself upright and returned to the death certificate. A quick glance through the section dealing with where buried and who officiated brought me to the final section of the certificate: the list of offspring.

Keith Millard was survived by three sons. One son had predeceased him. It gave the ages of the surviving sons. My most recent estimate of their ages tallied with those shown on the certificate. My thoughts the boys were still young when their father died were right. Although both their parents were dead, the thought they still had their stepmother, Ruby, to care for them gave me some comfort. But, it gave rise to another question: was any of the surviving sons Ruby's child?

No calculator was required to establish, based on their ages recorded on the certificate, the three surviving sons were born prior to their father's marriage to Ruby. In fact, their ages confirmed they were the three sons mentioned as surviving their mother's death. Just to give myself another question to ponder, what about the deceased son mentioned on the certificate? Was he born after Rose Millard's death and, therefore, likely to be Ruby's son? Of course, it was possible he was the first child – or an early one – born to Rose and Keith Millard. Perhaps he died soon after birth.

So many questions with no answers was not a good way to start the day. After a quick check to ensure I'd made a note of all the pertinent facts, I put the death certificate aside and turned my attention to Keith Millard's will. The document itself was brief. I discovered the bulk of the pages I bought and printed related to the probate process. As I set them aside to read later, I told myself they too could harbour interesting information – although I had no idea what it might be.

The will contained no surprises. Everything was left jointly to Keith's three sons. My eyebrows crawled towards my hairline when I found no mention of Ruby. From the point of view of an outsider looking in, it seemed a little unfair. I could understand his leaving the bulk of his estate to his sons, but his not making any provision for his wife, Ruby, seemed harsh. Even if the marriage was a disaster, wouldn't he expect her to continue to look after the boys? And, in order to help facilitate such care, shouldn't she be provided for in some way?

Move on, I told myself, there's no point in dwelling on things you can't understand. I turned to the inventory page. Again, this was brief and spoke in generalities rather than specific items. This probably was due to the fact the will was made some years before Keith Millard's death. At the time it was made, he would not have anticipated dying until a few decades later, and there might have been changes to his property during the ensuing period. Listed were house and contents, vehicle, and cash.

With nothing more of any consequence to be gained from the will, I moved on to the many pages relating to the granting of probate. Among those was a detailed inventory. It gave the address of the house, its current condition and approximate value. There was a Ford sedan of some vintage. Its valuation suggested it was not in great condition. The values given on a long list of pieces of furniture also suggested there was nothing great amongst them. I was interested in the cash component of the estate. Only one bank account was listed. It had a balance of a few thousand dollars ... and creditors' claims against it for close to two thousand dollars. But, as Keith Millard died as a result of an industrial accident, a Workers' Compensation payment also was held in trust pending the granting of probate.

Okay, even I could see the Millard sons didn't inherit a wealthy lifestyle on the death of their father, but I was curious about how the boys lived after their father's death. No guardianship or care arrangement was mentioned in the will although the boys were still young. Again, such arrangements probably seemed unnecessary at the time the will was made, as Keith would have contemplated being around until after the boys reached adulthood. Once again, I noted the absence of any mention of Ruby.

Having extracted everything of interest from the Archives' files, I decided I needed coffee to help me make sense of all I had discovered. In spite of my best efforts, the coffee didn't work as hoped, but it did produce a suggestion for further research. While an avenue for further research came to mind, the reason to pursue it eluded me. Although I planned to call James Whitby as soon as I finished my coffee, I decided to delay the call until I followed up on my latest idea. After all, I was sure it wouldn't take long, and then I could be confident of giving James the whole story.

Driven more by some subconscious thought than any real knowledge, I raced upstairs and went online to check the death index. Familiarity does save time. I was becoming an 'old-hand' at this online research lark. It took me no time to have the death index up on my screen. My only problem: what was I supposed to be looking for? Millards… Millard deaths are what I needed. Start from the 1960s I told myself.

Although I kept an eye out for the death of a son sometime during the first decade, Rose Millard's 1973 entry was the first one I encountered. The next one was from 1976. It was for the death of Raymond Millard, whose parents were given as Keith and Ruby. So, Ruby had a son, but he died in December 1976. Even I could work out Raymond Millard had a direct Cavendish family connection through his mother, Ruby, but it was extinguished with his death. As there didn't appear to be any other unaccounted for Millard offspring, I was feeling a little more reassured about the situation regarding Lillian's estate.

In spite of it, I decided to continue my check of the death index up to the time of Keith Millard's death. When no further entries were found in the 1970s, I wondered whether it was worth pursuing the exercise further. While I was trying to decide, I kept trawling the index. The entry for a death in 1981 almost leapt off the screen at me. Ruby Millard was dead. So, Ruby wasn't mentioned in Keith's will because she died five years before he did. Still stunned, I sat staring at the entry on the screen for a few moments before deciding I had to have a copy of her death certificate. After providing my credit card details and pressing send, I realised a depressing truth resulting from my research.

The online resources I had used did provide information and proof much quicker than wading through book after book of Lillian's journals, but they didn't provide the same insight into what was happening at the time. I couldn't help wondering whether Lillian ever learned of Ruby's life after she absconded the last time, or whether Lillian had gone to her maker never knowing what had become of her adopted daughter. And, my only way of finding out was to keep reading the journals.

Time had slipped away, and it was now later than when I intended calling James Whitby. I grabbed my phone and keyed his number half expecting him not to answer. When he answered after the number only dialled twice, I was surprised. "Sophie, you must be psychic. I was reaching for the phone to call you when it started ringing. This is your call, so you go first. What can I do for you?"

"I was hoping I might be able to do something to help you. I've done some research since we last spoke. It has produced quite interesting results."

"Ah well, maybe it fits in with what I was going to call you about. First, I need to apologise for not having done much of anything about Lillian's estate since our meeting. Although I'm retired, 'retirement' seems to be a fairly relative term. Every time something crops up involving one of my former clients, I find myself embroiled in legal matters as much as I ever was. It has seen me spend the last couple of days in court over a situation relating to a historical case of mine. Nevertheless, I have achieved one thing. Everything is now in place for us to access Lillian's lock-up at the secure storage place. I've spoken to the operator and sent him the relevant documents. So, if you're free, I thought, sometime this afternoon, we might take a look at what she stored there."

"Do you have a pair of sturdy bolt cutters, or do we need to obtain the required tool beforehand?"

"No bolt cutters required. The man assured me only a key was necessary and he holds a copy we can use."

"Well, I am free to go whenever it suits you."

"Okay, how about I collect you in about half an hour? We can have lunch at a little restaurant I know of on the way out to the storage place, and then go and enter Aladdin's cave afterwards."

"Wonderful… I'll bring copies of all my research notes for you to take home with you."

Half an hour didn't allow me much time to organise and copy the information I wanted to hand on to James but, somehow, I was downstairs with a bulky folder tucked under my arm when he pulled up out front.

Chapter 18

The lock held fast. I was holding my breath, fully expecting the key to break off. A bit of wriggling and jigging provided just enough persuasion for success. Although still requiring some effort, the key turned through ninety degrees and, with an ominous grating sound, the recalcitrant lock yielded. I drew the bolts securing the doors in place, and James and the owner of the place dragged them open.

"Good God," James exclaimed. "This isn't what I expected."

"It's bound to be pretty horrible in there," Brian, the owner of the secure storage place, commented as he peered past James and into the gloom. "It's a bloody long time since it was opened. Don't worry about the dust and cobwebs too much. It's the spiders you need to watch out for. …Bound to be a few Red Backs, and those big hairy ones. Those ones jump at you. Sorry, Miss. Don't mean to frighten you, but you'd be wise to keep your eyes open in there." Having delivered his helpful advice, he went back to his office, leaving James and I – probably with our mouths hanging open –staring into the darkness of the interior of Lillian's storage facility.

"I'm pleased she didn't find anything else to store," James quipped. "She wouldn't have squeezed another pocket handkerchief in there. We should be thankful we are not faced with having to explore two such storage lock-ups."

James was right. The shed-like building was crammed all the way to the doors with stuff. Most of it large, lumpy objects as far as I could tell through the gloom and the clouds of dust we created when we opened the doors. "Might be a good idea to let it air for a while," I suggested. "All the dust, and whatever is causing the awful smell, probably aren't good for us."

"Hmm… I am of the same mind. Let's leave it open while we go and have lunch. We'll see what it's like when we return."

Although our initial plan was to eat before going to the secure storage place, speculating about what Lillian might have stored there fanned our curiosity to the point where we decided to forego lunch. From Lillian's house, we went straight to her lock-up. Now, having made the decision to air the shed, I became aware I was hungry. After explaining the situation to the owner of the place and asking him to keep an eye on our open building, we backtracked to the little restaurant of James' original plan.

Lunch consisted of wonderful food and a glass of excellent house wine. It provided opportunity to brief James on the outcomes of my research and hand over the file I created for him. As there seemed little point in hurrying back to the lock-up, we sat and discussed – and speculated – on the information I dug up.

"So, thanks to your recently acquired bloodhound-like abilities, we now know Ruby died a long time before Lillian, and the only possible Millard connection died before Ruby. We'll follow up on it all of course, so we are prepared in the off chance those Millard lads try their luck. Do you think Lillian found out about Ruby before she died?"

"I don't know… yet. Now I have some dates to work with, I can go directly to the relevant times in Lillian's journals. While I might be wrong, I think she would have recorded an event as major as Ruby's death. But, it is not correct to think the Cavendish connection was severed with Ruby's death. There is also the first child Ruby had back in the 1960s, and there might have been more before she married Millard. What we still don't know is what happened to any child Ruby had before she married Keith Millard."

"Yes, it is something we still need to look into: what was the outcome of Ruby's pregnancy when she was sixteen?"

"We know she didn't marry Ken, the child's reputed father … or, perhaps, it was Ken who didn't marry Ruby, choosing to abscond interstate instead to escape matrimony."

"If you are basing your thinking on the fact she is recorded as a spinster on the Millards' marriage certificate, you need to be aware people often lied, and it was common when providing information to go on a certificate. Every bit of 'information' provided might be doctored to paint the best possible picture of the person involved."

"Are you suggesting Ruby and Ken might have married as planned, and then later went their separate ways?" James nodded and I continued thinking aloud. "If they did, there would need to be a divorce before Ruby could marry Millard. Thank you, James, for helping me realise what I'm going to be doing this weekend: more research."

"My pleasure… And, remember, things are not always as you think they should be. While it is possible Ruby and Ken married and later separated, it also could be Ruby chose to dispense with the bother of obtaining a divorce before marrying Millard. She wouldn't be the first one to do so… and not all of them were found out."

"I think my plan of attack will be to start with Lillian's journals to see if they answer any of the questions now piling up. What about you, James, what's your next move?"

"For the moment, the only move I have planned is to return to Lillian's lock-up to see what was so important she spent the money to purchase a private lock-up to store it. Who knows what we might find in there? I'd like to think we might find answers to some of our questions, but I'm a realist and, as such, I know better than to hold false hopes."

When we checked in with Brian at the secure storage place, he handed us a handful of face masks. "Thought these might be useful if you're determined to enter the lock-up," he said with a grimace. "If you are still on the premises when I'm ready to finish for the day, I'll send for an ambulance. If you spend too much time in there, you're likely to expire."

"Cheerful soul…," James muttered as we drove off.

As I examined the pile of masks resting on my lap, they did nothing to bolster my confidence in what we were about to do.

"I suppose these things will be of some use, but I'm not sure they will be up to the job of protecting us from whatever we are about to encounter in that shed."

On our return to the lock-up, we found its condition not much improved. Nevertheless, in a display of bravado, we donned our masks and stepped inside. James carried the torch he kept in his car's glovebox, and I had the small torch I slipped into my bag before I left home. Then, suitably armed for the task ahead, we began trying to pick our way around and through the material stacked in there. It looked as though, in the first instance, large pieces of furniture were jammed up against one another in neat rows. Then, smaller objects appeared to have been shoved wherever they fitted, or thrown up on top of everything else.

"How are we supposed to inventory all of this?" James demanded.

"In spite of knowing nothing about how to undertake an inventory, it strikes me the only way we will ever know the full extent of what is in here, is to remove it piece by piece. I don't know what to do with it after it's been listed – other than put it all back in here again. Is this likely to be the furniture from the Cavendish family home which Lillian inherited from Isabelle?"

"It's the first thought to come to my mind. I wonder if the silverware and 'other collectables' are in here somewhere as well," James said as he shone his torch in a wide arc over the shed's contents.

We worked separately starting on either side of the shed. Silence hung heavy over us for the next half hour, punctuated only on occasion by the odd expletive from one of us. The dust and grime of decades of undisturbed storage formed a thick coating on every exposed surface ... and transferred to me as I poked about. Cobwebs were plentiful and hung like Christmas decorations but so far, thankfully, there was no sign of their creators. More than once during the first half hour of inspecting the contents I asked myself why I was wasting my time on this exercise. What did we hope to gain? Apart from confirming there was a mountain of furniture stored here, everything was packed in too tightly for us to discover anything more specific.

"I need fresh air," James shouted from the other side of the building, and caused me a moment of panic. James was an old man – fit but old – and rummaging around in these conditions might not be in his best interest. Come to think of it, it might not be in mine either.

What little light entered through the open door suffered a temporary interruption as James exited the building. I decided to copy his example and followed him out. "There's not a breath of air enters the shed," he complained. "And, these masks don't make it any more pleasant. Whatever possessed us to pick the warmest day in a while to go digging about in there?"

"Yep, I agree, and we haven't achieved anything to crow about so far. All we've done is assume this is the furniture Lillian inherited from the Cavendish family home. We don't know what it consists of, or the condition it's in, and we don't know what else might be stored in there as well."

"So, what are you suggesting?"

"Now, therein lies the problem. You don't happen to know of any good – reputable, I mean – antique dealers, do you?"

"As it so happens, I do know of one. But, what do you expect him to do when it comes to sorting out this lot?"

"Again, I don't know – exactly. I suppose I thought maybe, if he had a look at a couple of pieces of the furniture, he might be able to give us some idea of its value or otherwise. We can't leave it sitting in this shed forever. It probably has already deteriorated from the years it's been stored here. From what I've seen of it so far, it is not to my taste. I'm not saying I wouldn't want any of it, but I know I don't want all of it. So, maybe we should think about finding it good and appreciative homes to go to … and make some cash while we are about it."

"Right… Well, I like your thinking, and my next move probably is to call the antique dealer. All we can do is to bring him here and hope he can work out what to do next. I'll make the call as soon as I'm back in my office. Having agreed on organising for antique dealer, what's our next move?"

"Well, you are welcome to make your own decision about what you might do now, but I am going back in there to see if I can get a better understanding of what Lillian saw fit to store here."

"While of no particular consequence at the moment, I had a thought which might prove important. Did Lillian have this lock-up and its contents insured? I've no idea how much selling all the furniture in there might realise, but I suspect it must be worth a bit."

"Perhaps it's something else we should follow-up. This place might have rules about insuring whatever is stored here. Maybe Brian can give us some clues to point us in the right direction."

"Something else you need to think about, Sophie – although this isn't the best time to mention it: what do you plan to do with all the cash you inherited? Maybe you should talk to a financial advisor about investing at least some of it. If you sell this lot, there will be even more money to worry about. I would suggest not leaving it too much longer to look into what to do with it all."

"Yeah, I know you are right. I had thought about it, but I suppose I don't feel it's really is mine yet. Until this business with the Millard brothers is cleared-up, I know I'll continue to feel tentative about Lillian's estate. As for whatever is in this shed, whatever comes in from its disposal, I tentatively had earmarked for a particular purpose. I don't have a plan as such but, if we can locate the child Ruby had when she was sixteen, I think it should go to the child. Don't look at me as though I've lost the plot. I did say I hadn't yet worked out how it should happen."

"…And we don't know whether there was a child, and if there was one, who and where it might be now. I think you'll agree, it's just another loose end to tie up. Still, it's a generous idea and worth considering – if we locate a child. There is something else to keep in mind with regard to a possible child born to Ruby when she was sixteen. The child would now be approaching sixty years old, and might believe they had entitlement to the whole of the estate and not just whatever comes from the sale of the stuff in there."

With our lungs somewhat recovered from whatever we breathed in during our first sortie into the shed, we both returned for another poke about in there. This time, I went straight to the back of the shed, and wriggled my way in amongst the furniture. A couple of large, tall cupboards occupied much of the space along the back wall. Access to the cupboards was barred by what looked like dining suite chairs stacked on top of each other in pairs.

I counted five stacks of chairs. Only two pairs needed to be shifted to provide access to at least one half of the first cupboard. After shoving the chairs, one by one, on top of already precarious piles of furniture, I examined the part I could see of the first cupboard. I initially thought it might be a display case – or a wardrobe. I hoped for the former, rather than the latter. But my hope was dashed when I realised the front of the cupboard contained no glass panels. Okay, probably not a display case.

Damn! My fanciful thinking had led me to imagine a display case might still contain the treasures it held in its former life. If it were a wardrobe, I would prefer not to open it. Any clothes still in it would be dusty and full of mould. While I didn't know the rating of the masks Brian gave us, I doubted they were up to dealing with those types of contaminants. Still, curiosity is a powerful emotion, and far exceeds the strength of my common sense.

The main problem I envisaged when I first saw the cupboards was a key would be required to open them, as was the case with most of their contemporaries. Again, I was wrong… at least, I was wrong about the one I could access. No keyholes were visible. The door-pulls featured a meatal ring resembling a laurel wreath hanging from a central post. I lifted the one nearest me for a closer look at the detailed design on the ring. The craftsmanship was excellent. As I went to flip it up to check the design on the back of it, it started to turn – but then jammed.

A bit of wriggling and jiggling back and forth was rewarded with success. The door-pull rotated through half a turn and the door, with a resounding pop and squawk, sprung open a couple of centimetres. With some degree of trepidation, I tugged it about half open. A bouquet of dust, lignum and mould, rushed out to greet me on the disturbed air my invasion created. In spite of the mask clamped firmly to my face, a fit of coughing and spluttering followed. Then, after one more application of muscles, the cupboard door stood wide open … well, as wide as the space I had created allowed it to open.

An array of silverware hiding behind a dark veil awaited me. A heavy coating of tarnish provided by its less than ideal environment cloaked every piece. The pieces I could discern in the failing light of my torch ranged from enormous (ice buckets and some form of table centrepiece) to tiny (diminutive salt cellars with tiny spoons, and napkin rings). The cupboard comprised four shelves all stacked with as much silverware as possible – without much thought to care and preservation. Objects were stacked in and on pieces to utilise every available space.

Was what I could see on the four shelves the extent of the collection? No matter how inflated its delusion of grandeur, how much more would a household need? The only way to find out was to explore the other half of the cupboard still protected by its closed door and guarded by the remaining six stacked chairs. It didn't matter how many other surprises the cupboard held, I wasn't going to discover its secrets today. My torch was reduced to nothing more than a dull glow. I used its failing light to shove two more chairs up on top of the surrounding stacks of furniture. Better lighting was required for my next visit, when I would remove the remaining four chairs to gain unhindered access to the contents of the other half of the cupboard.

By fixing my eyes on the light coming in through the shed's open doors and feeling my way gingerly around objects in my path, I eventually stepped out into sunlight and fresh air...and found James, already out there and leaning against the car.

"I was beginning to wonder whether I should call in a search and rescue squad to retrieve you. Are you okay? You look a bit the worse for whatever you got up to."

"My torch has died but, as long as I haven't contracted some fatal lung disease from the foul air in there, I'll be fine as soon as I've had a long, hot shower."

"If you've finished poking about for today, I'll take you home … after we ask Brian about insurance on our way out."

Brian assured us, for an owner to store property on the premises, they are required to maintain insurance cover over their property. In Lillian's case, it meant insuring the building, its contents, and holding public liability insurance – in case, by some chance, her stuff should cause damage to someone else or their property stored there. It was looking like I wouldn't have to worry about what was on TV tonight. I would be occupied going through Lillian's papers for an insurance policy.

By the time James dropped me back at Lillian's house, I was tired, grubby and in need of caffeine. I asked James in for a coffee but he declined, saying he needed to go back to his office to tidy up a few things before the end of the day. I wasn't sorry he rejected the invitation. As soon as he drove off, I flew up the stairs and had the shower running while I stripped off. Even my clothes, as well as my hair, retained the shed's aroma. Ignoring any water restriction in force, I stood under the shower for a long time before emerging pink, shrivelled, and with wet hair clinging to my face and shoulders.

Dinner was one of those something-on-toast nights followed by a mind-in-neutral session watching the seven o'clock news. Then I was back upstairs and wondering where in the office to start looking for the documents I needed. From the moment I entered the room, I experienced the overwhelming feeling something was not right. I was on high alert with my antennae twitching. "What is wrong with you?" I demanded of myself. While there was no one other than me in the house, I did have a surreptitious glance under the desk to check for monsters … and then checked over my shoulder to make sure no one had seen me. The strange feeling of something being amiss persisted, but I shoved it to the back of my mind and got on with the task I came to do.

Perhaps I should be thankful the little voice in my head kept telling me I wouldn't find what I was looking for in the office. It helped take my mind off my earlier uneasy feeling, and forced me to focus on looking for the insurance policy. An hour or so later, I had to admit the little voice had been right on the money. But, it wasn't only the insurance policy I hadn't found. There were other important documents I didn't find either.

Lillian was cautious. Excessively so at times, as I'd discovered in the past. While her passport and several other documents I could think of were personal, and I could understand she might want to keep them somewhere less obvious than in the office, but an insurance policy document…?

With a nightcap for company, I spent some time pondering the situation while sitting in a less than comfortable ancient lounge chair. The uncomfortable chair helped keep me awake, but it was no help in solving the problem of the missing documents. In the end, I admitted defeat and headed for bed. My uneasy feeling from earlier in the night had stayed with me and, the moment I turned off the light, it came back to haunt me. I tried blocking it by thinking about the missing documents. My last thought, almost like the dying flare of a fire, was 'safety deposit box'. "Of course…," I murmured, but don't remember another thing until my eyelashes finally untangled themselves this morning.

*****

I revisited the safety deposit box idea over breakfast. Keeping important documents in a safety deposit box at the bank made sense. But, why hadn't such a repository been found in the process of preparing everything for probate. All Lillian's bank accounts were identified and their balances recorded. It seemed logical for the bank to mention the deposit box to Tom Breen when he was collecting details of the extent of Lillian's estate.

Maybe I need to have a chat to James Whitby again today. I knew my call probably should be directed to Tom Breen who was Lillian's solicitor in the end and who had handled the probate paperwork for her estate. While I couldn't explain why, I hadn't found Tom Breen as easy to deal with as James. Besides, I sometimes felt Tom tried fobbing me off rather than answering my questions if he found them uncomfortable. Yep, I was more likely to achieve better results if I set up James to ask Tom the hard questions.

Chapter 19

Without consulting the clock, I called James … and then checked the time. By a retiree's standards, it probably was not yet a civilised hour for phone calls. James' phone had been dialling for a while when I realised what time it was, and I was tempted to end the call in the hope of saving myself some embarrassment. Too late. James answered.

"Apologies for taking so long to answer; I had to search every pocket of my golf bag before I found my phone. So, what can I do for you, Sophie? Did you have an epiphany of some sort overnight?"

"Not exactly... When I couldn't find the insurance policy for Lillian's lock-up, I wondered where else she might keep it. It's when I realised I hadn't come across other important personal documents as well. When all the work was done to prepare Lillian's estate for probate, was a safety deposit box located anywhere. I imagine if there were one at her normal bank, they would have mentioned it when Tom Breen was sorting out the bank accounts."

"It would be standard procedure, but I'm almost sure there was no mention of a deposit box in the inventory of her estate. Now, for me, it raises a couple of interesting questions. Did your thoughts on the matter produce any clues worth following up?"

"I'm not sure I would call any of the outcomes a 'clue'. One possibility did capture my attention, even though it seemed a bit far-fetched."

James encouraged me to share my thinking. While I felt self-conscious about telling someone who knows more about how to hunt down personal information than I do, I did as I was asked. "What if she kept certain stuff at a different bank?

I know, I know. Before you say anything, I know it sounds ridiculous, but is it a possibility? If it is, then I suppose the big question is, why? Why would she consider it safer to keep such stuff somewhere other than at her usual bank?"

"You do come up with the very best questions… and this is another one for which I do not have an answer. But, I will say this, your thinking could be running close to the mark. I'll go into my office straight after I finish this round of golf. As soon as I have something to report, I'll let you know what I discover. Where will you be today?"

"So far, I'm still based at Lillian's place. The jury is still out on where I'll be living in the future, but today I will be at Lillian's house all day."

His response was more than I'd hoped for after my call at such an early hour and having interrupted his game of golf, but I knew time would drag on while I waited to hear back from him. I needed something to occupy my mind and help time to at least seem to pass faster. The only thing I had to continue with was the stack of Lillian's journals. At first, the thought of a day spent reading journals did nothing to improve my outlook. Then I remembered my recent research had produced a couple of dates for significant events. Reading what Lillian recorded in her journals around those times could prove useful.

Back in the office, I went straight to my makeshift desk where I had left one of Lillian's journals. As I sat down to check the date range covered by it, the uneasy feeling from last night returned. "This is ridiculous," I told the universe. What was happening to me? Was it something about the room? But nothing had changed. Everything in here was as it had been for the last however many days. Why have I started feeling this way every time I enter this office?

No answers were forthcoming from the universe or anywhere else, but I had to find the cause. It wasn't possible for me to work while such uneasiness prevailed. First things first, find the cause, I told myself as I sat upright and pushed myself away from the desk. Slowly, I let my eyes scan the room. Nothing and nowhere escaped scrutiny.

Everything was normal … well, as normal as it had been since I started using this office. But, my eyes kept coming back to Lillian's desk. Why? The desk was where it always had been, and everything about it was as it should be, or so I told myself. It had no effect. The feeling persisted, and my eyes kept suggesting I should pay attention to the desk. "Okay, okay… I'll have a look at the desk." I hoped I sounded braver than I felt as I moved towards it.

I stood beside it and let my eyes drift across its surface. "No explosive devices and no monsters underneath, so why is it worrying me?" After flopping down on the chair, I tried to shut everything else out of my mind and just let my eyes focus on the desktop. I don't know for how long the exercise lasted but, it was time to abandon it and go fetch another of Lillian's journals.

"There it is! I know what's not right." Surely it can't be what this nonsense is all about. Yesterday, when I printed my research notes to give to James, I also printed a second copy for Lou Radford – whenever she appeared again. A file the same as the one I gave James would bring Lou up to speed on what had happened during her absence more quickly and efficiently than having me tell her. I used the only folder available for James' copy, and intended finding another folder for Lou's copy after I returned from the secure storage place.

Before I left to go to Lillian's lock-up yesterday, I stacked the pages of Lou's printout and held them together with a large clip. It was not how things were now. I had left the clipped pages on the desk when I left, and I hadn't used the desk since returning yesterday afternoon. Now, the clip was removed, and several of the pages were a bit askew. I wasn't responsible. I hadn't been near the document since I returned from the lock-up. So, who else had been here? Who had removed the clip and disturbed the pages?

Now, the uneasy feeling dogging me since last night turned into something more. Something akin to fear. Was there someone else still in the house? If there were, they had been quieter than the proverbial church mouse. What else in the room was not as I'd left it? A slow and steady scan of every inch of the office identified a few other anomalies. They were not major, just instances of things having been moved slightly so as to be no longer quite where they had been.

As my eyes travelled down the right-hand side of the desk, they came to an abrupt halt at the third drawer. I checked the drawers on the left-hand side of the desk. All the drawers on both sides of the desk were closed properly … EXCEPT the third drawer on the right-hand side. Almost closed, but not quite, it remained only about three millimetres out from being closed. Not much to go on I suppose, except I knew the drawer had been as properly closed as all the others.

Stunned, I sat slumped in the chair behind the desk, incapable of any clear thought or action. I felt cold, as though chilled to the bone, and my stomach had tightened into a lead ball. Someone had been in this house during my absence. Had they taken something – anything? Who else had a key? As far as I knew, no one else had a key to the house since Lillian's death. It meant there had to have been a break-in. I'm sure I would have noticed if there was damage to the front door, but what about the rest of the house? From where else might they gain entry?

On my way downstairs, I was on high alert, with my eyes flittering about all over the place and my head swivelling from side to side. Not a sound – apart from my thumping heart. And no ghosts, monsters or other frightening apparitions were seen. So, I made it safely to the backdoor and inspected it. No sign of its having been forced. Next, I made way around all the downstairs windows, checking each one for any sign of forced entry. Again, I drew a blank.

In the silence of the empty house, my phone seemed louder than I ever heard it before. It frightened the life out of me, and

I'm sure I leapt about a metre in the air. I was on my way to the kitchen to arrange a caffeine fix when James called. When I answered the phone, all I could manage was a strangled croak.

"Sophie, are you all right? What has happened?"

"Ah, James…ye-es, I'm fine thanks. At least, I think I am. There's something funny…"

"You don't sound okay. I was going to talk to you about the follow-up work I've done since our visit to Lillian's lock-up, but now I think I'll come over to talk to you in person. I'll see you in about twenty minutes."

He received no argument from me. The idea of having someone else here in the house with me had a lot going for it. I decided to delay coffee until James arrived, and spent the intervening time going from room to room on both floors. Perhaps I was becoming a bit paranoid, and my imagination was running away with me, but I identified a few things not quite as they should have been.

Even in Lillian's bedroom, I detected a couple of things had been disturbed. People would be entitled to question how I knew. Her bedroom had been a scene of much activity in recent times. It would be reasonable to accept objects were accidentally bumped or deliberately moved out of the way to safety. But, the things I saw as having been interfered with did not fit with such a scenario. A distinct cold numbness surged through me when I noticed a couple of personal items in my room were out of place.

Before I could work myself up into too much more of a panic, James Whitby rang the front doorbell. I rushed downstairs and threw open the door. "James, come in. I'm dying to hear what you have discovered. He didn't respond for a few moments, but stood there studying me intently. His eyes sprung open wide the moment he saw me. I noticed, but chose to ignore it rather than comment. When he spoke, his voice was deep and hesitant.

"Perhaps we might leave such discussion for the moment. I think it might be better if we had a chat first … Over a coffee maybe…?"

Conversation was non-existent until we were seated at the kitchen table with our coffees. I felt myself start to relax from the moment James arrived but, now it was time for our 'little chat', the relaxation process seemed to stall. How was I ever going to explain to James the ridiculous notion I have about someone having been in the house yesterday afternoon while we were at the lock-up? But, James is an experienced interrogator and all the details of my current nervous twitch came spilling out.

He didn't interrupt. Just sat silent and attentive all through my ridiculous ramblings. I had focused on some indeterminate spot on the tabletop as I recounted my supposed findings. As I came to the end of my story, I looked up at him. His composed countenance betrayed no emotion, but I felt as though his eyes could read my soul.

"I suppose there is one natural first question anyone would ask: how many people hold a key to this house? It's obvious you do, and I assume Lillian's key is still here somewhere. Who else might have had a key, and were any other keys returned after Lillian's death?"

"Those same questions have been bugging me all morning. No, I don't have a conclusive answer, but I'm inclined to think no other key holders remain out there in the community."

"Well, as you have found no evidence of forced entry, but have reasonable grounds to assume someone gained unauthorised access to the place, it stands to reason a key was involved. Don't take offence, but have you lost your key recently, or lent it to someone perhaps?"

"Of course not. I still had my key when I arrived home from the lock-up yesterday, and I haven't left the house since. It's the same key I've had since I was a teenager. I'm not in the habit of lending keys to anyone, and certainly haven't given anyone the use of my key. So, if we agree something strange is afoot here, what's to be done about it? I suppose I could call Gail Olsen, the day shift police officer from my protection detail, but her involvement with me and this place are consigned to history. I imagine she is involved with other cases now."

"Before we do anything else, do you know where Lillian's key is?" I nodded. "Good. Please check if it is still where it's supposed to be." I gave him a sceptical look. "Yes, I'm sure it still is where you expect it to be, but we do have to be sure of our facts before we talk to anyone. So, please check on the key."

James had a valid point. A few moments later, I was pleased to report Lillian's key remained where it was supposed to be. While it was good news, it didn't bring us any closer to an explanation of how someone might enter the house without having to force their way in. A sudden idea thumped in from out of left field. "James, I checked the doors and windows for any tell-tale damage, but might it be possible they didn't use a key? Could they have picked the lock on one of the doors?"

"It's possible, but they would leave marks confirming how they gained ingress. We could sit here speculating about this whole episode, or we could do the intelligent thing and talk to the police. What do you think?"

"They probably will think I've lost the plot and will send the men in white coats to come and take me away."

"I doubt you need worry. Just give me a moment to call Warren Tyson."

"Okay, but who is Warren Tyson?"

"He is the Detective Inspector I was playing golf with this morning. He's also the bloke who outplayed me as though I'd never played a game of golf before."

James had his phone pressed against his ear as he walked away to speak to his golfing partner. It wasn't a long conversation. When he returned to the table, I sensed he was buoyed up by whatever had been said. He checked his watch before asking, "What's the current state of your larder? Is it able to provide us with lunch, do you think?"

"So long as you don't want anything too fancy… Oh, and how many might I be feeding at lunchtime?"

"Just the two of us. Warren Tyson will arrive shortly, but he won't expect to be fed. He will be 'on-the-job' so to speak, and will want to ask a lot of questions and look around. There is no need to be concerned. He is a decent sort of bloke and easy to talk to."

Although I didn't know how much time I had before Detective Inspector Tyson arrived, I decided to put it to good use. Earlier, James had said he wanted to talk to me about what he had discovered after our visit to the lock-up but, so far, there had been no mention of it. I initiated the conversation I wanted to have, and it caused James to glance at his watch again.

"Goodness, I'd forgotten about wanting to talk to you today. We won't have time to go into details, but I'll give you an overview of some of what I've achieved. I called the antiques dealer I mentioned yesterday. He was almost salivating by the time our brief conversation ended. I expect him to text me dates and times of when he will be available to look at the contents of the lock-up. He also recommended one of the silversmiths who is part owner of the Silver Shop in the city, whom he thought would be equally interested in some of the collection. I had a brief conversation with him before I came here this morning, but we have yet to set up a time for him to have a look at the silverware."

"What about the possibility of a safety deposit box, or something similar? Was there any mention of something of that kind in the probate documentation?"

"No. I went through the file last night and found no mention of anything. So, as soon as I went into my office this morning, I asked Tom Breen what he knew about such a possibility. He had no idea what I was talking about, and assured me there had been no mention of a safety deposit box at any time during the process of compiling an inventory of the estate. So, I suppose the question remains a work in progress for a bit longer.

I think I just heard a car pull up. It's probably Warren Tyson."

Apart from whatever other attributes Warren Tyson might have, he was definitely eye candy. The tall, slim, swarthy detective inspector had a mischievous look about him. It was there in the twinkle in his eyes and his ever-lurking smile. Spending all his time with bad guys was a waste of this bloke.

When James introduced me, he also added how concerned I was Tyson would think me a nut case. The DI's deep rumbling laugh lit up his whole face and caused crinkles at the corners of his eyes. Yes, I was beginning to think James had nailed it. This bloke would be easy to talk to. So, I told my story.

It was no surprise I suppose when he asked to see those things I had identified as anomalies. After a 'look but don't touch' inspection of the place, including all the doors and windows, it was time for the keys… how many were there, who had them, and all the other stuff I'd already gone through with James. Not content with just my answers, he wanted to see the keys. Over yet another coffee at the kitchen table, James and I sat in silence as Warren Tyson examined the three keys lying in his hand. Two were attached to fancy keyrings, while one was just an unadorned example.

"Tell me again, whose is this one?" Tyson asked as he held up the one attached by a short chain to a St Christopher medal.

"It was Lillian's key – the deceased owner of this place." I told him for the third time since he started examining the keys.

"I never had Lillian down as being religious," James commented.

"She wasn't. Why did you… Oh, I see: the medallion. A client brought it back from overseas as a gift for her. I don't think the religious aspect meant anything to her. She just liked the how the thing worked as a keyring and how it felt comfortable in her hand."

"And, I think you said this one was yours…" Tyson held up my key attached to its big fluoro pink plastic heart key tag. I nodded. "So, tell me again who this other one belonged to." He waved the unattached key at me.

"Rita Moreno… It was the one Lillian gave Rita. I suppose she also gave it to Mavis Larson before Rita, and maybe even back in the earlier days, she gave it to Lorna Green."

"Eh..? Who the hell were all those women – and why would they be given a key?"

There followed a reasonably short – and, no doubt, confusing – explanation of the women who helped out in Lillian's household over the years. Tyson proved no slouch at soaking up information and processing it.

"Right… so Lorna Green, who was a housekeeper/nanny, was employed some time ago. Then, in more recent times, there were the two other women you mentioned. Why did they need a key?"

"In the beginning, Mavis Larson came in on a daily basis for a while as a housekeeper before becoming a live-in housekeeper/carer for Lillian. When her brother, who shared a house with her, suffered a stroke, she resigned to take over caring for him full-time. Rita Moreno was the replacement housekeeper/nurse who was still with Lillian when she died. As 'live-ins', they both had keys during the time they were employed here. Rita left her key with me the last time she was here."

"Okay, we've narrowed things down a bit. This key was cut sometime in the last few years – within the last decade. So, it's unlikely Lorna Green had this key while she was employed here. Do we know what happened to her key?"

"I don't know. Lorna came to work here in 1946. By about 1963, there no longer was need for a nanny. Lorna was getting on a bit by then, so she retired. It was all before my time, I'm afraid. After Lorna left, Lillian did for herself until I came along to help her out a bit over a number of years. Then, about eight years ago, Lillian's health was deteriorating and I persuaded her to engage a housekeeper. Mavis Larson started by coming in three days a week to do housework but, as Lillian's health continued to decline, Mavis moved in to care for Lillian as well as running the house. She was a retired nurse and only wanted to work for a few years to build up her retirement nest egg. When she left after about four years, Rita Moreno, who also had been a nurse, was engaged and came to live-in."

"Was Rita an elderly lady as well?"

"She took early retirement from nursing and was only about sixty when she came here."

James had remained silent while the question-and-answer session was in progress. When there was a brief respite and silence settled over the kitchen table for a few moments, James seized his opportunity to comment.

"A live-in position such as Lillian offered must have been ideal for those retired women. It provided all-found board and lodging as well as an income. It took care of the transition period between retiring from full-time career employment to living on a pension in a retirement facility of some sort."

"No, James, not for those three women. Lorna Green owned the family home after her husband died. Mavis was a widow and had her brother, a confirmed bachelor, living with her. He was living alone in the house until Mavis moved back home to care for him after retiring from here. Much the same was true for Rita. She was a widow who owned her own home. In her case, her daughter – and I think maybe a grandchild or two – lived with her. They continued to live in and look after the house while Rita worked here."

The detective inspector's next question took me by surprise. I hadn't realised he was paying attention as I explained to James about the women's situations.

"Rita's daughter, was she a widow too – or maybe a divorcee?"

"I don't know … Er…, no, I don't think so. I have a vague recollection of a comment Rita made one day. I don't remember the exact words, but my interpretation of it led me to believe the daughter wasn't married and her children were illegitimate. Of course, I might have misinterpreted it, but it was what I thought at the time."

Tyson checked his watch as he murmured, "I see." His action was infectious and caused both James and me to check ours. I realised it was almost one o'clock and I was feeling more than a bit peckish. As I was about to offer people lunch, Tyson saved me the trouble.

"There isn't much else I can do here today. I'll send the forensic boys in to dust for prints and anything else they find which might be helpful. With any luck, they should arrive later this afternoon. In the meantime, I would like to keep this key for a while. It's a long shot, but I'll see if I can locate where and when it was cut."

"How can it be of any help when the key has been here the whole time? And, before you ask, the only people who have been in the house other than me are your three police officers and James. Oh… and Lou Radford was here a few times, but it was a few weeks ago."

"You might be surprised by the information it could help us uncover. I'll be back in touch as soon as I have something to share, or more questions to ask. In the meantime, stay safe, pay particular attention to locking doors and windows, and keep an eye out for any unusual people or activity about the place."

With those few words, he stood up and made to leave. James sprang up and rushed to show Tyson to the door. I intervened. My next comment brought the pair of them rushing back to the kitchen.

"It's not the first time this has happened." I hadn't intended to blurt it out as I did, and I wasn't even sure it was true.

"Maybe you had better explain," Tyson suggested.

"Maybe I shouldn't have mentioned it. I already feel as though I'm jumping at shadows. But, the other afternoon, I spent some time at the supermarket and then, after coming back here and dealing with the groceries, I went for a walk and roamed around in the park for a while."

"When exactly was this?"

"The last day my police protection detail was here." I noticed James looked exasperated as I spoke to DI Tyson. I decided an explanation was needed. "When I went up to the office later in the evening, I couldn't find something I thought I had printed out earlier in the day. I had a bit of a look around in the office but there was no sign of it. At first, I tried convincing myself Police Officer Gail Olsen might have picked it up with other bits of paper and it was now not where I expected it to be. When another search failed to find it, I began questioning my own mentality. Had I printed it out, or had I meant to, but not done so? While I decided at the time the latter probably was the case, I don't think I ever really convinced myself it was true. Now, I'm almost prepared to swear I remember printing it out – but it still hasn't turned up."

"Good grief, Sophie, why didn't you tell me?" James exclaimed.

"Tell you what… I'm losing my marbles?"

DI Tyson jotted a few comments in his notebook before again heading for the door, with James trailing along behind him. I heard them have a brief conversation on the doorstep, followed soon after by the slam of a car door. Moments later, James was back in the kitchen.

"Do you think we might find somewhere more comfortable to sit while we finish the conversation I came to have with you?" he asked as he eyed off the chair he recently vacated. I was relieved my interrogation over the 'other' incident was finished.

We moved to Lillian's ancient lounge chairs – not comfortable but a definite improvement on the kitchen chairs. In a bid to bring it to the front of my memory again, I reiterated the information about antique dealers and silversmiths James gave me earlier. "Okay, but what about a safety deposit box or something similar, did you have success there?"

"As I started to tell you before, I went through all the documentation looking for any mention of stuff squirrelled away somewhere. When I found nothing, I asked Tom Breen about it. He was a bit offended I was asking and thought I was suggesting he had been less than thorough in preparing Lillian's estate for probate. After I smoothed his feathers a bit and explained the reason I was asking, he agreed there had to be somewhere else Lillian kept certain papers and perhaps other material as well."

"Right… Well, I guess, as there's nothing helpful from Tom Breen, what's our next move? I know it was only because of an insurance policy we started this treasure hunt, but I can't help wondering what else she might have thought necessary to hide from everyone."

"Yeah, 'what else' is the question isn't it? While I don't expect a speedy result, I asked one of the investigators we use to have a dig around to see what he can find. I don't think she kept stuff at one of the other banks, so we probably aren't looking for a safety deposit box. When word of Lillian's death circulated, and a call for creditors was published, any bank holding anything of Lillian's would have come forward. There are rules about such things."

"If we rule out a safety deposit box at a bank, where else could there be for her to keep stuff safe and away from prying eyes?"

"Perhaps our investigator will find an answer for us. The only other thing to come to mind for me is a safe somewhere. Before you ask, I have no ideas about what sort of safe or where it might be."

With nothing much else for us to discuss, and James had plenty of other things in his life to attend to, I walked him to the door… and met DI Tyson's forensic team as they arrived on the doorstep.

Chapter 20

I spent the rest of the afternoon showing the forensic team around the house. It seemed anything which stood still long enough was dusted with horrible black powder. As they were beginning to pack up, I walked into the office and shrieked, "What a bloody mess! How am I supposed to clean this up so I can work in here? Are you lot just going to leave it like this?"

"Yes, Miss, unfortunately we are leaving it as it is," the bloke who seemed to be in charge said quietly. He might have used his most soothing tone, but it didn't work. I spun around to face him, ready to deliver a few home truths. He cut me off before I started.

"If there is anything you must clean tonight, don't try brushing or wiping the powder off. It will only make a bigger mess and make it harder to clean off. Use warm soapy water to remove it on anything safe to wet. It might be a bit inconvenient, but it is too late now to do anything today. I'm sure DI Tyson will send in the specialist cleaners to clean the place for you tomorrow. Just try to work around it tonight if you can."

As much as I hated accepting defeat, I know when I'm beaten. Within a few minutes, the forensic team were gone and I was alone in a now filthy house. The one thing I was sure about was no work would be done in the office tonight. But, what I wasn't sure about was where I would spend the night. My inclination was to collect what I needed for breakfast and take it home to my place. It was clean and comfortable. If I returned early enough tomorrow morning, I could be here to let in the team of cleaners when they arrived. So I thought initially but, before it had time to settle and gain the tick of approval, another thought occurred to me.

Leaving the house unattended tonight might not be the wisest move. What if uninvited visitors arrived again tonight? I suppose it was only likely if they didn't find what they were looking for the last time. And, as I don't know what they might have been looking for, I have no way of knowing whether they found it or not. They will be in for a shock if they do come back tonight. There is barely a square inch of the place they could touch without leaving clear fingerprints behind. I wonder how easily the black powder cleans off skin.

Would I be safe if I stayed here tonight? While there hadn't been any rough stuff so far, they might resort to violence if they had become desperate to find whatever they were looking for. In the midst of trying to deal with so much indecision, my phone chirped, shattering the silence of the house. It was DI Tyson.

"The forensic team just called to say they had finished at your house. I can imagine the mess they left behind. I will send the cleaners in first thing in the morning. Are you planning on spending tonight there?"

"I was just debating what to do. I think I would rather go back to my place than risk ending up with this black powder all over me and my clothes, but I am reluctant to leave the house unattended tonight."

"It won't be a problem, regardless of whether you choose to go back to your place or stay where you are. The place will be patrolled again for the next few days… or, at least until we receive the results of the forensic team's investigation. I'll leave it to you to decide what you are going to do, but tonight's officers should be there within the next hour. Let them know whatever you decide."

For a few moments I thought his information had solved my problem, but then the doubts returned. The officers who were here tonight wouldn't be able to move about or touch anything without being covered in black powder. My decision making hadn't advanced any by the time the two officers arrived. They were new ones who hadn't been part of my earlier protection detail.

Night pulls down its dark shades early at this time of year, and the officers used it to their advantage. It was almost seven o'clock when I heard a knock on the back door. I rushed to answer it ... and then hesitated. After demanding to know who was there, I relaxed when they identified themselves as the officers who would be minding the place tonight. The senior officer sorted out my dilemma by his explanation, and encouraged me to go back to my place.

"It will be more convenient for all of us if you return home for tonight. Our operation will only succeed if anyone interested in poking about in here thinks the place is empty. After we make sure everything is locked, we will then settle down to spend the night in the dark. If we are to attract a return visit, the perpetrator must think no one is at home. I doubt you would enjoy spending the night here in complete silence and darkness."

He was right. It did not sound like a fun way to spend the night. Even having to play Scrabble would be preferable. I loaded a bag with what I needed for breakfast, told them I would return before they were to be collected at eight o'clock tomorrow morning, and was on my way home – via a take-away place for something for dinner. I was accompanied by the expectation of a night of total relaxation in my own home again – and in my own bed. Disappointment is a terrible emotion.

Far from feeling relaxed, I was on edge the whole time, jumping at even the slightest sound. When TV didn't do the trick, I decided the best way to occupy my mind – and help me relax – was to throw myself into my work. My editor expected an article from me by the end of next week. So far, there was no progress of the project. Once I settled in my office, work mode found me again. I remembered some work I did a few months ago with a view to turning it into an article at some time in the future. I dug out my file.

By midnight, the article was written, edited and licked into shape ready for submission. Discretion counselled I should wait until tomorrow before sending it off ... in case further inspiration occurred to me in the meantime. Working on the article had a cathartic effect. When I fell into bed, sleep was only moments away, and it kept me company until seven o'clock next morning when I went into panic mode. The plan was to return to Lillian's house before the police officers left at eight o'clock.

*****

With no time to spare, as soon as I was dressed, the stuff I brought for breakfast went back into a bag and I was on my way to Lillian's. It was early and traffic was light. I arrived at my destination less than twenty minutes later. And, after a further five minutes, the officers hoisted their backpacks over their shoulders and disappeared out the backdoor and into the lane behind the house. It seems a car was waiting to pick them up in a street some distance away. I learned their departure was the reverse of the process for their arrival at my backdoor last evening.

Breakfast was the next thing on my agenda, and it would give me something to do while I planned how I might fill in my day. After all, who knows when the cleaners might arrive to make the place liveable again, and the office fit to work in? In its own perverse way, my mind didn't want to focus on today. It kept wandering back to my final conversation with James before he left yesterday afternoon. His increasing scepticism of our chances of finding a safety deposit box containing Lillian's missing documents didn't fit comfortably with me. To put it in simple terms, it wasn't what I wanted to hear.

If no such deposit box existed, there had to be a safe somewhere involved. No matter how hard I tried, I could not shake my belief there was more material stashed away somewhere just waiting to be discovered. "Okay, where would she find an available safe?" I demanded of the empty house. "…Some type of facility offering the same level of security as a bank's safety deposit arrangement provided?"

I was halfway through my second mug of coffee before the fog started to lift and my brain stepped up a gear. What if…? What if…? What if such facilities don't exist? What if Lillian

213

didn't look to the outside world for somewhere safe for her select material? She wouldn't keep it anywhere in the building where she ran her accounting practice. If she had, she would have taken it with her when she closed the practice and retired.

My protracted dawdle over breakfast took me through to almost nine o'clock and probably would have continued for some time longer if it wasn't for the front door bell. I found an industrial-looking group of six people waiting to come in. Tyson's special cleaning brigade had arrived accompanied by what to me appeared an inordinate amount of equipment. After the person in charge allocated pairs of his team specific areas to clean, the place became a flurry of activity. At a loss as to what I should do, other than keep out of everyone's way, I parked myself in one of the lounge chairs and continued my contemplation of the matter of the missing documents.

To my mind, the key to the puzzle continued to be where Lillian might have found a safe repository for sensitive material. Again, I conducted a mental audit of each room in the house in search of such a place… and came up with exactly the same answer as before: zilch! I returned to the kitchen. No, she wouldn't hide such things in the cookie jar or one of the canisters, I told myself, but it didn't stop me looking through every cupboard and in every container. It was after eleven o'clock when the team leader came to tell me they would be finished all the cleaning in about another ten minutes.

After seeing them off the premises, and having elected to defer lunch for a while, I ventured upstairs. I poked my head into each room as I made my way along the landing to my room. They did a great job. The place was spotless. Once in my bedroom, I had to admit I had no idea what I was looking for. Everything about the room and its furniture was 'ordinary'. The wall from the doorway to the corner of the room consisted or floor-to-ceiling built-in cupboards. Furniture comprised a bed, bedside table, dressing table, chair and cheap student's desk. Why did the room contain a desk as well as the other desk-like piece of furniture we moved into the office to use as my desk? Although unusual, I was sure there was nothing sinister about it.

Working my way around the room, I examined each piece of furniture in turn before pulling it out to examine the wall and floor behind it. The bed was the last piece to be examined and it required some effort to move it. By the time I had everything back where it belonged, I was exhausted, starving, and still no closer to solving my mystery of the missing documents. So, back to the kitchen for sustenance and to rethink my approach to sleuthing. So far the score was: Lillian = one, Sophie = zero.

Midway through my sandwich, Tyson called to ask if he could come to talk to me about progress to date. Why not? He was easy on the eyes and good to talk to … and I didn't feel up to moving more furniture yet. I had about half an hour to finish lunch and tidy myself up a bit before he arrived. Needless to say, lunch was dispatched in no time flat, and washing my face and combing my hair didn't take long either. The few minutes I had spare before his arrival, I dedicated to coming up with ideas for a better/more efficient way of searching the house. Just as something lurking deep in the back of my mind struggled to come forward, the doorbell rang.

If his opening was anything to go by, Tyson's report would not take long. For a fleeting moment, I wondered why he bothered coming all this way to tell me what he easily could tell me over the phone. Apart from the fingerprints they expected to find, only one other set was located in various places throughout the house – including the office. Okay, no surprises in any of his findings, just disappointment when he confirmed they were unable to identify the rogue prints. He explained it was because they did not hold those prints on file, but they were checking other sources in the hope the prints would turn up on some other database.

I was surprised when he announced he had more to tell … and please would it be okay if he kept the key a bit longer? It was of no consequence to me how long he kept it, so I told him to hold it for as long as he needed.

"Good… We had something of a breakthrough on the key. The forensic boys, who know about such things, told me where they thought the key might have been cut. The locksmiths checked their records and confirmed the key had been cut about eight years ago for Lillian Cavendish. At first, they said it was the only copy of the master they cut, but a check further back in their records proved them wrong. It was fortunate some of the paper records created by the founder of the business had been computerised in recent times. In 1946, an earlier copy had been cut from the same master."

"1946…? The key cut back then would have been the one Lillian gave Lorna Green when she came to live-in as housekeeper/nanny. While, the one cut eight years ago would be the one Mavis Larson and then Rita Moreno had used. How does any of this help us with what happened here?"

"On its own, it doesn't. But we didn't give up then. We sent one of our junior detectives around all of the places which offer key cutting services to see if anyone could tell us anything more about the key. He struck gold at the local hardware store. The supervisor who works the area where keys are cut looked up a particular register they keep. It appears, if they encounter trouble cutting a key, it's recorded in the special register. We were lucky the supervisor had a vague recollection of something happening when a new trainee was still learning the ropes. He messed up two attempts to cut a copy of a key and, eventually, the supervisor did the job instead."

"But, you're saying a copy was cut for someone. Who and when?"

"Yes, a copy went out into circulation about a month ago according to the register. The person who collected the copy signed for it as 'Pat Smith'. Neither the supervisor nor the young detective thought it a particularly convincing name. The supervisor took our detective through to meet the manager, who was both intrigued and obliging. As it was only a month ago, the manager thought 'Pat Smith' might appear in early CCTV footage. They hold the computer files for up to six months, so it took a while to find the right file to examine. It proved worth the effort when the supervisor identified the woman in the CCTV footage as the one who collected the copy of the key."

"This is beginning to sound too good to be true. If you don't mind my saying so, you don't seem particularly excited by what's been discovered. I'll assume you've told me the good news, so what is the bad news?"

"Ye-es, the next part of the story is not good news. We were able to establish the true identity of 'Pat Smith', and went to her last known address to have a chat to her about the key. She wasn't there, and hasn't lived there since around the time she had the key cut. We are still trying to locate her."

"Yes, okay… So, who is she and how did she get hold of the key to have a copy cut from it?"

"The last person to have the key, before it was handed in to you, was Rita Moreno. The person we are looking for is her daughter, Seraphina, who is more generally known as Fina. In case you're wondering, Mrs Moreno swears she never gave the key to her daughter or anyone else, and always kept it safely in her bag. I have no doubts about the truth of her statement."

"Forgive me if I seem a bit dense about all this but, if she had the key cut about a month ago, doesn't it suggest some premeditation about its future use. Although you haven't said the copy of the key was used to gain ingress into this house, it's the inference I've gained from this conversation. Apart from straightforward theft, what other reason would Rita's daughter have for entering this house? As nothing appears to have been stolen, what was the point of it all?"

"…Nothing definite to share with you yet, but there is something you will find interesting. Our sources tell us Miss Moreno is the long-time girlfriend of the oldest of the Millard brothers. It's rumoured her two children are his. Mrs Moreno claims to have no knowledge of where her daughter or grandchildren are now, and I'm inclined to believe her."

"I came to know Rita well while she worked here, and found her to be as trustworthy as they come. She never spoke much about her daughter or the grandchildren, but I formed the opinion she didn't approve of whatever was going on in her daughter's life. Perhaps it was the Millard connection she didn't like."

"Although she didn't say anything specific when I interviewed her, I also gained the impression she did not have a high regard for her daughter's life choices."

"The Millard connection has me intrigued. Given the Millard brothers were casing this place, and then tried unsuccessfully to break in, were Fina Moreno's efforts with the key a part of their grand plan? And, I suppose the big question is: what was their grand plan? Did they want to ransack the house, move in and turn it into a squat, or were they after something in particular?"

"Good questions, but here's another one: was Fina Moreno a part of the original plan, or did she become involved when the original plan fell through without achieving its objective? I collected a few objects belonging to Fina Moreno from her mother's house. The fingerprint boys should be running some tests on them this afternoon. By morning, we might have more to add to this story. I've arranged for officers to be stationed here for the next few nights, or at least until we have a better handle on what this might be about. If you feel safe enough, it's fine for you to stay here. But, if you feel at all uncomfortable about it, just let the officers know where you will be spending the night."

Our meeting was over. Neither of us had more information to share. I offered Tyson a coffee. He declined and was soon out the door and on his way to somewhere else. A coffee still seemed a good idea. I took it through to the lounge to sip while I reviewed Tyson's information. Hearing Rita's name linked to the Millards and what might have been happening here was upsetting. While a part of me knew she wouldn't have any part in any of this, I still felt concerned about someone I trusted without question now somehow being implicit in illegal activities.

In a bid to shove Rita Moreno to a back corner of my mind, I forced myself to concentrate on anywhere in the house which might present as a safe hiding place for sensitive documents. Of course I knew it was 'mission impossible'. Hadn't I spent the last day on exactly such a mission, only to come up with nothing and nowhere? There had to be a more strategic way of approaching it. As I peered at the bottom of my empty mug and subconsciously debated whether to make another coffee or not, a new thought slammed in from left field.

What if Lillian had installed a safe in this house? Where would she install one? Would it be a floor safe or in a wall somewhere? While not dismissing it out of hand, a wall safe seemed unlikely. In all the good movies, a wall safe is usually hidden behind a painting or some other decorative paraphernalia. Lillian's house did not have much of either of those. I almost convinced myself a wall safe could be hidden behind a sliding panel in one of the built-in wardrobes. The idea wasn't too far-fetched but, somehow, it didn't send me into raptures – and neither did it fit with what I knew of Lillian.

But, the notion of a floor safe was not so easy to dismiss. In fact, it had a certain appeal. Yes, a floor safe was more in keeping with Lillian. Okay, so, in which bit of floor might one install a floor safe? I didn't have to be a genius to work out it had to be somewhere on the ground floor – but where? The little voice in my head was yelling at me to get off my backside and look. I took it up on its suggestion.

From my vantage point halfway up the stairs, I scanned the lounge room area. The ancient carpet showed no sign of any area having been disturbed in a long time. A couple of large pieces of furniture had never been moved in all the years I had come here. Still, it did not indicate they should be disregarded. If I were going to install a floor safe, where would I locate it: in the middle of a room or beside a wall? Never having considered the question before, my logic settled immediately for somewhere beside a wall. If I was honest, it was as good an option as any other. The only thing I didn't like about it was the prospect of having to shift those large pieces of furniture occupying much of the area along one wall.

In this exercise, the carpeted floor made it easy to see if the carpet had been lifted or folded back in the past. A quick inspection of the carpet adjacent to the walls – where possible – produced no evidence of any such past activity. After eyeing-off the two large pieces of furniture along the fourth wall, I decided it was unlikely a safe lurked beneath them, and I deemed my inspection of the room complete.

The kitchen struck me as an unlikely place for a floor safe, but I wandered in there to confirm my thinking before discounting it as a possible site. Not many potential sites existed on the ground floor and, with surprising rapidity, I was eliminating them. All I had left to consider were a small bathroom, laundry and the 'back room'. The bathroom and laundry weren't genuine possibilities. Their ceramic tiled floors didn't present much opportunity for concealing a safe anywhere beneath them.

So, only the 'back room' was left to consider. The room, lacking a more imaginative title, was tiny. I often wondered whether the original intention was for it to be a storeroom, but the plan changed somewhere along the line. In all the years since I first remember visiting this house, the room had contained only a day bed, a chair and a small side table. Although, I remember my mother telling me Lillian used it as her home office when she first moved in. Recollection of Mum's story stirred my interest. If it was Lillian's office for a time, might it be the logical place for her to install a safe?

I rushed into the room, and soon had the chair and side table dragged out into the hallway. A visual scan of the now cleared floor area found nothing to become excited about. The little voice in my head demanded to know why I thought it would be obvious. There was no point in installing a safe so anyone entering the room immediately could determine its location. Having accept the point of my thinking, I embarked on a more physical examination of the room. Pounding the floor with my clenched fist, I worked my way methodically all over the cleared floor space. The exercise told me nothing … well, nothing other than I now had a tender fist.

"One lone possibility left to investigate," I told the universe as I stood and eyed off the day bed. It was old, made of solid, dark stained timber, and resembled an overgrown sofa with a trundle tucked underneath. The bed featured railings at both ends and across its back. It didn't matter how long I stood there looking at it, it didn't change my mind about how heavy it was going to be to shift. First, move the trundle out of the way, I counselled myself.

Then, after a couple of deep breaths, I stepped in close and positioned myself. Taking a firm grip on the railing at one end, I pulled back, using my legs and shoulders for leverage. Although reluctant to budge at first, it finally yielded just as my strength was about to give out. I didn't lift it much more than about forty centimetres, but it was the first stage of moving the bed out of the way. Ten minutes later, I stood up and stretched my back. I was exhausted and a lather of sweat … But, I had dragged the day bed out about fifty centimetres from the wall. I allowed myself a few moments to regain my breath and down a glass of water before exploring the new area of floor I had exposed.

Chapter 21

There it is! The moment I slid in behind the bed, I could see the barely-visible rectangular outline on a section of floor adjacent to the back wall of the room. So, now I've found what I thought I was looking for, what do I do about it? There was nothing so obvious as a handle or knob of some sort with which to lift out the rectangular area of floor. I tried applying pressure to the corners and along some of the sides in the hope it might thrust the opposite side upwards to allow me to get my fingers underneath it.

When all manual efforts failed, I realised there had to be a particular way in which the piece of flooring could be lifted out. Instead of attacking it, I ran my fingers all over it, paying particular attention to all the edges. I discovered a shallow notch cut into the side against the wall. It created a very narrow gap about two centimetres long, but only two or three millimetres wide; far too small to insert a finger. Further scrutiny suggested the blade of a knife was about the right size for the notch.

A quick dash to the kitchen and I was back with a table knife. It fitted perfectly in the notch, but it didn't take me more than a moment to realise it was likely the knife would snap before it lifted the piece of the floor. I needed to find something more substantial than a table knife, but something with much the same dimensions as the blade of the knife. A large straight screwdriver might do the trick. The only problem was, I didn't carry one of those around my back pocket… And I was sure Lillian didn't either. So, what did she use to access the safe?

Damn! I was sure I'd find a safe under the piece of floor if I could just lift it out of the way. Maybe there was a special tool of some sort Lillian used. If there was, where would she keep it? There was a small shed in the corner of the backyard but, somehow, I didn't see the shed as the place where she would keep such a tool. Squatting there looking at the offending area of the floor was getting me nowhere. Applying some thought to the situation, and maybe conducting a bit of a search for a tool, was more likely to produce better results than what I was achieving now.

Shuffling in a crab-wise fashion in and out around the bed had lost its appeal. It was obvious I was going to be spending more time behind the bed, so it made sense to convince my muscles we were going to move the bed a bit further to provide easier access. While it was a good idea, there was one major drawback: as the room was so tiny, it was difficult to manoeuvre the bed out of the way to any substantial degree. The only obvious way to clear a space was to lift the bed up so it stood on its end rather than on its base. Did I have the muscle power to achieve it – without the thing coming down on top of me of course?

"Only one way to find out…," I told the empty house, "but let's see if we can lighten it a bit first."

It didn't take more than a minute or so for the bedclothes, mattress and pillow to join the chair and side table out in the hallway. The mattress was quite thick and heavy. I hoped its removal made a difference to the challenge ahead. It took a few moments of consideration before I had devised what I thought was a reasonable plan for how to stand the bed on its end. After a bit more dragging and shoving, I had the bed positioned and ready as well as it could be for the big lift.

Common sense told me I should have someone else here while I attempted it. If something went wrong while I was lifting it, and it came down on top of me, I was likely to sustain serious injury. I checked my watch. In about an hour, the two police officers should arrive to spend the night. Maybe I should delay the lift until they arrived. At least then I would have someone around if something went wrong … And, if I was lucky, they might help with the lift. Yep, I could find something else to do for the next hour or so while I awaited their arrival.

The time wasn't wasted. My thinking focused on finding the 'special tool' which I was firmly convinced must exist. I went up to the office and searched every drawer and on every shelf, only to come up empty-handed. While I knew it was a long shot, I repeated the performance in Lillian's bedroom, and produced the same result. As I was familiar with the kitchen, I doubted I'd find a tool there, but it was worth a search. I had just finished going through all of the drawers when a knock on the back door told me the police officers had arrived.

I watched their eyebrows climb skywards as, on their way through to the kitchen, they encountered the collection of material now occupying most of the hallway. Cocking an eyebrow in my direction, the senior officer asked, "Is there something we should know about happening here? I wouldn't have thought this was a good time to be redecorating."

"It's nothing for you to be concerned about. And, the word 'redecorating' does not exist in my vocabulary. But, if you've had your Weet-Bix today, I do have a small job I need a little help with."

After exchanging looks, the other officer said, "Well, I'm up for it. Whatever it is, it will help break the monotony we have ahead of us tonight. What about you, Sarge, are you up for it?"

"Perhaps I should acquaint you with the task before you commit yourself. If you will come this way, I'll show you what I want to do."

To say they were enthusiastic about what I was asking them to do would be a gross exaggeration. But, after I'd explained the situation and showed them the area of floor in question, all hesitancy disappeared. With the three of us gathered around the bed, we talked through the strategy we would employ to stand the bed on its end. Then, it was time for the hard work.

It was surprising how much easier it was to lift with three of us; how much lighter it seemed. Although not without a certain amount of grunting and struggling, within a couple of minutes, we had the bed standing on its end and with its other end resting against the room's side wall.

"Now what happens," the younger officer asked as she stood with hands on hips studying the relevant rectangle of floor. "I assume you have to lift the obvious bit over there out. How does it come out?"

"I think you just identified the next challenge," her senior partner commented. "I can't see any way of getting hold of it to lift it out. Do you have any ideas, Sophie?"

The three of us had focused our attention on the area of floor under which we believed we would find a safe. As I turned to and looked up at the much taller senior officer to respond to his question, I spotted something. It ramped up my pulse rate for a moment or two. "I'm not sure how we're going to do the next bit but, as you're a fair bit taller than I am, could you come over here for a moment please?"

They crowded around me as I pointed up at the end of the bed now up in the air. "See up there, attached to the inside of the base frame… It looks like some type of metal tool held in place by a couple of brackets. Can you reach high enough to fetch it down?"

Of course he could, but it involved a fair stretch. As he handed me the tool, he grumbled, "It would have been easier to unclip it while it was on the floor."

"True. It would have been easier – if I knew it was there. But, I didn't. Still, now we have it, let's see what we can do with it."

I went down on my haunches beside the relevant area of floor and took a moment to work out how the tool might lift it. It wasn't too complicated. The bent end of the tool slid into the notch and acted as a kind of hook which locked into the notch on the slab. As you pulled on the tool, it lifted the slab high enough to slip your hand in under it to grab hold of it. Less than a minute later, I had lifted out the section of floor and was staring down at a substantial-looking cast metal floor safe.

"I hope it's not a Pandora's Box," the female officer quipped. "Do you know how to open it?"

"How could I? I didn't even know it existed until I lifted the piece of the floor. So, no, I don't have a clue about how to open it, other than it looks like it requires the use of a combination of some sort. And, before anyone asks, no, I don't have the combination, and I have no idea where I might find it."

"If you can't find the combination, you might consider giving one of the better locksmiths a call. Some of them have had success in the past at opening safes. Alternatively, you might see if DI Tyson will send over our safe-cracking team," the senior officer suggested, and then paused before continuing. "Is it possible the person who gained unlawful entry – and was the reason we are here every night now – might have been looking for this safe?"

"No-o, I don't think so. I suspect they were looking for some documents for whatever their reason, but would have been unaware there was a safe somewhere in the house. While they did move about within the house while they were here, their main focus was on the office area first, and then on cupboards and drawers generally. To me, it suggests they were not looking for a safe. I'm not surprised. In spite of all the time I've spent in this house over the last couple of decades, I had no idea there was a safe."

"So, what are you going to do?" the young woman asked.

"…No real plans at this stage. But, maybe straight after dinner, I will initiate a search of the office for a combination. I'm hoping inspiration about where I might find such a thing will come to me over dinner."

Although it was probably not the best time, I called James Whitby. He answered almost as soon as it started dialling. "For you to be calling me at this hour, either Armageddon has arrived, or you have something to share with me. I hope I don't end up wishing I hadn't answered this call."

"I'll leave it to you to judge. James, I have found a safe. What I haven't found is the combination for it. I don't suppose there's any chance it's been squirrelled away in some of Lillian's paperwork held in your office?"

"Anything is possible, and stranger things have happened, but I think it unlikely. Leave it with me until tomorrow. I'll give you a call if I get any bright ideas."

With little else we could do as far as the safe was concerned, the three of us traipsed out to the kitchen to organise our evening meals. As soon as we had eaten, the senior officer said he was going to undertake a patrol of the yard. He stopped on his way out when he reached the pile of material in the hallway, and then came back to the kitchen to speak to me.

"I know we are here to prevent any unauthorised intruders but, if anyone should happen to get in, the stuff in the hallway is a dead giveaway. It will lead them straight to the small room and the safe. While I'm not expecting visitors, it might be best if we move the stuff back into the room. I'm not suggesting putting everything back where it was, just piling it all back inside the doorway."

By the time we dumped it all in an untidy heap on the floor just inside the door, the room tended to look as though it was undergoing 'redecoration'. And, with the slab of flooring back in place over the safe across on the far side of the room, it was virtually invisible.

Where does one start looking for a combination, I asked myself as I sat behind Lillian's desk. In my mind, what I was looking for probably would be a slip of paper with some numbers on it. It could be a tiny strip of paper, or something more substantial which included instructions on how to operate the safe. Although I had been through the desk drawers several times in recent days, I went through them all again, checking every skerrick of material I found. An hour or so later, I had gone through them all and found nothing even vaguely resembling what I needed.

It was time to stop doing and start thinking. If I continued this random scattergun approach, I could spend a lot of time looking for the proverbial needle in a haystack. The trick was to try to think the way Lillian did. If she had something she wanted to keep absolutely safe, what would she do with it – where would she put it? I had been close to Lillian for years and believed I knew her well, but trying to think myself into 'her shoes' proved more difficult than I expected. It didn't take me long to work out my new approach was a lost cause. I abandoned my search in favour of a mug of hot chocolate, a not so comfortable lounge chair, and nothing but rubbish on TV. With no new inspiration having brightened my night, just after ten o'clock I gave up and went to bed.

A hell of a commotion somewhere in the house woke me. The place was in darkness. I had to shake my smartwatch a couple of times before it decided to tell me the time was just before three o'clock. I realised the ruckus coming from downstairs was what woke me. I scrambled out of bed and tiptoed out onto the landing. Flashes of light were coming from an area of the ground floor directly below me. Throwing on a robe, I snuck down the stairs in the darkness, and stopped about three parts of the way down to assess what was happening.

It turned out I had missed the main performance and the show was just about over. While I stood there on the stairs, the situation below died to nothing more than a bit of scuffling and rustling on the floor. In the light from the officers' headlamps, I saw someone dragged up off the floor and slammed down on a kitchen chair – at about the same time as kitchen lights came on. Almost blinded by the sudden glare from the lights, I blinked a few times to clear my vision. When my eyes focused again, I saw the senior officer restraining a person on one of the kitchen chairs.

The female officer suggested I should go back to bed, or at least go back upstairs. She assured me everything was under control on the ground floor, and it would be better if I left them to get on with their job. I hope she really didn't expect me to comply with any of her suggestions. This was my property and, once again, someone had entered uninvited … and, no doubt, with unwelcome intentions. I strode past the young officer and over to where a struggling, slightly-built person dressed in dark clothing was being held down on a chair by the senior officer.

He snarled something about 'not being there', but I had no interest in whatever he had to say. I strode straight up and stood in front of the person on the chair. Then, in one quick movement I reached out, grabbed the balaclava and yanked it off. A mass of tightly permed black curls spilled down around the face I had revealed. It was definitely female, but belonged not to any woman I knew.

"Who the hell are you, and what are you doing in my house?" I bellowed at the woman on the chair, who now appeared to have decided it was pointless to struggle any longer.

"Miss," the senior officer growled, "please leave the room while we process the prisoner."

As I turned to leave, the female officer came back into the kitchen. I hadn't noticed her leave. "Tyson is on his way," she said as she walked over to the kitchen table.

For me, the wisest thing was to do as I was told. I went and flopped into a lounge chair. At last, my faculties seemed to be returning. Since being woken by the racket downstairs, I'd been in a semi-zombie like state. Everything was going on around me, but I wasn't able to take it all in. As I sat in the lounge, I dredged my memory banks for everything I remembered happening since I came downstairs.

I had reached the part where I ripped the balaclava off the woman. The woman… It was a slip of a woman who had broken into my house. Why was the fact she was a woman ringing a bell in the dark reaches of my mind? "Of course," I yelped and bounced up out of my chair … just as the doorbell rang. Detective Inspector Tyson had arrived. And… Yes, DI Tyson had mentioned a particular woman during our conversation earlier today – oh, I mean it now was 'yesterday'.

"Your officers are in the kitchen," I said as I let him in. He gave me a curt nod in reply as he strode past. Perhaps he is not a morning person either. With the police officers occupying the kitchen and nothing for me to do in the lounge, I was at a loss as to what to do and where to go. While my brain was alive and functioning now, there was no way it, or the rest of me, was up to doing anything in the office. After wandering around in the lounge like a lost sheep for a few moments, I climbed a little way up and plonked down on the stairs.

It was time to let my mind roam free. Now, what did Tyson say earlier about a young woman. It came back to me in a flash: Fina Moreno, Rita's daughter, who was a close associate of one of the Millard brothers. Is it possible the woman in the kitchen was Fina Moreno? Even in my befuddled, sleep-deprived state, I thought there was a fair chance she was. But why…? Why would Rita's daughter sneak into my house? What was she looking for?

My mental interrogation of tonight's incident, and its possible links to the Millards, only lasted a couple of minutes before Tyson came looking for me. I scrambled down the stairs to meet him – and to demand answers to some of my questions. He was brusque and made it clear he hadn't come to answer my questions. While I acknowledged his stance on the situation, he was not leaving until he had answered at least some of them. He threw his hands in the air and heaved a theatrical sigh of resignation when I made my position clear.

"Right, let's get this over with so we both might be able to catch some sleep before it's time to get up again. What do you want to know… and don't waste time asking anything other than your most critical questions. You have me for five minutes and no longer."

"Is the woman out there in the kitchen with your officers Fina Moreno?"

"I believe so, but we won't be able to verify it until we take her in. So far, she is refusing to say anything. Next question…."

"Have you determined if the unknown fingerprints collected by the forensic team belong to her?"

"We have confirmed the fingerprints in question belong to Seraphina Moreno. Whether they belong to the woman in your kitchen or not is yet to be determined. And, before you ask it, no, we have no idea why she has entered your house or what she might have been looking for. Your time is up. Depending on what happens, I might talk to you later in the day. Are you likely to be here?"

He was already on his way to the door when I confirmed I would be spending the whole day at Lillian's house. Then, I watched him drive away as another police vehicle arrived to collect the prisoner. The two 'night shift' officers indicated their night wasn't over and they would spend the next few hours on high alert on the off-chance the intruder had accomplices who might feel inclined to finish whatever she had started. Although I didn't think I would be able to sleep, I took their advice and went back to bed… and fell asleep moments later.

*****

Overslept this morning, missed the departure of the police officers, and had a sluggish start to the day. Then checked my emails and found the bad news (or maybe good news!) from Lou Radford. No reasons given, but her return would be delayed for a further few days. After giving it some thought, I decided it was good news. My investigation of any Millard connection to Lillian now did not focus so much on family history as on trying to unravel the stories behind some of Lillian's behaviour over the years.

A good example of which is the safe found in the back room, and my subsequent quest for its combination. Thinking about finding the combination stopped me in my tracks. Did I stand any chance of finding it? Given all I've learned over the last couple of days about Lillian and her propensity for safety and security, she was unlikely to have filed it away in an envelope with *Safe Combination* scrawled across the front of it. Two almost insurmountable hurdles confronted me: where to look, and would I recognise it if I found it.

The little voice in my head came through with a new suggestion: would she have hidden it in some form in one of her journals? It was a longshot but, in the absence of any other ideas, I allowed it more credence than I believed it deserved. Short on ideas of how to proceed, I reached for my phone – and managed to stop myself before I keyed the number. Just because I have nothing better to do with my life doesn't mean other people's lives are the same, and the latter includes James Whitby. I did not want to interrupt another round of golf. Besides, it was becoming all too easy to turn to James for assistance every time I encountered a difficult question.

Until I had explored all possibilities myself, I would not be ringing James again. Nevertheless, it would be handy to know when she installed the safe. If nothing else, it would give me some idea of which journals to explore. As, not only was there no record of the combination, I also didn't recall seeing any owner's manual relating to the safe. Where else might there be clues about its installation, or even its make and model number? The part of the safe visible when the cover was removed gave nothing away about its origins; not even a brand name was visible.

My day was going nowhere. As loath as I was to return to the journals, they seemed my only option. As I lowered myself to sit cross-legged in front of the stack of books in Lillian's cupboard, I murmured, "Right, now how am I going to attack this?" I would never have known about the wretched safe if it wasn't for the missing insurance policy. Now, all I could think about was what else might be residing in her secret repository.

Thoughts of the insurance policy took my mind down another track. If it were a requirement of the secure storage facility for owners of private lock-ups to insure their property, wouldn't the secure storage place demand proof of insurance cover? Somehow, I didn't think they would be satisfied with seeing the renewal notice every year. Might they require a copy of the policy to be kept on file? The more I played with the idea, the more credible it became. At about ten o'clock, I was looking up the storage place's phone number and preparing to have a deep and meaningful discussion with Brian. The only doubt I had about this course of action was why Brian didn't mention he held a copy of the insurance policy earlier when we asked about insurance.

Chapter 22

Again, I found myself dithering about whether to call James Whitby or not. Perhaps Brian wasn't convinced we held the right authority to see such documentation. But, James had made our situation clear to Brian, so I couldn't see how he would have any qualms about mentioning the insurance policy to us. In the end, I decided I wouldn't seek James' help, not yet. I'd save the 'big guns' until later if I encountered a problem with Brian. Within moments, I was listening to the phone at the secure storage place dialling. It took a while for Brian to answer and, when he did, he didn't sound pleased to be speaking to me.

Well, his tone proved a bit like waving a red rag at a bull. Perhaps it was because I was female. Regardless, speak to me he would, and I would know if he was being anything less than honest. Rather than go into combatant mode, I opted for friendly and apologetic. "I'm sorry to be annoying you again so soon, but we've run into a bit of a brick wall. A search of Lillian Cavendish's papers has failed to produce a copy of the insurance policy for her lock-up. As we have no information on the cover, or when it's due for renewal, we find ourselves in a bit of a dilemma. Is it possible you might hold a copy of the insurance policy as part of your operational procedures?"

His tone became abrupt. "I've no idea what you're on about but, yes, we need to know the privately owned lock-ups are insured. Have I answered your question?"

Okay, the way he wants to play it is not how I'm prepared to play it. Perhaps I will be calling James Whitby after all. Still, I wasn't done with this bloke yet. "Apologies, it seems I didn't make myself clear. The question I asked was: do you hold a copy of Lillian Cavendish's insurance policy for her lock-up? If you have any doubts about my authority to be asking this question, or some other reason for not answering it, I will go back to my solicitor. You met him the other day, James Whitby. Now…"

"There is no need to carry-on about it. If you wanted to know about the policy, all you had to do was ask. There is absolutely no need for you to be running up legal expenses just to find out about an insurance policy."

"It appears the threat of legal action is the only way I was going to find out about the policy. Now, if we can stop playing silly buggers and move on, when may I come to have a look at Lillian Cavendish's policy? Oh, and will I need to bring James Whitby with me?"

"I'm here all day. Come any time you like, and you don't need to get your solicitor involved."

After arranging to meet him at about eleven o'clock, I decided I would call James Whitby … just to let him know what had occurred and what I planned to do. He was in his office at Whitby and Breen. For someone who is retired, he spends a lot of time working. Our conversation was brief. And, there was no question about it, James would accompany me to the secure storage place – whether I wanted him to or not.

Brian was brusque but not uncooperative, although he did have a little dig about my bringing my tame 'legal eagle' with me. Without any further preamble or niceties, he slapped Lillian Cavendish's file down on the reception counter in front of us. "You may look at it but you can remove nothing from it," he snarled.

"We wouldn't dream of removing anything from it," James said in a much more affable tone than I could have managed. "We would be happy with photocopies of the relevant documents, thank you."

"You'll be lucky… If you want photo copies, you'll need to get a court order or something similar before you take anything away from here."

"Then, it's just as well I've brought one with me and, Sir, I'd be very happy to go back to the court and tell them about my concerns regarding the way this place is being run. Later today, or by tomorrow at the latest, it won't be me who is back here with a court order to investigate your operation. The next court order you see will be accompanied by a lot of police officers. Now, I would suggest you start warming up your photocopier." Having said his piece, James slapped the court order down in front of Brian.

The change in the man was amazing. All of a sudden Brian changed from hostile to affable; couldn't be more helpful. Half an hour later, James and I were driving away with a pile of photo copies on the back seat of his car. On the way back to his office, we again stopped for lunch at James' favourite little bistro. While lunch wasn't a rushed affair, we didn't waste too much time over it, as we were keen to study the documents we'd acquired from Brian.

I queried how James managed to obtain a court order in what must be record time. "Nothing record-breaking about it. The documents in his file should have been included in the probate paperwork. As we didn't know about it, it wasn't. Call it sixth sense if you will, but I had a feeling – a premonition perhaps – our friend Brian would be less than cooperative. So, I applied to the court yesterday, and picked up the court order on my way to collect you this morning. And, I'm afraid Brian could be in for a rough time in the next little while. During our six o'clock round of golf this morning, I mentioned to Warren Tyson my concerns about the way the secure storage place was being run."

"So, you've set the police on him anyway?"

"I've done nothing of the sort. In the course of social conversation, I just happened to mention, to the man I was playing golf with, how things at the storage facility seemed a bit iffy. What, if anything, he does about it has nothing to do with me." The serious and indignant tone of his comment was undermined by his wink at the end of it.

My phone chirped as we walked out to James' car. DI Tyson wanted to know if I would be at home at around three o'clock. I suggested about half an hour later would suit better. In the end, we agreed we would meet at Lillian's house at four o'clock. James asked whether he too should attend, but I thought it unnecessary.

For the next hour or so, Tyson's impending visit wasn't my main consideration as James and I pored over the photocopies from the security storage place. The insurance policy gave me the approximate date Lillian purchased the lock-up. It tallied with when she would have cleaned out her family home in readiness to lease out the property. A number of other documents James pounced on as we flipped through Brian's file were of less interest to me. When James' took me home, I thought it gave me more than enough time to return to Lillian's house and prepare for Tyson's arrival. It was just as well I left when I did. Tyson arrived about fifteen minutes earlier than expected.

His reason for the visit was to update me on progress subsequent to last night's arrest of the intruder. It was now confirmed the woman arrested was Fina Moreno. It came as no surprise to hear she was not co-operating with the police, and had not given any indication as to why she had a key or why she had illegally entered the house on at least two occasions.

"So, in effect, there is nothing new in what you have to tell me today. What happens to Fina Moreno now? Is she being charged with anything? More importantly, is she likely to be released on bail, and be free to visit me again?"

"She has been charged with a number of offences, but investigations are ongoing into other matters in which she is implicated. The list of charges is likely to increase. She remains in custody pending those further investigations. So, you should be able to relax and feel safe. In the off chance others were involved, police officers will continue to be posted here every night for the foreseeable future."

"Thank you. I feel relieved. On another matter, can I talk to you about the safe I found in the back room? While we are anxious to access important documents we believe it contains, we have been unable to locate any record of the safe's combination. I'd appreciate your advice on whether to engage a locksmith to open it, or if the police should open it in case it contains whatever the Millard/Moreno mob are trying to find."

"I'm inclined to think it would be best for the police to open it. I'll confirm it with our safe-cracking team and, if they agree, I'll find out when they might be able to do it."

Although I expected him to decline, I offered him a coffee. As I was in need of caffeine and was going to make one anyway, the polite thing was to offer him one too. To my complete surprise, he accepted my offer. While I don't remember our discussing anything of any consequence, it was well after five o'clock when he left… and I was thoroughly smitten. God, how adolescent! Anyway, he probably has a wife and kids at home. All of the good ones do.

As I dried the mugs and put them away, my police officer guardians arrived for the night. After letting them in the backdoor, I informed them there would be no rearranging of furniture tonight. Their comments indicated they were much relieved to hear it. I left them downstairs to do whatever it is they do, while I went up to Lillian's bedroom. I needed to pick up the threads from where my research was at when the lock-up and safe interrupted proceedings.

My first task was to find Lillian's journal covering the period around Ruby Millard's death in 1981. I half expected to find no corresponding entry in the journal as it appeared to be so long since there was any contact between Ruby and Lillian. Having found the journal covering the required date range, I flicked through until I found entries from around the right time. There was no mention of Ruby on the day of her death. Then, I turned the page, and there it was:

Police came today to notify me of Ruby's death. She died two days ago. Her funeral is on Friday. No suspicious circumstances. They said she had been unwell for some time.

I skipped forward looking for more information and something about the funeral. Lillian provided nothing more until her entry on Saturday, the day after Ruby's funeral:

Ruby's funeral was yesterday. I hope it went well. After her start in life, she at least merited a decent end to it. I wonder what her husband was like.

The next few entries were about things relating to Lillian's work and social events she attended. I was gutted by the coldness of her response to whole issue of her adopted daughter's death. Those questions I encountered earlier about what type of parent Lillian might have been returned to haunt me. Did she have any feelings for Ruby during the time she was growing up with Lillian as her mother? Were any feelings Lillian had for Ruby destroyed the last time Ruby absconded and never returned? There is a fair chance I'll never have answers to any of my questions about Lillian and Ruby's relationship, but I'm more inclined than ever to believe it was not close.

In an absentminded way, I continued to glance at journal pages as I flicked through them. Several pages after the entries relating to Ruby's death, her name leapt off the page at me. I flipped back a couple of pages to what appeared to be the first in a series of entries relating directly or indirectly to Ruby. I read the next couple of pages, and then went back and read every word of every one of them again.

It made for a fascinating, if somewhat tragic, story. From the information the police provided, Lillian knew Ruby was married to Keith Millard at the time of her death. Lillian appeared to have some reservations about trying to make direct contact with Ruby's husband, but her journal entries don't provide any specific reasons for this. Instead, through a 'friend-of-a-friend-who-knew-someone' route, Lillian set about gathering information on Ruby's life. This provided her with the name of a relative of the Millard family who agreed to meet with Lillian.

From her references to the meeting, I discovered the woman she met with was an elderly maternal aunt of Keith Millard's. It seems the woman did not hold back in telling Lillian about Ruby's life. Ruby, a single mother with a daughter, began her association with the Millard family when she accepted a position as their household help after Keith Millard's then wife became ill during her third pregnancy. The family needed help to keep the household running smoothly. Ruby's job involved a few hours work every day to do the washing, ironing and cleaning.

Mrs Millard's condition deteriorated after the birth of her third son. The boy was about only six weeks old when Ruby became the Millard's live-in housekeeper. She brought her daughter, Jane, who was about twelve or thirteen years old at the time, to live with them too. Ruby was kept busy running the household, caring for the ailing Mrs Millard, looking after the Millards' three sons, and caring for her own daughter. After Ruby and Jane were there for only a few months, Mrs Millard died. Ruby and Jane continued to live with the Millard family afterwards.

If only I could have been there to witness Lillian's reaction to the next part of the story. I know what she wrote in her journal but, somehow, I don't think she would have been too impressed.

Maggie [Keith Millard's aunt] said Millard married Ruby about four or five weeks after his first wife's death. She hinted at the couple's relationship having been open to speculation for some time before his wife died. Their subsequent marriage then gave it some degree of respectability. A son followed soon after. But, tragedy struck again when their son died when he was about a year old. The marriage produced no further children.

It's hard to imagine the consequences of so much tragedy in one family, and to understand how well, or otherwise, its members coped. The next few entries in Lillian's journal provide a glimpse of how Ruby and Jane coped with the tragedies which had dogged their lives since Esme's death so soon after Ruby's birth.

From Maggie's account of the Millards' life after the death of their infant son, it appears Ruby did not cope well. She turned to the demons of her teenage years for solace: drugs and alcohol. Maggie didn't think the drugs were too bad and were just a passing phase, but Ruby became an alcoholic. From an outsider's perspective, Maggie believed Ruby's alcoholism wrecked the marriage. The couple remained together but Keith was running the household and caring for his sons himself. According to Maggie, the wider Millard family saw Ruby's death as something of a blessing in disguise.

When Ruby died in 1981, she was still only thirty-five years old, and Jane was eighteen or nineteen. My heart went out to Jane. I had lost my mother when I was about the same age. But Lillian was there for me. I hoped there was someone there for Jane. A page further on, I learnt a little more of Jane's life after her mother's death:

After Ruby's death, the Millards wanted Jane to stay on as housekeeper. Maggie intimated the stories around at the time suggested housekeeping wasn't all they had in mind for her. When the Millards were away at some family gathering, Jane fled. She lasted only a few months after she absconded. It is rumoured drugs got her in the end. Dead at about 19.

Oh God, I wish I hadn't read the entry. What a tragic year 1981 was for the Cavendish family: Ruby dead at about age thirty-five, and her daughter, Jane, also gone so young. How did discovering she was the last surviving member of the Cavendish line affect Lillian? I had no way of knowing so long after the event.

As well as I thought I knew Lillian, I found I couldn't quite picture how she might have reacted. Lillian never spoke of her family, so there was nothing residing in my memory banks to help me assess how she took the news.

For a few moments, I sat staring into space, while trying to imagine what it must have been like to discover your whole family was gone and you, childless and beyond childbearing age, were the last of the Cavendish line. A thought slammed in in from nowhere to interrupt such morbid thinking. It stunned me and reduced me to a shattered and vulnerable mess for a couple of minutes. While I didn't know how Lillian coped, *I knew what it had meant to me.*

I was a couple of years younger than Jane when my mother died. There were no other family members around to support me, no uncles, aunts or grandparents. Yes, I had Lillian, and Lou Radford to some extent, but it is not the same as having family around you at such a time. It wasn't until a few years later, when a friend from university was getting married, the truth hit me. We were at a hens' party for her. Conversation turned to whether she and her soon-to-be husband were planning a family. She made it clear not only did they want kids, but her family expected her to produce offspring to continue the family line into the future.

I was the last of my family line. Oh, there were plenty of people in the world with the Sinclair name, and with variations of its spelling, but none of them belonged to my line. I have a vague memory of being drunk for much of the next few days after the bride-to-be's revelation. I remember feeling so vulnerable and alone. Of course, I wasn't. Lillian was always there for me. I was lucky. It appears Jane wasn't. Revisiting those emotions brought something else home to me, something I had never thought about until then.

Time was running out for me! If I was to continue my family's line, I needed to be doing something about it – and soon. The realisation reduced me to a fit of laughter. Do something about continuing the family line… what a joke. I didn't even have a romantic interest… and hadn't had one for years. Being single had never been a problem. 'Footloose and fancy free', as I had heard people call it, suited me and my life. Why would I change it? And, more importantly, why was I even thinking these thoughts. There was no opportunity to do anything about it right now. Did it matter a damn in the overall scale of things if my family line ended with my demise? I doubted anyone would notice.

In spite of my best efforts, those thoughts were depressing, and caused me to revisit a couple of other aspects of my life. Did my mother suffer these same thoughts all those years ago? Mum was a career woman. As a doctor, she went on to specialise in a couple of areas, before joining a number of other

GPs to establish a significant medical centre in the city. She never married, and probably never had time or opportunity for such distractions in her life.

The circumstances leading up to my arrival in the world were not a topic for discussion. Over the years, there were times when I was desperate to know who, how, when, and even where. But, nothing to do with those topics was ever going to be discussed with me – or anyone else I suspect. Somewhere along the line, I did gain the impression I was not an 'accident'. Not some loss of control at the wrong time. It was some time ago, I came to the conclusion I was here not by accident, but by 'intention'.

If Lillian knew the facts… and I am sure she would have known … she remained a faithful confidante and never revealed the story. Lou Radford too might know something of how I came about, but I think my mother was less likely to confide in Lou than she was in Lillian. Christ, I have to stop these thoughts. I've now managed to revive another question which has plagued me on and off for most of my adult life.

Why were my mother and Lillian – Aunt Lillian – so close? Mum always said they had been friends for a long time, for much of her life. But now, through my adult eyes, they had a closeness which suggested more than friendship. Perhaps 'closeness' is not the most accurate description. Maybe it was an understanding and tolerance of each other, such as you might find within families, where people, inextricably bound together by family ties, learn to rub along well enough together and support one another, without intruding in each other's lives.

Then the BIG question shuffled to the forefront once again: why was she 'Aunt' Lillian? Whose aunt was she? Was she even the aunt of anyone in my familial line? If so, how did she fit into my 'tree'? Or was the term 'aunt' just a mode of respect given to an older woman – much as the Indigenous community does? Now I was disappointed Lou Radford had delayed her return for a few more days. Forget the Millards and the Cavendish mob. Was Lillian my mother's aunt?

I slammed the journal closed and replaced it in the cupboard with the others of its kind. It was late. I was tired, and I was foolish enough to have opened an all-consuming can of worms too close to bedtime. A further depressing thought came to me just before my eyelids closed. By reading those journal entries tonight, I had saved myself a whole load of additional research. I now didn't need to try to locate Ruby's child born in 1962. The child was Jane, and she died only months after her mother. It also made a mockery of my grand plan to sell the Cavendish family's furniture and silverware and hand over the proceeds to Ruby's child.

*****

Although I woke at my usual time this morning, a restless night had left me with a thick head and no enthusiasm for anything this morning. After I watched the night shift police officers let themselves out the backdoor, I spent the next hour parked at the kitchen table indulging in breakfast and two enormous mugs of coffee. I eventually managed to lever myself off the chair and was heading for the stairs when the doorbell rang.

The police safe crackers had arrived. There were three of them and a toolkit of some description. With the three of them, their toolkit and me in the tiny back room, there barely was enough room to breathe. Their presence had stirred me to life. I was excited to see what Lillian thought so precious it belonged in a safe. As soon as I lifted the slab of flooring, I stepped back out of the way. They crowded in around the safe.

"Aw, bloody hell, it's one of those," I heard one of them murmur to his colleagues.

"Yeah, we might be here a bit longer than we thought," someone replied.

I couldn't help myself, I felt compelled to ask. "Is there a problem of some sort with the safe? I don't know much about it, or if there is anything I can help you with if there is a problem."

"No, Miss, there's no problem, but these little darlings can prove difficult and time consuming to open. I don't suppose you know how old the safe is, when it was installed, anything else about it?" the most senior member of the trio asked. After explaining only recently becoming acquainted with the safe, and sharing my speculation about its being installed around the time Lillian cleaned out the family home and purchased her lock-up, I told them I would be upstairs if they needed me, and then left them to get on with it.

While I wasn't expecting any exciting emails, checking my inbox is a good way to start the day while I try to convince myself there are more important things I need to be doing. Two emails caught my eye. One was from my editor. The layout had allowed a little more column length for my article. Could I add another paragraph of about fifty words or find another interesting photograph to go with it? The other item of interest was from Lou Radford. She was on her way home and would see me in a couple of days.

Today is starting to show real promise. If it keeps going this way, it could develop into a good day. I wondered if the safe crackers' news would keep it humming along in the same vein, or ruin it altogether.

Chapter 23

On my way to harass the safe crackers, I was about halfway down the stairs when the doorbell rang. I hesitated for a moment. No one was expected and, in my experience, this was not a house used to having people just drop by unexpectedly – not even those of various religious persuasions promoting their beliefs. The bell rang again.

I rushed the rest of the way to the door, flung it open, and found DI Warren Tyson about to press the doorbell button yet again. "Good morning. We seem a touch impatient today," I snapped.

He gave me a sheepish grin and shuffled his feet. "When nobody came after the first ring, I became alarmed, and was concerned all was not well in here. I see our safe cracker squad's van is parked up there." He pointed to a dark blue van parked beside the kerb about two houses further along. "I don't imagine they were too happy about having to carry their gear all the way back to here. As their van is still here, I take it their endeavours haven't yet met with success."

"I'm not sure how they are progressing with the safe. I was on my way to find out when you arrived. It's almost coffee time. Maybe I should make coffee for everyone while they tell you how things are going."

"Good idea," he replied over his shoulder as he made his way through to the back room.

It wasn't quite the response I'd expected, but I did offer… Having swapped the small stove-top coffee maker for the 'real' coffee machine, I set out five mugs and sugar and milk while I waited for the machine to warm up. A few left-over biscuits I found lurking in the cupboard went on a plate just as the machine indicated it was ready for me to make the coffees. It was ages since I used the big machine. Although everything was happening as it should, it took until I'd made the third mug before I felt confident using it again. The gang from the back room arrived as I plonked the fourth mug of coffee on the table. While they fussed about with milk and sugar and selecting biscuits, I made my coffee.

Tyson fetched the chair from the back room as we all shuffled around the table a bit to allow the extra chair to slot in amongst us. Once the shuffling and fussing settled down – and no one had thought it necessary to update me on the situation – I initiated the conversation. "So, how is opening my safe going? Thanks to my lack of knowledge about such operations, I expected the job wouldn't take more than an hour."

It earned me a chorus of raucous laughter. Tyson stepped in to ease my embarrassment. "In most cases, your assumption would be reasonable, but not in this instance. Your particular brand and model of safe is amongst the most difficult to open. On occasions … granted, it's when the safes are bigger than yours and in very different locations … they have to bring in cutting gear to open them to avoid taking too long to do it. It is not the preferred approach for your safe. Pete, maybe you could explain what's happening and how much longer it might take."

"Yes, Miss, DI Tyson is right." I discovered the nominated spokesman, Pete, was the older-looking member of the team. "A more delicate approach is required in a situation such as this, and then it takes a bit longer. But, we are almost there. Give us a few minutes after coffee and we will have it open for you."

Almost as though they appreciated how anxious I was to see what was in the safe, the team didn't dawdle over coffee and were soon back on the job. Tyson, on the other hand, wasn't in any hurry to finish his coffee. Of course, it could be his intention all along was to hang around until the safe was opened. As soon as he drained his mug, I gathered up the others, rinsed them and added them to the dishwasher. Tyson rinsed his own before handing it to me to add to the collection.

Did I imagine it, or was there a brief moment of something as we stood together at the dishwasher? Before I had time to think on it, a call from the back room had the pair of us rushing out of the kitchen. Hunched down on their haunches around the safe, the three team members looked pleased with themselves. Tyson stepped aside to allow me to move up and stand beside the hole in the floor. Two of the team members stood up and moved away to one side.

Pete, still down on his haunches beside the safe, looked up at me and said, "If you're ready for this, I'll open it for you." I nodded and went down on my knees to join him.

While a whole host of fanciful notions about the safe's contents had flowed through my thinking since the safe was discovered, if I'm honest, I didn't expect there would be anything exciting, or much material, in it. Now the big moment had arrived, I kept reminding myself of my earlier expectation as I struggled to contain my excitement. Pete raised his eyebrows in question at me. I swallowed hard. Words caught in my throat. I settled for another nod instead.

My expectations were wide of the mark. Far from containing only a few bits and pieces, the safe was crammed full. I was stunned. Too stunned to react for a moment or two. DI Tyson, noticing my hesitation, moved over to stand beside me. "Is everything all right, Sophie? Do you need help to remove the articles from the safe?"

"No... No, I can manage. I was just a bit surprised. Do you need to see the material stored in there? I don't know if any of it is likely to be relevant in any way to recent incidents here."

He said no, but asked me to show him anything I thought he might want to see. I heard him step away and pause for a heartbeat before leaving the room, presumably to join the safe cracking team now lounging around the kitchen table. While a part of me wanted to dive in and rip everything out of its hiding place, most of me couldn't work out how to start. A hand on my shoulder made me jump.

"Sorry, Sophie, I didn't mean to startle you. I saw this basket in the kitchen and thought it might be handy to put things in as you remove them from the safe. I'll be in the kitchen with the others if you need me. While I don't think they are in any particular hurry, the team will need to come in here before too long to pack up and collect their gear."

The basket was the long, narrow, and relatively shallow one we used when picking fruit from the trees along the back fence. Within not much more than a minute, the basket was full. It now held all the documents and other paper-based objects from the safe. Only a number of small wooden boxes remained in the bottom of it. Their sizes varied, but they had one thing in common: none of them was labelled in any way. The little voice in my head urged me to take a photo of them lying there in the bottom of the safe. Although I had no idea why I should do so, I complied.

One by one, I removed the four boxes from the safe and balanced them on top of the other material in the already full basket. All the boxes appeared to be craftsman-made and sported brass hinges and clasps. There were four boxes. Two were cube-shaped and about twice the size of a box for a ring. The other two boxes were rectangular, about 150mmillimetres x 100millimetres and about 30millimetres deep.

It seemed prudent to move the basket to somewhere safer before exploring its contents. Lillian's big desk upstairs was just the place for the job. I stood up, taking great care not to spill anything from the basket when I picked it up.

As I made my way past the kitchen, Pete commented, "You look as though you expect something in the basket to explode at any moment."

"Did you find anything I should know about?" Tyson asked. "There isn't an explosive device of any type amongst it is there? Where are you taking it? Do you need a hand with anything?"

"If you have a minute, would you mind grabbing those boxes off the top and carrying them up to the office for me? If I leave them where they are, they are bound to fall off when I'm halfway up the stairs."

Once everything was cleared from Lillian's desk, I plonked the basket on it and unpacked its contents onto the desk. Tyson added the boxes in a neat pile on one corner. The moment I had started unpacking the safe, I knew I had found Lillian's passport. Now, with everything spread out as much as possible, I also had the insurance policy and a copy of the purchase contract for the lock-up at the secure storage place. One of the bulkier items looked like a tightly-folded, large map. I would come back to it after I had explored everything else.

So far, I had restrained myself, but self-restraint had just about reached its limit. My curiosity about what was in those boxes claimed precedence over everything else. The brass clasps were stiff. So stiff, I couldn't budge them with my fingers. I remembered a letter opener resembling a miniature kukri lived in the desk's top drawer. Tyson held the boxes down firmly on the desk as I levered their clasps open with the letter opener.

"Okay… let's see what treasures these contain," I said. After a deep breath to steady my hands, I lifted the lid on one of the small cube-shaped boxes. Mystified, I stared at the single item it contained. "It's only a pebble. Why would someone go to so much trouble to store an old stone?" I murmured as I lifted the golf ball sized 'egg' from its velvet-lined nest. I placed it in the palm of my hand and held it out for Tyson to see. I heard his sharp intake of breath.

"Unless I'm mistaken, that is no pebble. It is a rock."

"Rock, pebble – what difference does it make what you call it? I'm more interested in why someone saw fit to treat it like one of the crown jewels." I was talking to Tyson's back. He had his back to me as he felt for the switch on the reading light now relocated to my desk along with everything else from Lillian's desk. Having switched it on, he swivelled it so it shone up towards the ceiling, and he was now examining the 'rock' as he called in the bright light of the desk lamp.

"Yep, I think I'm right," he murmured. "I think it is a rock, but you probably were correct in the first place when you called it a 'stone'." His face was aglow with excitement when he looked over at me. "Sophie, I think this could well be an uncut diamond. If I'm right, have you any idea how much this is worth?"

I couldn't answer. No words would come. Nothing was making any sense. How and from where did Lillian Cavendish come by such a huge uncut diamond? Was it possible it was a diamond? Whatever it was, Lillian thought it warranted going to a lot of trouble to keep it safe. Then a terrifying thought struck hit me. Did Lillian come by it illegally? Was it a 'blood diamond? And, should I mention such a thought to DI Tyson? I decided against it. By the time I found my voice again, Tyson had opened the second cube-shaped box to expose another huge uncut stone. Two such large diamonds…?

"I don't know anything about them. And, I can't believe your assumption is anywhere near correct about these stones being diamonds. Assuming they are diamonds, where would Lillian come by such stones? I'm not aware she ever went mining and, quite frankly, I can't picture Lillian with pick and shovel digging for diamonds. And, I'm not sure I want to know too much about them or their origins. They have a definite illegal smell about them."

"Did I say anything about Lillian digging them up? These boxes are old. I suspect they were made for these stones a long time ago."

"Lillian was old too."

"Yes, I know she was. But, I think an expert would date these boxes to before Lillian's time. Do you know when she was born?" I gave him Lillian's birth date. "Okay. If she dug up these stones, it would have been in the 1940s or 1950s. When she was an adult. I think these boxes date from way before then. What do you know about her father?"

"Her father…? Frederick Cavendish? Not a lot, other than he probably was married in the early-1920s and died in 1940. Why ask about him?"

"Whether he is important or not depends on how old he was when he died. If he died young, he doesn't fit with my thinking."

"Can't help you with his age. I haven't bothered – or needed – to find out too much about him. But, I suspect I will be digging into his past after this. Do you have any ideas where the stones are likely to have come from?"

"Not so much ideas, as vague speculation at the moment. Let's leave it until we have more information on Frederick Cavendish before we pursue it any further. Are you planning to open the other two boxes, or are you saving them for some special occasion?"

In my befuddled state brought on by the discovery of the first two stones (my tiny mind still refused to consider them diamonds), I had forgotten about the other two boxes. I told myself whatever they contained could not be as stunning as the contents of the first two. The remaining boxes were too shallow to contain anything like the huge rocks in the previous boxes. Nevertheless, my hand trembled as I tried the clasp on the first of the rectangular boxes. It presented the same resistance as the earlier ones, forcing me to resort to assistance from the letter opener again.

No huge single stone greeted me this time. Instead, cocooned in velvet-lined channels across the interior of the box was a kaleidoscope of coloured gemstones. Even with my limited knowledge of jewels, I could identify rubies, emeralds and a couple of sapphires. Some of the other stones were familiar colours, but I had no idea what they were. All the stones were cut and polished. After giving a low whistle when I opened the box, Tyson now stood gazing at its contents. "Very nice…," he murmured. "I can't wait to see what's in the last box."

He didn't have to wait too long. I already was applying the trusty letter opener to the clasp. It proved the most recalcitrant of all of them. Perseverance paid off and it finally sprung open with a loud 'clunk'. The tremble in my hand had become more pronounced with each box, to the point I felt compelled to pause for a moment before lifting its lid.

This one's contents provided a more limited coloured palette. Rubies and emeralds were there, but my eyes were drawn to six other stones nestled in the velvet. As with the previous box, all these stones were cut and polished and sparkled in the light from the desk lamp. But, none sparkled so brightly as the six colourless stones which captured my attention and refused to let it go. Probably zircons, the little voice in my head whispered.

"May I…?" Tyson asked. I nodded, and he lifted one of those colourless stones free and held it up in front of the desk lamp. His low whistle was longer this time. "Look at the clarity," he exclaimed, "and the colour."

While I could see the stone he examined, I knew it and its five colleagues were colourless. I was about to take him to task about the colour, when he murmured again. "What clarity… there's not a blemish or impurity of any type."

"What are you on about?" I demanded. "They are colourless gem stones, probably zircons or crystals I imagine."

"For God's sake, Sophie, have a look yourself. These are not zircons. I'm no expert, but I would bet my pension these are diamonds … and they are magnificent. Well, this one is, and I assume the other five are the same quality."

Still sceptical, I held one up to the light. It took my breath away for a moment. The clarity and beauty were stunning and, as it sparkled in the desk lamp's light, its blue pinpoint of colour was unmistakable. Maybe they are diamonds. The frightening question in my mind was: how did the Cavendish mob come by them? It spawned another concerning question: What to do with them now I've found them? And, yet another question I dared not dwell on lurked in the background.

"Tell me I'm wrong, but I suppose there is little chance these stones were acquired legally, and I can now claim legal title to them. What happens to them now? What am I supposed to do with them?"

"Slow down. Don't get yourself all worked up over this stuff. But, since you ask, no, I doubt they were acquired legally. What I don't know is when and by whom. The first thing you should do is to safely lock these stones in a bank safety deposit box. Then, there are two other things you should do: have an expert examine and value them, and find out all you can about Lillian's father. But, those two things don't need to be done sequentially or in any particular order."

"And just where am I likely to find such an expert – an honest one – who is able to assess the stones?"

"Ah, well now, I might be able to help you. We know people." He gave me a knowing wink and tapped the side of his nose. Cheeky sod… and I was about to tell him so when he continued. "As to finding out about… was Frederick Cavendish his name? … You and James Whitby will have to work it out."

"No problem," I said in a supercilious tone. "We know people." I tapped the side of my nose and gave him a wink in reply. Lou Radford's image came to mind as I spoke. She might be my only chance of finding out anything – when and if she reappeared. Still DI Tyson didn't need to know I harboured any doubts about Lou.

In the midst of the turmoil, James Whitby called. Before I had a chance to ask why, Tyson gestured for me to give him my phone. Although he wandered off as he spoke with James, I heard him invite James to the house. When he handed back my phone, James was gone. I gave Tyson a 'what-the' gesture.

"James will be here in about five minutes. He was in the neighbourhood and called to ask if he might drop in. I think James needs to know about this development." Tyson made a sweeping gesture over the stones.

As indicated, it was no more than five minutes later when James rang the doorbell. I was surprised when it took only about fifteen minutes to show James the safe and the stones, and tell him about their discovery. He agreed we needed to look into Frederick Cavendish's life, and perhaps identify a possible source for the stones while we were about it. James also supported Tyson's suggestion the stones be stored safely in a bank and for it to happen *now.*

To emphasise his thoughts on the issue, James said, "You get those stones to a bank. I'll go now so you can get on with it. Sophie, I'll catch up with you later to work out our plan of attack on the Frederick Cavendish matter."

Once James was out the front door, Tyson returned to the matter of safe keeping for the stones. I agreed a bank safety deposit box was the best option. He offered to transport me and my boxes of treasure to the bank, and to help arrange their safe storage. As we also agreed it should happen without delay, about ten minutes later, we were on our way to my bank.

My mind remained a writhing turmoil of questions and doubts. We had travelled only a few blocks before a flock of new questions developed and managed to break free. "Is it possible those stones were the reason for my recent unwelcome visitors?"

"It's possible I suppose, but I don't see how they would have known about the stones. If Lillian never mentioned them to you, is it likely people with little or no direct link to the family might have known about them?"

"Well, while we've managed to establish there was no familial link between the Millard and Cavendish families, we don't know if there was some third-party who knew about the stones, and passed on the information to the Millards. If my intruders weren't looking for the stones, what else might they have been looking for? You've been right through the house. Did you come across anything else they might want to steal?"

"No, but I don't think it's so simple. If we've only just discovered the stones, who knows what else there still might be to find? They might have been looking for something not as valuable as stones, but valuable in other ways... Like documentation of some sort which might prove valuable to them."

I suppose he had a point. While we don't know what they were looking for, somehow, I don't think they were looking for details of a lock-up full of old furniture and silverware. From the outset, I believe their interest was in obtaining the house through whatever means possible. It is a valuable piece of real estate, and would fetch a considerable bucket of cash on today's market if it were sold. By then, Tyson was edging into a parking spot almost in front of the bank and further speculation on the matter was put on hold.

Our time at the bank was brief. What I had expected to be a long, complicated process turned out to be less so. About half an hour after our arrival, we were on our way back to Lillian's house. Silence prevailed for much of the return journey, and provided each of us with opportunity to indulge in our own thoughts. When we were only a few streets from Lillian's house, Tyson broke the silence.

"I'll have a word with our expert about examining those stones. It's going to take up a bit of your time when he's ready to do so. While I don't know how he might want to go about it, we will be guided by his expertise. Whatever he needs to do, I suspect it will be done within the confines of the police precinct. At least, it is the approach I favour, and I will be making it clear to all involved."

"Okay. I'm sure it won't be difficult to organise a time suitable to everyone. In the meantime, I'm going to be trying to get a handle on a bloke whom I've never met, whom I don't know the first thing about, and who has been dead for about eighty years. It shouldn't take up too much of my time… if a miracle or two come my way."

While trying to sound flippant, I was silently praying Lou Radford would materialise tomorrow and she would know exactly how to go about finding all there was to discover about Frederick Cavendish.

Chapter 24

Who has time to wait for Lou Radford? In my current state of mind, I certainly didn't. Armed with a coffee, I settled down in the office to confirm what I already knew about Frederick Cavendish. It didn't require much time, or energy. My research notes produced little, and none of it useful in understanding the possible origin of the stones.

Adopting a positive approach to the task ahead, I tore about a metre-long strip from a roll of butcher's paper I'd found in one of the cupboards and laid it out on Lillian's desk. From the pocket in my folder, I retrieved Frederick Cavendish's death certificate. For the first time, it registered with me how sparse the information it provided was. Regardless, the next few minutes were spent transferring its information onto my new chart.

It was hard to believe his wife, or some other relative, didn't know where Frederick Cavendish was born. I was at a loss to think of some other reason the information was missing from his certificate. The missing details also suggested Frederick's parents either predeceased him, or were not around for some other reason at the time of his death. I didn't think it too far-fetched to expect his parents knew when and where their son was born.

In what I considered almost a stroke of genius, given my recent introduction to this family history research lark, I searched the pockets for a copy of the marriage certificate for Lillian's parents, and discovered I didn't have one. Then, it was onto the computer and back to the online marriages index. I remembered the first rule I learnt: start from what you know and work backwards.

Okay, how does the rule apply to looking for Frederick and Annie's marriage certificate? The first thing I know about them is the birth of their first child, Lillian, was in 1922. In spite of my lack of knowledge about contraception a hundred years ago, it was a safe bet they had been married not too long before their daughter arrived. I took a moment to congratulate myself on yet another stroke of genius, before locating the list of marriages for 1922 and beginning what I knew could prove a long plod backwards through the years.

In reality, it wasn't such a long search after all. The couple had married in late-1920. After a bit more action on my credit card, a copy of their marriage certificate was ordered. Then I discovered my muse had left me, taking every shred of inspiration with it. Maybe I hadn't learnt so much about how to do this family history stuff after all, because now I was stuck. Rather than confront the situation, I told myself it was late and I should be making something for dinner... and then come back to this after I'd eaten.

My phone chirped as I was loading the dishwasher after dinner. "Lou, it's good to hear from you. Where are you, and what are you doing with yourself these days?" I didn't want to sound too desperate, but my heart skipped a beat when she told me she was home, and asked if she could come here tomorrow. Again, not wanting to appear desperate, I said, "Of course, you're welcome any time, but don't rush around here if you still got work to do settling in at home." She confirmed she would see me tomorrow at about ten o'clock.

I suffered a singular flash of inspiration just as her call ended. The only other place I knew to look for family history type information was in Trove, the National Library's online newspaper archive. If it had visited me earlier, I probably would have mentioned it to Lou as a possible source, and it would have ruined everything. I was determined to show her how much I'd learnt in her absence, and would enjoy gloating over her surprise. Of course, I won't mention how much help Gail has been, or the brick wall I've hit now.

*****

257

The first couple of hours this morning were spent tidying the office and preparing to relinquish the big desk after Lou's arrival at ten o'clock. My grand plan to have progressed my research into Frederick Cavendish before Lou arrived fell in a great heap after dinner. While I find searching the newspaper archives something of a challenge at any time, I was tired last night and, in the end, didn't have what it took to take on the challenge. After all, I told myself Lou would be here today and she probably has a black belt at navigating her way through ancient newspapers.

In typical Lou fashion, she arrived late and insisted on coffee as soon as she set foot in the place. Too much of the morning already had been wasted, so I made my position clear. "I'll make coffee, but we will take it upstairs and begin work while we drink it." Perhaps I should have been more circumspect. She could have been offended and left again but, thankfully, she accepted the situation without argument.

Once we were settled behind our desks, and without mentioning discovering the stones or any other reason I was interested in finding out about him, I explained my need to know about Frederick Cavendish's background. When I checked my emails first thing this morning, the marriage certificate I requested yesterday hadn't arrived. As soon as I finished explaining the situation to Lou and showing her the new chart I'd started, I checked my emails again. The certificate was there.

Before printing it out, I studied it on the screen. "Aha, that explains it," I exclaimed.

"It explains what?" Lou demanded. "What have you found? Should I see whatever it is your reading?"

"Yes, of course. I just printed it out. Yesterday I requested a copy of Frederick and Annie's marriage certificate. It just arrived and gives me a little more on Frederick's background. The intriguing thing it explains is why nobody seemed to know the information when it came time to fill in his death certificate. Surely his wife, Annie, knew he'd been born in England."

"As you say, you would expect her to know. Who were Frederick's parents?"

"Here's a copy of the certificate. See what you make of it." I slapped one of the printed copies on the desk in front of Lou and took the other one to my desk to study it further.

Frederick's father, Thomas, had been a military man. Good to know, but perhaps not the most useful piece of information. The question bouncing around in my mind was about when, and how, Frederick came to Australia. But, the certificate did have another interesting fact to share. After some simple maths, I realised the supposed age at which he was married did not tally with his reputed age at death some twenty years later. I mentioned the anomaly to Lou.

"Yeah, it happens. It's not unusual to find those sorts of discrepancies. Sometimes, some of the parties don't even know when they were born, so age becomes an approximation. Then, later in life, for whatever the reason, they remember things differently. At this point in time, I wouldn't worry about it too much. After we check out a few other things first, we'll have a look overseas to see if we can establish his birthdate with a little more accuracy."

She had booted up her laptop and was searching the screen as she spoke to me. As she offered no insights into what she was doing, and looked preoccupied with whatever it was, I decided not to ask. With no other ideas about what I might do in the meantime, I returned to Lillian's journals. As I sat on the floor in front of the stacks of books, I realised I didn't have any particular event to pursue. But, after a moment's thought, I realised there was something specific I could look for.

While I accepted Lillian was only about eighteen years old when her father died, I wondered whether she might have maintained a journal around the time of his death. There wasn't one. Her first journal started about two years later. But, in my search for a journal, I found another old photo album. It contained images of 'Mum and Dad' and of her young sisters.

The surprise came about halfway through the album; it became a combination journal/album.

Her first few journal entries weren't particularly interesting. Then it became *very* interesting. The next long entry dealt with her father's death. The tone of the writing seemed 'off' somehow, so I made myself read it again. No, there was no mistaking it. The entry suggested Lillian and her father were not close. In fact, the clinical nature of the entry seemed to suggest his death hadn't left her bereaved. Was there a deeper, darker story involved? My enthusiasm for the journal went up a few notches, and I settled down to read every last word she had written.

Before I finished reading the entries, Lou shattered the silence of the place with a yelp. "What? Ooh yes, there is more to dig up on this one."

"Well, don't just sit there. Come on, share what you've found. I'm assuming it's something about Frederick – or maybe his family."

"I found a snippet in a newspaper about the return home from the Boer War of Frederick, son of the local merchant, Thomas Cavendish. He returned at the beginning of 1903. I don't know what he got up to in all the years between then and when he married Annie in 1920, but I will find out."

Nothing more of note was discovered until after lunch. Again, my journal reading was brought to a sudden halt by Lou's excitement. I had reached the last page in the old photo album and was open to anything interesting to go on with, but I had to wait a couple of minutes longer before Lou shared her latest find.

"On his death certificate, what did it give as Frederick's occupation? I know I've got a copy of the death certificate here somewhere but it's under all these bits of paper I printed out."

A quick look at my new chart and I could tell her, "It claims he was an 'agent', whatever one of those was. Why? What have you found?"

"If you remember the last bit I read out to you, Frederick's father, Thomas, was said to be a merchant. It's quite possible

Frederick was also a merchant but, by the 1940s, merchants were sometimes called 'agents'. The name change reflected nothing more than a slight change in the way they did business. In part, any change in operations was, more often than not, due to changes in the commercial environment of the time. Make a note to remind me about it, and I'll try to explain it to you later."

"You seem excited by what strikes me as being interesting but of little relevance to the object of the exercise. Am I missing the point in what you are trying to tell me?"

Lou didn't answer my question. Her only response was to hold up her hand to stop me speaking while she read something on the screen. It captured her interest and no further communication occurred until I dared to shatter the silence by announcing lunchtime had come and gone, and I suggested we should take a break. I was more than ready for a break, if not so much for something to eat. My morning hadn't produced much useful information, but I was keen to hear about all Lou had found. While my time was spent reading journal entries, Lou had spent her time attacking her keyboard and printing off a stack of paper.

She looked over at me and blinked. "What? Oh, lunch… Yes, lunch would be nice. Let's take a break. I need to get up off of this chair and walk around for a bit anyway. Bits of me I didn't know I owned have gone to sleep. Need to get the circulation flowing again." And, walk around downstairs she did, while I fixed us salads for lunch. This is what happens whenever Lou is around for more than five minutes. I end up wanting to shake her until she recognises everyone around her wasn't there just for her convenience. Still, she was helping with something I didn't know how to do… and she wasn't charging me for it. Well, so far I hadn't heard any mention of fees.

As soon as we sat down to eat, I demanded to know what her morning's work had produced. She seemed taken aback by the firmness of my request.

"Okay. You only had to ask. The problem is, now I can't remember what I've already told you. So, you will just have to put up with me if I repeat myself." After I assured her – perhaps a tad too pointedly – she had told me nothing, she sniffed and began sharing her findings between each mouthful of salad.

"Well, it seems the family was well-heeled and Frederick was well-educated. On completion of his education, he went to work in the family business. Then, when he attained the age of twenty-one, he was given a grand tour to explore the world. I think 'the world' comprised parts of Europe and England, and he was away for almost two years. But, it seems a wee problem followed him home: a breach of promise situation."

"He was supposed to marry someone overseas, but ran out on her?"

"It seems it was more like he left her standing at the altar. Her family was well-to-do and everything was in place for a big wedding. When the family hadn't seen or heard from him for a couple of days, on the day before the wedding, the bride's father tried to contact him. He had boarded a ship the day before and was already on his way home. Slighted and humiliated by what had happened, the bride's family sought compensation. They made the mistake of letting the Cavendish family know, if they didn't pay a particular sum of compensation within ten days, the bride's family would take legal action."

"So, it appears they were not trying to reinstate the wedding; only seeking a payout as compensation."

"Correct... They had no interest in his returning to England to marry the girl. They just wanted money to salve their embarrassment and humiliation. So, from long distance, they hired an Australian attorney. As you might imagine, his ability was no match for the capabilities of the legal representation the Cavendish's money could buy. The local newspapers lapped up every moment of what went on. It seems, being forewarned legal action might ensue, Frederick Cavendish, complete with rank commensurate with his education and position, was packed off to the Boer War."

"Were they not concerned Frederick might not come back; he might be killed in a skirmish over there?"

"Who knows? Perhaps his rank protected him from any direct involvement in the fighting. His absence from Australia suited the Cavendish family's lawyer, who claimed Frederick had denied all charges. And now, as he was not available to fight the accusations, all charges against him should be dropped. It appears the court agreed and threw it out. As one journalist noted, by the time the case was closed, the girl's family had arranged another marriage for her. This time, they chose a good old English junior aristocrat; a bloke with a title."

"It seems the lesson to be learned here is: a title can mend a broken heart and restore a family's dignity. Then, in 1903, Frederick came home from the Boer War. Do we know what happened after he returned?"

"He went back into the family business, of course, and life went on as though nothing had happened. But there were problems ahead for the family. Frederick became something of a lad about town. He and his drunken mates – all from moneyed backgrounds similar to his own – often appeared before the local magistrate on various drunk and disorderly charges and were routinely charged the grand sum of £1 or £2 for their hijinks."

"If he came home from the war in 1903, and didn't marry Annie Morgan until 1920, it gave Frederick plenty of years in which to cause the family concern, and to upset a large part of the community. I'm now wishing I knew exactly what he got up to during those years."

"I don't know the whole story, but I can tell you about one part of what went on during those years. As I don't have my notes in front of me, I think it was in about 1908 when the next major incident occurred. One of his mates had a yacht. Frederick and several others spent a boozy weekend out on it. Sometime during the Saturday night, one of their number disappeared. None of the others realised what had happened until they discovered he was missing the next day. A coroner's inquest was held sometime later, and its finding was death by misadventure. While nobody, including Frederick, was held responsible, the incident focused the journalists' attention on Frederick again for a while."

"His family must've breathed a sigh of relief when he married Annie and settled down. Am I safe in assuming there were no further major incidents between the coroner's inquest and his marriage to Annie?"

"Not exactly, no. As I indicated, Frederick had become a favourite go-to for journalists during periods of slow news. On one such occasion, one journalist hinted at something inappropriate between Frederick and a young woman who worked in the packaging section of the Cavendish warehouse. It was suggested 'child support' might have caused the family their next dose of consternation, but the journalist couldn't follow-up on the story as the girl seemed to have disappeared. Just before Christmas, it was reported she had reappeared and was back at work in the warehouse."

"Are you suggesting an illegitimate child –Frederick's illegitimate child –was the cause of the family's next upheaval?"

"There was only a suggestion that was the case, but no further comment appeared in the newspapers."

"Aw yeah, and not for one moment am I buying there wasn't more to the story. A journalist with a potential story to embarrass the big end of town would not back-off until he got to the bottom of it, and he had exposed all the grubby details."

"…Unless he was 'bought-off', of course. Then, the story would drop like a stone. One of two possibilities might apply in this case: either the journo was bought-off, or the publisher was. In the publisher's case, not only might he be paid not to publish further stories about Frederick, but part of the deal could have been for the journo to get the chop from the paper."

"Insisting on the journo's being fired might have backfired. He could publish a more damaging exposé through another media outlet, and mention of how and why he was fired would only serve to give the story added credence."

"Yep, there always was such a possibility. Although I still have miles of research to do, I haven't noticed the particular journo to be missing from the same newspaper. So, maybe it was the journo who was paid off."

"While I acknowledge the degree of speculation involved in this event, I'm inclined to believe there was a child, and I can't help wondering what happened to it. After all, the child would have been Lillian's half-sister. I don't suppose there is any way we can find out?"

"Perhaps, when we go back upstairs, you might check the births index for anything which might be a possibility worth following-up."

Back at my desk, I tried to summon up some degree of enthusiasm for the task allocated me. Aware I was not an expert at using such resources, I doubted my likelihood of success. I scribbled myself a note of the details I needed to look for as I trawled through the index entries: 1912, sometime before Christmas, illegitimate indications. Not much to go on. Something more to help narrow the field would be handy. "Lou, do you have a date for the journo's first suggestion of something improper involving Frederick and a female employee?"

"Uhmm… yes, here it is: 08 March 1912."

A few moments later, I had the online index of 1912 births filling my screen. If the journo knew of something by early-March, it was likely the woman already was a few months into her pregnancy. With nothing better to help pin it down, I assumed the child would be born in the second half of the year, and possibly no later than around September/October.

It's unfortunate the index is alphabetical, and then by date for each surname. Damn! It would be handy if the woman's surname was Abbott but, with my luck, it will turn out to be Wallace or Zanzibar. Stop moaning and get on with it, I chastised myself, and began the slow and tedious process of checking every entry. By three o'clock, I was struggling to keep my eyes open and was in danger of crashing headfirst onto my keyboard. Lou rescued me. "Sophie, do you think it might be time for another coffee? I'm going cross-eyed reading these old newspapers and need something to liven me up again."

We looked like a pair of zombies as we sat nursing our coffees at the kitchen table. I didn't have the mental capacity left to indulge in conversation, and Lou didn't appear to be in any better condition. Nevertheless, we didn't linger long over coffee before returning to the hard slog awaiting us upstairs. The coffee had reinvigorated my grey cells, and I seemed to move through the births index at a much increased pace, but it proved a temporary fix.

By four o'clock, my search had reduced to a crawl. I closed my eyes, and slumped back in my chair. The little voice in my head kept chanting 'don't fall asleep, don't fall asleep'. I knew falling asleep was a real and present danger, so I allowed my eyes only a few moments rest. As I refocused on my screen, I heaved a sigh. I was only part way through surnames beginning with the letter S, which meant I still had a long way to go.

A quick glance at my notebook confirmed I had nothing much to show for my efforts so far. I had recorded three entries, but one of those I figured to be too early to be a possibility. "Nothing ventured, nothing gained," I murmured, and then forced my eyes again to focus on my screen. Although not fully committed to the task in hand, I picked up from where I left off and continued down the list of names.

My approach had been not to worry too much about the names for each entry, but to concentrate on the parents' names and the date of the birth. I thought this worked well for me and saw no reason to change my *modus operandi*. When I encountered a birth with only the mother's name beside it, I checked the date to see if fell within what I considered the likely timeframe. I hadn't been back on the job for more than about five minutes, when one such entry caught my eye and caused a double-take. Yes, the date was reasonable, and there was only the mother's name.

"What the…?" I yelled.

"What's happened, Sophie? What have you found?" Lou asked. She was peering over her screen at me, but didn't seem overly excited.

"No. Nothing, just me going cross-eyed and reading stuff that's not there. As you were… everyone relax again."

Lou gave an audible sniff and disappeared down behind her screen once more. "I really didn't think you had found anything. If you ask me, we are unlikely to have any success with such a random approach."

Why had I said what I did? Why did I lie? I too disappeared behind my screen … to once again read the entry which took my breath away.

Chapter 25

Maintaining the subterfuge was difficult. After noting the relevant entry, I continued skimming the births index without taking on board anything as I scrolled down the screen. But then, I was at the end of the 1912 index and didn't know what to do next. I found whatever compelled me to lie about the last entry still had a hold over me, and it insisted I not share my discovery with anyone … or, maybe it was just Lou I wasn't to share it with. In a bid to maintain the impression I was still scanning the index, I started scrolling through the 1913 entries.

A couple of minutes later, Lou exclaimed, "Look at the time." She sprang up out of her chair and retrieved the last few pages she had printed. "I needed to be out of here by five o'clock if I'm to be on time for tonight's show. I'm beginning to wish I hadn't arranged to take Nancy with me. I'll have to go almost clear across town to collect her."

"Well, go now, Lou. I'll straighten up in here when I'm finished. I'm almost done now. So, go, don't be late and end up having to rush."

"Yes, all right, I will. I don't have anything to report anyway. I printed out a few things, but only because I thought they might point me to something useful sometime in the future. Right, I'm off now." With one last glance at the desk, she picked up her bag and her laptop and was heading for the door.

"Okay, drive carefully and enjoy yourself tonight. I'll see you tomorrow," I called after her." She came to a sudden halt and spun around to face me.

"I forgot to tell you, I'm not sure about tomorrow. If I do come tomorrow, it won't be until after lunch. Tomorrow is a bit tentative until I receive an email I'm waiting for. If you're stuck for something to do in the morning, you could go online and check out the English census for 1881 to see if you can find Thomas Cavendish and his family, and also have a look to see if you can find an entry for Frederick in the UK birth index." She called the relevant web addresses to me as she was on her way out the door.

Until I heard the front door close behind her, I didn't relax. Then there were a couple of deep breaths to help me focus, before returning to the last entry in my notebook. There it was. It had to be… Stunned, I slumped back in my chair to contemplate the implications of the entry I had found in the 1912 births index. I raided my memory banks and dragged out everything I could find to help confirm my speculation.

Within a few moments, I had three generations of my family tree scribbled in my notebook. There were only three generations I knew anything about, and it had *only a maternal line to it.* While a male was involved in producing me, my mother would never identify my father or tell me anything about him. The last time I tried prising it out of her was only days before she died. She took it to the grave with her. I put it down to one of two things: either he was of no consequence to her, or she didn't know anything about him. Either way, he was just a means to an end.

Then there was Grandma, a woman who died before I was old enough to remember her. Her name was Alice: Alice Sinclair. Although there wasn't much to contemplate, I sat studying my family tree for a minute or so while a vague question wormed its way through to the front of my thinking. *Who was my Grandfather?* Of course… why had I never asked about him; never looked him up in any of the records? Well, now I had become something of a dab hand at such research, I would. I didn't need to know all about him to start with. All I needed was basic information about him to get started on my mother's birth entry.

It was easy. I knew her birth date. All I had to do was find her in the appropriate year of the births index. And it's then my whole plan came unstuck. Her birth was too recent and, therefore, fell within the 100-year privacy closure period. Still, she was my mother. Surely they wouldn't deny me her information. I would send off an application for her birth certificate… But, something made me hesitate.

The little voice in my head was back again, urging me to think about the information I had collected. I decided to comply. The three people I had on my family tree were: Grandma, Alice Sinclair, my mother, Margarite Sinclair, and me, Sophie Sinclair. And, of course, there was the other woman I was leaning towards claiming: Catherine Sinclair. Nothing registered at first. Then it hit me.

These were four women whom I thought represented four generations of my line. But, they all have the Sinclair surname. I knew, due to illegitimacy, I had my mother's surname, but what about the others? It appeared the same might be true for Alice Sinclair, if she were the illegitimate daughter of Catherine Sinclair – as is suggested by the 1912 births index entry. And that then brings me back to Mum, Margarite Sinclair. I didn't want to have to wait until a copy of her birth certificate arrived. There had to be some other way I could find out about her father.

Devoid of inspiration, and having run slap bang into the proverbial brick wall again, I abandoned family history in favour of staving off hunger and went in search of something for dinner. An omelette was quick and easy, and it was a mind-in-neutral task. It was as I loaded my plate into the dishwasher, I remembered the file I had back at my place. It contained all the documentation relating to winding up my mother's estate. Perhaps, as in the case of other wills I had seen lately, a copy of Mum's death certificate might be amongst the probate documentation. Did I dare leave this house unattended while I went back to my place to fetch the file?

My police watchdogs were called off a couple of days after the arrest of Fina Moreno, but I remained nervous about the possibilities of other unwanted visitors. Nevertheless, tonight my curiosity won out over cautiousness. I grabbed my keys and minutes later, I was unlocking my own front door. The probate documentation yielded what I was looking for. Rather than be away from Lillian's place for too long, I stuffed everything back into the file, tucked it under my arm and was out the door and on my way back to Lillian's in record time.

This line of Sinclairs seems to have a thing for illegitimacy. I remembered the faffing about which went on when I provided the information for Mum's death certificate. I didn't know who her father was and the relevant section was left blank. When the documentation was prepared for probate, it appears the court was not happy with the death certificate, as it didn't provide all the information they required.

The court requested a birth certificate be provided as well. And there it was! Mum's birth certificate was attached to the back of her death certificate. Surprise, surprise! …No father's name appeared on her birth certificate either. Now, how did I feel about her illegitimacy? …About the last three generations of my line all being illegitimate? If there was any reaction to it, it wasn't an adverse one. But, the revelation did have me wondering about Catherine. Was she illegitimate too?

It took a few random assumptions about when she might have been born and how long she might've lived but, by midnight, I felt certain I had established she was a legitimate child of her parents. I had done all I needed to do. No further research was required. I made the last few notes in my book, shut down the computer, and closed the office behind me. The only things left for me to do tonight were to have a shower and to go to bed.

Both of those created ideal environments for thinking, and plenty of it occurred. If, as the newspapers had hinted, Frederick Cavendish was the father of Catherine Sinclair's illegitimate daughter, Alice, then my mother was Frederick's granddaughter. And… it would make Lillian, my mother's *Aunt Lillian* – or whatever the correct term is for Alice's half-sister.

From in amongst all my thinking, a stray thought slowly elbowed its way through to the front. Lou referred to a newspaper article which indicated Catherine Sinclair was back at work in the Cavendish warehouse. How awkward would her return have been for the family – or at least for Frederick? In my mind, the family would be more inclined to want the girl as far away as possible from them and theirs. But, according to whatever Lou found, there she was back at work as though nothing had happened.

How did Frederick react to the situation? I assumed their relationship had ended when the girl became pregnant, but did it? Or did their relationship continue in the hope one day he might make an 'honest woman' of Catherine. Well now, there's another interesting question: did they perhaps marry at some point in time? I doubted they did. After all, he already had left one woman stranded at the altar. Was he legally able to marry Annie when he did? If he had married Catherine, had she died in the meantime?

The questions kept coming, but brought no answers along with them. All they did was prevent sleep from making an appearance. Trying to sleep was hopeless, so I climbed out of bed and wandered along to the office. I didn't have anything specific in mind – until I sat down in there. Once I was seated at the desk, my mind revisited the basketful of stuff extracted from the floor safe. Having identified the material I was looking for relevant to my interest in Lillian's lock-up, I didn't bother with the rest of the material.

With no particular purpose in mind, I dragged the basket of material down from the top of the filing cabinet where I placed it out of the way. Apart from the bulky, folded-up document I had decided was a map, the other item of interest was a large envelope with reasonably thick was of contents. The envelope was old, yellowed, stiff, and brittle with age. Exercising the utmost care, I opened the flap and slid the contents out onto the desk. It appeared to be a contract. I gasped as I read the cover sheet.

As clearly indicated on the cover sheet, this was a contract between one Catherine Sinclair, and Thomas and Frederick Cavendish (henceforth to be referred to as the Cavendish Family). Sleep was now the last thing on my mind. Wide awake now, I settled down to the hard slog of making sense of the contract's legal jargon. As I interpreted each major point, I noted it in my file.

An hour or so later, I sat back to browse through what I had recorded. The first thing of note extracted from the contract was the confirmation by all parties of Frederick Cavendish as the father of the illegitimate child Catherine Sinclair was carrying. The document then went on to outline how the situation should be managed henceforth. At the expense of the Cavendish family, Catherine was to become a 'guest' at a 'health spa' located in the Blue Mountains area until after she had given birth and spent at least two months recuperating.

Other conditions covered by the contract included the purchase of a small cottage for Catherine in which she could live for the rest of her life, or until such time as she married. A nanny or other suitable person was to be provided at no cost to Catherine to assist with caring for the child until the child completed its education. Catherine could return to work at the Cavendish enterprise at some mutually agreed point in time within six months following the birth.

A small trust fund set up by the Cavendish family, and administered by a couple of people whose names meant nothing to me, was to be maintained for the child until it reached the age of twenty-five years. Although the fund was established and maintained by the Cavendish family, the administrators were to ensure no Cavendish family connection ever was to become known. …And, finally, the BIG condition: any mention or inference in any way, by either party, to the child's being associated with the Cavendish family, or being the product of any relationship with the said family, would render the contract null and void.

Although so many questions were answered in just this one document, they were not all laid to rest, and a couple of new ones had joined the group. Did Annie Morgan know of Frederick's background before she married him … or, did she ever know the story of his previous life? An overwhelming feeling of disgust accompanied me as I pondered those questions. There were no answers of course. But, one big question tended to sweep all the others aside: how could the family have the hypocrisy to treat Esme the way they did? With those 'skeletons' residing in Frederick's cupboard, how could they disown Esme for her indiscretion? And, if Annie knew of his background, how could she drag Isabelle into being complicit in the way they treated the youngest daughter? Still, the way both Frederick, and then Annie, treated Isabelle, suggested a sinister pall hung over both the parents?

It's become obvious to me, Lillian, by whatever means, knew of her father's illegitimate daughter from prior to his marriage to Annie. Although I don't know when she became aware of it, she knew my mother was the daughter of his illegitimate child and, therefore, Mum was Lillian's niece. In the end, perhaps this aspect of the family's history was what motivated Lillian to reach out to Esme and her baby.

Although it wasn't too long before the sun came up, I was hopeful of at least a couple of hours of sleep, but one last issue delayed it a bit longer. From amongst the swirling mass of thoughts keeping me awake through the earlier hours, recall of an item from Lou's research crashed its way back in, elbowing Catherine and her child off centre stage: Frederick Cavendish had served in the Boer War.

Where are diamonds found? Young Frederick spent three or four years in just the right place to collect diamonds and other gems. Was it possible, how he went about collecting them might change the status of those stones from illegally to legally acquired? Although it would be nice to believe it might be a possibility, I doubted it was. From the picture I'd developed of Frederick from his behaviour, both before the War and after he came home, I found myself harbouring strong doubts those stones were acquired by anything other than questionable means.

Chapter 26

Over breakfast this morning, I mentally ticked off all the people I needed to call today: DI Tyson, James Whitby, and Lou Radford. The latter, to tell her I thought my research was now complete. Tyson called me before I had made any of those calls. He had arranged for a jeweller/gemmologist to evaluate the stones, and could I meet them at the bank at ten o'clock. Of course I would, and I'd bring James Whitby with me, if I could get hold of him in time. In spite of interrupting yet another of his games of golf when I called him, he would be at the bank at ten o'clock.

A text message from Lou saved me having to call her. She would be heading out of town again today on another job. She probably would be away for at least a week and would call me when she was home again. I smiled. By then, I hoped to have my life well and truly sorted out, including all of the ghosts in my family tree laid to rest, and where I was going to live in the future.

Tyson's expert was suitably stunned by the quality of the stones he was asked to appraise, and asked what I planned to do with them. The confused look on my face must have been obvious. Tyson stepped in to tell him, I had no plans to do anything with them, except to leave them in safe storage for the time being. It started me thinking about what Frederick had planned to do with them. Maybe they were to be his version of superannuation… or just a nest egg in case his father ever threw him out of the business.

Whatever his thinking at the time, a part of me was grateful he never had to sell them to fund his lifestyle. I don't have any need or use for them, but they are gorgeous, and it is nice to know they are there – just in case. And, just as the stones have remained a secret for so long, they will continue to do so. They are a legacy from my great grandfather… another longstanding secret, who will remain so.

Our time at the bank took longer than I expected. By the time we emerged, and Tyson's expert had departed, it was lunchtime. We all agreed we were starving, so we went back to Lillian's house and dined on take-away Tyson picked up on his way there.

After lunch, I updated Tyson and James on all I had discovered about 'my family' over the last couple of days. It seemed odd calling the Cavendish mob 'my family' but it's what they were – in a convoluted roundabout way. Everyone sat in stunned silence for a few moments after I finished telling my story. James Whitby was first to recover.

"Well, I never; how interesting. As the sole remaining member of the Cavendish family, everything does belong to you after all. Everything in Lillian's estate rightly belonged to you from the moment of her death. The only thing still to have me intrigued is why the Millards thought they had some claim to the house, and/or whatever they were looking for here."

A couple of days later, I had the answer to the last part of the riddle as well. Rita Moreno, Lillian's last nurse, came to see me. She had been allowed to spend some time with her daughter, Fina, who was being held awaiting trial. She persuaded Fina to tell her why she had broken into Lillian's house, and what she had been looking for. It seems, when Keith Millard married Ruby Cavendish, an old woman, whom the Millards' Aunt Maggie had known for years and whom she was caring for before the woman died, felt obliged to tell Maggie a story she had heard many years earlier.

As the story went, when Frederick left Africa, he smuggled out a horde of diamonds. Nobody knew what became of them, but stories circulating in parts of the community at the time were of some incredible hidden horde. At some point after the Cavendish connection entered their lives, Maggie shared the story with some – or all – of the Millards. Thanks to an abundance of creativity at some point, the Millard brothers decided Lillian must have ended up with the 'horde', and they saw her death as an opportunity to capitalise on their pseudo-Cavendish connection. It was the stones, they and Fina Moreno were looking for following Lillian's death. They figured the stones probably were illegally acquired, and they would be hidden somewhere, rather than stored in any reputable repository such as in a bank. So, their creative logic led them to believe the stones had to be secreted somewhere in the house. It was the legendary stones, rather than the house itself, they wanted.

I was able to share the information when Warren Tyson came to dinner the night after Rita told me the story. And, when he came for dinner again last night, the matter of the stones became a closed book for me. He confirmed no legal action was likely regarding ownership of the stones. They were mine to keep with a clear conscience.

Tonight, James Whitby is joining Warren and me for dinner, so I will be able to tie up the last of the loose ends for him too. And, tomorrow I have a string of builders, painters and other tradespeople coming to discuss refurbishing Lillian's house. With the renovations I have planned, the place will be a very different house when I am finished. Hopefully, the refurbishment will exorcise the last of the ghosts who, in some form or other, have lingered here for generations. There will be no room for ghosts here in the future. Maybe sometime after all the work is complete, I will be able to start thinking of it, and referring to it, as my place, and no longer as Lillian's house.

…And, who knows, if things continue shaping up the way they are, maybe sometime in the not too distant future, Detective Inspector Warren Tyson might come to think of it as his home too. Perhaps the time is right for a hitherto one-sided family tree to add a male line to it.

The End

Also by the Author

Revenge is not Enough
Harbour Plaza: built on dreams
On the Way to Istanbul
An Unsuitable House
A Land Too Far
Paradise Interrupted
Unwelcome Mail
By Any Other Name

About the Author

KAYLA DANOLI spent her early years traipsing around Australia and then Europe with her parents, and then completed her tertiary education in England before returning to Australia. There were a variety of jobs in various parts of Queensland before eventually making her way towards the coast. She now lives in a small coastal town on the Queensland coast where she works part-time on a charter vessel.

In the early days after settling in that small town, to fill in her spare time, both when at home and while on cruises, she started scribbling down her ideas for stories. These days, she writes whenever time permits. Her *Harbour Plaza* series, previously released in 2015 as monthly eBook episodes, was updated, extended and released in 2016 as the *Harbour Plaza: built on dreams* compilation. *Revenge is not Enough,* also released in 2016, was her first full-length novel.

House of Secrets is Kayla's ninth full-length novel.

Discover more about Kayla and her work by visiting

www.eaglemountbooks.com.au/kayla-danoli

or contact her at

admin@eaglemountbooks.com.au